The Secret Books

MARCEL THEROUX

The
SECRET BOOKS

FABER & FABER

First published in 2017
by Faber and Faber Limited
Bloomsbury House
74–77 Great Russell Street
London WC1B 3DA

Typeset by Faber and Faber Limited
Printed in the UK by CPI Group (UK) Ltd, Croydon, CR0 4YY

A CIP record for this book
is available from the British Library

ISBN 978–0–571–28194–7

2 4 6 8 10 9 7 5 3 1

This hour I tell things in confidence,
I might not tell everybody, but I will tell you.

WALT WHITMAN, 'Song of Myself',
from *Leaves of Grass*

1: LOST BOY

WEARYING OF THE TRICKERY of arresting opening sentences – their flavours of honey and brimstone, their glimpses of drama to come, their syntax weighted to draw you to the full stop and beyond – all I can honestly say is: *reader, come with me.*

I've never been a fan of epigraphs in books; there's something arch and writerly about them, like a cupped chin or an ostentatious scarf in an author photo. They're a cut-price way of giving both of us a literary feeling – instead of flowers, a burst of ersatz laurel from a can of air freshener. Psssht. *Mmm, is that . . . Whitman?* But I chose that fragment of *Leaves of Grass* as a kind of promissory note, as a token of good faith between us. It says: let us be equal partners, let us be the sort of friends who share secrets. Is there flattery here? Perhaps a little; friends must be inclined to think well of each other.

My friend – and I'm aware of sounding overfamiliar in my eagerness to assure you of my good intentions – in order to save you time and money, I'm going to put the argument of this book on its opening page: the world we inhabit is only a story we tell, and neither the truest nor the best.

The wisdom of the conventional metaphors says that stories resemble bridges, gifts and medicine; they join, they are bestowed, they heal. But stories are less pure and less benign than these images suggest. Human beings are compulsive

3

makers and believers of stories. And stories can be many things – banners round which a mob will rally; masks to signify enemies; blades even, to cut, and sever, and kill. If novels are good for anything, which I occasionally doubt, perhaps it's for revealing how stories arise, where they end, and when to stop believing.

Still listening, camerado?

Towards the end of the year before last, I began swimming every day at Tooting Bec Lido. Looking back, I don't recall a particular day when the resolution to swim throughout the winter seemed finally to crystallise. It's not easy to explain – even to yourself – why you would undertake such an unpleasant daily commitment. The pool is a hundred yards long and unheated. From October to April, the water is varying degrees of icy, sometimes frozen. The first immersion is bewilderingly painful. No amount of repetition makes it easy. Sometimes I would spend the whole morning before my swim haunted by a vague sense of dread. Worst of all were the days when the walk from the changing cubicles exposed shrinking flesh to wind and rain, or sleet.

Shuffling across the poolside in my flip-flops, I would pause by the water's edge. For a long time, I was in the habit of easing myself in slowly and waiting at the shallow end for my legs to go numb before I submerged my whole body. It took me a while to realise that this was a method used by none of the small number of people who continued to swim through the winter months and who all regarded the use of a wetsuit as beneath their dignity. They would plunge in without hesitation, committing themselves to the scalding immersion that left them gasping for breath.

4

By January and February, most swimmers are doing a width or two at most, though some physiologically gifted people are capable of swimming eighteen lengths, a mile, when the temperature of the water is close to freezing. I discovered that my natural distance was two lengths, not for reasons of machismo, but because any fewer and the experience was abbreviated to something approaching pure pain.

For me, the first fifty yards were like being in a fight, or having a tooth pulled without anaesthetic, or any experience where your consciousness contracts to the immediate struggle to keep breathing. Your skin feels as if it's being stripped off you with wires and your head aches. There is no space to think of anything. Abandoned by your higher mental function, you regress to the state of a floundering reptile. The first few times you do this, it seems like pure insanity. Gradually, experience shows you that this moment will pass. As you relax, you begin to notice that there is no pain in the place where the breath enters your body. If you can abide there long enough, by the time you reach the midway point of the pool the pain has not only diminished but been succeeded by a sensation of well-being that verges on euphoria. On the return length, you are no longer cold. There is no feeling whatsoever in your lower body. Hauling yourself out of the water, you experience the air as warm. You can then walk the fifty or so yards to the sauna – a gift from the Finns on the occasion of the lido hosting the World Winter Swimming Championships in 2008.

At this point, you know that nothing you have to face that day will be more difficult than what you have just done, and whatever anxiety or stress you've been carrying has been purged from your system.

The sauna comfortably seats eight. At the times of day when I swam, there were usually no more than three or four other people in it. Many of the long-time winter swimmers regarded it as an unwelcome novelty and talked fondly of the old days when the amenities of the club offered nothing more than a cold shower and a cup of tea.

I should point out that there is no evidence that swimming in icy water is good for you. Only cod science and the attractive but unproven intuition of hormesis – the notion that something bad for you in large doses is good for you in small ones – suggest otherwise. In my first winter, I contracted a stubborn case of bronchitis for which the doctor prescribed steroids and antibiotics. I felt sure the swimming was to blame. And yet, all the other swimmers seemed in rude good health. I, in my forties, was one of the youngest. Some looked decades younger than their calendar ages. These people seemed to have found in the freezing water the elixir of eternal youth.

The conversations in the sauna circled constantly around three unchanging topics: the temperature of the water, the inaccuracy of the lifeguards' thermometers and the prospects for the weather. If you stayed in there long enough, your opinion would be canvassed on all three. The discussions we had often resembled the dialogue of an absurdist drama, full of repetitions, non sequiturs and strange bathos. One elderly woman vocalised every thought that came into her head, from what she was intending to have for lunch to the brand of ointment she used for her piles; clad in a drooping towel and citing weak hands, she would ask the nearest male to wring out her swimming costume. There seemed no appropriate way to decline.

6

Still, for someone like me who works in solitude, it's important and restorative to connect with other people. Something we shared was our baffled curiosity at the motives that drove us to participate in such a painful activity. Our general inability to explain it fitted with my growing disillusionment about stories. It seemed to me that the true source of all our desires was mysterious and inaccessible and never disclosed by our belated explanations. First we do things, then we make up stories to explain why. Of course, being a writer, I could invent plenty of reasons. One was that it was something to do with death. It made me think of the Japanese delicacy fugu, the deadly pufferfish; its real aficionados like to enjoy it with just enough of the highly toxic liver to induce euphoria, but not so much as will kill them. When you saw the blotchy ice-milers mumbling incoherently in the hottest corner, as their core temperature rose slowly back to normal, it seemed that they were drawn to some threshold experience, to peering over the lip of the crater at the spectacle of their own dissolution.

But the experience of swimming in the cold also offered less grim rewards. It was often beautiful: the ice sang with the vibration of the water; the pool in sunshine glowed an extraordinary submarine blue, all the more wondrous when you were in it; a pair of Egyptian geese honked by the changing cubicles, like guardian spirits. One sunny midwinter morning a septuagenarian swimmer towelled off his brick-red body and declared to me: 'If paradise is one tenth as good as this, I'll settle for it.'

In the water, when the pain eased, I would turn over ideas for stories in my head, wondering at my presumption in telling untruths for a living. I seemed to have lost the gusto for inventing facts that is at the root of what a writer does – but in the bracing grip of the water, I couldn't feel sorry about it. I assumed that either something would turn up or it wouldn't. And it didn't really matter which.

Now and again, I would hear the story I wanted to tell like a shortwave broadcast from a distant country, the swooping signal fading in and out, carrying unintelligible fragments. But at the moment I turned my full attention towards it, it would vanish.

My long apprenticeship, almost twenty years of it, had at least taught me patience.

At my desk, I made a list of the books I wanted to write: a counterfactual thriller in which Britain had been colonised by India; something about a Viking; something about a psychoanalyst on a spaceship. But each time I started writing, my nerve failed me after three or four pages. Whenever I considered committing to one of the ideas – and I think I knew by now that I could force my way to the end by an act of will – I felt a great weariness.

The problem I kept encountering was that fiction, which I had used for consolation all my life, had somehow lost its charm. Whenever I read a novel, I found myself resisting the necessary conspiracy between writer and reader. I was inhabited by a spiteful internal heckler who would utter a flat denial after every assertion of fact. 'Hale knew, before he had been in Brighton three hours, that they meant to murder him.' *No, he didn't.* 'In the latter days of July in the year 185—, a most important question was for ten days hourly asked in the cathedral city of Barchester.' *No, it wasn't.* The weak magic of novels was powerless before this malcontent's jeering non-co-operation.

There seemed to be nothing special any more about the enchantments of fiction. On the contrary, in every area of human life, someone was trying to tell a story. Sports commentators, politicians, revolutionaries, religious leaders, business people, accountants, advertisers, actors – all were peddling selective and self-serving interpretations of the world. I told my wife I no longer believed anything I read in a newspaper, and she said I was driving her nuts.

Everyone was suddenly talking about *narratives*. These bogus *narratives* could justify invasions, absurd inequalities of income, murder, torture, and every kind of cruelty and selfishness. It seemed that people thought that by shouting loudly and insistently enough they could talk any version of the world into existence. I began to understand the peasant distrust of what educated people do with words, of the smooth and lawyerly language that talks you out of everything you own. More and more, I felt that true goodness must be mute.

Assailed by empty words, I longed for something preverbal, an unmediated experience of the world, and the cold water provided it. It told no story.

Back at my desk, I began another book, about a haruspex, one of the Roman diviners who scrutinised the entrails of animals and who are memorialised as emblems of charlatanism. But my haruspex was entirely sincere, someone in thrall to his own baseless claims of expertise, little different from the people I heard on the radio every morning: pundits pretending to make sense of the aggregated chaos that no one could really understand; reporters being invited to speculate on a country's 'mood'. I half expected someone to describe the speckled appearance of a sheep's liver and pronounce the economic recovery therefore in full swing.

I wondered if was possible to write a story that bore witness to the unrepeatable crisis of its own creation. But I was constitutionally hostile to experimental fiction, and when it crossed my mind that I might be inadvertently writing some kind of deconstructed novel, I felt like punching myself in the face.

One afternoon, after my swim, I went for a fruitless meeting with a film producer who told me in passing that the secret to producing a masterpiece was to organise a story around a single word. His explanation worked something like this:

Play: *Macbeth*; theme: ambition; result: masterpiece.
Play: *Hamlet*; theme: not sure; result: qualified failure.

He was rich and successful and the idea had an attractive simplicity. But afterwards, it struck me that one of the many ways of understanding *Hamlet* is that its central character is someone who has lost the capacity to believe in stories. Once a conscientious person has shared Hamlet's glimpse of the way the stories we tell mask instinctual motivations for power, and sex, and status, it's hard to believe in anything ever again. A series of strange and problematic plays clusters round *Hamlet* in the Shakespearean canon: *Troilus and Cressida*, *Measure for Measure*, *Othello* and *All's Well That Ends Well* – the work of someone rattled by the insight that justice, love, honour, history and progress are all just *stories*.

At the end of August that year, I flew to China to write an article about its surplus bachelors – a result of the country's one-child policy. It was part of a larger demographic anomaly: the world's missing women. In many countries – South Korea, India, China – men greatly outnumbered women. Abortion, cheap ultrasounds and a preference for boy babies meant that girl foetuses were terminated for being girls, and boys were growing up in a world shaped by their absence, a world of fewer daughters, fewer sisters, and fewer wives.

In a tiny hamlet outside the city of Huayin, I sat on the floor of a dusty brick shack. It belonged to a family of farmers who seemed to have been vaulted from the distant past into the twenty-first century. The soil still yielded ancient stones from buildings that had stood there millennia before, part of the great riparian civilisation that had grown up beside the Yellow River. An old woman called Qin Yu Lan, who was bird-thin and bowed from a lifetime of hard graft, cooked a meatless dinner over handfuls of blazing firewood and wept about her son's failure to find a wife. He was forty, and she was lamenting the lonely old age that faced him. She might well have been shedding tears for her own predicament. She had lived her life like an ox in harness, dragging unimaginable burdens, and there was no possibility of respite in old age, no daughter-in-law to share her labour, to care for her or her decrepit husband. Now and again a train rumbled along the track behind the house. The old terraces above us were overgrown with thornbushes and wild date trees. Forty years earlier, there had been wolves roaming in the woods. Now this was the last bit of village left as the urban sprawl encroached.

Mrs Qin's plight touched a chord with my belated understanding that I had arrived in a world wholly shaped by the decisions of previous generations. She and I were part of a species that was living through the reverberations of a slow-motion car crash that had begun in the long nineteenth century. The filthy air we breathed, the fictional division of the globe into nations, planes, penicillin, dentistry, the plastic detritus in the grass by the outside toilet: all were products of this sudden period of change; something that, for want of a better word, we must be tempted to call *modernity*.

The axiom of storytelling is that a person defines their life through their choices. From 'Little Red Riding Hood' to *Hamlet*, a protagonist desires, and then acts, and then lives through the consequences of their decisions. We parse the events of our lives in this way, turning them into stories – of triumph and failure, of odds overcome, moments of insight and redemption, and lessons learned. But for millions of people, ourselves included, the truth of a life lies in shadows and absences, roads not taken, unborn daughters-in-law. The Qin Yu Lan I met was only one possible version of her. And who's to say whether it was the most accurate, fairest or best? Even starting with such difficult ingredients – being born poor and female in Shaanxi province in 1942 – we can still conjure numberless variations of the life she might have led. Her husband, who had arrived to work on the railway in the 1960s, might easily have been dispatched to another village. She could have caught the eye of a well-connected Party member; or perished in a famine; or learned English; or become a Red Guard; or moved to the city. But now we are entering the territory of the haruspex, engaging in activity that is futile and tempts absurdity. And yet there is a stab of compassion in remembering this: glimpsed in her crib, or at her mother's breast, with her hopeful bright eyes and tufts of ebony hair, tiny Yu Lan was already *someone*; she surely had an inner essence, which would struggle to find expression in the world; which would be shaped and thwarted by circumstances over which she had no control.

It seemed to me then that the people we didn't become, the lives we couldn't lead, and the worlds that never were, were like so many secret books, whose pages supported with certainty one single knowable assertion: *things might all have been so different*. And any other conclusion or story was a shameful collaboration with the tyranny of this accidental world.

Nabokov writes, on the final page of *The Real Life of Sebastian Knight*, that 'any soul may be yours, if you find and follow its undulations'. Back in London, hauling myself through the icy water, I felt an ambition stirring: to gather one soul, just one in its entirety, from the oblivion of the secret books.

*

FICTION SHOULD HAVE PREPARED me for this inevitable reversal: the soul I went looking for was not the one I ended up with. In the beginning, I was searching for one of my distant relatives. I wanted to write about a lost boy.

In August 1914, my great-uncle, Leonard Castle, joined the Royal Norfolk Regiment to go and fight in World War I. At that time, he lived above his father's shop on Moyser Road, in Streatham, south London. The building stands about one hundred yards – a pool's length – from where I'm sitting now. If I open my window and stick my head out, I can just see its chimney pots.

Today it's a hair salon; in 1914 it was a hardware shop. About four times a year, I go in there to buy shampoo, or get my daughter's hair cut. I feel no special connection to the place, which passed out of my family before World War II. I have to remind myself that important family dramas were enacted here, that this is the house where, in 1906, my grandfather was born.

This was then the fringes of the great city. Sometimes still you can recover a sense of it. Squint at Mitcham, and the duck pond and the cricket green seem to belong to an English village, announcing the lavender fields and medicinal herb gardens of Purley, where the big Ikea now stands. At night, when the flight paths are diverted, the hum of aviation ceases and the sky falls silent. The pregnant darkness of prehistory seems to hang over south London. On an icy winter evening, the snow can bring traffic to a standstill. The common rings with the bark of foxes. The city is gone. You

14

are reminded that one day the two of us will be no more than memories.

Leonard's dad, my great-grandfather, also called Leonard, dealt in ironmongery and oil derivatives – paraffin, lamp oil, turpentine, paint. His was the forgotten trade of the oilman. The sign of their occupation was an amphora fixed to the shopfront.

What seems most distinctive about young Leonard's life in retrospect are its absences: no electricity, no wireless, no television, no telephones, no car, no bathroom, no expectation of travel abroad, no knowledge of other faiths or cultures, no central heating. In his brief childhood, on cold nights, he would uncurl his legs an inch at a time as the warmth of his tiny body penetrated the bed sheets. The tarry odour of the prepared kindling that was stashed in the backyard must have permeated the house, along with the smell of smoke, and washing, and stewing meat.

The Castles were not literary. The only books of theirs that survive are the volumes of my great-great-grandfather Elijah's collected Dickens. These battered brown editions with their purgatorially tiny print have inhabited both our worlds. But did Leonard read them? I somehow doubt it. The only book I'm certain he knew well is the Bible.

The family way tended towards dour. Sundays were long. Days were long. Their God was a vigilant boss, omnipresent and not inclined to give you much of a break. The business's success turned on accurate accounting. They lived amid flammable stock. And their religious faith was exacting. Twice a day on Sunday, the Castles worshipped at the Baptist Church in Balham. When war was declared,

Leonard's God bolstered his desire to go and fight. Searching online, I found a complete record of his military service, including a copy of the commissioning papers he signed in St Paul's Churchyard a century ago.

My grandfather, Leonard's younger brother, was six foot two. His height was one of the things that defined him in an era when tall men were less common than they are now. So I was surprised, when I saw a copy of Leonard's medical exam, to learn that he was only five foot five and a half, and 110 pounds. Perhaps he was of a different build from his younger brother; perhaps his late-Victorian diet was less nutritious than the Edwardian one my grandfather grew up on; more likely, Leonard just hadn't finished growing. The first category on the document is 'apparent age' – a bureaucratic wink to encourage volunteers to lie? Leonard's apparent age is nineteen. In fact he was seventeen, almost a child, putting on khaki and going to fight for his country.

There's no extant photo of him, but the corporeal facts on the exam flesh him out a little: he had grey eyes, a sallow complexion, light-brown hair. It's not much, but enough to fool the eye into thinking it has glimpsed a young man's face. With a similar economy, his war record compresses a handful of details into the facsimile of a life.

On the 8th of October 1915, Leonard suffered shock and concussion on the Western Front and was sent to hospital. He rejoined his regiment a month later and was promoted to corporal in February 1916. The handwriting on the form is hard to decipher, but it seems as though he was out of action again for ten days with influenza in July 1916. The final entry on the form is dated 12th October 1916 and bears a stamp for 'Wounded in Action'. Beneath it is written by hand: 'S.[hell] W.[ound] Chest and Abdomen. Died 5:30 AM.' He was nineteen.

I imagine the news being brought – by bicycle? – to the little shop on Moyser Road. I can guess at the habits of faith and stoicism being stretched and tested by the shock. For some reason, I see his father wearing a black armband, manfully accepting the condolences of his customers. I expect Leonard Senior was present in 1920 at the dedication of the parish war memorial: fifty-three names from half a dozen streets. Did he look around at the other bereaved parents? Was the early rawness of their grief calloused a little with time? What on earth did they say to one another?

Some version of that loss reverberated through my grandfather's life for close to a century. It was still present in the timbre of his voice, seventy years on: *he was a good bloke*. That laconic epitaph contained as much grief as he ever allowed himself. It was a family trait never to revisit the past.

Leonard's death closed off a whole branch of possibilities for people who never knew him. Each of those names on the memorial expunged an alternate future. The hundreds of thousands of absent men left a whole generation of women without their future partners.

And, unthinkable as it seems, maybe Leonard took lives; maybe he was a killer, setting off a chain of absences on the other side.

The fiction of a nation is invariably written with the blood of young men: Thermopylae, Masada, Kosovo, Crécy, Culloden, Gettysburg, Gallipoli, Stalingrad. The unspeakable things that happened in these places become the totem that defines a tribe. But in every story that sings of feats of arms, heroism, noble sacrifices, there's a voice that whispers something else, that insists that all that's real is young men getting chewed up in a bloody accident.

I say that not as a pacifist. The haruspex in me can invent circumstances where I'm compelled to give or take a life. I hope I'll be able to face my own death with the appropriate gravity and courage. I hope I'll remember that death is less often a tragedy, more often another regrettable fact.

But it's one thing to imagine your own death – brief, one hopes, as the shock of immersion in freezing water. It's quite another to imagine your child – or a whole generation of children – out there in the darkness, mortally wounded, dying alone.

You can't help wondering about the world where this didn't happen, a world without Sarajevo, where the dead of Passchendaele never left home, a France unhaunted by the mutilated *gueules cassées*, where the Anzac regiments never embarked, where Leonard took over the shop on Moyser Road and married a girl from the Baptist Church. What would that world have been like? We can't know, of course; but it would say in the secret books.

I regularly cross paths with Leonard's shadow. He knew the outside and the inside of these houses. There are still trees and shopfronts he would recognise. I think he'd feel at home in my front room, with his grandfather's collected Dickens on the bookshelves. And I often wonder if he swam.

Leonard would have been nine when the lido opened. Three decades earlier, Captain Matthew Webb had swum the English Channel for the first time, larded with grease and using a head-up breaststroke. A mania for sport was as British as tea and imperialism. I know that after the war my grandfather swam in the lido year-round and, with a touch of eccentricity characteristic of him, used to condition his eyes to seeing underwater by holding them open while he immersed his head in the kitchen sink.

I think of the family admiring the newly excavated pool. The big oak trees that frame it would have been much smaller then. And I think of Leonard back there, a decade later, on leave, looking at the innocent green of the plane trees and the chestnuts with the grateful eyes of someone who, chastened by reality, turns to the consolation of the secret books.

As a Baptist – he states it clearly on his army papers – he knew about the symbolic properties of immersion, about purification and rebirth, about the water of life. I believe that more than orthography connects swimmers and sinners. And in the pool, perhaps still, there may be a homeopathic trace of him.

*

HOPING TO LEARN MORE about Leonard, I began to make speculative enquiries down at the lido. I told some of the other swimmers about my family's history in the area. I explained that my grandfather, Raymond, used to swim there in the 1930s with his cousin Charles, and I cast around for witnesses to that and earlier eras, in vain.

One lunchtime, a man called Catford John – whose name probably doesn't require even this much explanatory parenthesis – was making a rare visit to the sauna, which he generally avoided for fear of picking up a fungal infection.

He had scrupulously cared-for feet and strongly held views about the poor podiatric hygiene of most of the swimming club members. John suggested I speak to Francis.

Francis was in his eighties, still a noticeably handsome man, with unexpectedly green eyes and olive skin, and what remained of his hair was black. Some recent catastrophe had deprived him of free movement. He came four or five times a week to swim, making his way painstakingly along the length of the pool with a walking stick. He was always accompanied by his companion, a Polish woman of about seventy named Jana, whom Francis had belatedly taught to swim. Her solicitude to him now seemed like a form of recompense for his teaching.

The novelist in me would like to write that swimming liberated Francis, that for a few minutes each day he moved freely and confidently in the pool; but he was as unsteady in it as out. The lifeguard would hover nearby holding a life preserver as Francis lowered himself down the rungs of the ladder, swam a few strokes in the shallow end, and slowly hauled his ruined body out of the water.

I approached him one day in the small common room where the winter swimmers went to drink tea and warm up. We chatted for a bit and it quickly became clear that, although he had been swimming in the pool since before World War II, he had no recollection of my grandfather, Raymond, and had never heard of my great-uncle Leonard.

Disappointed, but not surprised, I asked Francis about his life and what trade or vocation he had followed. He said he still ran a small business, selling and maintaining office equipment, principally typewriters.

I was pleased to hear this. I told him that I was an enthusiastic user of manual typewriters. In fact, I owned three, one
of which – an Olivetti Lettera – was no longer working. He
suggested I come by his shop and let him take a look at it.

A few weeks before Christmas, I drove out to see him in a
terrible rainstorm that presaged one of the wettest winters in
British history. I had all three of my typewriters in the back
of the car.

Francis's shop stood in a little parade of others along the
A217, between Cheam and Sutton, which it shared with
a cafe, a drycleaner's and a newsagent. The sign over the
shopfront read DITTAMI OFFICE EQUIPMENT. Its phone
number was still listed with an 01 prefix, but even without
that anachronism it was evident that the sign had stood un-
changed since the 1970s.

I found Francis inside, seated at a desk, under a brown
Anglepoise lamp, using a jeweller's loupe to inspect the wear
on some type. The space was made oppressively small by
the typewriters from every era which packed its shelves. I
showed Francis my Olivetti and he wrote me out a receipt.
He said his engineer was dealing with a backlog, but they'd
do what they could. His engineer turned out to be a man
called Simon who worked in the basement and must have
been at least eighty. I told them there was no rush.

Driving back home in the rain, I felt distinctly gloomy about
what I'd seen. It might have served as a *vanitas* motif – two
elderly men padding about in a building filled with obsolete
technology.

Francis turned the repair around faster than expected. Less
than a week later, I returned to collect my machine and the

bill cured me of any sentimentality. Francis charged me £90 for the repair and £10 each for two new ribbons. This time, I took a closer look at the price tags of the typewriters on the shelves and I understood that nostalgia was not his motive for continuing in his occupation. As one of only a handful of people in the country still selling and servicing manual type-writers, he was able to charge what he liked. The twenty-first century, confounding all expectations, was a good moment to be in the manual typewriter business.

'Castle, wasn't it?' he said, as he passed me my handwrit-ten receipt. It took me a second to understand.

He led me to the back of the shop and worked himself slowly down the stairs into the basement. The room was lit by a series of naked bulbs that he frugally switched on and off as we made our way along a narrow corridor between wooden shelves piled with old machines. They weren't just typewriters: there were old fax machines and printers, as well as various primordial computers. I had the impression that the basement had been extended out far under the main road, and I wondered if it was entirely legal.

Finally, in a puddle of yellow light from a bulb above it, stood a shabby pine roll-top desk. 'Castle,' he said, and jabbed a brown thumb at the picture that lay on the desktop.

It was a team photograph of men and boys in woollen bathing suits. They were standing in formation in front of the building that once served as the main entrance to the lido. Beneath it was written 'Streatham and Surrey Swimming Club, 1914'. Francis turned it over. A piece of yellowing pa-per was glued to its reverse side, with a list of names typed on it. Between 'G. L. K Townsend' and 'A. P. Quinlon' I read

'W. L. Castle'. The man it referred to looked uncannily like my son – something about his pointed chin, and the way his eyes crinkled against the light.

Was it Leonard? It struck me that someone might easily have transposed the letters of his first and second names. I wasn't sure of Leonard's middle name, but my grandfather's was Wallace, and that seemed like a form of confirmation.

I asked Francis if I could borrow the photograph and show it to my mum. A careful, shrewd look came into his face. He said it was too precious to let it out of his sight, but he'd see if he could make a copy.

*

YOU'D THINK WRITERS would be story-proof, would understand how all narrative attempts to understand the world are partial and misleading. Not a bit of it. The writer is usually the most wedded to a story, the most deceived, his own first dupe.

In the close darkness of that basement, I think I may even have persuaded myself that I felt some throb of recognition. It was only much later that I saw how quick I'd been to bend the facts to fit my preferred story. Read them again: the list of names explicitly denies that any of the swimmers was Leonard. But I'd instantly turned that evidence into its opposite, on the basis of a hasty typist, in whom there is no reason to believe, and some conjectured facial similarities.

*

I WATCHED THE FILM *Philomena* with my wife last night. Its mainspring is another page from the secret books – regret about an absent life. Everything was slightly muted and underplayed, and yet the film never felt small or insignificant. The combination of Steve Coogan and Judi Dench in the main roles seemed to hark back to an archetype: head and heart, intellect and wisdom. And while it was clear that she had found a surrogate son in him, and he a mother in her, that was never made explicit in the film. I admired that restraint.

And I thought, while watching it, that what's so far lacking in this book is that anima, the feminine principle, which Dench embodied. The best stories have an inevitable shape. The smart-aleck boy *must* find his complement in a grounded image of the eternal mother.

Authenticity and enchantment are the twin poles that generate a story's vital energy. Authenticity is the sense that a story bears witness to reality, that the storyteller has some privileged insight into an aspect of life, a world, a particular set of circumstances. At a minimum, authenticity demands that the experience described is *real for someone*. Even in nonsense literature, the whimsy of Lewis Carroll and Edward Lear is redeemed by an obscure sense of real feeling, by Alice's tears, by the broken heart of the abandoned Dong.

The other pole is *enchantment*: the power to persuade us both, you and me, that something which is not real truly exists. It's a magic spell we generate together. The reader conspires with the enchanter. I would say *surrenders to* but its connotations are too passive. The casting of this spell is something we both participate in.

24

Adults are suspicious of this aspect of writing. They are uncomfortable with the notion of make-believe. It's childish. It's also frightening – because who knows what you might be revealing about yourself in your fantasies? But enchantment is the only magic we have that might unlock the secret books.

To accomplish this magic – to cast this spell – demands technique and patience: careful word choice, attentiveness to the rhythms of the prose, the ability to fill the reader's five senses with the illusion of life, an intuition about pacing and the push–pull rhythm of a satisfying structure. It requires the co-operation of a gifted accomplice, a reader who can see through the words the way a conductor hears the black dots of a musical score: this is a string section, this the melancholy quack of an oboe, this celestial brass. Some of it, of course, is simply sleight of hand and confident patter – and this too is craftsmanship. But there is also deeper magic at work: there is necromancy, the summoning of the dead.

It's not that Francis fails to convince, but that I have an instinct that the spell's not right. For the alchemy of the tale to work there needs to be a sense of balance.

The thesis of this book is that we are trapped in stories but that we may be able to imagine our way to better ones. There are other stories than the ones we have collectively chosen. There are second chances and redemption. So let us say not *Francis*, but *Francesca*.

Francesca: yes, it rolls satisfyingly off the tongue. I see her as an incarnation of my Italian grandmother on my father's side: round-faced, with an aquiline nose. The shop of office equipment is less gloomy with a woman in it, somehow. Immediately, we attribute a kind of pluck to her; she is a pioneering businesswoman. Even her avarice is more likeable than that of Francis, who now shimmers and fades from our tale, as though he never existed.

As if by magic, her disability has gone too. Francesca is stout and commanding, with a rustic directness. Her loud voice is the only symptom of her poor hearing. 'I won't let this out of my sight. No offence,' she said, packing away the photo. ('None taken,' I murmured.) 'It's too precious to me. That one – the man in the back row. That's my father. But I can see about getting a copy for you.'

She left it in a manila envelope with my name on it by the signing-in book at the entrance to the pool.

*

TODAY WE FACE an unanticipated problem. So far, things have been going swimmingly, if a trifle slowly. True, I've switched the gender of one of the minor characters and we're still in the portico of the story, waiting to enter the front door. But there's so much inside that I want to show you: there is a man called Rachkovsky who will be the best character I have ever written; there is a fearless female journalist called Wednesday MacGahan who stands six foot tall in her socks, is a lapsed Mormon, and carries a swordstick. And already I know how the theme of the secret books is going to pay off in various subtle and unexpected ways. I'm even going to take you to a place called the Department of Secret Books – a phrase I actually considered at one point for the title.

It's just that today is the problem. I know you have days

like it: one-magpie days, when a sourceless melancholy settles on everything you do.

Sometimes, stories are just not enough. What do you do on the days when your own story seems meaningless and poorly constructed; when even the stories of art, and therapy, and religion provide no consolation; and whatever is objectively good about your life seems to have nothing to do with you? Sometimes what needs repair won't respond to reason and remains beyond the reach of words and stories.

The writer John Gardner said authors should consider the possibility that someone who picks up their novels may be contemplating suicide. (Don't do it, reader!)

But how can writers be depended on to find a *raison d'être* for the reader's life when so many can't scrape one together for their own: Sylvia Plath, Ernest Hemingway, Stefan Zweig, David Foster Wallace, Yukio Mishima? Don't their suicides give the lie to the argument that stories are a source of life-giving wonder? Mostly, I would say, they are the efflux and chatter of wounded egos. I know a lot of writers and by and large they are a bunch of embittered narcissists, like me.

*

I WAS JUST THINKING it would be funny if I now turned my resentment on you, reader, and abused you for making things worse. That, after all, is how unhappy people usually behave: lashing out at the people closest to them. It would be a dangerous game, though. If you close the book in exasperation, I will actually cease to exist.

*

NOW THE DOWNSWING is levelling off. I can feel myself pulling out of the plummeting gloom. The key thing here is to avoid rocketing up into mania. Ease back on the stick, moderate the clever-dickery, and let's get on with the story we're charging good money to hear.

*

OVER THE NEXT few weeks, I spent more time with Francesca. She travelled by bus to the lido and whenever I saw her at the pool, I'd offer her a lift home and quiz her about her life, partly out of curiosity and partly in the selfish hope that I'd learn something I could use in a book. It turned out I was in luck.

She told me her father was from Genoa. He was a child of the *ruota*, the revolving hatch set in the walls of foundling hospitals in which unwed mothers deposited unwanted babies. The system, a curious blend of shame and compassion, was supposed to maintain the mother's honour and the father's anonymity. His surname, Dittami, was assigned to him on arrival. There were others like it – Esposito, Projetti, Ospizio, Casagrande – that marked their owners with a badge of disgrace. The word was that Vincenzo was the natural child of a village priest from Chiavari – and far from his only offspring.

He'd come to England as a teenager. His plan had been to travel to New York, but he only had enough money for passage to Liverpool and on his first week in the city he met Francesca's mother and began to court her.

28

Francesca's mother was the youngest daughter of a family of Irish immigrants. They looked kindly on the match: Vincenzo may have been Italian, but he was a Catholic and hard-working. He'd found himself a job with the Victograph Office Machine Company. Ambitious and personable, Vincenzo impressed his bosses and was offered a promotion to the head office in London, where he moved with his new bride shortly before World War I. He joined up, ready to serve his adoptive country, but his aptitude for fixing machines kept him away from the front line.

It wasn't until after World War II that Vincenzo set up the business that Francesca still ran. He remained an uncomplicated Americanophile, finally making it to the United States in the 1970s. A bleached-out photograph of an unrecognisable old man at the Washington Memorial was pinned to the wall on the ground floor of the shop.

'In another life,' Francesca told me, 'he would have ended up in America, working as an inventor. That was really his dream.' She didn't seem to dwell on the implication that the life her father had ended up with was second best, that she and her siblings represented a dream deferred.

She showed me the ancient typewriters that Vincenzo had collected and restored in retirement: one had no keyboard and was operated by a dial on a drum. 'Dad once had a customer who told him that no weapon had been invented more deadly than a typewriter,' she said. 'That became one of his sayings.' Vincenzo had been fascinated by all sorts of machines, and alongside the pre-plastic objects were more modern relics: an old Atari console, a Sinclair Spectrum, a range of fax machines. What seemed at first like a coda to his life, the inevitable diminuendo of old age, was nothing of the sort. This had been his most important work. He had been building a kind of ceremonial tomb – a subterranean temple to the god Qwertyuiop.

Francesca had an idea that the objects might be worth a great deal of money one day and that they ought to form a bequest to a museum of office technology. There seemed no harm in encouraging this notion, but privately I was sceptical that anyone would pay to visit.

In an alcove at the rear of the basement stood four dusty mahogany cabinets. They were the last incarnation of nineteenth-century recording technology, rendered finally obsolete by the advent of magnetic tape. 'From the old Victograph days when Dad sold dictation equipment,' Francesca explained.

One was no more than a carcass; its insides had been ransacked for spare parts; the ancient cable of another terminated in fraying copper, but a third had been rewired and fitted with a three-pin plug. I held it up to the light and could see that it wasn't recent work. The plastic had yellowed with age.

In a pile of boxes beside it lay the wax cylinders on which it recorded. I picked one up. It was the size and heft of a rolling pin. The putty-coloured wax beneath its paper sleeve was grooved with an almost imperceptible spiral. It seemed miraculous that some voice from the past, someone's actual breath, had been preserved upon it.

*

ORDINARILY, AT THIS POINT, I would write a scene that culminates in one of those wax cylinders being played. If I invented lots of obstacles, I could squeeze a thousand words out of it, possibly more.

Right now, though, I'm not sure what else would be achieved by that scene. I'm very conscious that I've been slow to unfold my story so far. Also, I'm mindful that you stuck by me back there, during my blue period. And I'm genuinely touched by that. So I'm proposing that we just play those cylinders ourselves, in Francesca's absence.

There's a certain knack to loading one onto the spindle, but it's easily acquired. The wood and brass parts are strongly reminiscent of my mother's old Singer sewing machine, a legacy from her mother, Betty Castle. A brass lever, its patina fogged by decades of idleness, snaps down to hold the roll into position, and the needle descends from the rear of the cabinet. On the front of the panel is a huge circular Bakelite on–off switch, like the lid of a coffee canister. If you would be so kind. Thank you. A yellow bulb flares unsteadily into life beside it.

Another click, and the basement fills with a muted crackling sound, followed by the noise of someone clearing their throat. A woman begins to speak. She has impeccable pre-war diction, but the slightly strangulated vowels of someone aiming at the accent of a social class above her own. 'Four score and seven years ago our fathers brought forth, on this continent, a new nation, conceived in Liberty, and dedicated to the proposition that all men are created equal.'

That's all there is of her. The raw crackle fades to a repeating bump and hiss, which continues to play out like the sonic counterpart to the shadows around the walls of the basement.

The paper wrapper on the next cylinder is marked, in thick pencil, 'Christmas '34'. It's a recording of half a dozen voices singing 'Silent Night'. The cylinder has warped and the melody seems to oscillate slightly between keys as the spindle turns. After two verses, everyone stops singing except for one tenor voice that carries on bravely in German, before finally dissolving in laughter halfway through the chorus.

We are silent for a while. A change has come over the basement. The temperature appears to have dropped a couple of degrees. Something is stirring. The dead are beginning to move among us. Our skin tingles at their approach.

It's time to unwrap the third cylinder. It comes from a set of containers kept separate from the others, five Harvey Nichols hatboxes whose lids are labelled in block capitals: NN: DO NOT ERASE. The inscription on the paper wrapper is consistent with the handwriting on the other cylinders, but there's something distinctive about it. Turn it towards the light. It's the neatness of the lettering. The words 'Volume I' are written with the scrupulousness special to the earliest stage of anything – work, love, friendship; that moment when a fresh start gives us the hope of shedding old habits and becoming a better person. I wonder – not selflessly – if this care can be maintained through the later stages of a long project.

A moment later, a sonorous male voice is addressing us. It is grave and deep, with trilled rs and unplaceably alien vowels.

There is, frankly, relief all round. We seem to be through the interminable throat-clearing, the exasperating hesitancy.

Finally, we are going to meet someone who knows how to tell a story.

*

IT'S A CRISP MORNING in early February 1933. Light snow falls out of a grey sky. Vincenzo Dittami sits in the cab of a delivery truck, heading to an address off the Finchley Road in north-west London. He generally makes his calls alone; however, today he is delivering one of his newest and heaviest machines, a Scriptovox Imperator, which requires at least two men to move safely. Alongside him in the cab of the truck is a man called Pierre Thibaut, a red-headed Frenchman of about twenty, who not many years later will receive a posthumous commendation for gallantry on his ancestral beaches in Normandy.

Pierre wonders aloud if the address on the invoice is correct as the truck turns into a residential street. Neither man has ever made a delivery to a private house.

The client answers the door himself. He nods to confirm that he is indeed Mr Nicolas Notovitch.

Mr Notovitch is wearing an extraordinary blue robe that gives him the appearance of a dervish or a conjuror. It is made of quilted velvet, worn and heavily patched, with voluminous sleeves and a hem that scrapes the floor. Vincenzo will later learn from Notovitch that it is an Uzbek chapan from Namangan in the Fergana Valley and was once the property of an old acquaintance. For now, such secrets belong to an unimaginable future. The old man has a fastidiously trimmed white beard, waxily smooth skin, and grey

33

eyes whose gaze is severe, mistrustful and wounded.

It takes all of Vincenzo and Pierre's strength to manhandle the Imperator from the truck to the spot Mr Notovitch indicates in the parlour, a north-east-facing room which, thanks to mahogany furniture and heavy drapes, seems nocturnally sombre even in sunshine. Vincenzo wipes their fingerprints off the Imperator with a handkerchief. The low flames of the coal fire glow dully in the cherry-wood cabinetry of the machine. Vincenzo is already one of the more senior men in the company, and takes the novelty of most of the machines for granted, but he is curious about the new Imperator – to our eyes a ludicrous antique, then the most sophisticated device of its kind.

Once the machine is in position, Vincenzo begins the induction. This is a short demonstration of the Imperator's features that is, for Vincenzo at least, the most enjoyable part of his job.

By the end of his career at Scriptovox, Vincenzo will have performed this induction close to a thousand times. All except one of those demonstrations follow the same pattern: a brief introduction to the machine, the insertion of the wax cylinder, the reading by a volunteer of the Gettysburg Address from a typed sheet Vincenzo carries with him, and then the extraordinary moment of its reproduction.

It requires an imaginative feat to understand how strange it was in the first decades of the twentieth century for a young secretary – such is his usual volunteer – to hear for the first time in her life her own disembodied voice. Seeing the reactions wrought by the sound is like witnessing the effects of real magic.

The audible astonishment that follows that *coup de théâtre* is the cue for Vincenzo's encore: he pulls back the spring-loaded brass footplate to release the recorded cylinder and then erases the recording using the shaving wheel – sometimes housed in a separate unit, but on the Imperator concealed beneath a hatch inside the main cabinet. Behold: the voice has vanished!

Only one of his demonstrations deviates from this pattern. On this occasion, Mr Notovitch stays Vincenzo's hand as he opens the hatch. Notovitch announces that he has no intention of shaving the cylinders. 'I intend to make a record,' he says. 'A record of my life.'

So, of the twenty-one cylinders that survive of Nicolas Notovitch, the first is that one. The recording appears to have degenerated, but this is an auditory illusion; our ears, accustomed to high-fidelity sound and Dolby noise reduction, are spoiled. This hissing, scratchy recording projects a dead man's low, faintly Eastern European voice into the present day.

'Four score and seven years ago our fathers brought forth, on this continent, a new nation, conceived in Liberty, and dedicated to the proposition that all men are created equal.'

There is a gap of a few seconds, and then, a little querulously, the voice enquires: 'Is that sufficient for your purpose, Mr Dittami?'

*

THE FOLLOWING WEEK, Mr Notovitch sends a scrawled note to the office asking for Vincenzo by name. His handwriting is very crabbed and difficult to decipher, but the note appears to say that the machine is giving him difficulties, which he does not specify.

That Saturday, Vincenzo returns alone and repeats his demonstration. Notovitch is, as on that first visit, watchful, imperious, guarded. When Vincenzo asks him to try loading the cylinder, he turns his back on the younger man, and wrestles with the mechanism in vain. Vincenzo can hear that he's struggling to release the catch of the footplate. He offers to oil it.

'The problem, Mr Dittami,' Notovitch huffs, 'is not one of oil.' He straightens up with a visible effort and extends his empty hands. The fingers are splayed and lumpy like the toes of a frog. 'You see? I suffer badly from arthritis in your climate. I simply cannot operate this device. Please make arrangements to remove it.'

It is true, Vincenzo concedes, that the mechanism of the Imperator is sometimes initially stiff, but it will yield after a period of moderate usage. No great strength is required to work it; for this reason, he adds, the model is extremely popular with lightly built female employees. His words fail to mollify the client.

'You have many competitors,' Notovitch says in a crotchety and disparaging tone. 'Glossophone. Dictascribe. One of them has surely foreseen the needs of customers such as myself.'

It is a matter of great pride to Vincenzo that he has never had a machine returned. He explains to the old man that there is no better product on the market than the one in front of them. He enumerates the failings of the machines Notovitch has mentioned: short recording times, poor fidelity, expensive cylinders. Notovitch dismisses his arguments with the wave of one arthritic hand.

As Vincenzo considers the loss of his commission – close to £5 on a machine of this price – and the ignominy of returning the Imperator to the showroom, he notices Mr Notovitch giving him a wary, sidelong glance. It dawns on him suddenly that this isn't a process of rejection, but negotiation. 'Mr Notovitch,' he says, 'you clearly have a very specific task in mind. We at Scriptovox pride ourselves on our flexibility. How can we render the service you require?'

Notovitch takes a step towards Vincenzo and studies his face for a long time without embarrassment, like a jeweller who in the dim light of a back room is trying some doubtful gold for marks of assay.

What does he see in that face? Who is he searching for? Notovitch is so close that Vincenzo can smell the lilac eau de cologne he used that morning to dress his whiskers. Finally the old man turns away and invites the salesman to sit down on one of the heavy chairs. He riddles the glowing coals with a poker and adds a few more pieces from the scuttle. When he speaks again, it is with a new note in his voice, more conciliatory and more sad.

'In my life,' he says, 'I have seen the written word falsified and abused. I wish to make a record that has unimpeachable authority. I want words that stand for all time.'

Vincenzo says something to the effect that all the company's products carry a minimum twenty-year guarantee and that, as long as they are stored in the correct conditions, the cylinders will hold his words indefinitely.

'That's as may be,' Notovitch says, wiping coal dust from his hands with the rag that hangs on the fire screen. 'I have important work to undertake. I'm an old man. I cannot afford mistakes.' He raises a crooked finger and wags it at the salesman. 'This is more than the story of a man's life. The well-being of humanity may depend upon it.'

Vincenzo is too attuned to the needs of his customers to laugh, but he finds something risible and pathetic in these claims. Who is this buffoon who has dragged him out on a Saturday to waste time with his grandiose boasts and self-regard? Vincenzo is closing in on middle age himself. He has a wife and children, and places he would much rather be. But he also has an understandable reluctance to write off the money.

'I need an amanuensis,' says Notovitch.

*

THAT DAY ESTABLISHED a pattern of acquaintance that lasted for two and a half months, until April of the same year. Once a week, after work, Vincenzo travelled to Notovitch's house from the showroom on Fleet Street. He went by suburban train, across his rain-washed adoptive city, whose smells of coal and laundry soap and stale beer he already took for granted.

The housekeeper, Mrs Maguire, would meet him at the door. Invariably, Mr Notovitch would be already seated in the parlour.

It seemed that Notovitch required nothing more than the services of an engineer. Vincenzo's ostensible job was merely to engage the cylinder of the Imperator and signal to Notovitch with a nod that the recording was under way, then signal once again after fourteen minutes when the cylinder was almost full.

In fact, I believe Notovitch needed Vincenzo for an additional reason. The old man had the gifts of a village storyteller: fluency, directness and an uncanny talent for mimicry, which is hard to render on the page. But a storyteller requires an audience. Notovitch needed the conspiracy of a listener, a human silence to contain and validate his tale. With a few significant exceptions, Vincenzo is absent from the recordings, but you can often sense his outline in those pauses, where Notovitch stops to reorient himself, like a bat navigating through darkness by the echo of its own cries.

At the end of their second meeting, he sealed Vincenzo's compliance with the payment of a guinea – a payment that he repeated after every subsequent encounter.

It was a relationship upon which Vincenzo embarked with misgivings and with no intention of seeing out to its conclusion. But over time, the transaction mellowed into something more cordial, despite Notovitch's habit of addressing Vincenzo sometimes as Victor, sometimes Lorenzo, and once Luigi.

On the day of the final recording, with the work concluded, both men sat on in the half-dark for a moment in silence, neither of them ready to dispel the ghosts they had conjured.

By then, both of them knew that time would be unkind to Notovitch's memory. His exit would be followed by the mortifying laughter of history – a fact that pained him deeply. And yet, Notovitch understood better than most that in some sense all lives are imaginary, beginning with the fiction of a name.

When their work was complete and Notovitch returned to Paris, Vincenzo saw him off at the station. Almost the old man's final act was to entrust the cylinders to Vincenzo's care.

The relationship of the story they tell to the historical character they name, the *real* Nicolas Notovitch, is a complex one. Naturally, it has occurred to me to transcribe the cylinders verbatim, but I feel that you and I are past that, reader. Why commit ourselves to such a tiresome formal obligation? We both know that the recordings themselves are only one ingredient in the spell. This is a story for which no tense properly exists in English: a tale in the subjunctive – contingent, supposed, doubted, wished for, feared. Its purpose will become clear to us gradually. There must be an act of faith on both our parts. The time has come to stand together in the illusory light cast by the enchantment and peer into the pages of the secret books.

*

*'I was born in the town of Kerch, on the northern shore of the
Black Sea . . .'*

THERE IS A SHOP. It is already familiar to you. You have
glimpsed it in another life, in Leonard's. Smells contend with
one another in the darkness: the sharp aromas of paraffin,
pitch and coffee; the oaky scent of hemp ropes; venereal hints
of dried fish, musky tobacco; the camphor tang of liniments
and cough remedies. Listen carefully and you are aware of
a faint sound, like the hoarse breath of a sleeping giant: the
steady motion of a gentle inland sea.

It is evening. A boy of seventeen is standing behind a
barrel, studying a medical textbook by an oil lamp's yellow
flame. He reminds us of Leonard, but he is not Leonard. He
is a young version of the man we have just met: Nicolas, or
more accurately Nikolai, but here we'll know him by an af-
fectionate diminutive, Kolya: sallow, grey-eyed, height five
feet five and a half inches, weight 110 pounds, with a silky,
incipient moustache of which he is inordinately proud.

The town of Kerch sits on the eastern tip of the Crimean
peninsula; it closes off the Sea of Azov to the north, and looks
across the water to the Cossack lands of the Kuban. Sometimes, when the wind blows from the east, Kolya fancies it
is carrying the scent of wormwood and incense across the
steppe from the caliphates and emirates of Central Asia.

From childhood, he has dreamed of visiting the Silk Road
cities, of tasting the wild apples of the Tian Shan mountains,
and seeing the blue-eyed Muslims of the Kashgar oasis whose

41

ancestors travelled east with Alexander's conquering armies.

At the Greek Gymnasium, founded for the children of émigré traders, Kolya has worked industriously, winning his teachers' approval, but is occasionally chided for sprinkling his compositions with bulbuls and minarets and harems and splendid thrones.

Since the age of eight, he has assisted in this shop, weighing, packing, keeping accounts with a neat hand in the ledger; making deliveries to customers who are favoured, or old, or sick.

The Kerch of the 1870s is small, but all varieties of life blow in from the sea: Turk, Armenian, Georgian, German, Greek, Italian and even English. A frequent visitor to the stores is a man named Horace Meakins, a Mancunian and the skipper of a packet ship. He comes in for supplies and to fill his pouch with pipe tobacco; he is married to a fierce Bessarabian woman who has borne him a family in Odessa.

Wait for a second in the warm darkness of this shop. Be careful what you touch. This place is as fragile as any enchantment. There is a feeling that a strong wind might ruffle its backdrop, expose the jars on its shelves as clever sketches. The ring of a mobile phone could intrude at any minute. Still, look at the child beside the barrel: pensive, hard-working, standing at the threshold of a long life of seemingly inexhaustible promise, but which will be reduced in conclusion to an inventory of disappointments and consolations. He is you, reader; he is me.

Now there is the sound of voices. The boy looks up, his eyes refocusing slowly on the door of the shop. (What a privilege it is to observe him unnoticed! Imagine if someone were watching over you in this kindly way.)

Meakins, the packet-boat skipper, enters. Beside him is an extraordinary creature. Kolya seems to see a tall man with a deeply tanned face, shoulder-length brown hair, and a dress. A man who is in fact a woman, but so tall, garrulous and swaggering that Kolya cannot, somehow, think of her as one. Her speaking voice is low, deeper than alto, a warm tenor like Kolya's own, as she talks to Meakins in English, listing the items she requires.

In spite of his long residence in the Russian Empire, Meakins's command of the language is shaky, but he seems keen to impress his guest with his local knowledge. He passes on the information hesitatingly. 'A cooking pot, a case of biscuits, lamp oil, tobacco . . .'

Kolya jots down the items in his neat clerical handwriting. Now he interrupts in English, addressing the stranger directly in order to clarify something. 'Tobacco to smoke?'

She holds his gaze for a second. 'To chew,' she says, and sends a gout of brown saliva onto the dust of the wooden floor.

Kolya fills her order as quickly as he can. She is no more than ten or fifteen years older than he, but already she has the air of someone whom the world can no longer surprise. Her face is as brown as a sailor's and the corners of her eyes are ribbed with crows' feet. She stands in a wide, unladylike stance and uses a silver-topped ebony stick to point out supplemental items from the shelves: dried fish, ink, wax candles, ten quires of paper.

'You speak English,' she remarks. 'They teach you that at school?'

'A little, but mostly I learn myself.'

Sixty years later, Notovitch will allow himself a smile as he parodies his rustic pronunciation. '*I lyorn myself.*' But there's a little dash of pride. In retrospect, it's clear that this is his defining talent. It comprises a combination of gifts – a facile memory, a bent for mimicry, a good ear, but most of all a special confidence. He plunges into each new language like an expert swimmer who knows that each lake or river or sea presents a fresh set of challenges, but that they're all water, an element he's conquered. The trick is in a kind of surrender. Kolya can pick up the rudiments of a new language in a week, get close to mastery in a month. He'll do it with an athlete's unthinking grace, surprised that others can't do the same. He'll notice too the slight transformation that each language works on his persona: more direct in Russian, more sprightly in French and Italian, more heavy and scrupulous in English; and in the oriental languages he's still barely dreamed of learning, he'll astonish himself with his subtlety and resourcefulness.

Her order complete, the woman draws a handful of unfamiliar gold coins from a leather knapsack to pay for the purchases. Kolya hesitates. She asks what is the matter. He says he can't accept the money, the coins are not a currency he recognises. 'These are gold dollars from the United States Mint,' she says. Kolya is steadfast. She names the usual rate of exchange and hints that she is willing to accept a punitive one. Still Kolya will not budge.

'I need to get under way before dawn to meet my schedule,' she says. 'What do you suggest I do?'

Kolya, by now, is flustered. He wants to help this stranger, but he is too much his father's son to accept the strange coins.

He asks her to wait, and, stepping into the street, rouses one of the drunks who patronise the liquor counter to go and fetch his father.

As the unsteady steps die away in the distance, Meakins and the woman sit down on two crates of Kazan soap. The woman quizzes Kolya about the book he is reading. He tells her he is studying to be a doctor. She is sensitive enough to catch a note of wistfulness in his voice; she presses him and learns he has dreams of making a living with his pen, of writing stories for newspapers and thick, learned journals.

'Imagine,' she says to Meakins with exaggerated irony. 'A writer!'

Kolya assumes he's being mocked. He explains, defensively, that it's not a dream that comes from nowhere. He has a cousin, Osip, nine years older, who grew up across the water in Taganrog. He lives in Saint Petersburg and edits a paper called *Novosti*. Each proper noun – Osip, Saint Petersburg, *Novosti* – seems to emerge from Kolya's mouth in a bubble of awe and pride. 'One day I will work for him.'

Not 'would like to', mind, or 'hope to': *will*. The note of certainty and upward reach is as out of place in the dingy shop as – what? – well, the woman herself.

She puts a hand into her knapsack and presents Kolya with a visiting card. He sounds out the roman letters in his head. *Wednesday MacGahan. London Daily News.*

'I am the chief foreign correspondent of the *Daily News*,' she says. 'Founded by Charles Dickens. The greatest newspaper in the world.' It's not a boast. She says it with a gravity that is intended to honour the boy's ambition.

'You're a writer?' Kolya's face has the naked amazement

45

of someone who has encountered a creature from a dream.

Indeed she is. The astonishing stranger tells him that she has recently travelled overland from India. Her paper has received intelligence of an uprising in the Ottoman lands of Bulgaria and she is intending to file dispatches. She has engaged Meakins to take her across to the Black Sea port of Varna. His ship is being coaled for its voyage.

Kolya's imagination snags on a single word: India! It conjures a jasmine-scented dream of geometric gardens, Mughal domes and ankle bracelets that is abruptly dispelled by the arrival of his father, who is carrying the fine scales and still sucking the remains of his supper from his teeth. Kolya feels an unaccountable pang at seeing the curve of his father's back as he stoops to fuss over the brass pans. With the hindsight of sixty years, such tiny things will seem like the mutterings of destiny.

The money is sound; the journalist accepts the poor terms she is offered. Within an hour, the provisions are being loaded by moonlight aboard Meakins's boat, the *Derby*. Only the visiting card tucked into the pages of the medical textbook is proof to Kolya that the apparition was real.

Later that night, lying wakefully in bed, Kolya hears the water lapping at the wharf. He thinks of the sea wrinkling under the moonlight as it spreads eastwards from Kerch to Jason's Colchis on the Georgian shore, and westwards past the Hellespont, to the pirate coast of Barbary and beyond.

He packs a canvas bag with a few possessions and creeps out into the darkness. He sees with the clear-eyed heartlessness of his seventeen years that this is a chance that will not come again.

'The Derby *was a vessel of sturdy English construction that had been retired to the Black Sea after the opening of the Suez Canal.'*

Slipping out into the warm night is like putting on a disguise. Kolya has become invisible. He is a sigh of breath in his nostrils. He is the strap of a bag cutting into a shoulder. He is the sound of footsteps.

The air at the dock is sour with tar and oil and the drainlike smell of bilge. But nothing can be more magnificent than the sight of the wharf in moonlight. Kolya hears murmured voices, singing, the notes of an accordion, the creak of a canvas hammock, as he swings his bundle over the stern of the ship and creeps below. He has provisioned the *Derby* on so many occasions that all her hiding places are well known to him. He finds himself an empty locker to the aft of the ship into which he crawls and falls asleep. This willing sleep is the property of youth that he will yearn for more than any other in old age.

Dawn breaks. Kolya is startled awake by the sound of pistons hammering in the engine room beneath him. In his bag is some rye bread and *brynza*, soft ewe's cheese that he has taken from the pantry. He looks at the stolen food with a sickening remorse. What has he done? Worse, he has forgotten to bring water and his tongue feels thick with thirst.

As he is cursing his oversight, the hatch above him lifts, and a bar of sunlight dazzles his eyes. A shaven-headed man with a drooping moustache and Cossack forelock reels back with an oath. *'Chert voz'mi!'* He drags Kolya out of his hiding place by his ear, marches him to the wheelhouse and presents him to the captain.

47

Kolya improvises a story quickly. He explains that he went over the account book in the store and realised that MacGahan's lamp oil had been forgotten. Returning to the ship, he carried it below decks, banged his head on a beam, and woke up to find himself a stowaway.

It is wildly incredible for many reasons, but it is the best he can do at short notice. In fact, throughout his long life, Kolya's lies will tend towards the audacious rather than the plausible.

Captain Meakins does a great deal of business with Kolya's father. It's difficult for him to be as harsh as the boy undoubtedly deserves. Meakins beckons Kolya over with a crooked finger and feels his head for a lump. The boy at least has the presence of mind to wince at his touch.

While Captain Meakins is interrogating the stowaway, MacGahan stands in a corner of the wheelhouse cutting a plug of tobacco and watching with mild amusement.

Meakins explains that the boy must work his passage to Varna; from there he will telegraph the father, put the boy on the next boat home and deduct the cost from his account at the store.

Kolya is assigned a mildewed canvas hammock and given a job in the galley. The ship's cook is a wiry, dark-skinned man called Dass, who came with Meakins from Alexandria and whose English Kolya finds incomprehensible.

Dass is a lascar, one of the Indian seamen who have provided the sinew of maritime power for centuries. Born beside the Hooghly in Calcutta, Dass had nothing we would recognise as a childhood. He'll spend his life on ships and die of tuberculosis in 1902 in a home for indigent sailors in Whitechapel.

It is a journey of four days to Varna. Kolya's mood alternates between exuberance and melancholy. Twice a day, after clearing the dishes from the mess, he spends fifteen minutes by himself on deck. His heart is lifted by the vast sky. The boat chugs westwards, into a future that seems all promise. But at low points, upbraided in gestures by Dass for being slapdash, for wasting water, or finding himself once again the butt of rough sailors' jokes, Kolya thinks sadly of home. Brought up among women, he is used to female companionship. There is a softness in his nature that he has not yet learned to hide.

MacGahan sees this. MacGahan sees everything. She is an aloof and puzzling presence on the boat. Her lack of discernible femininity upsets the sailors, particularly the Cossack, who revenge themselves with vile jokes about her, but dare say nothing within her hearing. She is paying for the passage. Besides, her indifference to convention compels a kind of respect. The Cossack's contempt begins to batten on weaker prey.

Supper time. Already flustered by a bollocking from Dass, Kolya hurries to clear the table for the second sitting. As he leans past the Cossack, he feels a big hand fasten on his wrist.

The Cossack supplements his meals with *salo*, glistening white pork fat, from a personal supply. He has cut off a slice and speared it with the tip of his knife. This he holds to Kolya's lips.

'Have a bite,' he says.

Kolya stammeringly declines.

'Try it,' he says, this time with a more explicit note of menace.

49

Once again, the boy refuses.

'Sit,' the Cossack says. He knows just how to lock Kolya's wrist back against the forearm to enforce compliance. Kolya drops to the bench beside the Cossack, who entangles him with an arm like a hawser, dragging on the boy's thin shoulders.

The Cossack smells of drink. His breath snorts noisily through the whiskers of his moustache. His veins pulse at his temples. Sweat glistens on his shaven head; slicked back against the naked skin, the forelock of bristly hair seems somehow obscene.

'Relax!' He rubs Kolya's scalp with his knuckles and sniffs them. 'Yid,' he announces, with the proud air of a wine merchant identifying an obscure vintage. A hush falls on the table. The Cossack places the blade of his knife against the boy's cheek, the tip with the chunk of pig fat so close to Kolya's eye that he can't see it. A roll of the ship could leave him blind. 'Christ-killer. Eat.'

Some vestigial spirit of defiance moves in Kolya, some loathing of the man, some resistance to having a story forced upon him, to being an accessory in the Cossack's personal drama of virility and orthodoxy. But silence is the only weapon Kolya has. If he opens his mouth, the Cossack will force the pig fat down his throat.

Silver flashes in the air before his face. Kolya feels the Cossack's arm go tense and resigns himself to being cut. Involuntarily, he closes his eyes. He thinks of home. He thinks of his mother. He hears a muttered oath. The Cossack's arm drops away. Kolya opens his eyes.

MacGahan is standing on the table. In one hand, she has gathered her skirts and lifted them clear of her knees;

with the other, she flourishes the blade of the ebony-handled swordstick. The Cossack is pinned by the throat. The tip of the sword grazes his Adam's apple. MacGahan holds his gaze. She bears down on him with a quiet intensity. Bread crusts are squashed beneath her bare feet. A pair of indigo wings have been tattooed expertly on each of her ankles to make them resemble Hermes's boots.

'Translate for me, boy,' she says. 'Tell him it's a rapier blade. Forged in Toledo, Spain.'

With eyes downcast, Kolya mutters his translation. 'She says the sword is Spanish.'

MacGahan continues: 'All I have to do is straighten my arm and the tip will go right through his windpipe.' She makes a forlorn bird call through her front teeth. 'Hear that? Tell him that's the sound the hole will make when he tries to breathe.'

'We were playing.' The Cossack is trying not to whine. 'The boy knows it was nothing serious. Manly humour, that's all.' He offers a conciliatory hand to Kolya. 'If I've offended you, I'm sorry.' Kolya accepts the offered palm. His tiny boyish hand disappears in the Cossack's paw.

'Look him in the eye, boy,' says MacGahan quietly. Kolya's afraid to meet his tormentor's gaze but does as he's told. He finds neither menace nor insincerity in the man's face. His eyes are as blue as the sky over his native steppe. MacGahan sheathes her sword.

'Give me that,' Kolya says, pointing at the *salo* on the table. He stuffs it in his mouth, chews the creamy fat, and swallows. The crew bursts into raucous laughter. The Cossack claps him on the back. 'I knew you weren't a yid,' he says.

MACGAHAN TAKES HER MEALS alone in her cabin. Dass serves the food himself – gussied-up versions of what the crew eat, prettified on the plate and embellished with linen folded into shapes. From the length of time Dass spends turning a recalcitrant napkin into a swan or a boat, it's clear this is something he takes a certain pride in.

That evening, Dass gestures at Kolya to carry in the tray.

'Me?'

'You,' the cook says, gruffly. Kolya understands he has been asked for.

Heat has been building in the ship all day. The boilers burn constantly, making steam to turn the screws; the sun sears the outside of the hull; the clamour of the pistons fills the galley. Kolya blinks as he emerges into the cool sea air on deck. He knocks on the door of the cabin and is summoned inside.

MacGahan has discarded her dress because of the heat. She is wearing red combination drawers and a pair of reading glasses. Tall and bony, she resembles a crimson wading bird. She doesn't look up from the charts spread across the map table in front of her. 'Put it down there,' she says, indicating a stool in a corner of the cabin.

Kolya does as he's told and turns to leave.

'How did you like the pork fat?' MacGahan asks.

The boy shrugs. 'More or less. I liked it.'

She takes off the reading glasses and looks over at him. 'Really? As good as your mother's? As good as home-made?'

He notes the sly humour in her eyes and decides to make no reply.

'I bet nothing beats your mother's cooking,' MacGahan says with a show of innocence. She folds up the charts and asks Kolya to pass her the tray, then flaps out Dass's painstaking recreation of a lotus to cover her drawers and grinds black pepper onto the food: another perk of the passenger cabin.

Kolya waits to be dismissed, but MacGahan is not done with him. Jabbing at the boy with the fork for emphasis, she asks him a question through a mouthful of cutlet. 'Tell me something, son: why did you come aboard this ship?'

MacGahan leans back in her seat and holds up an admonitory finger as Kolya launches into the explanation he gave the captain. 'Not the crap you told Meakins. When there are stories to make up, I'll be the one to do it.'

Kolya's lips form a guilty smile. From the moment he saw MacGahan, she awoke a bud of longing in his heart. He recalls that sensation in the shop – that imagined jasmine blossom whose perfume seemed to snag inside him like a silver fish hook. But he knows he can't say *that*. He shrugs. 'It's hard to explain.'

'Then let *me* tell *you*. Your father wants you to become a doctor, right? You think, five years of study? Forget that. It's a third of my life on earth . . .'

'I'm nearly eighteen.'

She dispatches his mathematical quibble with a contemptuous wave. 'You've had it with the chandlering business. You see me and you're saying to yourself, I'd follow her into the cannon's mouth. Right? It's the fantasy of mousy clerks everywhere. You all dream of being Tamburlaine. But you can't guess what it cost me to live this life. And if you could guess, you wouldn't pay it.'

Working as a shopkeeper in a port city has given Kolya a thorough grounding in human nature: drunks, misers, traders, swindlers, repentant spendthrifts trying to return ruined merchandise. Kolya knows MacGahan is in the market for something. He recognises her rudeness as a haggler's gambit, one he'll adopt as his own: disprizing the product you plan to buy.

The truth is MacGahan has taken a shine to Kolya. She liked him from the start, from the moment her gold coins failed to dazzle him. Now he works hard to impress her further. He tells Dass she's asked for him to deliver her trays. He scurries back and forth from her cabin uncomplainingly with hot tea when she is laid low by the sickening swell. He makes it clear that she could do a lot worse than hire him as a servant. She knows it doesn't hurt to travel with a male companion. Above all, she needs a translator. When she asks if he knows any Bulgarian, he has no hesitation in claiming fluency. Is it even a lie if he can make it come true eventually?

'My recollection of these incidents has raised an issue which I had hoped to delay addressing . . .'

A clock chimes four in the parlour on Finchley Road. Vincenzo unwraps a fresh cylinder and mounts it in the Imperator. Notovitch gets slowly to his feet and holds a taper to the mantles of the gas lamps.

The light deepens the shadows in the old man's face. It's hard to see any trace of Kolya there. Indeed, it's sometimes difficult to believe that any such creature ever existed. But Notovitch has lived a handful of different lives.

Nicolas Notovitch. It's a name he has grown into. *Nicolas* suits him. He pronounces it without its terminal *s*, a Gallic style that's very close to the Russian original. And the family name carries some pre-revolutionary distinction: the exoticism of the unformalised old-style transliterations – Tchekoff, Turgenyeff, Pouchkine. Certainly, he has as good a claim to this name as anyone else on the planet. But at the time of the events he has described, such a man as Nicolas Notovitch had barely begun to exist. Until he stowed away aboard the *Derby*, he had gone by another: Naum Moiseich Abramovich.

Can we credit the Cossack with preternatural powers of Jew-detection? No. He sees Jews everywhere. He has a long record of false positives: an Italian aristocrat, a Scottish banker. He's even drunkenly accused Dass, a Hindu, of being Jewish. And once Kolya's eaten the *salo*, it never crosses the Cossack's mind that he might have been deceived.

But Kolya is a Jew. His grandfather on his father's side, now dead, was the hazzan, or cantor, of a synagogue in Odessa. His mother counts among her relatives the Litvinoffs of Chernobyl. Kolya's family has declined in observance after moving to Crimea. Perhaps the sea air has moderated their piety. Since he began at the gymnasium, where all the students wore a round-necked Prussian-style uniform, Kolya has borne no visible signs of his religion.

Is he a coward? Perhaps. It would have been courageous to affirm his faith in the face of that bigot. Jews from the shtetl made a virtue of displaying the symbols of their rites defiantly.

But Kolya – as we must continue to call him – is on a different quest. And it takes another kind of courage to violate

55

your tribe's taboos. This is what he has seen in MacGahan, foul-mouthed man-woman, seemingly careless of anyone's opinion. Kolya is beginning to confront the questions that he is fated to encounter for his entire life: What of us is truly real? What are the limits of our nature? What freedom do we have to rewrite or discard our own stories?

The cylinder turns. The old man sorts through the sheaf of notes on his lap. Sometimes, of course, he must wish he'd been a doctor. It is a noble calling. And there is a special grace in pleasing your parents. But then he thinks about what happened to the Jews of the Pale – what was done by the Cossacks and their ilk in Odessa, Rostov, Kishinev, Kiev, Bialystok and elsewhere; he knows he's lucky to have left when he did.

'The Cossack appeared to bear me no ill will.'

The passage of time has erased all recollection of his name. Was he Ivan? Let us suppose so.

Satisfied that Kolya was not a loathed Jew, Ivan took it upon himself to begin the boy's nautical education. He showed him with great patience how to take a reading from a battered sextant, how to forecast weather from the clouds, and how to give a death blow with a knife. Once, he stood in the bow and persuaded a wild seabird to take bread from his hand; he talked matter-of-factly of killing a man. He liked to get drunk and sing loud, impassioned songs out of one side of his mouth, while his eyes rolled back into his head. He was vain, a bully, as fanatically loyal to the Tsar as one would expect; though not the least character in this story, he is far from the greatest. He was a sworn enemy of the Jewish people. The old man has no grounds to be fond or sentimental about his memory. Why does he dwell on him? Maybe it's because a steppe-warrior making a home on the sea is as great a break with family tradition as Kolya's.

It seems to the old man that so much that is deemed to be great or profound is merely tawdry when inspected, particularly the abstractions for which people are prepared to kill or die. Nowadays, he believes in nothing at all. The universe is a dark space which men fill with their own meanings. The mystery of a human being like Ivan only deepens on reflection. Each is an infinite paradox. But perhaps he presumes too much on the listener's patience with his sermonising.

'When we reached Varna, MacGahan took me on as her valet.'

From the deck of the *Derby*, which is riding at anchor, awaiting a visit from the port authority, Varna seems to sing an eternal song of seafaring and trade. The Black Sea port has been part of the Ottoman Empire for four centuries. Doubtless, there are harlots and spices, strong drink, and men with tattoos: the eternal ingredients of every maritime spell.

Yet sometimes, I feel this is not an enchantment at all, but a jury-rigged assembly of mirrors and lenses that enables us to peer back into the past. *Valet. Swordstick. Combination drawers*. The archaisms of our great-grandparents can lull us into a sense that their world was remote from ours. It's not.

To Captain Meakins's annoyance, there is not yet a telegraph station at Varna. But elsewhere, submarine cables are knitting the world into a web of synchrony. Time is becoming

57

the same everywhere. The long and varied beats of the medieval year have given way to shorter cycles. It's a meaningless cliché to say that the world is changing, but stories that have done for centuries are losing their place to newer ones. In Baku, oil wells have been sunk where the Zoroastrians once worshipped the fire god, Ahura Mazda. Steam trains rumble past temples honouring the *Siva lingam* on the Deccan Plateau. Even Japan, in occultation for more than two hundred years, is opening itself to the world. Everywhere printing presses and electric wires accelerate the passage of news and propaganda, multiply the intercourse of opposing fictions.

A great empire is falling to bits. That's what's brought MacGahan here from India. The catch-all term is the Eastern Question. The rule of the Ottomans, which once swayed subjects from Baghdad to Belgrade, down the Levant, and across Northern Africa, is in terminal disarray. It's menaced by the fresher energy of younger empires – British, Russian, French – and the new stories of nationhood. For a few decades more it will limp along before collapsing entirely. It will be wound up at Sèvres; its possessions reapportioned by the Great Powers in ways that we're still killing each other about.

The story MacGahan is chasing is this: restive Christian subjects have risen up against their Muslim rulers. Or some have. There are rumours the uprising has been put down with excessive bloodshed. From Varna, from anywhere, the truth is unclear. Spokesmen for the Ottoman government, the Sublime Porte, insist they have simply dealt with a revolt. After all, what imperial power has ever managed to get by without slapping down unruly subjects? The British government, led by Disraeli, is inclined to agree. On the Olympian chessboard of the Great Powers, the Ottoman Empire serves a useful strategic function as far as the British are concerned, blocking further thrusts by Russia towards the West.

But tales of terrible cruelty are leaking out of the Balkans. Disraeli's old nemesis, Gladstone, denounces the Turks as bloodthirsty tyrants and Disraeli for supporting them. It is an oddly familiar pile-up: geopolitical abstractions, business interests, personal ambition and moral outrage. MacGahan, employed by a newspaper that voices liberal opinion, has been sent to find out the truth. Or, more accurately, she's been sent to gather evidence to support one version of it. Already, in 1876, the world is inundated with competing stories. We have to try to choose wisely between them; or better, perhaps, to disbelieve them all.

MacGahan and Kolya settle the terms of his employment at the dock. She insists he writes a letter to his father to be sent home through Meakins. He borrows paper, ink, and sets to work.

It's better to be brief than lie. He frames it as a short absence. There's much he can't say. (I think of Uncle Leonard, writing from the Western Front, standing on duckboards, shells passing overhead, the corpses in No Man's Land already food for rats: 'The meat paste arrived safely. Thank Winifred for the socks.')

Kolya leaves out making friends with the Cossack and the part about eating pork. Perhaps that's what his transgression meant on board the ship: an act of severance with all that lies behind. The choice seems very clear: to go home and be chastised as a child, to go on and become a man. At least, that's how it seems to him. No parent who has ever worried about a child's absence – in other words, no parent – will agree.

*

JULY TURNS TO AUGUST. At the port, the sea air provides some relief from the heat. But MacGahan's assignment is taking her inland, to Peshtera, and to Batak, where there is word of a massacre.

Russian and Bulgarian are just enough alike for Kolya to make himself understood; a few times he mumbles something about the dialect being unfamiliar. If MacGahan's noticed his deception, she doesn't show it. They travel in carts to Peshtera, but the difficult journey into the hills can only be made on horseback; the Turkish authorities forbid the local inhabitants from hiring them any.

Over coffee and honey pastries, the governor of Peshtera tries to foist a minder on Kolya and MacGahan. 'The people are unpredictable. Liars. A woman travelling with her son . . .' (such is their deception) '. . . surely I don't to need to tell you what they're capable of?' MacGahan refuses point-blank. At night, Kolya slips out and haggles for horses and donkeys.

In the hour before dawn, Kolya and MacGahan head off with a train of twenty animals. Sunrise brings heat and the soothing buzz of insects. Pans and water bottles rattle as they move. The world smells of hot grass and donkey shit. There are four local guides and a dozen women on foot bringing up the rear, villagers from Batak, too scared until now to return home.

Kolya's a novice rider, but he's young and adaptable. He

copies the Bulgarian guides whose movements on horseback combine looseness and brutality. Their heels pound the mangy flanks of the horses, urging them up the hillside paths.

In MacGahan, the men know they have a champion and they show her the utmost deference. Her eccentricity and ambiguity appear not to be noticed. She rides like a farm boy, has taken to wearing breeches and tucks her hair under a straw hat. The sun tinges her brown tresses with gleams of copper.

The fields are full of wheat and rye, but no one is there to harvest. The black-haired Bulgar peasants passing the other way are melancholy and silent. It's not until 1903 that we'll get the right word to describe them: *traumatised.*

We have a hard job ahead of us. Can we summon up outrage about an obscure massacre that has long ago been trumped by bloodier and better-documented ones; whose record is barely more legible than those in the secret books? Perhaps outrage is not the word. Can we care without sentimentality? Can we show sympathy to the victims without being pulled into the trap of immediately taking sides?

Let's stay with what Kolya sees.

Cresting a rise – on foot, leading the horse by the reins, because the path is too steep – he enters a wide upland valley. There's a sawmill by a stream. Further on, wooden roofs, a church. This is Batak, hardly prosperous, but previously orderly and thriving. The women in the rear fall silent. The buzz of insects grows ominously loud. The ungathered corn has collapsed on its rotted stalks. Two dogs are fighting over a bone. One of the Bulgar guides chases them off with a whip, but they only retreat a few yards and inch back as soon as he takes up his reins again.

The earth is a carpet of bones. Corpses three weeks dead have been pulled apart by the dogs. The sun has turned some skin to leather. The dried-out sockets of a severed head stare blindly into the sun. Kolya stumbles. His boots drag. It seems like sacrilege to walk upon the dead. The accumulation of horrors begins to turn him numb. Chemises of violated girls. Dried blood. The tiny bones of dead children.

Bashi-bazouks – Turkish irregular soldiers – have burned or smashed every structure in the village. The women who followed MacGahan and Kolya into the mountains begin to ululate with grief. As they approach the churchyard, it seems prurient to dwell on the stench; it seems oddly fastidious not to mention it all. MacGahan passes Kolya a handful of tobacco. He holds it to his nose and breathes.

The churchyard is three feet deep in putrid bones. A desultory attempt has been made to cover some with gravel. The church is crammed with more dead bodies.

Kolya sits on a rock. He feels wretched and strange. He keeps seeing the leathery faces, piles of heads, embroidered ankle socks around what's left of feet. He hears the ghastly buzz of sated insects. He closes his eyes and wishes he were home. This isn't the world he left for. What he cannot know, what he cannot guess, is how scenes of cruelty like this will come to seem typical of the approaching century, and how they will be woven into tales of war. But looking back, he will recognise this as the first moment that he felt a dizzying sense of living in history, and that the world that had once seemed so new to him was being pressed upon by blind and ancient forces.

There will be many massacres in the decades ahead. Some will seem to merit the coining of new words: holocaust, genocide, ethnic cleansing. Historians will weigh relative amounts of suffering in the scales of professional dispassion. The significance of each act will never be absolute, but will be determined by a large number of other concerns, like the number and credibility of its witnesses. Some dreadful deeds will take place in a kind of historical silence. Others will be memorialised in images, photographs, cine film, video. Some vast acts of murder will be reconceived as regrettable necessities.

Here, MacGahan has her pen. Kolya watches her counting, making notes, oddly detached from the horror. In the churchyard alone, she estimates a toll of three thousand corpses. Two hundred women and children were burned alive in the schoolhouse. She is shown children's skulls bearing sabre cuts. She will match the numbers of the dead to estimates of the population from the taxation rolls. She will bear witness to the murder of five thousand villagers. And around this slaughter, she will weave a tale of Muslim terror that is both apocryphal and eerily familiar: 'When a Mohammedan has killed a certain number of infidels, he is sure of paradise, no matter what his sins may be.' From this devastated mountain valley, the tale of the massacre will go out to the world. Amplified by print, her words will reach powerful ears in every capital.

Disraeli's opponents will pronounce his support of Turkey monstrous. The voices calling for Russian intervention in the Balkans will grow louder. The Tsar will declare war on the Turks a few months later and enter the conflict. Turkey will turn to its old ally, Britain, for help, but the British will demur this time, citing the public outrage over the massacres. Russia will crush the Turkish army. Bulgaria will throw off

Ottoman rule and begin to govern itself for the first time in five hundred years.

'After that,' the old man says, 'who could doubt the power of a story?'

'I often asked myself: what kind of woman was she?'

MacGahan consigned her report to the United States Consul in Istanbul on 10th August 1876, to be carried in the diplomatic bag to London. There would be a delay of almost two weeks between the lighting of the fuse and the explosion.

In the interim, Kolya saw her visibly wilt. Returning from the consulate to the pension where they were staying, she took to her bed with a high fever. She talked to herself and appeared to hallucinate, addressing Kolya by unfamiliar names. He was concerned enough to fetch a doctor.

The landlady recommended a Frenchman, a portly Lyonnais gentleman who was a disciple of Charcot. He palpated MacGahan's tongue, and prescribed quinine and plenty of rest.

'Nervous exhaustion,' he confided to Kolya. 'This is something very common in cases of sexual inversion. The constitution is subject to special strains—'

MacGahan spat a filthy oath from the sweaty bed sheets. 'Tell the quack to go—'

Kolya reddened and ushered the doctor through the antechamber and out of the door. He could hear the springs squeaking as MacGahan rose angrily from the bed. 'I'll give him sexual inversion!'

It was a while before he could persuade her to lie down,

but the outburst of rage seemed to do her some good. The colour returned to her lips as she settled her head on the pillow.

Kolya offered his own prescription: vodka, the panacea of the Russian Empire. The dubious rationale was that it would help sweat out the fever. But vodka was nowhere to be had, so he fetched a bottle of raki, stoppered with a twist of brown paper, a loaf of bread, and a lemon.

MacGahan swallowed half a tumbler and made an extraordinary face: she looked glassy-eyed and breathless, like a carp in a fisherman's basket. Kolya handed her a cube of bread to sniff. Unaware of the correct etiquette, she ate the bread, then took the bottle and splashed some liquor in a tooth-mug, saying, 'I don't like to drink alone.'

Kolya had never drunk spirits before, but his father ran a profitable sideline in alcohol, which was served from a little hatch adjoining the hardware shop. He had witnessed enough drinking to know exactly how it should be done: expelling the air from his lungs, he knocked back the raki in one gulp, and inhaled strongly through a cube of bread held to his nostrils. One eye watered a little. MacGahan poured each of them another shot.

That long-ago afternoon now ceases to conform to the constraints of sober time; it lurches forward with the sudden disjunctions of inebriation: another drink; MacGahan drunkenly recites a prayer in Spanish and demonstrates a balestra lunge with her swordstick; Kolya falls off the bed and crushes his own hat; MacGahan challenges him to arm-wrestle. Kolya sings a Ukrainian folksong in a reedy voice; suddenly, MacGahan is dressed. Despite the heat, she's wearing a Bulgarian sheepskin jacket, riding boots, a straw hat and a taffeta frock. Kolya stumbles after her, down an alley, pressing himself into a doorway to allow a donkey loaded with copper pots to struggle past. The touch of its warm flank lingers where it brushes his hand, innocently alive.

Everything is available in this raucous city; it's just a matter of looking. It doesn't take long for MacGahan to find what she's after. A succession of middlemen, all working on the speculative hope of a final tip, lead them to a blue door in a quiet backstreet. It has the inconspicuousness of real iniquity.

MacGahan requests a private room. Drunk, unable to speak a word of Turkish, Kolya 'translates' by repeating her words verbatim. From this pantomime and MacGahan's remarkable appearance, their hosts deduce the patronage of rich eccentrics.

They are shown to a shady boudoir, lit with yellow lamps, where musky perfumes conceal the smell of sweat. Two oiled boys, naked from the waist up, carry in a water pipe. MacGahan waves a hand. 'I don't know about you, Nick, but my tastes don't run that way.'

Kolya clarifies the situation to a grateful proprietor, who sends in girls this time, three of them. They are ebony-haired, brown-eyed, painfully young. Kolya thinks of his sisters, back in Kerch. It is a thought melancholy enough to kill off any prospect of tumescence.

MacGahan has settled on a pile of cushions and gestures to one of the girls to join her. 'I ain't going to hurt you, little one. I just want to daddy with you for a while. Come here, you pretty thing.'

There is something both tender and flirtatious about MacGahan here. She's enacting something Kolya doesn't understand, some gentle, mutual version of ecstasy. It's not like the busy Kerch brothel, where sailors go in and come out five minutes later, carrying the boots they're too drunk to put back on.

Kolya is not blind to the effect MacGahan has on these village girls with their cheap bracelets. Whatever she may be, she is all they have eyes for. He might as well not exist. They take off MacGahan's hat and play with her long copper-tinted hair, cooing over it in the liquid and guttural sounds of their language.

'What are they saying, Nick? You're supposed to be my translator.'

The girls turn their uncomprehending smiles towards him.

Kolya's drunkenness seems to have sharpened his eyesight. He sees with an extraordinary clarity: the black hairs along the pale arms of the young girl refilling his glass; MacGahan's weathered face; the bottle-green thorax of a fly against some orange peel as it catches the lamplight. 'They want to wash your hair,' he says.

'She told me the story of her birth and parentage.'

Kolya, as Notovitch, in his mid-seventies, is still a magpie. Vincenzo sees it in small things at first – a word or inflection lifted from him and handed back as though it's newly minted. One day, he arrives to find the old man wearing a carefully folded cravat in the open collar of his shirt – Vincenzo's unvarying attire. Where others might be embarrassed to mention the cravat, Vincenzo is one generation up from peasant and exercises the licence it gives him to be blunt. 'You've copied me,' he says.

'I often wear a cravat,' the old man replies, with a disarming innocence. 'You haven't noticed?'

If Notovitch could appropriate such trivial plumage from a virtual nonentity, imagine his debt to MacGahan.

This story is Kolya's. I'm trying to tell it economically, but completely. I'm confining myself to the events and characters that gave his life its particular shape, which led to the incident that defined him in the eyes of posterity. These aren't formless imaginings – though perhaps it seems so at times. We are working towards a point where the conjectured happenings of a fictional past converge with the account of history. And I'm keen to avoid those breaks in energy that can affect a discontinuous narrative. The supreme ambition you can have for a book is for it to be one thing: a single utterance in which every word plays a part.

But MacGahan's story is so pertinent to Kolya's, the story of her life, her apostasy, her disavowed religion; they influenced him so strongly that we're going to have to risk another digression.

Of all the stories of which our world is made, the tales of the creator and the redeemer, the tales of the spirit and the Holy Word, are the most powerful. I know in my bones that when Leonard went to war it was for many reasons, but not the least was for an idea of duty sanctified by religion.

Kolya belongs to the oldest monotheists of all, the Jews, the trunk of the Abrahamic tree; MacGahan to one of its youngest offshoots: the Mormon heresy.

68

Imagine, then, me and you, on a distant planet, scrutinising light and sound waves that have drifted through the dark emptiness of interstellar space. Imagine, sifting through the effusions of eternity, that we could home in on a single speaker at a single moment in time. Imagine we've found MacGahan reclining on the cushions of the Turkish seraglio, all washed and anointed by her handmaidens, and Kolya recalled from a long exile in the hallway to share a sobering coffee, seethed in a copper ibrik and tasting like thimblefuls of mud. Now imagine we could hear her speak.

'Her family were Latter-Day Saints.'

'You know what a Mormon is?'

Kolya shakes his head. Two of the girls play with each other's bracelets. The third snoozes in MacGahan's lap; the pallor of her sleeping face makes the rouge on her cheeks look garish.

'Every farming family now and again throws up a son who doesn't have it in him to make a farmer. Maybe he's simple or dreamy or lacks the steadiness for work. Joseph Smith was one of those. He was a fool for farming, but he had a special head for other things.'

A muezzin's call from a nearby mosque punctuates MacGahan's speech and is met with answering echoes across the city. The sleeping girl stirs and then subsides back into unconsciousness.

'I've seen his portrait: a tall brown-haired man with the radiant blue eyes of a virtuous prophet. Handsome too. He was the kind of man that other men will follow. And women.'

69

MacGahan straightens up on the cushions, soberer now; perhaps she was never as drunk as she seemed. She's not one to drop her guard, ever.

'No one was more serious on matters of conscience than those Yankee farmers. Marx calls it the idiocy of rural life, but out there in the darkness, those men had commerce with the stars. In my childhood, our blacksmith was an alchemist, you know. At the symposia of our cider press, the topics under discussion were salvation, and infinity, and the right way to God. We loved a talker. And Smith had a story for everyone.

'You've got to know something else. The way I'm telling you this is not as a believer would. It's cost me most of my youth and pints of my own blood to understand this story in this way.

'The country of the United States was different then. The past was bigger and nearer. Vermont, where Smith was born, was dotted with big tombs, holy to the tribes who'd lived there, and people naturally believed they had precious things hid in them. Smith got a name as a treasure-finder. He claimed he had sticks or jewels that would find out treasure wherever it was hidden. But the only thing he got as a result of his seeking was a pile of trouble and a name for being unreliable.

'Now you and I might pause there and decide to knuckle down, try to make a sober living for a while, but it's tough to go against your nature. Sometime in his twentieth or twenty-first year, Joseph was visited by an angel. Yes, he was. That's what he told his friends. The angel led him to some golden plates that were the rarest kind of treasure of all: a gospel, written in an old Egyptian tongue. Over the next few years, he Englished them and found a publisher. He called his gospel *The Book of Mormon*.

'Given that Joseph was unlettered, you must be wondering how he read the plates, especially in a language not his own? Well, luckily the angel had seen to that, bestowing on him two magic stones which gave him the power to understand the ancient writing.

'He was hounded and disbelieved as prophets are apt to be, but many people took his writings for the truth, my parents among them. They followed him to Far West, Missouri, to Nauvoo, and on his death they made the great trek west to the red lands of the Salt Lake Valley, where I was born.

Kolya's head aches from his dissipation. His tongue is dry. But he feels emboldened to speak. 'Was Smith a fraud?'

'Of course, *I* think so. But I've found some sympathy for him in my heart as I've gotten older. He was a farmer's son who wasn't cut out to be a farmer and I was a girl who wasn't cut out to be my family's idea of a woman. We both had to alter the world a little to find our place in it.

'The other thing is this: there are some kinds of belief that make stories come true. The kindest take I can have on old JS is that he saw something in the eyes of his congregants that made his lies seem real. It's as though you said *abracadabra*, or *talitha kum*, but not in earnest, and yet you found it made a dead child breathe again. What would you make of that? You'd doubt your own insincerity then. Either you or the words must have some magic.'

'What about you?'

'My own story is one I'm not comfortable telling.'

'How did you come to leave?'

'There was the wife of a minister I'll always be grateful to. In the Civil War, I nursed and I learned I could write and that I was brave. I followed a woman I loved to Paris and was there for the Commune. I filed dispatches for the *New York Globe*. That was the beginning of another life that in a roundabout way brought me here. That's as much as you need of my story, Nick. And it's time for us to be going.'

*

MACGAHAN RISES WEARILY from the cushions, clean, sated, talked out. She makes small gifts of money to the girls and settles the account with the obsequious patron.

Night is falling in the streets outside. Ovens are being lit. A crescent moon hangs over the Bosphorus. Many miles to the east, in Kolya's home, the sabbath has begun.

Out of all that he has heard, what stays with Kolya is one image: Joseph Smith, scrying the gold tablets with his magic eyepiece, dictating the gospel to his confederates. Hold that in your thoughts.

'For two years, I travelled with MacGahan.'

The drumbeat of war means good business for arms-dealers, ship-builders, brothel-keepers, and journalists.

MacGahan and, increasingly, Kolya, are in demand. Embedded with the Russian Army, MacGahan writes for the *Daily News*. Kolya begins sending articles to his cousin Osip in Saint Petersburg who writes back excitedly to commission more. Quick, brave, energetic: Kolya makes an excellent correspondent. He also has a flair for local colour and a tendency to manufacture quotes, though is neither the first nor last young journalist to do so. He is exhilarated to be living by his pen. He borrows his cousin's new surname for his byline: Notovitch.

The money's never quite enough, payment can be slow, and it helps to have items to pawn; but for a young man of twenty, even this erratic living is a living to be proud of.

And what stories! Kolya crosses the Danube with the Russian Army in the first weeks of the war; he interviews the victims of Ottoman cruelty; he trembles at the fierce Cossack regiments in their sheepskin burkas; he watches from hand-cut steps of ice on the frozen mountainside as General Gurko leads his spearhead into the valley of Sofia; he is a witness to the signing of the final peace in a whitewashed villa on the Sea of Marmora.

During the months of fighting, he becomes fluent in the language of war. He speaks confidently of supply lines, debouches and enfilades. Through MacGahan, who knows him from Central Asia, he moves from nodding terms to speaking terms to drinking terms with the massively bearded General Skobelev: known to his adoring troops as the 'White General' for his white uniform, his hat of curly white astrakhan, and the white horse that he unfailingly rides into the thick of battle.

Kolya reveals an unsuspected ability to hold his liquor, joining the general in the deepest realms of drunkenness, long after MacGahan has exercised her female privilege to cover her glass with her hand. Kolya and the general move together across the spectrum of inebriation beyond informality, hilarity, philosophy and clarity, to a strange realm where the general turns pale and weeps at the recollection of all the blood he has spilled. MacGahan and Kolya learn to leave then, with Skobelev sitting in his camp chair, muttering prayers for forgiveness in the Old Slavonic language of the liturgy. The next day, of course, it's as though nothing has happened. The top of his cheeks freshly shaved, his eyes clear, his boots gleaming in the stirrups, he'll simply offer a nod of greeting to them both.

On the quiet days between battles, Kolya rides with MacGahan in search of copy. 'We just need to find him,' she says, in a sentence that becomes a kind of catchphrase between them. 'The fellow they're all looking for: a passionate man with a story to tell.'

Kolya's success emboldens him to write home more frequently. He wants his parents to be proud. What he gleans from their sparse correspondence back is that their fortunes have declined. They've left Kerch and moved to Kiev. His older brother has stayed behind in Crimea to sell the business. Father's been unwell, but is better now.

At the villa in San Stefano outside Istanbul, Kolya watches the glum Ottoman signatories put their pens to the crushing terms of the peace treaty that concludes the war. Its text will be transmitted in full by telegraph to the world. Standing by a window, through which the sunshine gleams off the Sea of Marmora, Kolya allows himself a moment of reflection: less than two years ago, he was manoeuvring pickle barrels around his father's cellar, having his head cuffed for inattention, dreaming hopelessly of the East. Today, he's a witness to history and nursing a hangover he acquired in a drinking bout with MacGahan and General Skobelev.

MacGahan glances at him. She's seen her protégé change, not always for the better. Two years of steady progress, two years of having his own means and bossing servants, two years of reporting on the suffering of others – it has deadened his compassion a little. Like many people on a lucky streak, he's rather too quick to give himself the credit for it. She stifles a cough. Kolya's young liver makes short work of an evening's drinking. Hers has grown less resilient with age. Last night, she was caught out in a rainstorm and got drenched. She's not ready to slow down, but being a war correspondent is a young person's game. Also, there's someone, an English governess she met on a brief leave in Saint Petersburg. (English governesses have supplanted the French in the affections of the Russian elite.) MacGahan fancies a new life where the two of them could hide in plain sight: perhaps as a pair of retired schoolteachers in a New England village. She's been promised a good price for her memoirs and knows she could sell out lecture tours for long enough to buy a nice parcel of land in upstate New York. She wonders idly how she would manage the winters now.

Kolya's thinking of home, too, but for another reason. He wants his parents to see the success he's made of himself. Even if they read the Russian papers – which they don't – they're unlikely to connect special correspondent Nicolas Notovitch with their absent son.

He says farewell to MacGahan, picks up a new suit of clothes from an Italian tailor and catches a steamer to Odessa, from where it's an overnight train to Kiev. He spends the journey in third class, sitting uncomfortably in his stiff new suit, trying to avoid the malodorous rustics. Buried in a French novel, he starts at the sound of a conversation in Yiddish: a Jew from the shtetl is upbraiding another Jew, a stranger, for concealing the long braids of his *tsitsit* beneath an overcoat.

*

ON KHRESHCHATYK, Kiev's main thoroughfare, Kolya stops at a bakery to add a cake to his other presents: a coffee pot, jewellery, Turkish sweets.

The address he's got is for a ground-floor apartment in a stinking courtyard. Inside, of course, it's spotless. His sisters – Rebecca, Feiga, Lera – coo over the gifts. His mother receives the cake box as though there's an anarchist's bomb inside it and glances at her husband. The prodigal son senses it's not going to be eaten here.

Kolya doesn't remember this: the menorah and the tin of polish on the table, his father's fringed shawl. He thinks of the earnest Jew on the train. What's happening here? Who's changed? Him or them?

The answer's both.

Two years with the fearless, godless MacGahan, who goes out of her way to antagonise clergymen, has recalibrated his sense of religion. The papers' appetite for news shows no consideration for the sabbath; he works every day he needs to. For long stretches of the war, the only food available was meat, butchered filthily in camp, and Kolya has acquired a taste for pork.

Meanwhile, his family has gone the other way. Something has caused them to cling more tightly to their ancient faith.

It's partly how they've responded to the loss of him, and partly reflects a wider movement, a religious renewal that's touched many Jews. 'You look like a real Russian gentleman,' his mother says, without joy.

His father sketches out the events of the last two years: the business slackened off after Kolya left; sickness. They wanted to be closer to his wife's family. In everything the old man says, Nicolas hears an unspoken reproach: *this is your fault*.

They couldn't be less interested in his war stories. He tries to tell them about MacGahan, but whatever he says is received with pained incredulity. He feels about thirteen again. His new boots chafe.

The atmosphere in the apartment presages a looming storm. Then, a mere six hours after he's arrived, a messenger turns up. It's a boy from the telegraph office who looks with envious eyes at Kolya's dapper clothes as he hands over an envelope. More than any of his abortive boasts, Kolya's ease with this strange interruption signals to his parents how much he has changed. He tips the boy and asks him to wait. It's from General Skobelev. Kolya's vision grows blurry as he reads the words: *MacGahan. Typhus. Istanbul. Regret.*

'This coat was hers.'

Chapan. Vincenzo repeats the word. 'From Uzbek,' the old man says, offering him the sleeve to touch, its hem rubbed shiny and soft from decades of use. 'Too big for me, in fact. I found it in a steamer trunk after her second funeral.'

Margaret Ann MacGahan – Wednesday, of course, was a fiction she devised in part to be eye-catching, in part to obscure her sex from her readers – was buried in the Greek cemetery in Istanbul and reburied in Salt Lake City two years later.

The change of venue, Kolya thought, would not have pleased her much, but seeing as he missed the funeral the first time around, and seeing that grateful Bulgarian-Americans were paying for the reinterment, and seeing that the paper *Novoe Vremya* had offered him good money for a series of reports on the American West, he made the trip out to Utah. At the graveside, he expressed his condolences to her thin and weathered mother, in whose face he saw the familiar stoicism of an Eastern European peasant. The old woman insisted he take something to remember her daughter. The chapan he chose accompanied him to New York, Boston, the Niagara Falls, and then back home to Paris.

By 1880, a volume of his war reporting had already been well received. He planned to write the next one in French to reach a wider market. Travel books, military history, royal biographies and current affairs would flow from his pen over the coming years, but he'd only be remembered for one.

On my desk is a jiffy bag from the London Library containing two of his forgotten books. It's been there for weeks, but I've yet to open it. I'm doing so now, tearing through the packet's yellow paper. One of the books is *L'Empereur Alexandre II*, published in 1884. It's the other volume that makes me gasp: *Russie et L'Alliance Anglaise*, published in 1906, but with the following inscription written shakily and belatedly on the flyleaf: 'To her Royal Highness the Duchess of Kent, respectful homage accompanies my highest regards for the health and happiness of your noble and gracious Royal

78

Family.' And then, beneath it, his signature in the same blue ink: *Nicolas Notovitch, 15th January 1939, Paris.*

Running my finger along the words, I have the uncanny and vertiginous sense of uncovering a piece of history. No one knew that Notovitch had lived so long. And I had forgotten in my enthusiasm for the story that under these inventions lies the kernel of something real. For a giddy moment, that assemblage of mirrors lines up perfectly. The prey I've been stalking through the secret books swims into view. Our eyes meet briefly. It's the one activity we've obviously got in common: inscribing copies of our work. There's something pathetic about this one: thirty-three years after it was published, after an interval that included the Russian Revolution and the Great War, Notovitch made a gift of this superannuated text to a woman who would never read it; judging from the tightness of its pages, I'd say no one ever has.

This isn't the book of his that will be remembered. By the time of its inscription, he was old, older than I've so far dared to imagine him: eighty, shortly to turn eighty-one. He handed her the book, after a dinner, a *soirée*. The country of his birth vanished in 1917 and he is by now an adopted Parisian.

'*Monsieur Notovitch, vous êtes gentil,*' the duchess says, when he offers to inscribe it. Did she associate the courtly old gent with a notorious tale of forty years before? Did the name stir a fragmentary recollection: the story of an old monastery, India, a suspected Russian agent? '*Notovitch. Notovitch. That name is familiar.*' 'Why yes, perhaps you've read my *Souvenirs of Sebastopol,* or *The Pacification of Europe*? Seen my drama, *Mariage idéal*?'

'No, no – it's something else, I'm sure of it.'

Looking at the title page through his reading glasses as he tries to shepherd the unruly syntax of his inscription, the old man feels his heart tighten. He's being mocked. A sly compositor more than thirty years before inserted a rogue word repeatedly in the fine print of the list of other works. It's there, and there, and there: three times, like an obscene sound from the back of a rowdy classroom. 'With illustrations *jésus*', 'Available in octavo *jésus*', 'In cloth *jésus* wrappers'. The word is street slang for a young male prostitute, but when applied to Notovitch it has other, obviously demeaning, associations.

He closes the book in consternation and gives it to the duchess with as much composure as he can muster. Decades before, he must have made an enemy at the printers, been high-handed to a fellow in dirty overalls who enacted this jeering, belated revenge. *jésus. jésus. jésus.*

Suddenly it's cold. The basement's empty. The needle butts against the run-off on the wax cylinder.

By 1939, history has already passed its judgement on the old man. The duchess will recall it as she's being driven home. 'Why, Notovitch! The scoundrel who—'

The book will languish unread and be bequeathed to the London Library on her death.

By 1939, everyone knows there's trouble ahead. Notovitch must have a better sense than most: he's seen Batak, after all. But no one can conceive of what's to come. This time the carpet of bones is going to stretch right across Europe.

So much for history. The secret books allow a different kind of man: alongside the ambition, the self-promotion and, let's face it, the outright lies, there is something else: an instinct for conciliation, a desire for the better story. He's taken more than an old coat from MacGahan. Her regrettably brief life embodied another lesson: not just the power that stories have, but their provisionality. They can all be rewritten. Hers, and his, and yours.

Because it's impossible to believe there's no shape to anything. It's impossible to shed the habits of the haruspex. Peering at the entrails of Notovitch's book, I read *jésus, jésus, jésus* and it makes a queer kind of sense to me. Qin Yu Lan gathering firewood by the railway track; Dass folding his napkins in the bowels of the *Derby*; Pierre Thibaut cut down by gunfire, his blood puddling on a Normandy beach; an overloaded donkey on a backstreet in Istanbul; a teenager from beside Lake Van pouring adulterated wine for two strangers in a brothel; Leonard winding his puttees round his ankles, waiting for the blast of an officer's whistle: out of all their infinite arrangements, there must be one that makes perfect sense. There must be a best story.

2: THE SAVIOUR ON BLOOD

THE SLEEPING CAR ATTENDANT rouses us with a sharp voice and tells us to get a move on. We take our bags and stumble blearily through the station concourse, past the new statue of Peter the Great that's supplanted the old one of Lenin.

I've always wanted to take you here, show you things that mean so much to me, astonish you with its history, impress you with my Russian. Taxicabs are waiting at the rank outside the station, but we'll go by foot, the better to adjust to our new surroundings. Along Nevsky Prospekt, damp May Day tricolours are flapping in the breeze that blows across the Gulf of Finland. Overhead is a tangle of trolleybus wires.

This is a young city, but over its relatively brief life it has had almost as many names as Notovitch: Saint Petersburg, Petropol, Petrograd, Leningrad, Saint Petersburg again.

To locals, it's sometimes just *Piter*, named for a Saint Peter but inescapably linked to the Tsar Peter who had it conjured from a swamp. It's an unnatural place. It didn't grow up over centuries organically – because of a harbour, say, or a confluence of rivers. It was built swiftly by *fiat*, like Astana, Pyongyang or Dubai. Like them, it's a boast in architectural form, and as with all boasting, there's a nucleus of insecurity that it can't conceal from everyone. In the works of Pushkin, and Gogol, and Dostoevsky, it's the background to nightmares. Flood-prone, status-obsessed, somehow heartless; it isn't good for a person's soul. It's a place where clerks are driven mad by endless light and unrequited love.

But on a warm day like today, the northern sky feels wide and hopeful. The spire of the Admiralty gleams like a raised sword, like the gold spike on a Buddhist stupa. I visited in 1990 when the whole place seemed to be crumbling. It's good to see it cared for again. I love these smells: diesel fumes, sunshine on old stone, garlic sausage, brackish canals.

It was built to mark a fresh start for the country. Peter wanted Russia to be a European power and he commissioned foreign architects to tell that story in stone. These stucco palaces, the canals: they are his legacy.

But the place I want to take you to is this: see? It bursts out of the elegant cityscape like a crazed assertion of Russianness. It's a luxurious reimagining of a peasant church. The multicoloured onion domes. The headscarved women lighting candles in the nave. The gold glinting on the iconostasis. The mosaics that cover every wall and reflect jewel-coloured light. The incense. At first glance, it seems like the oldest thing in the city, but it wasn't finished until 1907.

It was consecrated as the Church of the Resurrection of Christ, but most people know it as *Spas na Krovi:* the Saviour on Blood. Here in the western apse, this canopy (rhodonite, jasper, serpentine) resembles a howdah; perched on four columns, it protects nothing more glamorous than a cobbled floor. Did you ask, *why?*

*

LET US UNDERTAKE AGAIN the trick of weaving the past from starlight. Set the dial for March 1881. As time spools back around us, indulge me by glancing at two snapshots. First, in 1990, that's me, wandering around the city, now Leningrad, with a satchel of scavenged brochures. How vulnerable I look. I'm trying to compile information for a guidebook to the Soviet Union – a country that will cease to exist in just over a year. In the lobby of a hotel – beige carpets, marble, one-armed bandits – I fall into conversation with a track-suited tough called Ruslan and his girlfriend, Masha. Ruslan is friendly but somehow on edge. He quizzes me about my job, smokes, fidgets, puts his feet up on the coffee table. After a few minutes, we're joined by another woman, Natasha, a blonde, who arrives in the elevator from an upper floor and an assignation with a Finnish tourist. She accepts a cigarette from Ruslan and shrugs in answer to Masha's questioning raised eyebrows. Seated next to me, she smells strongly and incongruously of sweat.

Look: that's also me, visiting for the first time in 1983, aged fifteen, on a school trip, using my rudimentary Russian to persuade a middle-aged man to buy me a bottle of red wine from the grocery; one more: me hung over on the coach tours of the city, and so clueless that when I got back to London I didn't know which pictures I'd taken in Leningrad and which in Moscow.

Now we're going back in earnest, past the grey decades of stagnation, Stalin's death, the terrible siege of World War II, the purges, the heady revolutionary years, through times when the deconsecrated church is a warehouse and a morgue. The buttress on which it stands draws back from the canal.

The building vanishes. The church is gone. We're standing on bare pavement. It's March. The air is damp and raw, just above freezing and the worse for it.

We should probably move to the other side of the canal. Here, in Russia, in 1881, there's a desperate edge to the search for better stories.

Pulled by a pair of horses and flanked by half a dozen Cossack outriders, the Tsar's carriage is approaching. It's somehow smaller than you would expect – smaller, anyway, than the armoured limousine with tinted windows a head of state would ride in now. His Imperial Highness, Tsar of all the Russias, has just come back from the trooping of two battalions of guards. A peasant woman crosses herself at the sight of her sovereign. A butcher's boy on an errand stops and gawps.

A thickset clean-shaven man steps in front of the carriage. It's just after 2 p.m. There's an unmistakable intent in the way he moves. This starlight is endlessly manipulable. I'm bending it so you can see his face up close. You are surprised by its earnestness and youth. It's an expressive, open face that would suit a young Midwestern farmer, except his jaw is set in grim resolve. His name is Rysakov. He's clutching a bundle, which he pitches beneath the wheels. It tears the air with a crack that hurts our ears. Grit and ice and blood spatter onto the slushy road.

As the smoke clears, there's an eerie pause, a rip in the fundamental story. Busily, people swarm back into action, like ants repairing a ruined nest, rushing, swearing, shouting 'Treason!', 'Catch that man!' and 'God save the Tsar!'

One of the Cossack horsemen and the butcher's boy lie

dying in the street. Rysakov is being held. A crowd is forming round the Tsar's carriage, which is damaged, but he emerges unhurt.

That's Alexander II – the Tsar liberator, who freed the serfs. He's sixty-three, tall, moustachioed and rather fine-looking. He's wearing a furred coat over a military uniform. From one of the sleighs that is following the carriage, Colonel Dvorzhitsky steps out. He urges the Tsar to leave the scene. The crowd is sympathetic, outraged, but the atmosphere is still pregnant with threat. How tentative and panicky everything seems, how different from the fixed lines of history in retrospect.

The Tsar resists the pleas of his aides, urging him to hurry away. He is conscious of a duty to show courage. He moves with a regal hauteur. First, he attempts to console the dying men. There's nothing to be done, the wounds are clearly mortal. Then he goes over to take a long look at his would-be assassin. Rysakov is a member of a revolutionary cell called Narodnaya Volya, People's Will, who are nothing if not determined. As far as the revolutionaries are concerned, the Tsar is a sinister tyrant in blood-stained robes, leading a filthy, backward slave empire. That's easy enough to grasp. The world will clearly be a better place without him. Over the last few years, they have mined Odessa harbour to destroy the Tsar's boat, tried to set bombs under the Royal Train on its way back from the Black Sea, and blown up part of the Winter Palace. They've failed repeatedly and now the secret police are on to them. This was a last desperate attempt.

Colonel Dvorzhitsky's hand hovers over the royal arm, eager to spirit the Tsar away. Alexander examines the revolutionary with a kingly contempt. Rysakov, in spite of his grounding in progressive political theory, is overcome with awe and cannot meet the monarch's eyes. The truth is, he's a little rattled by the sight of blood. The butcher's boy is dying loudly and messily.

There's something about human pain that rightly shakes our confidence in stories. It was supposed to work like this: a cruel tyrant lying dead, joyful citizens pulling down statues of the despot. But in the forlorn stories that we know in our hearts to be truer, good and evil are more hopelessly mixed.

This doesn't feel any nearer to Utopia. There's just a young boy crying out in pain for his mother, panic, injured horses, and the smell of blood. Even the broken Cossack, so martial in life, the incarnation of Orthodox prowess, draws our sympathy.

And then the second bomb goes off.

Rysakov set out today with three accomplices. The second lost his nerve. But this third one, Hryniewiecki, was standing by a railing just a few yards from the Tsar. At the point when Alexander was about to leave, he threw his bomb. The blast has removed both Alexander's legs below the knee. Even now, he could still survive if someone has the presence of mind to stem the bleeding: apply a tourniquet, put pressure on the femoral artery – just raising his shattered legs would help. But no one does. There's general panic. They can't get him into the carriage so they put him in an open sleigh, which leaves a trail of blood in the slush as it carries him dying to the Winter Palace.

The canopy preserves the spot on the embankment where the Tsar fell.

'I visited Russia at least twice a year.'

Tsars, anarchists, divine rule. It's all so remote from 1930s London. Religion will decline, Vincenzo thinks, and some form of socialism will be the answer everywhere: rational economic planning and an end to the curse of unemployment. There's no reason nowadays that anyone should go hungry. He gets up to reload the Imperator.

'So you were in Saint Petersburg when the Tsar was killed?'

'By chance, I was,' the old man says. 'I was visiting my cousin, Osip.'

I'm tempted, naturally, to put Nicolas at the scene of the assassination, have him perhaps minister to the dying butcher's boy – a real character, incidentally, who figures in eyewitness accounts.

But Nicolas – now, at almost twenty-three, I think he merits his full first name – is at the offices of *Novosti* that day, the newspaper his cousin edits and for which he sends regular reports from Paris. Sales of the last two books were slow. Nicolas feels the envious glances of the paper's younger staff, but he can't pay the rent with those. 'I loved your piece on Plevna,' one young man tells him, a bit too eagerly. 'And the profile of Skobelev. What a man! How well did you get to know him?'

That was three years ago, Nicolas thinks. What about the comic sketches of Paris life? The articles about the United States? What about the big think piece on the ten-year anniversary of the Commune that he slaved over for months?

Osip's apartment is a short walk from the office and the

cousins head there for lunch. 'Irina nags me. New carpets at home. But she'll be delighted to see you, of course.'

After Haussmann's boulevards, the Tuileries, the mild south, it's hard for Nicolas to summon up great enthusiasm for Saint Petersburg, which strikes him now as a demented Russian vanity project – a tyrant's idea of rationality and elegance. Osip hums an anxious trumpet voluntary as he picks his way past the black puddles of melted slush. He is thirty-four, but looks older: paunchy, balding, henpecked. He calls out to his wife as he opens the apartment's inner door. 'Sweetheart! It's me.'

Big, handsome rooms, but all in disarray. The shutters are closed, fireplaces dark. The cold and cheerless place smells of ink and sour milk. Osip seems not to notice. He is an intellectual, Nicolas thinks, and resides principally in the lofty book-created space inside his head.

Irina lies on a divan pulled right up to the single tiny fire, wearing a dressing gown, nursing a baby. 'You said you'd be home at twelve. The soup's cold. Hello, Nicolas.'

Osip manages to work his face into a smile that produces deep lines on his forehead. He kisses his wife's hair. 'Soup! Excellent!' He dishes out two bowlfuls from the tureen. It is, as Irina warned, barely warm. With a single cautionary glance, Osip advises Nicolas against saying anything.

Nicolas babbles to fill the silence. 'Real black bread. It's the taste of home. There's nothing like this in Paris.'

'Paris!' laments a sad voice from the divan. 'Paris! Why can't I be in Paris?' Irina bursts unaccountably into tears and flees from the room.

Osip looks relieved. He butters some bread and eats it

quickly. 'Since the baby, she's been a little like this. The nurse said that sometimes, when the milk comes in, it makes them blue.'

Nicolas nods and thinks: *I'm never going to get married.*

'Hear anything from home?' asks Osip.

'Everyone's well. And you?'

Osip gives a non-committal shrug and pours vodka into two little glasses.

This is their major point of contact: two ex-Jews, making their way in a Christian world, both severed from their origins.

Osip seems eager to pick up the glass. 'It's cold today,' he says, as if to rationalise drinking at lunchtime. Nicolas joins him: he has no choice, really. It would be rude to let Osip drink alone. The drink improves Osip's mood and the tune he hums as they walk back to the office is in a major key.

Around 2.30, word reaches them of the bombing. By three, the Tsar's death is confirmed. Osip convenes an editorial meeting. 'We should publish with black borders. A series of pieces on his legacy. Reaction from around the globe.' He lays out an imaginary headline with his hands. 'A lamentable tragedy. The world mourns.'

This direction is heartily approved. There's one dissenting voice. A younger journalist, a non-Jew called Stepan Bogomilov. He was the one who expressed such admiration for Nicolas's work in Bulgaria. 'Do you think it really was the anarchists, this time? I mean, of course it was the *anarchists*, but how come they got so close? I just think we should dig a bit more deeply. Who benefits from this? It's just, like, so convenient. When the Tsar's pressing for reform and there are so many people who oppose him. This works nicely for the conservatives. Now they'll have one of their own in power.'

'You think the army are behind it?' Nicolas finds himself irrationally annoyed.

'Not the army . . .'

'Then who?'

'Forces of some kind. I don't know.'

'Forces? Who are you thinking of? The English? Free-masons? The Jews?'

That's a very direct challenge. Nicolas and Osip's ethnicity must be obvious to the other journalists.

'Let's not squabble, people,' says Osip. 'We have a paper to produce. I want a big piece on the Emancipation. The other major achievement is the Turkish War and the liberation of the Balkan nations.' He lets his glance alight briefly on his cousin. 'Now, if only we had someone who could give us the inside scoop on that.'

The other journalists laugh. Nicolas feels, in spite of everything, flattered.

After the meeting, Osip takes Nicolas aside. 'I hate to sound opportunistic, cousin, but I think this is crying out for an instant book.

'Consider it started.'

'Suvorin, too, was a great champion of my work.'

The most powerful figure in all of Russian letters is a fellow called Aleksei Suvorin. He is an impressive man, big, upright and very hairy. He's also irascible, impatient and more than a bit intimidating. A fan of Nicolas's writing – high praise, given that Dostoevsky was a personal friend – he has Osip's

94

old job as editor of *Novaya Gazeta*, a liberal paper that, like everything in Russia, is now gravitating to the right.

Nicolas didn't tell his cousin about this meeting. He reassures himself it's not disloyal ('It's just a *meeting*!') but he has a misgiving about it in his heart. Still, what's a freelancer to do? Perhaps Nicolas also has a sense of the way the wind is blowing. The next years will be chilly ones for the soft-left liberal intelligentsia. A man like Osip, who has difficulty standing up to his wife, is going to wither in the coming reactionary winter.

'Take a seat,' Suvorin says. The sound of the presses rumbles up from the basement. Suvorin wears a copy editor's green-tinted visor that looks, to our eyes, like a baseball cap. Maybe it is a baseball cap. The past of the secret books is not wholly one we recognise. It contains unrealised possibilities. It's penetrated with strangeness and anachronisms. 'This is some heavy shit. First Dostoevsky, now the Tsar.'

'He was a good man,' says Nicolas, sincerely.

'That's the thing in all this,' Suvorin says. 'He was a reformer. Why the hell would they blow him up? This guy that's coming in now, his son, Alexander III, he makes Genghis Khan look moderate. And, by the way, you're right about the other thing.'

'Which thing was that?' asks Nicolas.

'A man. *That's* what he was. The day he died, the Tsarina pleaded with him not to leave the palace. He threw her on the sofa and fucked her right there. Then off he went to review the troops. A man, I tell you. Sixty-three years old. They don't make them like that any more. He was a real *Russian*. It's a dark hour, son. Smoke?'

Feeling distinctly un-Russian himself, Nicolas thinks he'd better accept. Suvorin's sources are impeccable and the story is almost certainly true.

Suvorin lights the cigarette for him. 'I think these things have done wonders for my weak lungs. What about you, what are you up to?'

'I'm working on a book about the Tsar for my cousin. A tribute.'

'An instant book. No shame in that. We've all got to eat. Have you read *Demons*?'

'By Dostoevsky?' Nicolas is stalling a little.

'The very one.'

'It's by my bed. I've been meaning to get round to it.'

'You really should. He predicted all this shit. The guy was a genius. We buried him a month ago – now this. Hey, you know what would be great? *Inside the Anarchists*.' Like Osip, Suvorin has the habit of writing headlines with his hands. 'That idea, but a better title. What makes them tick. That's what people really want to know. The fascination of the abomination. You live in Paris, right? It's supposed to be crawling with terrorists.'

'Absolutely.'

'See? What I'm telling you. And for an assignment like that, we're talking good money. Better than your cousin pays.'

Nicolas exhales smoke and feels light-headed. Maybe *Among the Anarchists*? It's certainly a more interesting proposition than rehashing his Bulgarian journalism.

*

THE NIGHT BEFORE leaving Saint Petersburg, Nicolas wakes before dawn. Disorientated by the early hour and the unfamiliar bed – a rooming house he came to after two days of being woken by the shrieks of Osip's baby – he takes a while to remember where and who he is. Sometimes, still, he's surprised by an overwhelming pang of sadness for MacGahan. This isn't like one of those. Today what he feels is an intense misgiving. He can't think why: he has an assignment from Osip, something potentially in the offing from Suvorin. Was it the drinking at lunchtime again? Is he coming down with an illness?

Spring has barely set foot in the capital, but in a few weeks, the lilacs in Kerch will be in bloom. The first wild strawberries will arrive in tiny punnets in the market. The vines at Massandra will put forth curly tendrils. First blossoms, then fuzzy green fruits will form on the boughs of the peach trees. Suddenly, unbidden, out of the shadows on the wall looms a familiar face: moustache, brown hair, crow-like dark eyes – it's his own. No, it's his father's. 'Son, I'm dying. Please come home.' The image fades.

Jesus, he thinks. Then: *Jesus?*

So: let Nicolas's steam train bisect that vast country, from the snowy north still labouring in the grip of winter, down to Kiev where the Dniepr is already flowing and the first green leaves are showing on the poplars.

Outside the train, parts of Russia are in flames.

For reasons we can argue about later, an idea has taken hold that Jewish names are over-represented in the roll call of would-be revolutionaries. As word of the assassination has spread, it has unleashed a wave of retributive violence against the Jews.

'It was craven murder.'

Nicolas is the last to arrive at the cemetery, unbuttoning his coat and leaving his luggage in the mortuary with the caretaker, who also lends him a yarmulke.

It takes him an age to recognise anyone in the army of mourners: a huge grieving tribe. The hopeful buds on the trees jar with the heavy mood of the crowd. Rebbe Volchiskii in his faded capote reads the prayer as the pine coffin is lowered. Many hands assist with the interment. One elderly lady measures the grave with a length of thread that she will later dip in wax, cut up, and sell as wonder-working candles.

The family return to their home for the seven-day period of formal mourning. Nicolas is trapped; the room feels steeped in grief. His mother is pale and inconsolable. Rage surrounds his brother like a static charge. His voice quivers with it. He stares fixedly into Nicolas's eyes. 'We weren't ready. Next time. We're stockpiling pickaxe handles. We've been too soft with these animals. You want to know what they did to him?'

'Not really. No.' Nicolas thinks: *for the love of God, don't tell me.*

His mother shrieks: 'He was coming out of the synagogue. Those bastards beat him and they took his shawl and they put it on a dog!'

Out of all the misery he's seen, even Batak, even Mac-Gahan's death, nothing has affected him as intimately as this. The idea of the old man in pain. The frail bones cracking under a Cossack boot. Avram sees the upset in his face and tries to offer him some consolation.

'At least it was quick, thank God. He didn't suffer.'

'Was he the only one?'

'I know of a dozen. And not just here: Kherson, Poltava, Chernigov, Odessa too. We're only just hearing what's been going on in the countryside.'

Time inches along for the mourning family. Friends drop round to pay their respects and bring food; neighbours too, artisans and shopkeepers who also make their homes in the courtyard. They join the prayers for the dead man. Among the visitors are the money-changers, men who had baize tables alongside Nicolas's father's. They talk warmly about him, about his patience, fairness and talent for conciliation. It turns out he stepped in between another Jew and his attack-ers to plea for cooler heads. One or two try to diminish the sense of siege. 'It was just envy and opportunism coming to the boil. The authorities will punish those responsible.'

Others see more sinister machinations behind the events: official involvement; a desire at the top level to punish the Jews en masse, to kick them out of the cities.

Another of the visitors is a policeman, a non-Jew. He's a big blonde Ukrainian with fat hands and the wide face of a steppe farmer. He nods at the family, looks uncomfortable, and leaves quickly. 'His grief is genuine,' says Avram, as the door closes.

'You sound very confident of that,' says Nicolas.

'Dad paid him a lot in bribes to protect his pitch.'

And of course, there is no *Nicolas* here. Here he is Naum. Avram, as the eldest, is the man of the house now. He re-ceives the lion's share of condolences. Saying the Kaddish prayer links him formally to a line of Jewish males stretching back into prehistory. He seems magnified by his new sense of duty, even in Nicolas's eyes. He tells Nicolas the conclusion he has drawn from the wave of murder and arson. 'We need our own land now, like your friends the Bulgarians.' Nicolas feels oddly touched by the allusion to his journalism.

Outside the house, spring quickens.

For a reason he cannot at first understand, Nicolas finds himself thinking of MacGahan, counting skulls at Batak.

Then he sees that fitting the violence into a story makes his feelings more manageable. Quantify it. Give it a name. This was a pogrom. It wasn't personal. This was part of the ancient enmity between the Slav and the Jew. Reasoning like this helps to inoculate him against the enormity of it.

And yet, the sadness catches him at times. The prayers touch his heart, in spite of his habitual unbelief. The words are sanctified with the pain of centuries, with all the previous griefs of a suffering desert people.

As soon as the week is up, Nicolas wires Suvorin to say he'll do the story on the anarchists. He signs for the advance in the paper's Kiev bureau and gives half to his mother. She takes the money without counting it, holding the paper notes loosely, as if to disparage them. 'This means you're running away again,' she says.

On the train home, a memory catches up with him. It's a recollection of a moment when his father abandoned his habitual parental reserve and in a word or gesture unambiguously revealed his love. But which? Scouring the shops of Catford for a particular ballpoint pen? Unconcealed pride when Nicolas won the Science Fair? His vocal and partisan concern after a bad foul during mini-rugby practice? The grip of his warm hand while having a tooth filled at the dentist? Or just the particular and reassuring smell of maleness when he hugged the boy at bedtime? (Because these visions only have life to the extent that we're willing to invest them with some of our own blood.) To his astonished relief, Nicolas is racked with heavy sobs. It's dark outside the train. Cinders from the smokestack glow momentarily in the black wind and disappear. Gone. Gone. Gone.

'I needed to find myself some anarchists.'

Ten years earlier, in Paris, MacGahan made her name with reports on the Commune: a revolutionary uprising that was brief and messy and abortive. Mystifyingly to many of those who were there, the happenings of 1871 have been idealised in retrospect: rather in the way that, roughly a century later, three days of mud and hallucinogens at Woodstock will seem to betoken the coming of a better world. The events of the Commune have entered the vocabulary of the world-improvers; they've made new thoughts thinkable, fresh stories possible.

In many of these, there's a hero called the working class whose struggle for emancipation is the driving force of the narrative. Since everyone has difficulty writing endings, no one can be quite sure what that emancipation will look like. But those brief moments in Paris have become talismanic to people of a revolutionary persuasion.

The Commune leaders were thoroughly squashed, but every now and again, belated youngsters show up in Montmartre looking furtive, trying to find a way to join the revolution.

Back in Paris, Nicolas thinks of all the bohemians he knows. A year before, he gave some money to an émigré artist called

Boris Volchkov who claimed he was on the verge of an entirely new technique for making portraits. Volchkov said he needed the money to buy some kind of special German lens. In return, he promised Nicolas a chin-cupping author picture to use in frontispieces, plus a share of the profits. Over a long evening drinking red wine, Nicolas was bamboozled into handing over quite a lot of cash. And then heard nothing more.

Volchkov lives at the top of a decrepit staircase that he doesn't repair because the squeaky treads give him advance warning of his approaching creditors. Nicolas knows this and sticks to the obviously sound boards, but before he can even knock, the door opens.

'I'm so close,' Volchkov says. 'I had a major breakthrough with the process.' Lank locks of dirty blonde hair frame a pale face that women seem to find attractive. His teeth are grey and there are red-wine stains round his lips. 'I've been meaning to get in touch.'

'Relax,' says Nicolas. 'I'm not chasing you for money. Do you know any anarchists?'

Volchkov draws a breath. 'Anarchists? Most of that's happening in Geneva these days. It's too hot here right now, brother. Besides, I'm sticking to making art, not revolution.'

Nicolas pushes past him into the dingy studio over the artist's feeble protests: 'I'm in the middle of—'

'Hello,' says Nicolas.

A chubby young woman with long brown hair that reaches her waist stands with one leg on the ground and one knee supported on a wooden chair, her calf and foot kicked back behind her, naked.

'—a portrait,' concludes Volchkov. A half-worked canvas

rests on an easel by the window. Blank canvases on stretchers are stacked around the room, among clothing, empty wine bottles, and wooden fruit crates that have been disassembled to be fed into the cast-iron stove. Volchkov throws the woman a dressing gown. 'Don't forget where you were. Nicolas, this is Isabelle, my inspiration. Isabelle, this is Nicolas, a friend from the old country.'

'Sorry I didn't say hello,' the woman says. 'Boris told me not to move for any reason.'

While Volchkov searches vainly in the detritus for a clean glass, Isabelle tells Nicolas how the artist used to patronise her fruit stall. 'He told me I had the necessary inner magic to become a muse,' she explains proudly.

'I'm confident, mademoiselle, that you will inspire his finest work to date,' says Nicolas. The girl glows with visible pleasure.

It's unfathomable to Nicolas, who is, at heart, sexually conservative, that a pretty Parisian like Isabelle should be willing to give her cherished virginity to someone like Volchkov who can offer nothing but a set of used paintbrushes, the strong likelihood of an unwanted baby, and a good line in pretentious patter. But then he remembers how he was talked into his investment in the lens over copious glasses of wine, all of which, if memory serves, he ended up paying for. He also recalls riding around Balkan towns during ceasefires, with MacGahan saying, 'We're just looking for what everyone is looking for: a passionate man with a story to tell.'

A passionate man with a story: Boris is certainly one of those. Over a glass of wine, he returns to his old theme: '*Photo-peinture*, Nicolas. Painting with light! Art's new frontier. We will see the world in ways you have never even conceived possible: a hummingbird's wing in flight, the remorse in the eye of a penitent murderer, the instant when life leaves the body of a dying man.'

Nicolas puts down the wine. That last image is too close to home. He remembers why he's come and he channels a little of his inner MacGahan's steely vibes. 'Think of this as a chance to work off the money you owe me, Boris. Just ask around. See what you can come up with. I need at most two names, three.'

'My landlady was a woman called Eugénie Gigout.'

Antithetical in every other respect, MacGahan and Nicolas's father shared a horror of going into debt. Nicolas too prizes his independence above any displays of luxury. His rented room is half the size of Volchkov's and scrupulously neat. He is an ideal tenant and his landlady adores him.

He begins work on his Tsar book for Osip. It will end up being hackwork like everything else he writes, but he approaches it with the sincere care of a craftsman. He wakes each morning at seven, breakfasts on coffee and rolls, works through to lunch and then spends each afternoon at the private libraries whose subscriptions are his only substantial expense. He eats modest suppers back in his room and makes notes for the following morning's work until ten. He's taken to reading the New Testament in French at bedtime, a project he undertook for the linguistic challenge, but which he now continues out of curiosity.

The non-fulfilment of the piece about anarchists for Suvorin presses on his conscience a little, but he's confident he'll find his way round to it once the Tsar book is off to the printer's. For the first time, he's writing in French.

At the libraries, he roves the coloured plates in atlases for stories: Amazonia, Africa, the Pacific, the unshaded but shrinking areas of *terra incognita* that still dot the world, still waiting to be named by their discoverers. And, of course, there's India. Somehow, he'll get himself to India. With his finger on Pondicherry, he closes his eyes and hears the waves on the shore of Coromandel, sees an elephant rolling a log beside a slow-moving river and the naked brown limbs of its mahout against the grey flank.

'A gentleman to see you,' says Mère Gigout with uncharacteristic hesitance. Something in her tone suggests part of the statement is bothering her: it's the word *gentleman*.

Boris Volchkov stands behind her, turning a disreputable hat over and over in his hands, looking excited or drunk, or both. He's speaking in Russian to forestall Mère Gigout's suspicions but only managing to inflame them.

'Good news,' he says, laying his finger against the side of his nose. 'I've been doing some researches and I found you those friends of the prince.'

'What prince?' Nicolas is genuinely puzzled.

Volchkov leans in and his warm brandy-vapour breath makes Nicolas's neck tingle. 'Kropotkin, you nut-bar, that's who. The most famous anarchist on the planet.'

'The meeting took place in one of the insalubrious quarters of the city.'

It's a mild June evening. A week of sunshine has magnified the stink of rubbish on these backstreets. At the side door of a tenement building, a man in a bowler hat lets Volchkov through but bars Nicolas from entering. 'He's with me,' says Volchkov. The arm lifts like the gate of a level crossing.

At the top of three flights of stairs an entire floor serves as a weaver's studio. The big Jacquard loom has been pushed against the wall to make space. 'Try not to stare,' counsels Volchkov through his teeth. 'They're really jumpy about spies.'

Nicolas daren't write anything down so he makes virtual notes in his head: air of expectation (underline twice), twenty-five people, average age mid-twenties, artisans and bohemian intellectuals. All men. No, three women. Two dressed in black. One covering her head with a blue shawl.

Through a pair of big windows, the sky outside is clear but moonless. All the faces are in shadow. The darkness and silence give it the atmosphere of a religious gathering.

A distant clock chimes the half-hour. For an age, it seems like nothing happens. Then there's the sound of footsteps. Two men enter. One drags a table into the middle of the room, its legs stammering against the unfinished floorboards, and sets a candlestick upon it, while the other lingers at the fringes of the crowd, muttering to himself. It's Pierre Verzilov, the man everyone's come to hear.

When the candle's lit, Verzilov sits down on the tabletop. His body is long and gangly but somehow folds easily, like a deckchair. He hugs his knees and stares into the flame. He's no older than Nicolas. The candle flame lights his features with a yellow glow, hollows his eyes, and makes him the focus of the room. Without warning, he begins to speak.

'I won't risk brighter illumination. It's not on my account. The Tsar's spies hold no fears for me. But I don't wish to compromise my comrades' safety.' Verzilov has a dandyish pointed beard and a moustache whose ends he plucks at while he thinks. 'The change is coming. The time when tyrants tremble. The time that will honour the blood of our revolutionary martyrs. The new Tsar is already revealing the true character of his tyrannical regime. My brothers and sisters will continue to heed the wise words of the noble communards: *Society has only one obligation toward monarchs . . .*' Verzilov pauses deliberately and looks slowly round the room. '*To put them to death.*' In spite of himself, Nicolas finds he has to suppress a shiver.

There's a murmur of approval from the assembled people. Verzilov continues to talk quickly in heavily accented French. He speaks of workers' insurrections, the will of the people, and secret printing presses pumping out antidotes to the poisonous falsehoods coursing through the veins of the body politic. It is stirring, passionate, outraged, and thin on facts. At the end, his silent accomplice passes round a hat. Many of those present have brought bags of money to put in it. Nicolas understands that they represent other cells of revolutionaries, from whom they have brought cash, to whom they will return with news of this sermon.

Verzilov continues to sit motionless on the table, cross-legged now, like a pagan idol. A woman in a blue shawl approaches to speak to him. Verzilov nods but doesn't meet her eye. Nicolas watches the candle flame illuminate her face: a neat oval, pale skin, tresses of brown hair.

Volchkov leans in. 'You'll have to donate for me, buddy. I forgot to bring my wallet.'

It's typical Volchkov. Nicolas is careful to unfold a fifty-franc note in a part of the room where there is enough light for his munificence to be visible and to speak French with a strong Russian accent when he praises the speech. Verzilov accepts the compliment grandly, as if to indicate that it's no more than he deserves. 'I'd like to be able to do more, comrade,' Nicolas says. 'My people are ready.'

The henchman intervenes. 'We'll let you know when the time is right.' Verzilov extinguishes the candle with a pinch. He appears to vanish in the ensuing darkness.

'The Turkish war had made me a patriot.'

Nicolas buys Volchkov dinner to say thanks and to pump him for further information. Volchkov is euphoric with the sense of an obligation successfully discharged and at the prospect of free food and drink. He orders for them both: beefy onion soup, herrings and potatoes, crispy squares of breaded tripe, red wine.

'How do you hear about a thing like this?' asks Nicolas.

A half-moon of translucent onion dangles from Volchkov's beard. 'You've got to be plugged in. There's a whole subculture out there. Our generation is going to change the world. Young people today: we're all *free love, down with the establishment, spread the wealth around*. It's entirely new shit. You saw that loom? It uses programmable punchcards to remember the patterns. It's a machine with, like, a fucking brain, Nicolas! People over thirty are just not going to get it.

It might honestly be kinder to just kill them.'

Nicolas feels unaccountably miserable. His first encounter with revolutionary politics has left him shaken. He tries to adumbrate the reasons why: the humourless sense of conviction; the confidence in the usefulness of violence; the disdain for other viewpoints. 'Don't you see? Verzilov is just telling you a story. His version of history is an amalgam of violence and lies. He says the world is going to be better, but why should you believe him? And what is the world anyway? There's no world. There's just . . . you and me, and two plates of this, whatever it's called.'

Volchkov smiles wolfishly through a big mouthful of fried tripe. 'It's called fireman's apron, and you, my friend, are failing once again to see the big picture. Didn't you hear Verzilov? There's capital and labour, and the bourgeoisie and an exploiter class, and a parasitic clergy sucking the life out of the workers.'

'Right. So when this glorious day comes and the wealth gets shared around, who is going to buy your art?'

Volchkov empties the wine pitcher into his glass and signals to the waiter for more. 'You're nitpicking. Under an anarcho-socialist-syndicalist system of workers' collectives, everyone would be paid to do what they wanted. I'd get a wage from the government. I could use my talent to entertain the proletariat. Photopeinture would be at the forefront of revolutionary art.'

'Good luck with that,' says Nicolas, with uncharacteristic bitterness.

'For the first time in my life, I experienced writer's block.'

It's not that the words won't come. The words come all right, it's just that they're the wrong ones. And Nicolas has two sets of publishers breathing down his neck for the Tsar book: Osip and a Parisian firm that is keen to take it too.

One morning he just stays in bed. We're all at it, he thinks: the making of stories. It's just words, words, words, no matter from the heart. The Tsar, a bra, catarrh. Behind it all flap the big black wings of unmourned grief for his father.

His moods shifts before lunch and he rouses himself to salvage something from the day. On the way to the library, his attention is caught by a flash of blue shawl in the crowd: like the azure of a kingfisher or a damselfly, hovering on the surface of a grey pond. He hastens to give chase. She's carrying a basket and is moving with surprising speed. Finally, he's behind her. 'Excuse me—'

She turns: that oval face; demure, brown eyes peer from beneath her lids. 'Monsieur?' The Russian accent in her voice is like the smell of home: specifically, lilacs and chestnut blossom.

'I believe you are a friend of the prince?'

'What of it?'

'May we speak?'

'She had trained as a midwife in Kiev.'

She lets him buy her a slice of cake, which she eats hungrily. She works among the city's destitute. Her eyes glisten with tears when she talks about the joy of delivering children.

There's outrage in her voice when she speaks of the conditions of the poor. 'It's a crime. The lack of sanitation. The poverty and ignorance. We should all be equal in the eyes of God.'

'If there was a God,' Nicolas adds carefully, feeling rather pleased with himself.

Her face wrinkles into a smile that displays big ivory teeth. Her nose strikes him as perfect and quite peppered with freckles. 'You are right. An old habit. My family are Jews.'

'Mine too,' says Nicolas. He can't believe this. The revolutionary activism aside, this is someone he could take home to his mother. 'You heard about the attacks, the pogroms?'

She nods. 'Pierre says anti-Semitism is the template for all forms of intolerance.'

'Does he?' Nicolas wishes that Pierre hadn't said something that sounds quite so intelligent; and he wishes she wouldn't look so worshipful when she mentions his name. 'He's probably Jewish too,' he says, aware of a note of envy in his voice.

'No, he's not.'

'You can never be sure of that. Look at us!' His gesture includes them both: a pair of freethinking cosmopolitans with no apparent Jewish heritage.

'I am sure.' Her revolutionary broadmindedness surrenders to a blush.

Oh God, thinks Nicolas. *She's seen his cock.*

'You and he are . . . intimate?'

'Pierre and I are close friends, but he is faithful to only one mistress.'

And now she's going to say 'the revolution'.

'The revolution?' Nicolas interjects.

'Exactly.' She pushes away her empty plate, burps adorably, and bursts out laughing.

'Lizaveta Gelfman was her name, but she called herself Bessie.'

Notovitch sits silently for a while. The sound of an angle grinder from a plumbing emergency in the room next to where I am writing these words penetrates his reverie. I wonder what extraneous sounds you are battling with. *That Theroux, he's always thinking of his reader.*

'Twenty-three is old for a first love, nowadays?' muses the old man.

'It always was,' says Vincenzo. 'Surely when you were fifteen or sixteen, there was someone?'

'Puppy love. That's not what I'm speaking of. The breathlessness, the sleeplessness, the yearning. The Himalayas of elation and despair. Some people never feel it, you know.' The old man goes still. He is a husk. His soul is elsewhere, taking refuge in the chamber of memories. When he returns, his voice is subtly altered, softer, mellowed by the recollection of this love. 'You know, not only did I persuade her I was a sincere revolutionary; looking into her eyes, I almost persuaded myself.'

'She was a member of Verzilov's inner circle.'

The revolutionary enthusiasm which seems to arise in Verzilov from innate narcissism, from a Napoleonic urge to crown himself emperor of the world's dispossessed, has more benign roots in Bessie. With her, it starts as a sincere wish to alleviate suffering. So much misery is avoidable. The planet is rich and fecund. Properly managed, there's enough for everyone. Progress is not some mystical belief in Utopia, it's just a series of practical steps: antisepsis, education, drainage, street lighting, universal suffrage, clean water and contraception so that women won't jeopardise their health from enjoying the one pleasure that belongs to poor and rich alike.

And of course she likes Nicolas too. Something in her has been nurtured to respond to the prospect of a nice Jewish boy from home. Have I mentioned how handsome he's become? He's grown into his slightly awkward face. The moustache has darkened and filled out. He has the thoughtful introspective features of someone who misses nothing and thinks deeply. He's dapper, too. He needs to be: his job means he could be called upon to visit an ambassador, or turn up for a press conference in the Elysée Palace at a moment's notice.

But as he grows closer in spirit to her, a conventional urge to marry and procreate comes to dominate his other feelings. Bessie is adamantly otherwise. 'Men and women ought not to live in bondage,' she says. 'But we can honour each other with our bodies, if you'd like.'

On a rainy afternoon in Nicolas's garret, Bessie takes his virginity. Imagine it as you wish, but the dominant notes were tenderness and love.

'She found our political differences insurmountable.'

Rain patters on the windowpanes. The wind cat's-paws the water in the flooded gutters. Nicolas wakes and stretches languorously. The sheets feel airy and cool. How long has he been sleeping? It must be close to eight. The light is fading. A single candle on his writing desk illuminates that corner of the room with a penumbra the colour of honey and love.

Bessie, naked except for MacGahan's dark-blue chapan, sees Nicolas rousing himself from sleep.

In a shrill, cold voice she reads aloud: '"The far-seeing Tsar understood that the yoke of serfdom must be lifted from the neck of his suffering people."' She waves the papers in the air. 'What bullshit is this? Don't you mean: "The blood-thirsty tyrant realised his days were numbered if he didn't stop enslaving his own subjects"?'

Nicolas hears the new note of harshness in her voice. Until now, he believed eyes flashing in anger were purely a literary device.

'Bessie, sweetheart, please. It's just a book.' He opens his arms in a gesture intended to placate her.

'Don't *sweetheart* me, chauvinist fucker! You lied! Stooge! Patsy! Reactionary scum!'

The change in her is so sudden and intense that he finds it, of all things, funny. She's surely joking? He risks a smile.

Bessie takes a step towards him and spits right in his face. She is shaking with rage. *Please, Lord, let this be a bad dream*, he thinks. He closes his eyes in the vain hope that when he opens them they'll be back in bed, lovers again, or at least on speaking terms. But all he feels is the spit, issue of her pert, lovable mouth, going cold on his face, paralysing him like cobra venom, turning his body into marble. He stands mo-tionless while she gathers up her clothes and leaves the room to dress abruptly on the landing.

In the coming days, Nicolas learns that the symptoms of a broken heart – lassitude, gloom, loss of appetite, an over-whelming urge to stay in bed – are very similar to influenza.

Viewed from where we're standing, somewhere up in the celestial eighth sphere, their tiff seems pointless: two young fresh folk, lovers, Jews, divided by irreconcilable opinions of the *Tsar*?

But Nicolas cannot dismiss her rage as the ravings of a fanatic. Her twin sister, Gesya, belongs to the ranks of revolutionary martyrs. Tried for capital crimes in Saint Petersburg two years ago, she was sentenced to hang. On hearing the verdict, Gesya revealed that she was carrying her lover's child and in the fourth month of pregnancy. Her punishment was commuted to hard labour in a northern penal colony. Whatever savagery and cold you can imagine, this place was worse. Gesya was separated from her child immediately after giving birth, contracted blood poisoning and died. The baby lived only a week longer.

Every time Bessie assists at a birth, she thinks of her sister. Every miraculous slippery child she lays with its purple umbilicus on a mother's belly is, however briefly, her niece. And for all Bessie's many good qualities, she lacks a capacity for forgiveness. Revolutionary virtue tends towards the pitiless. Mind you, Nicolas is hardly innocent. Imagine if she knew the scope of his project for Suvorin – presenting the anarchists to bourgeois readers like prepared slides of microbes, or stuffed exotic birds.

Believe me, it breaks my heart that they can't be together. How much I'd like to write of their love mellowing, the minutiae of their shared life, of all they might undertake with each other. But in this version of the secret books, the two of them dwell in incompatible stories.

'In 1883, I was received into the Orthodox Church.'

Yes, Nicolas became a Christian.

That is the *what*; but why?

The old man we and Vincenzo know tends to pooh-pooh the religious stirrings of his younger self – a reversal that implies to me the frustration of a disappointed mystic. We needn't be so dismissive.

I think that behind the urge to faith somehow lies a primary experience of love: something Nicolas felt dimly but certainly in Bessie's presence: awe, the communion of things, the sense of brimming with melancholy at the transience of this beautiful life. He has an intuition that he doesn't end where he thought he did and that the world penetrates him deeply; he knows we are spiritually involved with it and with each other, whether we acknowledge it or not.

Well, speaking of the ineffable is bound to make fools of us.

In his thorough way, he visits a variety of priests: Protestant, Roman Catholic and Orthodox. Why not a mullah, why not a rebbe? What is wrong with the faith of his parents?

I can only offer you reasons: He feels it is a fault in him to lack certainty and overcompensates by choosing something that feels like decisive progress. It is a final break with his past. It is a calculated step to enhance the prospects for his career, which will go more smoothly by far for a proper Christian than a wavering ex-Jew. It is a refutation of Bessie's anarchism. He feels called to honour his father's death by committing himself to something obscurely serious. It is some or all of these.

The priest who instructs him is a Georgian called Father David Chikladze. Explicating the parable of the yeast in Matthew 13, verse 33, the priest recalls his childhood in Khaketi, and the annual vintage of saperavi grapes. Trodden in the press, the grapes produce a juice the colour of arterial blood, which the action of the wild yeasts transforms into something intoxicating, something more fully alive. Just like this, he continues, the Holy Ghost animated the red clay of Adam.

When Nicolas quizzes him about the afterlife, a lacuna in Judaism, the priest offers the vaguest of imaginings: 'I know only this: we will be with God, and it will be better.' Nicolas finds himself moved by the tentativeness and hope of the formulation. But at his baptism he feels nothing. The myrrh applied to his face during the ceremony of anointing unfortunately recalls the sensation of Bessie's spit, turning from hot to cold.

Naturally, he chooses the baptismal name *Nicolas.*

'I offered to return Suvorin's money.'

The Tsar book sells respectably. Giving a talk at a Paris bookshop to launch the French edition, Nicolas fields questions about Anglo-Russian rivalry in India, free speech, the Pussy Riot protests, and the prospects for a triple entente between Russia, France and Britain. He's halfway through one answer when he glimpses a flash of blue at the window and a woman with an oval face shading her eyes to peer in.

'Would you excuse me for one moment?'

He rushes to the door of the shop and looks both ways. The boulevard is a sea of indifferent grey faces.

His heart drops into his boots. Returning to the podium, Nicolas continues with an explanation of balance-of-power politics and regional hegemons that now seems to him fatuous and unconvincing.

At the back of the room, Volchkov, who has thrown over the brown-haired fruit-seller for a new interest, is working his way through the bowls of Twiglets.

After the talk, a representative from *Novaya Gazeta* presents his card. He's a Russian with a German name, Ludwig Ganz. 'Mr Suvorin sends his warmest regards,' he says. Nicolas is momentarily anxious. He hasn't heard back from Suvorin since he wrote to say the piece on anarchists was a non-starter. 'Mr Suvorin was curious to know what difficulties you encountered with the story?'

Ganz is blonde and pinkly clean-shaven. Nicolas knows he owes him an explanation, but he's not sure how to begin it. Fortunately, there are immediate grounds for an adjournment: at one side of the room half a dozen people are waiting to have their books signed. Nicolas suggests the men meet another time. Ganz bows and clicks his heels.

'Who's that stiff?' asks Volchkov. 'He looks like secret police. Since the Tsar got whacked, they're all up in our shit, oppressing the youth.'

'Don't be an idiot. And why are you talking like a hoodlum? He's another journalist.'

A day later, Ganz calls at Nicolas's apartment. 'An artist's garret!' He pauses at the door to catch his breath and pulls off his gloves a finger at a time. 'Suvorin sends his compliments and asked me to tell you how much he enjoyed the book. I'm only halfway through myself, but I'm a slow reader and there's so much to savour.' He lists a handful of the extracts that have given him special pleasure.

Like any writer, Nicolas finds it hard to resist flattery. Ganz's praise seems unfeigned and there's something about his open demeanour that encourages the sharing of confidences. He is that rarest and insufficiently praised thing: a gifted listener.

Over dinner at a restaurant called The Blue Wheel, it all pours out: the anarchists' meeting, running into Bessie, the sudden end of the affair, the continuing ache of loss.

Ganz listens, non-judgementally, sympathetic, reassuringly unsurprisable. 'It sounds like you've been through the mill, old chap. Suvorin's a gent and has known a broken heart or three in his life. I'm sure he won't demand his money back. I think probably a letter from you – just setting down what you've told me – is the best way of straightening things out.'

Suvorin couldn't be more understanding. He not only writes back personally, but also encloses a banker's draft for the balance of the fee. 'I've taken the liberty of sharing your contact details with an old friend at the gendarmerie,' adds Suvorin in a PS. 'As a fellow patriot, you'll understand, I'm sure.'

'At that time, I began to entertain doubts about my choice of career.'

Nicolas is glad of the money, and yet something about the transaction doesn't feel entirely wholesome. Who pays and expects nothing in return? What service has he, however obliquely, provided? He was careful to change Bessie's name in the letter; the address of the weaver's apartment he can't even remember himself. Perhaps he might have given away one or two details about Verzilov, but surely nothing the secret police don't know already?

Now Nicolas's passion for writing begins to falter a little. He learns what all writers eventually learn, that the path he has chosen is not a career at all, but a series of crises, or solitary trudges uphill and down, with a peak that's only visible in retrospect. It starts crossing his mind that his talents might be more pleasantly and lucratively applied in another field.

He begins to dabble in the wine export business. Then as now, there's a healthy global demand for upmarket French wines. He has the necessary languages, a background in retail, and a good grasp of the transport links. He buys a share in a firm of vintners and works three days a week in their offices, moving claret, burgundy and champagne by rail to Moscow and Saint Petersburg; by boat across the Black Sea to Kiev and Little Russia. He subcontracts some of the work to his brother, and thereby maintains a thread of connection to his family and former life. Things at home are a struggle, he learns. The general hostility towards the Jews has only intensified.

Late one afternoon, Ganz stops by the shop. 'I heard you were working here. I hope we can still expect a sequel to your last volume?' Nicolas says yes, he's halfway though a book of political analysis. 'I brought a friend,' says Ganz. 'Suvorin, I think, may have mentioned him.'

A bowler-hatted Frenchman entered the premises the

same time as Ganz and has been perusing the racks of wines. He carries a bottle to Nicolas's desk and asks to buy it. Nicolas has to explain that they're not that kind of wine merchants. They sell *en primeur* and by the case, but principally for export. That bottle belongs to the display. Nicolas feels unaccountably angry. This job only works for him if he can believe it has nothing to do with the world he came from. With one remark, it's as though he's found himself back in his father's shop. Ganz smoothes out the misunderstanding, but it's an inauspicious beginning.

The Frenchman, Monsieur Chabrot, is monastically bald: the removal of his hat reveals a tonsured pate and a fringe of dark hair. His upper lip is covered with a bristly, animated moustache. He's here to request a favour. Suvorin's name comes up again. Nicolas feels as though he's being prodded with it.

'Could I have a word in private?' Chabrot says.

Ganz sits at the desk, flicking through the brochures, as though born to the job, while Chabrot and Nicolas go to the rear of the store. Chabrot shakes out a handful of mugshots from an envelope in his breast pocket. 'I wondered if any of these look familiar?'

Nicolas scrutinises the pictures: the technology is still relatively novel, and there's something unsettling about confronting the gaze of the photographic subject. The sight of a familiar oval face in the spread of images causes his heart to shut oyster-tight. 'No, I've never seen them,' he says, almost too abruptly.

'If I might draw your attention to this one, Monsieur Notovitch.'

To Nicolas's relief, it's not the one of Bessie, but another, of a man. 'Why, yes.' Clean-shaven, with his hairstyle bizarrely reversed, it's still unmistakably Verzilov. 'Yes, I know the man. But I think that must be a wig. And not a very good one.'

'I hate to presume again on your time but our mutual friend Suvorin assured me you would be keen to render assistance. We won't need to trouble you again.'

There is a cab waiting outside. By now it is close to dusk. A bank of violet cloud has massed beneath the setting sun. They reach their destination – the Imperial Embassy on Rue de Grenelle – and are ushered into the basement through a side entrance. There's a lime-green metal door with a spyhole. 'Please take a look.'

Within, it's brightly lit. The angle of the spyhole takes in a seated man whose face appears in Nicolas's mind as instantaneously and indelibly as a photographic image: the head lolls back; blood dribbles and clots in its beard; one purple eye is swollen and half-closed. He's motionless, dying, possibly already dead. Nicolas manages a nod and turns away. Yes, Verzilov.

Walking shakily out of the building, Nicolas justifies himself with boilerplate phrases: My duty as a citizen-subject. Enemies of order. Terrorist-fanatics.

But the bloody face haunts him for a long time. He thinks of Bessie. He thinks: *Judas*.

*

FATHER DAVID, the priest who received Nicolas into the Church, retains a soft spot for his converted Jew. Nicolas brings him a fine old burgundy and tries to articulate his feelings of betrayal and loss.

'What is bitter is truly sweet, and what is sweet truly bitter,' says the priest, who has a fondness for paradox. 'The gift of poverty is to make us more attentive to the world; the gift of pain is to open our hearts to the suffering of others.'

The priest's words are no comfort whatsoever.

'Suvorin came to Paris.'

It's strange to see Suvorin the newspaper magnate in these unfamiliar surroundings. He's here on unspecified business, has taken an apartment on Quai des Célestins and invited Nicolas to dinner. Suvorin's tired from the train journey so they order room service and Suvorin tucks into the minibar, mixing himself a Cuba libre with miniatures of rum and a tiny can of Diet Coke.

'So what did you think of *Demons*?' Suvorin wants to know.

Nicolas has read it finally and thinks it's a surprisingly bad book: unlikely characters, a poorly worked-out plot, and a first-person narrator who can't possibly have witnessed any of the things he's talking about. Technically, it's all wrong. But there are a couple of scenes that stand out with an unearthly power: the dissolute characters visiting the holy fool, Tikhon; the young people desecrating the icon. 'I loved it,' Nicolas lies. 'So well achieved, and prescient.'

Some part of that is true. The book, now ten years old, eerily foreshadows the activities of People's Will. Pyotr Verkhovensky, the novel's dark and charismatic anti-hero, is a dead ringer for Pierre Verzilov.

'We lost a prophet when Dostoevsky died,' sighs Suvorin. 'The last of the great ones.'

'Well, there's still Tolstoy,' ventures Nicolas.

Suvorin waves a dismissive hand. 'I liked his early stuff, but he's lost the plot: all this vegetarianism, pacifism, bearded-guru shit. You know he even makes his own shoes? What's up with that?'

'I've been meaning to ask. They never said what happened to Verzilov.' Nicolas picks up his club sandwich with great care and poses the question as though wondering aloud: 'How did he actually die?'

'He fell out of a window, trying to escape.'

'From the basement?' says Nicolas, unable to conceal his incredulity.

Suvorin gives him a sharp, reproving look. 'One of the upper storeys,' he says, through a mouthful of French fries. 'Ganz told me you helped to ID the body. It was probably in a bad way.'

Nicolas nods and his appetite for food dies as he fails to suppress the recollected image of Verzilov's mutilated face. He puts the sandwich back down on the plate.

'Listen, it's all very well talking about a free press,' Suvorin continues, as though answering an inaudible accusation, 'but what kind of freedom would you have if those people come to power? They're brainwashing the nation's youth with their lies. Who says the system we have is perfect? Not me. But change isn't simple. You don't pick up and discard political systems like they're a bunch of old LPs at a yard sale.' Suvorin wipes his mouth with a paper napkin and changes the subject. 'I have a more inspiring theme to raise with you, young man.'

Nicolas feels something in him rise with excitement. A man like Suvorin, with good news, for him?

'The only question is, are you ready for an adventure?'

'Always, sir.'

'That's what I want to hear. My guy in Ashkhabad has come down with something. It's not incurable, but he's going to be out of action for quite a while. I can't stress enough the importance of boiling the water out there before you drink it. Anyway, things are getting interesting in that whole area. It's a great story: Britain and Russia duking it out for control of the region. There's plenty of reporters keen to go, but I wanted to offer it to you first.'

'India had always felt like my destiny.'

It's a long, wearisome journey by rail to the Caspian Sea and then overland through the deserts of Central Asia, but Nicolas wakes up each morning at whatever godforsaken whistle-stop or dusty caravanserai and thinks: *the best thing in my life is happening now.*

Coming back to this kind of work after a break, he feels close in spirit to MacGahan, he enjoys it more than he remembers, and he notices how good he is at it. He's quick and organised and has the gift of winning people's trust at once. Doing satisfying work and being appreciated: the secret of life seems simple.

Another thing restores his sense of well-being. The British he meets are the most insufferably smug, complacent, patronising and presumptuous tribe of fools he's ever met. Furthermore, where other conquerors at least perpetrate honest pillage, the British he encounters constantly claim to be acting in the best interests of their subject nations, as though they are the world's strict parent. It takes no prophetic gift, Nicolas thinks, to see that this is an unsustainable hypocrisy.

Nicolas finds a deep enjoyment in holding this entire group of people in contempt. Furthermore, it stabilises his somewhat shaky Russian identity.

On a trip to Simla, he meets a precocious young jingo called Something – Rudolph, Rudiger? – Kipling, who tells stories in funny voices and whose eyes grow moist when he toasts the Queen. Sitting next to him, Nicolas feels invincibly and proudly Russian. Whatever in him is still Jewish or non-Slav shrinks to a tiny pencil-point.

One of his ongoing assignments is to report on the smouldering conflict between the Russian and British Empires. Nicolas travels repeatedly to the dusty and contentious border that runs through Afghanistan, where he smarms up to subalterns on one side and bribes homesick muzhiks on the other for all the information he can get. It strikes him that the jostling for control of India and the territory around it must inevitably bring the two empires into open warfare one day. But for now, despite the posturing of rival diplomats and the hostile words of puffed-chested generals, Nicolas concludes that it's really no more than a staring contest.

He is in the region for two and a half years. The nature of Nicolas's work, his ability to roam and ask questions, his allegiance to the country of his birth make him useful to a cohort of shadowy fellow Russians who flit in and out of the country. He travels now and again under an assumed name: Polish, French or Armenian, as the situation demands. The line between journalism and espionage grows blurry. One day he asks himself if this was Suvorin's intention all along and realises the answer is yes.

Nicolas is the go-to guy for all his paper's regional stories and he even finds time to send a few dispatches Osip's way. But he earns more and more of his income from writing reports on transport links, troop numbers and the shifting allegiances of the rulers of the princely states. These secret pages leave India in diplomatic bags and swell the files of the Foreign Ministry in Saint Petersburg.

Everything about India and Central Asia exceeds his expectations: heat, frustration, sublimity, dirt, exoticism, crushing squalor. There are moments of both transfiguring beauty and low comedy, sometimes simultaneously: at Agra, viewing the Taj Mahal in moonlight, he is ravished by the soul of the place, then has his toe bitten by a squirrel and spends two days worrying about rabies.

In one of the Rajput kingdoms, he joins a crowd of barefoot pilgrims making offerings at a temple to Hanuman. Groups of sacred grey langurs eye them from the rocks. Their size and human-seeming gestures make them uncanny. A monkey mother suckles a monkey baby at her hairy breast. Another snatches a garland of marigolds from a startled human child and munches it, wearing a truculent expression on its mangy face. Inside the temple, the air is close and hot, the noise overwhelming. Watching the worshippers prostrate themselves before the monkey god, Nicolas experiences a wave of nausea and has to force his way outside to vomit. The culprit is some buffalo-milk barfi he has unwisely accepted from a friendly Brahmin performing darshan. Looking out on the scrubby hills through still-watering eyes, Nicolas sees tattered shreds of plastic bags fluttering to the accompaniment of cheap transistor radios.

When his time is almost up, he spends a couple of months volunteering at an orphanage outside Madras in order to satisfy some vague notion of 'giving something back'. He makes an attempt to teach the children English – more use to them than Russian – but they're not interested and the heat is so overwhelming that he soon abandons the pretence of work. In the mornings, he eats a hearty breakfast with the nice Swedish missionaries who are putting him up and then goes for a walk along the beach. Sometimes he'll swim, or watch the local fishermen landing their catch. Most afternoons he takes a nap, has a half-hearted Tamil lesson, and reads or plays carom until supper time. Still, in later years he'll earn a surprising amount of kudos from people when he tells them about this humanitarian interlude.

In the centre of the city, beside the sea, he watches blocks of ice being loaded into the thick masonry of an icehouse. Parcelled up in straw and sacking, the ice blocks have been carried across the ocean from the lake in Maine where they are cut each winter. They lose half their weight in transit, but there's enough of them left to be sold as a luxury in the tropical heat, to chill the sahibs' gin and tonics and make iced puddings for their wives and children. Nicolas feels grudging admiration for this evidence of British ingenuity. It's further proof that the world is shrinking. He's moved to buy a postcard of the icehouse and send it to his brother with cheery greetings. 'The Twentieth Century, here we come!' he writes.

Towards the end of 1884, he makes his slow, touristic way

north. He hasn't slept with another woman since Bessie – opportunities are scarce and he's fearful of contracting something from the native brothels, but in Goa he enjoys a minor romance with a German backpacker from Cologne. They agree, insincerely, to stay in touch. As he leaves, it crosses his mind how nice it would be to be going home to someone.

A month later, travelling north out of Uzbekistan through the frontier statelets of the new Russian Imperium, Nicolas sees a huge earthwork rising out of the desert floor. It is a ghost town: all that remains of the once-prosperous city of Otrar. Nicolas scrambles onto one of its embankments. The top is flat. Lizards scuttle through the rust-coloured dried grass. Under his feet, shards of bones and fragments of broken pots testify to a previous existence as a thriving desert oasis. 'I'm king of the world!' he shouts, to the amusement of his local guides. 'Look upon my works, ye mighty, and despair!'

This barren space was once a city of a quarter of a million people. Most of the pot shards underfoot are simple pieces of terracotta, but one or two have the striking blue glaze of precious azurite, which Nicolas has seen being laboured out of the ground on a tour of the lapis lazuli mines in Badakhshan. The raw mineral gives little hint of the celestial blue with which it has clothed portraits of the Virgin Mary for more than five hundred years, but Nicolas still buys a chunk from the gift shop as a present for Father David.

Author, journalist, man of business, adventurer, and now spy: Nicolas Notovitch is on his way home.

'I owe the next phase of my career to a louse.'

The return journey to Paris devours Nicolas's cash. He's un-characteristically free-handed with his money, assuming that – worst-case scenario – his investment in the wine business will have held its value.

But the vintner's has gone belly-up: the shop is derelict, the signage peeling, and half a dozen dusty bottles are the only remnants of the once-pristine display.

Two unforeseeable events have bankrupted it. First, the phylloxera louse, which has continued to munch steadily through French vineyards while he's been away; then the eruption of Krakatoa in 1883, which plunged the entire world into several years of unusually cold weather. The output of French wine has crashed as a consequence.

'Bummer,' says Volchkov, tearing chunks off a baguette with a practised wristy action that reminds Nicolas of the way his older brother used to give him Chinese burns. Volch-kov has changed almost beyond recognition. Nicolas expect-ed to find the old reprobate drink-stained and roistering still, but he's married, with a tiny daughter on whom he dotes. He's cut his long hair off and is working as a teacher in an art school, still poor, still talking about his plans for photopein-ture, but with less conviction.

Nicolas takes him out a couple of times, in the hope of en-ticing him on to some serious dissipation, but Volchkov heads home early on both occasions and speaks with an eerie but sincere enthusiasm about the pleasures of being a parent.

At least Mère Gigout, his old landlady, has hardly changed, or so little that it's assimilated at once into the mental im-age Nicolas carries within him. She offers him his old garret. Cashing the last of his traveller's cheques, he's able to scrape together the money for six months' rent, and begins to scribble his way back to solvency.

And what of Nicolas himself? What changes have these two-plus years wrought?

I notice a change in his writing about this time. An orotund manner creeps in. The rough edges that give his early books their energy are planed off, and his output begins to bloat into longer and longer volumes – writing that conceals more than it enlightens. Stories can be fog as well as knives, to veil the truths we'd much rather avoid.

Out of his own extraordinary facts, out of Naum, out of Kolya, out of the particles of MacGahan that he's absorbed into his own being, he weaves the stuff of a sober bourgeois: a patriot, a Russian, a reactionary. He turns his eyes from inconvenient truths and picks facts to confirm his stories: about his good intentions, the basic decency of people, the flawed but necessary institutions of state power. And out of all these approximations to the truth, a false self is formed: an outward shape, whose interior conceals the doubt and bliss and honest confusion that comprises the living man.

He gives the chunk of lapis lazuli to Father David, who puts it on his mantelpiece. 'You have grown older,' says the priest, who, alongside his fondness for paradox, has a liking for stating the obvious.

'Yes,' says Nicolas. 'I've been thinking it might be time to settle down.'

'To take a wife?' says Father David with a mixture of surprise and approval. The priest has an unofficial role as matchmaker in Paris's small Orthodox community. 'I know just the family.'

After church on Sundays, Father David hosts small gatherings of his congregants; at one of these he introduces Nicolas to the Rozenfelds. Mr Rozenfeld is a converted Jew from Lvov who owns a chain of fashion boutiques. He's married to a Polish woman. The two of them have a daughter, Anya, who is training to be a teacher. Petite, dark-eyed and curious, Anya's nineteen but has the preternatural self-possession of a doted-on only child. She is intrigued by the polite and well-travelled young man. Her parents invite him to stop by for tea and malt loaf.

'I received an invitation to dine with the head of the Third Section on my return.'

While Nicolas has been away, the previously slipshod operation of the Russian secret police in Paris has been put on a more professional footing. Paris is the destination of choice for the Russian revolutionary in exile. It is, depending on your political outlook, a freethinking Eden of creative dissent or a swamp of ideological contagion that needs to be drained.

The man brought in to head things up is sometimes Pierre, sometimes Pyotr, sometimes Peter; but his last name is always Rachkovsky.

Rachkovsky: it's worth saying that out loud; a surname to conjure with. Its sound evokes the turn of a key in handcuffs, the click of a lock in a cell door, the scrape of a chair leg on the floor of an interrogation room. Such onomatopoeia, though it fits his job, is strangely discordant with the appearance of the man himself.

He's five years older than Nicolas, but his age is hard to

determine from his face. As genial as a talk-show host, endowed with big appetites for food and sex, he's large, giggly, bearded, and has black curly hair like lambswool.

At their first encounter, he simply holds Nicolas's hand and stares at him with unconcealed delight. 'This is terribly shame-making. I can't think where to begin. It's too-too wonderful to meet you. A fellow lottery winner.'

Nicolas has come dressed to the nines and with his hair brilliantined. He is keen to make a good impression and was intending to project gravity and reserve. He's pitched himself too formally, he realises, and it's going to take him a few drinks to match Rachkovsky's energy. 'A lottery winner?'

Rachkovsky chuckles in a hiccoughing, schoolgirlish way. 'That's what I call us! People like us.' He looks around himself and grins. 'Here we are! In Paris! For goodness' sake, somebody pinch me!' Momentarily distracted by the curve of a waitress's backside, he follows her motion across the room, and then turns to raise an appreciative eyebrow at Nicolas.

People like us? What can he possibly mean? The two men are chalk and cheese. Russians? Writers? Expatriates in Paris? Spies?

'Suvorin has told me everything about you. He said you could speak all the local languages and had practically gone native. I half expected you to be carried in on a palanquin. And the word from Saint Petersburg is that your intelligence from India was breathtaking. Let's have champagne. I hear too you have quite a palate.'

Nicolas shrugs. 'I don't know about that. I used to dabble in the wine business.'

'You clever *molodets*. My cellar is full of absolute filth

because as soon as the wine merchants hear me speak French they assume, quite rightly, that I'm an ignoramus. Tell me something, is the outlook for French wine really as bleak as all that?'

Rachkovsky asks a hundred questions, but Nicolas senses that he already knows the answer to every single one. He orders a stupendous meal, even by Parisian standards: oysters, foie gras with jelly of Sauternes, sea bass in a pastry crust, and for the main course a Bresse chicken. It comes to the table in the pig's bladder it's been poached in. Rachkovsky catches his eye as the waiter carves the wings off expertly and ladles morels and cream over them. 'Non-kosher, I'm afraid,' he says slyly. And Nicolas gets it: *people like us*. He means ex-Jews, men like them, living large in Paris. 'I still have a sentimental attachment to Judaism,' Rachkovsky adds, 'but the dietary laws make no sense whatsoever. I mean, no rabbit, but *grasshoppers*?'

'What's your mission in Paris?' asks Nicolas, who's never been afraid of a direct question.

Rachkovsky goes suddenly serious and leans in close. 'My mission, young man, is nothing less than to get the whole place annexed to Russia!'

'Really?'

'No – of course not. But imagine! Oh, you can keep your ghastly Perms, and Volgograds, your Irkutsks, and Petropav-lovsks.' He says the names of the provincial cities as though they're unpleasant tropical illnesses. 'Imagine if Paris, beautiful Paris, were a Russian city. This, my friend, is civilisation.' Rachkovsky sighs like a lovelorn puppet in the Guignol and raises his glass. 'My mission, as I see it, is to stay in this city as long as possible. So we should drink to the revolution-aries who've given me a *raison d'être*.'

The wine glasses touch. Rachkovsky's green eyes hold Nicolas's gaze and then close with a slow feline blink. It's an enigmatic look, presumably intended to be some kind of salute, but which might equally express sleepiness, contempt or ecstasy. Nicolas has no idea why he's he been invited here.

Rachkovsky, veteran of many similar sieges, knows just how to pursue Nicolas. At this first meal, he lets the demon-stration of largesse speak for itself and merely suggests that Nicolas pay him a visit when he can find the time.

The next morning, Nicolas writes a bread-and-butter let-ter to thank Rachkovsky for dinner and receives a chummy, handwritten reply by return of post. 'A pleasure, my charm-ing one. Come by for tea sometime.' It's signed with a single ambiguous initial, which can be read as a *P* for Peter in the Roman alphabet or an *R* for Rachkovsky in the Cyrillic one; it perches on a bed of curlicues.

Rachkovsky runs his kingdom from two modest base-ment offices in the Imperial Embassy at 79 Rue de Grenelle. This is the Paris headquarters of the so-called Third Sec-tion or Okhrana, the organisation set up in the aftermath of the Tsar's assassination to maintain the security of the next monarch and his family. The sinister-sounding word simply means: *protection*.

Small but well funded and – under Rachkovsky – well or-ganised, the Paris office controls agents across Europe, mon-itoring the activities of revolutionaries in exile. The primary threat is political terror. No one is in any doubt how danger-ous that is.

Nicolas is given a laminated name badge by the reception-
ist and asked to wait while she tells her boss he's there. Rachkovsky's first act is to tut, remove the badge, and pitch it in
the bin. 'We won't be needing that,' he says. The reception-
ist, a modest, dark-haired young Russian woman, apologises
profusely. 'Don't worry, Ksenia, Mr Notovitch is a personal
friend. You weren't to know.'

The basement is furnished with filing cabinets, a dedicated telegraph room, cipher books, equipment for perlustrat-
ing letters – steamers, bright lights, magnifying glasses – and
trays of hectographic gel for copying them. Rachkovsky
shows it all to him proudly, and talks about his plans to build
a darkroom. 'And that,' he announces, 'is the armoury. Do
you like guns? I love them! Let's have tea.'

They sit together in a glassed-in meeting space with a
whiteboard. Along one wall are WANTED bills for various
agitators, and flow charts showing the interrelationships between the different factions of the revolutionary movements:
anarchists, socialists, communists, syndicalists and so forth.

Nicolas is surprised that Rachkovsky is so open with his
intelligence and says so. Rachkovsky waves his hand. 'All
old hat, dear boy. It's like cutting heads off a hydra. No: that
makes them sound too glamorous. They're like a classroom
of sixth-form girls: one minute besties, the next *loathing* each
other. Sixth-form girls with a taste for savage violence.'

Rachkovsky's frankness emboldens Nicolas to ask a question that has been bothering him: *why me?*

'Why you? Dear boy!' Rachkovsky still makes tea in the
Russian way: he pours a syrupy decoction into the bottom of
a glass and tops it up with hot water. 'Why you? Reliable.

Russian-speaking. Multilingual. With a great cover story – and an ex-Jew to boot. Professional endorsements from the great and the good and a track record from Macedonia to Madras. Why you? I can't *possibly* imagine! Surely you mean to ask, *What's in it for me?'* Rachkovsky dithers over a box of chocolates, takes two, and pushes them towards Nicolas.

What's in it for me? Nicolas knows the answer to that one. It's the gravity of Rachkovsky that's so persuasive. His world is heavy and solid. For someone like Nicolas who's been travelling so much, who's been making his living with evanescent words, the prospect of drawing a regular salary, paid holidays and a pension is very attractive. Added to that there's the whiff of power, the sensation of proximity to the centre. That is the secret conviction Rachkovsky projects: wherever he is, that is the inner chamber. No one knows more or sways more than he.

On the way out, Nicolas notices that the gleaming refurbishment has omitted one detail of the basement. In the far left-hand corner, the interrogation room with its green door and spyhole has been left untouched.

Rachkovsky's used to quick responses, but after leaving, Nicolas vacillates. He's barely aware of the reason. Something stirs in the depths of his consciousness, something whose shape is indistinct, but from which bubbles of discomfort rise and disturb his sleep.

Sensing hesitancy, Rachkovsky makes his pitch again.

Candlelight gleams goldenly on heavy silverware. Crystal glasses, clearer than the conscience of a sleeping child, ring to the touch. The waiters speak in hushed voices. Rachkovsky has promised a special treat tonight.

The recollection of Verzilov has been nagging at Nicolas. The black blood in his beard. The broken face. It can't be right to do that to a man. In spite of all his outward changes, Nicolas retains the fundamental conviction of the small-*l* liberal that the worst thing a human can be is cruel. He hears Suvorin: *You eat meat, don't you? You sound like that crazy vegetarian Tolstoy.*

'Whatever happened to Verzilov. I wasn't comfortable with that. Will I . . . ? Do you . . . ?'

Rachkovsky shakes his head. 'I didn't like that one. The Verzilov business was a mess. Not necessary. And before my time, of course. I don't approve of pain – except recreationally. Have you read the Marquis? You simply must! Why, here they are!' He rubs his hands excitedly.

The waiter sets down a dish of tiny roasted birds. Nicolas doesn't even recognise the name in Russian when Rachkovsky tells him: *ovsianki*.

'You're a townie like me, dear boy. As far as I'm concerned, the countryside is made up of *birds* and *trees*. Any finer distinctions are simply lost on me. Now watch carefully.' Rachkovsky takes one and pops the whole thing in his mouth. He closes his eyes orgasmically. Leaning his head back, he veils the lower third of his face with a napkin and removes the tiny bones discreetly from his mouth one by one. 'Now your turn.'

These ortolans, like most delicacies, in Nicolas's view, have had their virtues overpraised. They're bony and taste more or less like chicken, but he does his best to seem to enjoy it. Rachkovsky is quick to see that his dinner companion is both intimidated and underwhelmed and dials back his enthusiasm. He dabs the grease from his chin and turns back to business.

'Bear with me, Nicolas. This is going to sound like a roundabout answer to your question.' He folds his hands while he collects his thoughts. When he finally speaks, his diction seems precise and rehearsed. This is a speech he's made before, to more important ears than Nicolas's. 'I am a servant of the Tsar,' he says. 'My task is to identify threats to the peace and security of his empire. My task is not to inflict pain and suffering. Far from it. What's more, I believe that pain is a clumsy way of changing minds. Pain tells no story. To the expert, to the artist of control, what is interesting is the stories that people tell: Who is to blame? Who is to be trusted? Who is at fault? Who benefits? Who is truly shaping events? Control the answers to those questions and you rarely, if ever, need to inflict pain. Fail to control them and you quickly learn this: nothing is more dangerous than a story.'

He pauses and sips his wine. When he smiles, Nicolas feels touched, in spite of everything, by Rachkovsky's obvious affection for him. The spymaster leans across the table and talks quietly. 'I have a somewhat different approach to my predecessors. Our enemies – and I don't shirk from that word – our enemies have a powerful story. There is a hero and a villain, they say. The villain is oppressing the hero. The hero must fight back and in doing so will either die or bring into existence a juster world. Well, we can't argue with the power or attractiveness of *that*. I dare say, as a youth yourself, you find something in you that responds to it. It's a sexy combination, frankly.' Rachkovsky flutters his fingers as though conjuring an analogy from the air. 'It has a chemical power – like a voltaic cell. Oppress them, hurt them, punish them, and what happens? The electrical charge only increases. Suddenly, we are duelling thunderbolts. A foolish endeavour. We must offer instead a more persuasive alternative.'

Rachkovsky signals to the waiter to remove the dish. The next course, much more to Nicolas's liking, is toast spread with the drippings of the birds and Roquefort. Rachkovsky sips the wine – a venerable, agate burgundy – and shakes his head. 'Divine.' His signet ring clicks against the glass as he lowers it to the table.

'So – what's your story?' asks Nicolas.

Rachkovsky, replete, eases back into his chair and gives his arms a long, catlike stretch. 'The story we have is a much older and better one than theirs. We say that the world is what it is. There is order and disorder. *Those* are real. Freedom and liberty are empty words, Nicolas. Really, it's the truth. Do you know what it was like here under the Communards? It was a fucking bloodbath. To a nineteen-year-old law student from Lvov, who thinks the Tsar is some kind of Darth Vader with a mask and scars, it sounds like paradise, but to everyone else it was just bloody frightening. You know poor Rimbaud got buggered by a gang of soldiers? Most people aren't concerned with the coming socialist Utopia. They just want to be able to walk to the end of the road and back to post a letter. Can the elderly leave their homes? Are your children safe? Are your parents safe?' He pauses meaningfully and looks at Nicolas just long enough to show he knows what happened to his father. 'These are the questions. Everything else is simply poses. The world is a terrifying place. Humans are beasts who must be restrained with order. Everyone knows this but the young, the zealots like Verzilov, and the Jews. The Jew is prone to a fantasy of melioration, a notion that the world can be improved, that divinity can be negotiated with.' He refills Nicolas's wine glass. 'I know because I had it in me too.'

'You were a revolutionary?'

'It sounds so absurd when you say it like that. But these men – they have compelling stories of change and hope. It's the most natural thing in the world to be seduced by them. I'm a curious person, Nicolas – how frank I'm being with you; Suvorin warned me of your talent for winkling things out of people. I was close to some attractive young enthusiasts. Things went awry. I was offered a choice: Siberia or sharing my information with the authorities.' He lowers his voice to a growl: 'I'm *not* a fan of cold weather.'

After the meal, Rachkovsky walks with Nicolas as far as the street lamp on the corner while his driver brings the carriage to the front of the restaurant. Standing in the pool of lamplight, the spymaster embraces his protégé in farewell.

'Look,' Rachkovsky says, a slight sway in his motion and a glitter in his eye the only evidence of all the alcohol he has consumed. 'I'm not going to waste your talents by sticking you in a green pea coat and having you tail anarchists through Batignolles. You're in a position to influence public opinion more efficiently: the odd favourable bit of journalism, smiling on Russian foreign policy in your articles for the French papers. Sexing things up a little to suit our interests. But not in an obvious way. The point about you, Nicolas, is that you're a serious-minded person with integrity.'

There's an unspoken question that seems to ask: *really, why wouldn't you?*

'I was assigned to penetrate a revolutionary cell.'

What Rachkovsky calls without irony his 'war on terror' is both lucrative and potentially endless. He doesn't bother to conceal the pleasure it gives him – or the rewards it brings. The work exactly suits his genius for intrigue and manipulation, his astonishing appetite for long hours in the office. Despite or perhaps because of his own brilliance, Rachkovsky carries an innate distrust for flair and flash. He likes solid, conscientious workers who are prepared to grind away at a problem for weeks. At the same time, he's a generous boss, and employment with the Third Section brings all kinds of fringe benefits.

International spycraft is a business that runs on cash: paying for safe houses, bribing postal workers and policemen, per diems for agents abroad. No one gives receipts and no one takes cheques. There's a lot of untraceable money swilling around and the rumour is that much of it ends up in Rachkovsky's own accounts, invested in the Bourse, and his big mansion in the suburb of Saint-Cloud.

Rachkovsky has most of Parisian publishing in his pocket, so Nicolas is receiving more commissions than ever – and being paid twice. Some of the articles he signs, some he doesn't. Now and then, Rachkovsky will send a whole piece to him to be published as is. Usually it's a gossipy insider's view of exiled revolutionaries that implies one of them is talking to the police. The intention is to sow discord in their ranks.

Nicolas enjoys being a pen for hire. He likes the money and he exults in his power to reorder reality with words. He doesn't notice the innate peril of the job: the dangerous frivolity of believing that the world of words is entirely separate from the one in which people love and suffer. 'The line between the improbable and the inevitable is tiny,' Rachkovsky tells him. 'Freedom for slaves. Votes for women. Rights for animals. Merely think it and it's halfway to coming true. Our battlefield is the mind. Our task is to control the plane of the real.'

In some ways, the work seems like a logical progression from his experience with MacGahan, another self-fashioning teller of stories. But when he attends honestly to what he feels, he notices a buried sense of disquiet. At least MacGahan's story-making was underpinned by her compassion and authenticity, by a sense of responsibility to bearing honest witness. He recalls her tenderness, her capacity to be moved by mute suffering. It's hard to imagine Rachkovsky shedding tears with a bereaved mother. It's not clear, in fact, if Rachkovsky actually believes in anything at all. Sometimes the spymaster insists that Russia's role is to stand firm as the Eternal Rome, a buttress against liberal decadence. At other times, he accepts change is inevitable: 'Of course change will come,' he'll say. 'But we want it to be at a time of our choosing.'

Rachkovsky's big idea ('everyone needs one, dear boy') is to bring about a closer relationship between Russia and France. It's certainly counterintuitive: the French Republic, despite its wobbles, is still the inheritor of the French Revolution, the global symbol of political progress, whereas the Tsar heads the most reactionary regime in Europe. But in balance-of-power terms, both states have something to gain from the odd pairing. Both fear a resurgent Germany, are envious of the British Empire, and have imperial aspirations of their own. Rachkovsky's short-term goals – keeping tabs on terrorists, developing a reliable partnership with the French Interior Ministry – are a kind of political foreplay. What's the endgame for Rachkovsky? An ambassadorship? The Foreign Ministry? Don't be deceived by his rumpled, cards-on-the-table bonhomie. He's a man of limitless ambition. He'll take everything he can get.

At this stage, what Nicolas is doing is more public relations than real espionage. He's part of a big stable of journalists who do Rachkovsky's bidding, a spigot of disinformation, a virtual claque that applauds whatever suits Russia and trolls whomever opposes it.

Nicolas tells himself that it's just a job, that he's putting his real self in the book he's writing: an account of his adventures in India which exaggerates the derring-do and omits the spying. Things have moved quickly with the Rozenfelds, the family Father David introduced him to at church. Every Saturday, he visits them for lunch, invariably brisket followed by apple pie. After the meal, Anya's parents discreetly withdraw for fifteen minutes. Anya plays the piano for him and talks about the books she's reading. Nicolas is always slightly relieved to hear the loud cough that precedes the dip of the door handle and Mr Rozenfeld's return.

Meanwhile, Rachkovsky gives Nicolas the impression he's a favoured associate of the Third Section, but he's skilled at giving everyone the same feeling. He senses that Nicolas has a father-shaped space in his psyche and manoeuvres himself to fill it. Every month or so, he invites Nicolas around for shashlik in his garden. Here, Rachkovsky plays the host and family man, squeezing lighter fluid over the charcoal, flourishing a fish slice at the kebabs and hamburgers, his pale, pudgy legs exposed in an ill-advised pair of Bermuda shorts.

At one of these Sunday gatherings in the early spring of 1886, the guests are crowded round the space heaters because it's much too cold for eating al fresco and Rachkovsky seems unusually subdued. Nicolas asks why. 'Office politics, old chap. Be grateful you're a freelancer and don't have to deal with the wankers I have to.'

'What's the problem?'

Rachkovsky presses the grilling meat with the spatula and fat sizzles onto the briquettes. 'Not everyone approves of my methods. Our current government is not renowned for its subtlety. It's not enough, apparently, that we're keeping tabs on everyone who could possibly do us harm and that we're working behind the scenes to bring the French government onside. They want a big fucking headline. I tell them until I'm blue in the face that peace and quiet is the best possible outcome. There's just a profound lack of intellect back in Saint Petersburg. They don't seem to see the importance of the stuff that never happens.'

'Well, if you need any help . . .' Nicolas offers mildly.

Rachkovsky looks away from the barbecue and seems to weigh a thought up in his mind. 'As it happens, I might. Are you serious?'

It's the easiest thing in the world for Nicolas to double his stake of polite interest with an affirmative.

'In that case, if you're free on Tuesday, why don't you stop by the office?'

Nicolas finds social gatherings like this hard work, but he persists in coming out of loyalty to Rachkovsky and because his work for the Third Section is now making up eighty per cent of his earnings. He gets cornered by Rachkovsky's long-suffering, much-betrayed wife, Maria, who talks about the difficulty of finding a decent school for her children. Behind her, Nicolas can see her husband flirting with someone else's wife.

Maria Rachkovskaia's tragic, aged eyes frame the same coquettish question she always asks at this point. 'And when are you going to bring this lovely girl of yours? I hope you know she's always welcome.'

'It's early days, Maria Vassilievna,' says Nicolas, using the polite patronymic that causes such confusion for English-speaking readers of Russian novels.

'Early days?' she replies, swatting Nicolas with her fan. 'It must be nearly a year. Get on with it!'

Nicolas manages a weak smile, sips his beer, and thinks guiltily of Anya.

Everything about Anya is right, on paper, and he gets on well with her parents. Something about their cosmopolitanism and their effort to assimilate strikes a chord with him, but whenever they make lame excuses to leave the room and give the courting couple time alone, Nicolas feels strangely exhausted and struggles to find things to talk about. Saying goodbye, last Thursday, Anya pressed her head to his chest and stroked his lapel with her tiny fingers. It feels like, at nineteen, she's just so young. Or, at twenty-seven, he's so old.

The world he sees in Anya's eyes is one shorn of all the pain and strangeness that he knows to be the true complexion of reality. He feels paternal towards her, and can't help contrasting those feelings with what he felt for Bessie, who always seemed to fit him like the adjacent piece of a jigsaw puzzle; at least, until she chucked him. The symptoms of his broken heart have a malarial tendency to recur whenever he's feeling particularly low. Still he persists, hoping something in him will change, hoping that he will find a way to consolidate his respectability with marriage. At the same time, if there were a button that could make the whole Anya situation vanish, he'd probably press it.

*

IT'S A RELIEF to see Rachkovsky in his business clothes and back in the more appropriate context of his basement office.

'Thanks for coming by,' he says. 'Sorry if I dumped on you rather at the weekend.'

'Not at all,' says Nicolas, but stops just short of saying: *that's what friends are for.*

'It's basically this. Our masters in Saint Petersburg want a coup. I've been working on something, but it lacks a crucial element. Now, Nicolas, this is a big step up from what you've been doing so far. It's a one-off, but don't be in any doubt about its difficulty. You'll be out on your own. An assignment as a penetration agent is the most challenging work of all. Of course, the remuneration is correspondingly generous.'

'What kind of thing would it be?'

'We set you up with a cover story. You'll have a temporary

new identity. You befriend persons of interest and report back to me. If things work out, we might dabble with some minor sabotage.' Rachkovsky smiles. 'I can see a light in your eyes, Nicolas. Remind me to play you at cards sometime.'

How does he read Nicolas? How does he know that what Nicolas hungers for above all is an opportunity to disappear?

Rachkovsky takes a folder from his desk. 'I'm rather pleased with this one.'

He reads his notes with evident satisfaction, drums his fingers on the desk. 'The protagonist – that's you – is a businessman; his name is Max Schneiderman. Originally from Kiev, you're alarmed by developments in Russia, and particularly worried about the treatment of the Jews. As we're both aware, the backlash since the murder of the Tsar has been substantial. It's not just the spontaneous violence . . .' (Rachkovsky ironises the word 'spontaneous' by making quote marks with his fingers) '. . . There's increased official prejudice. Quotas at universities, job restrictions, yada yada. You want to see a more just dispensation. You're a wealthy man. With the help of an associate, you're offering substantial means of support to the appropriate recipients. You say that history needs a push sometimes to give birth to a fairer future, and all that revolutionary bunkum.' He closes the folder.

Does it cross Nicolas's mind that this invented alter ego could have more in common with his true self than the role he's been performing for the last decade? Almost certainly not. The reasons that attract him to it are, in descending order: a desire for adventure, a chance to escape from Anya, and the cash. Striking a blow for the Jewish people is not a goal he's ever entertained, even in fantasy.

'I'm in.'

Rachkovsky stands up and offers Nicolas his hand. 'This is excellent news. Give me some time to draw a few threads together. We'll set you up with someone who can make the necessary introductions. Who can back up your story. We need to be vigilant. One really mustn't underestimate these people. You remember what happened to Arkhipov?'

'I'm not familiar with the name,' says Nicolas.

'It's a cautionary tale.' For a moment, Rachkovsky hesitates. He doesn't want to put Nicolas off; on the other hand, it might come back to haunt him if Nicolas hears the story from someone else. On balance, the old fox decides he'd better tell it. 'He was my mentor. An exceptional operative. Five years ago, he was running an asset called Degaev in People's Will. He was this close to the mother lode.' Rachkovsky measures one eighth of an inch with his surprisingly feminine thumb and forefinger. 'Arkhipov went to meet him in a hotel room in Saint Petersburg. Two men were waiting. They beat him to death.' Rachkovsky's eyes cut blankly up and to the right as stored images are retrieved from his memory. He sighs and shakes his head as though to rid himself of them. 'I was the first on the scene. It was . . . horrific.' The words are shockingly bare of his usual contrivance.

In spite of knowing it's a bad idea, Nicolas feels compelled to ask why.

'The teeth. Simply everywhere, dear boy, and so many of them.'

'It was time to break things off with Anya.'

When Anya's mother sees Nicolas in his Sunday best on a Tuesday afternoon and carrying a bunch of flowers, she sends the maid out to buy a cake, assuming there will be good news to celebrate.

Anya sits on the sofa between her parents. The tea remains unpoured while they wait for Nicolas to speak. He clears his throat. 'This is for all of you to hear. I have to go away for work. For a while. I don't know when I'll be back.'

In the silence that follows, the tick of the carriage clock on the mantelpiece seems as ominously loud as the footsteps of an executioner. Nicolas feels compelled to fill the pause. 'I don't want there to be a misunderstanding. It's not that my feelings have changed. It's just that I don't want Anya to be placed under an obligation.'

Anya looks confused. 'I don't understand what you mean, Nicolas. Of course I'll wait for you.'

Her mother folds her arms contemptuously. 'He's throwing you over, you simpleton.'

'Not at all, Mrs Rozenfeld,' lies Nicolas, who naively thought that this would be so much easier. 'That's not what I'm saying at all.' If only he'd had a female friend to run this through with. The lone operator is always in danger of catastrophic tonal lapses.

'Then what *are* you saying?'

What *is* he saying? He just thought they'd understand. There's been no exchange of intimacies. He's trying to say: *let's just be friends.* But the hectic colour in Anya's cheeks and the imminent tears are making it impossible.

Nicolas thinks: *she's going to cry, she's going to cry, she's going to cry.*

'On my return, if Anya's still unattached, I would be honoured to ask for her hand in marriage.'

The parents look puzzled. Is he or isn't he? On his *return*? What kind of conditional-tense proposal *is* this?

'Or, in fact, right now.' He kneels down on the carpet. 'Would you consent to, erm, consent when I get back?'

Anya pulls him to his feet. 'Oh, maman, I'm engaged!'

The maid brings in the cake. The almond icing tastes like ashes in Nicolas's mouth as he munches, his cheeks blushing hotly.

'Rachkovsky set me up in the wool business.'

Nicolas tells everyone that Suvorin is sending him to Bishkek, a distant outpost in the Kirghiz highlands of Central Asia. It means at least a month of travel. Before he leaves, he borrows money from Rachkovsky to pay for an engagement ring. Anya gives him a woollen scarf she's knitted and a volume of love poetry. Looking at her parents' eyes he notices residual distrust, which doesn't diminish when he insists that he'd rather not be seen off at the station.

In fact, having bid his intended a heartfelt goodbye, Nicolas simply moves out to the perimeter of the city. His temporary new home is two rooms above a bonded warehouse near the stockyards of Belleville.

Rachkovsky's chosen wool because the props are cheap, unlike, say, jewellery or haute couture. He's given Nicolas two fake labourers and a fake clerk called Lipmann. The list of employees actually includes a dozen names. Nicolas is confident their salaries are going straight to Rachkovsky, who, he senses, is hedging against the plan's failure and an inevitable recall to Saint Petersburg.

At first, Nicolas loves his imaginary job, sauntering round the warehouse, inspecting the plump and faintly ovine parcels of fleeces, leafing through fictitious paperwork and taking extended lunches. After five days, the sense of leisure is just threatening to turn to boredom when Lipmann brings him a note, written by Rachkovsky himself and sealed with his ring. 'Go to the Café de Jura on the corner of Rue Dupin at 5 p.m. tomorrow. The contact will be waiting for you there. They'll make the approach. Forgive the melodrama, but it's best if you destroy this after reading.'

Nicolas considers for a moment the optimal way of destroying the note. Tear it into tiny pieces? Put it in the fireplace? Throw it into a canal? Clearly, the important thing is that it gets completely obliterated. He settles on lighting it at the grate and juggles it from corner to corner until the paper is consumed. A grey ash skeleton lingers for an instant, like the quintessence of the note, lighter than air, then crumbles into powder.

On the way to the cafe the following day, Nicolas is caught in a rainstorm. The sign on the door is turned to CLOSED but the patron, a tall man in sleeveholders and a white apron who is polishing glasses, waves him in.

Nicolas has put on his soberest, most businesslike suit. He takes a seat at the rear and orders a pastis. The addition of water turns the crystal liquid to the cloudy colour of the Parisian sky. He unfolds his damp newspaper and browses the personal ads, but his eyes skitter across the print and take nothing in. Five minutes pass. Now ten. There isn't provision in the plan for a no-show. He decides to give it till half past.

On the stroke of 5.15 the door opens. Someone backs in slowly, shaking out an umbrella, and then turns, undoing her bonnet as she addresses the patron brightly to order a glass of red wine.

'Bessie.'

Vincenzo, ordinarily the best of listeners, lurches in his chair and there's an audible bump on the wax cylinder at this point.

But, really, who else could it be?

'It's good to see you, Mr Schneiderman. I'm sorry to have kept you waiting.'

Nicolas understands immediately that she knew it would be him. It's been five years since he's seen her face. He's not cold-blooded enough to be able to conceal what this means.

But Bessie is well coached. 'The weather is atrocious, I'm afraid. Still, we have an hour until curtain up. Chin-chin.' She sips her drink. Her glance never quite alights on him. As a performance, it's not noticeably false, but to Nicolas, who's known her, who's worked hard but unsuccessfully to expunge that face from his dreams, it's clear that she's withholding the real essence of herself.

He reaches across the table and tries to seize her gloved hand. 'Bessie?'

She slips his grasp, checks a hatpin, and corrects him in a firm, low voice: '*Yulia.*'

For the first time, she looks at him properly, to underscore her admonition. The alterations in her face are still those benign changes of our twenties, before time starts unravelling its work; changes which reveal deeper beauty in the beautiful. Or maybe it's that Nicolas, whose eye has been educated by suffering, sees more in her face than he ever saw before: soulfulness, melancholy, a faint shadow of sleeplessness beneath the eyes.

'We'd better go,' she says, with a lightness that's for the patron's benefit. Outside she's businesslike. That brightness is gone.

'How are you? What are you doing these days?' he asks.

'I work as a pharmacist.'

'Really do, I mean.'

'That. This. This is who I am.'

The light from the street lamps just being lit breaks in the surface of the puddles, winking up at them. The wet streets seem as dark and slick as oiled hair.

'And you? Still writing books?' She's walking quickly, lifting her skirts as she steps over puddles and tramlines. There's no real curiosity in her voice. This is just a job.

'I'm in the wool export business these days,' he says, intending to sound ironic, but it comes out as a statement of fact.

At the entrance to an apartment building, she takes his arm and leads him in.

The moment has none of the drama of his encounter with Verzilov. The apartment is crammed with couches overstuffed in tired velvet and great swagged drapes, and smells of cologne and stale chamber pots. It feels like it must belong to someone's great-grandmother. The four men inside could be estate agents or clerks. They've gone to some trouble to look as forgettable as possible. They're sitting on dining chairs, all dark-suited, whiskered, dark-haired. Seen on the street, none would draw a second glance.

There are no introductions. The atmosphere is one of mutual suspicion. Bessie works hard to break the feeling of distrust. She sits beside Nicolas and holds his arm. His cover story said only that he and his contact are close acquaintances. She's vouching for his credibility with this masquerade of love. Nicolas is too nervous to find it painful, but he's aware that afterwards he will probably recall the touch of her hand with sadness.

'We're speaking to a number of investors,' says the shortest of the four men, who appears to be their leader. Nicolas notes a smudged brown birthmark the shape of a comet on the side of his forehead. 'Tell us a little about yourself. Your reasons for wanting to involve yourself in our enterprise.'

Nicolas feels their stares on him. Bessie smiles, but he sees anxiety in her slightly glazed look, in the tense muscles around her eyes. What on earth made him think he could do this?

'Vanity,' he says. It's the answer to both questions. 'I suppose I'm vain enough to believe I can make a difference.'

One of the seated men, who is distinguished by a deep and grating voice, says: 'We do not undertake our endeavours for the purpose of gratifying a man's vanity. Our task, the task of all of us, is impersonal and scientific.'

'That's commendable,' says Nicolas. He feels a slight quaver in his voice, which he can only master by talking very quietly. It has the paradoxical effect of compelling the men's attention. 'My motives are entirely personal. Four years ago, my father was murdered by pogromists.' He infuses his words with a triple sense of loss, a compound of MacGahan, his father and Bessie. 'I have no time myself for the superstitions of religion, but my father took a great deal of comfort from his faith in old age. Are you familiar with the rites of Judaism?'

Apparently not, judging by their reactions, but Nicolas feels confident that at least one of them, the fellow farthest from him, listening with steepled hands, shares his background.

'My father was set upon as he left a synagogue in Kiev. Not content with assaulting an old man, his attackers took his prayer shawl and phylactery – you understand what I mean by this?' His listeners affirm their understanding with brief nods. '. . . And defiled them by parading them around the city on a dog. They said' – Nicolas pauses for effect, partly moved and partly enjoying his power over his listeners – 'they said, "The Jew-dogs killed our saviour and they killed our father the Tsar."'

'Animals,' murmurs the man with steepled hands.

The revelation has won him a moment of sympathy. He is quick to build on it, speaking of the five million Jews of the Pale, the failure of the old order, the necessity of bringing into being a new one, the brotherhood of all mankind. 'History needs a push,' Nicolas says. 'We have an obligation to future generations. What's standing between us and a better world is a reactionary government and our own sentimentality. Both we will do better without.'

'And what will it be like,' muses the rabbinical revolutionary, from over his folded hands, 'this coming world of yours?'

156

'I don't know,' says Nicolas. 'No one does. All I know is that it will be better.'

This thought, of course, is plagiarised from Father David. For the priest and for the revolutionaries, the coming of the better world is an article of faith.

In the silence that follows, Nicolas has the feeling that his performance has exceeded expectations.

'For now, you will deal directly with us,' says the man with the birthmark. 'We'll hold internal discussions to determine if you are a suitable investor for our factory and our school.'

'And have you settled on a location for them yet?' Bessie asks. Nicolas is impressed. The tone of her question is perfectly judged. It sounds like revolutionary impatience rather than suspicion or curiosity.

'The school will be sited in Geneva,' says the man with the birthmark. 'The factory—'

'We're still appraising sites for the factory,' interjects the man with the harsh voice. He's less ready than the others to assume that Nicolas is to be trusted. Nicolas senses that this man is the senior figure here, but one content to leave the questioning to his underlings, the better to observe.

'Is there any further information on the payment of wages to the workers?' Bessie asks.

Mr Birthmark and Mr Grating Voice exchange looks. 'Not yet.'

'On behalf of all of us,' says Grating Voice, 'I'd like to thank you for coming. We'll be in touch to let you know of our decision.' Nicolas is less certain now that it's gone well.

The men remain seated while Nicolas and Bessie stand and put on their coats. She takes his arm once more as they leave and descend the wide stone steps of the apartment building together, not relinquishing it even when they pass out onto the street and onto the damp pavements. Nicolas feels the warmth of her, the swell of her bosom against his upper arm. And it infuriates him.

He shakes her off his arm. 'Wait a second,' he says. 'Is this really you? This *Yulia*? Where's the mistress of the revolution? Where's Verzilov's long-suffering lover?' His voice is full of an uncharacteristic contempt. 'Where's the woman who spat in my face and called me a traitor? Or are we both traitors now?'

She looks left and right nervously, moves towards him to close down the gap between them, and speaks in a low, reproachful tone. 'Listen to me: we're both adults who answer to our own consciences.'

As he begins to formulate another angry question, she grabs his face with both hands and kisses him hard and lovelessly on the mouth. Nicolas is too surprised to do anything but yield as she backs him into a doorway.

'You idiot,' she hisses, the weight of her pressing him against the door. 'We're a hundred yards away from their apartment. Don't you dare take risks with my life. You're getting well paid. Now earn it. Be a professional.'

She holds a single gloved finger on his lips and stares wrathfully at him until she sees his eyes assent.

'Rachkovsky's offices were staffed day and night.'

Nicolas doesn't believe in this new Bessie. Knowing what he does about her, remembering her commitment to the cause of revolution, her rage about the fate of her sister, he finds this turn of affairs impossible to accept. Of the two Bessies he knows, only one can be real. In his mind's eye, he sees a hotel room with its door ajar, a trail of shattered teeth on the carpet. He thinks: *this is a trap.*

He wanders around the city for hours, making sure he's not being followed. Just before midnight, he enters the offices on Rue de Grenelle, his head swathed in Anya's scarf to preserve his anonymity.

A security guard lets him in. The basement rooms are ablaze with gaslight. Pizza boxes and bottles of soda on one of the desks suggest the staff are pulling an all-nighter.

Rachkovsky, in an open-necked shirt, emerges from the meeting room. His face wears an expression of sincere concern. He leads Nicolas into the meeting room and sits him down. 'What is it?'

Nicolas apologises for violating the cardinal rule of his new identity by visiting the offices, but says he simply couldn't wait to air his doubts.

'Why this loss of nerve, my dear?' Rachkovsky asks. 'You're exactly who you've said you are. A businessman with some outside interests. Believe me, none of them have told you their real names. The only thing that will put this whole project in jeopardy is your being seen here. Although I dare say I could, in a pinch, finesse that. Still, let's try to keep things simple.'

'Nothing about this is simple. I knew Bessie before. She was a zealot. There's no way she'd turn.'

'Yulia's taking precisely the same risks as you. And from what *I* hear, your assignment went very well indeed.' On the table sits a sheaf of handwritten pages, joined at one corner with a treasury tag. Rachkovsky picks them up and glances at the cover sheet.

'Is that what Bessie said?'

'Absolutely not. I would never risk speaking to her in person.' Rachkovsky licks his forefinger and turns the page. 'Ha! You understand that these men are fond of the most absurd Aesopian language? The school is a printing press, the factory is of course a bomb-making operation, and wages for the workers are the chemicals required for their manufacture: fulminate of mercury, nitroglycerine and pyroxylin.'

It both puzzles and reassures Nicolas that Rachkovsky has such detailed knowledge of the conversation. 'How do you know this, if not from her?'

'There were six of you present at the meeting?' Rachkovsky asks.

'Yes.' The spymaster inclines his head and Nicolas feels obliged to offer further details. 'There were the four of them and me and Bessie—'

'It's really best if you think of her as Yulia. Holding two different names in your head can lead to messy situations. What do you remember of the four?'

Nicolas counts them off on his fingers. 'There was the guy with the birthmark.'

'Burak, Yurii.'

'The guy with the croaky voice.'

'Seliverstov, Ivan.'

'The Jewish one.'

'Yes. Mandelbrot, Osip.'

'And a fourth.'

'A fourth. Mmm, yes. And what do you recall about *him*?'

Nicolas thinks. In his recollection the man's face is obscured. The fourth man.

He searches his memory. It's like pounding a broken telegraphic key. The circuit's dead. There's nothing.

'The fourth man is an agent?'

A kind of humorous look in Rachkovsky's eyes. 'Do you think so little of me, dear boy? Do you think I'd risk losing a man of your considerable talents for the scalps of some C-list provocateurs? I *always* triangulate my information.'

Rachkovsky continues. 'Since you're here, there's someone I'd like you to meet.' He opens the door to his office and calls to a skinny, fair-haired man of about Nicolas's age whom he introduces as Mulhouse. Mulhouse is busy tracing a signature from a letter. He completes the task before he looks up.

'I wanted you two to meet. You're both writers,' Rachkovsky says. 'One day, perhaps the two of you will collaborate on something for me.'

Never, Nicolas thinks to himself, but expresses cautious enthusiasm for the vague project. 'What kind of thing do you write?' he asks.

The other man is sullen, entitled, and oddly sure of himself. 'Science fiction, and fantasy.'

'Like Jules Verne?'

The young man wrinkles his nose. 'Albert Robida's more my guy. There's a bunch of others.' He hands Nicolas a visiting card. 'Check out my blog, Mulmaison.com.'

'Oh yeah, Robida. Cool.' Nicolas pockets the card and makes a mental note to find out who he is.

'Mulhouse, my dear, if you've finished with that book I lent you, would you be so good as to give it back?'

'Yeah, sure, I'll get it now.'

'A young man of great literary gifts,' Rachkovsky says, gallingly. 'Now, much as I enjoy seeing you, Nicolas, we need to preserve the integrity of your cover. Agreed?'

Nicolas feels faintly abashed at his panic. 'I knew Bessie. I still have difficulty believing she'd be willing to help.'

'Yulia has her reasons, as you have yours.' Mulhouse is at the door, clutching the yellow pages of a pamphlet, which he gives to Rachkovsky. 'Thanks, Mulhouse.' Mulhouse nods in rather indifferent farewell and heads back to his desk.

Rachkovsky flicks the pages absent-mindedly as he searches for words to reassure Nicolas. 'I'm not able to betray her confidence in me. I hope you understand. Let's just say she faced a crisis of her own.'

'What kind of thing?'

'I can't say, dear boy. I'm a locked vault where my agents' private lives are concerned. That should in itself set your mind at rest.'

Nicolas senses that there is one gap in Rachkovsky's knowledge: he doesn't seem aware that he and Bessie were once intimate. At first it touches him that she's kept this secret. Subsequently, he feels wounded that the episode was too embarrassing or forgettable to be worth mentioning.

'And by the way, this is something you might like.' Rachkovsky hands Nicolas Mulhouse's pamphlet. 'Political satire. Let me know what you make of it.'

'At that time, The Black Cat was the centre of bohemian Paris.'

Too fizzed-up to sleep, Nicolas takes his broken heart out drinking. Le Chat Noir in Montmartre is a place he only knows by reputation, and he's always been curious to go there.

The luxury of the age is light and Paris is its greediest consumer: it hisses out of mantles; it's refracted through crystal and dazzles in gilt and mirrors; it shines from the pioneering candles of the ingenious Pavel Yablochkov, a countryman of Nicolas's, who has found a way to harness the incomprehensible power of electricity. As Nicolas makes his way through the dressed-up crowds in Montmartre, he sees a group of girls wandering about in not much more than underwear; another in black flared trousers and white shoes. The fashion in cosmetics is to paint your face an eerie verdigris. Nicolas feels old and past it, weary as the Ancient Mariner, and thinks: *nothing is worse than this, getting old, facing obsolescence.* He is, I should remind you, still only twenty-seven.

At Le Chat Noir, Nicolas gets drunk in character, downing cocktails that are equal parts cognac and absinthe, curses the Tsar loudly, and wins pats on the back from the *bien pensant* crowd for his revolutionary toasts. Before he knows it, he's reached the stage that Russians call *green-snake drunk*, and can't be sure if he sees or dreams what follows.

Lights dim. A screen unfolds. It's one of Le Chat Noir's famous magic lantern shows: shadow puppets and rear projection are about to give the crowd an early hint of cinema.

The story tonight is one that Nicolas will soon know well: a tale of love and revolution, of two young people separated by ideology, but brought together to undertake a hazardous adventure.

163

Applause greets the first *mise en scène*: a den of terrorists. They're recognisable by the casks of TNT, their beards and piercing eyes. The hero and heroine enter and conduct negotiations with the revolutionary anarchists in an atmosphere of tense mistrust. A railway journey follows, a *coup de théâtre*, which shows a locomotive pulling a train of carriages up and down a series of vertiginous papier-mâché Alps, until it's waved across the border into Switzerland by a suborned customs official.

An arc of moon is lowered jerkily from the ceiling. The agents, accompanied by a would-be terrorist, enter the premises that hold the secret printing press. And now the double-cross! What resourceful cunning! The hero and the heroine aren't who they seem at all. The heroine draws a gun and forces the hapless anarchist to the floor while the hero pies the cases of type, casting the letters in handfuls on the ground, and splashing them with acid.

The denouement shows the hero unwinding a length of fuse across the screen. The characters crouch. Their limbs on wooden sticks approximately block their ears as the press is blown sky-high by an explosion that's rendered exquisitely with coloured paper unfolding in red and yellow like a chrysanthemum to oohs and aahs.

'We were supposed to travel on different trains.'

Such, broadly speaking, was Rachkovsky's plan: a dramatic act of counter-revolutionary sabotage that would destroy a subversive printing press, demoralise the Tsar's opponents, and impress the Third Section's bosses in Saint Petersburg.

And Rachkovsky, whose scheming always tended toward the rococo, had also supplied Nicolas and Bessie with manifestos to leave at the site, claiming the outrage on behalf of a rival revolutionary organisation.

Nicolas travelled alone from Paris with the acid and explosives packed inside rolls of linoleum. At Basel, a customs man named Zwingli entered the compartment to receive the necessary bribe. He stamped Nicolas's passport and carnet and saluted before dismounting from the train.

It had been arranged for Bessie and Nicolas to meet at a cafe in Geneva before making contact with the members of the revolutionary underground. Bessie's train had arrived early. She was waiting at a rear table and seemed almost pleased to see him before she remembered herself and reverted to her habitual indifference.

The two revolutionaries were improbably young – twenty-one or twenty-two at most – and both boys: one a Frenchman called Pascal with crew-cut hair and the soulful brown eyes of a painter, the other a garrulous Ukrainian named Leonid. They seemed awestruck by their foreign visitors. Leonid, in particular, bragged foolishly about the prolific accomplishments of their press.

They drove their guests to a yard on the outskirts of the city with a shed that housed the printing workshop, and unloaded the cargo of acid and explosive, speculating excitedly on its final intended use: which tyrant, which crowned head, which hypocritical cleric, which bloodsucking financier would it terminate? As soon as the cart was empty, Bessie drew a small pearl-handled revolver from her pocket and ordered the two boys to lie down on the chilly floor. 'Oh,' said

Pascal, faintly, as the scope of the deception was revealed to him with sudden clarity. Leonid made a vain attempt to run to the small window, but a single warning shot was enough to bring him to a halt, trembling, with his hands above his head. Nicolas handcuffed both of them and locked them in an outhouse safely at the perimeter of the yard.

As soon as dusk fell, Nicolas and Bessie began the destruction of the press. Nicolas laid the explosive charge while Bessie unspooled twenty yards of fuse wire in a zigzag pattern along the floor. Nicolas overturned the trays of type and slopped gallons of acid onto the letters; the disfigured lead hissed and bound into unusable bunches.

Finally, the two of them paused on the threshold as Nicolas struck a safety match and set a serpent of fire on its slow course through the dark shed.

The getaway vehicle – a light trap with two horses – stood half a mile away. Disoriented by the darkness, Nicolas was momentarily uncertain of the cause of the flash and *crump* that split the silence like an artillery shell.

It was only afterwards that Nicolas realised that in his haste he'd forgotten to put on his rubber galoshes and had spilled acid on his shoe. Anaesthetised by the adrenaline and excitement, he felt only a slight stinging at the time; later, in the first light of dawn, the injury was revealed to be more serious: most of the fourth and fifth toes on his left foot had been eaten away. At the sight of bone, Nicolas passed out like a damsel in a romance novel.

Bessie and the getaway driver helped Nicolas into the train carriage. She was supposed to depart on a later express, but chose to remain with him as the train pulled out of the station, treating the injury with the calcium gluconate gel that she had presciently brought in her midwife's bag. Despite the wound, both she and Nicolas felt reckless, powerful, and giggly with disbelief at their triumph. The risk they'd undergone together was a fresh kind of intimacy. They noticed it at the same time and were both suddenly self-conscious. Their eyes met briefly. Bessie was the first to look away and continued to bandage his foot.

But later, in the darkness, Bessie whispers Nicolas's name and pulls the blanket from his bunk. He wakes instantly and yields without hesitation. Even in the dark, Nicolas is aware of a change in her body. Her breasts are not the high, halved apples he remembers from the rainy afternoon in his apartment. She's more tender, more soft, more passionate.

At breakfast – fresh baguette, filthy coffee, ravenous appetites – he broaches the subject hesitantly. 'Did you . . . conceive a child?'

The way she sets the baguette down, the flush in her cheeks, the suppressed consternation, all say *yes* before her mouth does. 'The baby was stillborn. A girl.'

'I'm sorry,' says Nicolas.

'She was Pierre's. He never met her, but he claimed he knew it was a girl.'

Nicolas is stirred by the revelation. He wants to say that Verzilov was never modest about his powers of prediction, but this isn't the moment.

Bessie smiles. 'It was a lucky guess. He wanted to call her Marianne.'

'The goddess of liberty?'

She shrugs as if to say: that was Pierre. From her dismissiveness, Nicolas understands that those dreams of revolution are old ones.

When does he realise? Is it then? Or later, parting at the station with muted farewells and suppressed smiles at his limp? Or afterwards, watching her make her way through the crowd, the flash of her bonnet vanishing in the press of people? Yes, it is then, it is at the last possible moment that he knows he loves her.

This is the tale of two stories. This is the tale of what Nicolas did next, and what Rachkovsky is about to create in the basement of Rue de Grenelle: a fire balloon that will float out of the nineteenth century with devastating consequences for an entire people. This is not the story of a lost love; yet all stories are stories of loss and love.

Weeks later, at the conclusion of the narration, Vincenzo will push Notovitch for evidence to support his wilder claims.

So much of what Notovitch had told him was, at best, a partial truth. He had embroidered, elided, omitted, exaggerated, fabricated, misremembered and forgotten. He had told a mixture of half-truths and truths-and-a-half. Vincenzo was compelled to do what we all do: piece together a workable version of the world from incompatible stories, knowing that no final truth is available. But inside every ironist is a romantic with a rose between his teeth, struggling melodramatically to get out.

Vincenzo will shake his head almost pleadingly. *Something. Anything.* He needs some token of authentication, if only to save Notovitch, whom he's come to like, from the accusation of being a liar.

'Very well. I must ask you a favour. Would you be so kind as to remove my left slipper?'

Vincenzo hesitates. He's reluctant to kneel before Notovitch: the act seems charged with an inappropriate deference. He slides a footstool towards the old man's armchair and seats himself on it. Notovitch raises his left leg. Vincenzo removes the worn carpet slipper and the heartbreakingly darned sock whose odd shape gives a premonition of its abbreviated contents: a foot with only three toes. The fourth and fifth have been tidily removed: a surgeon's work. But the splash marks on the skin, and the livid gouges, show where the acid had fallen.

'We had enhanced the Third Section's reputation at a stroke.'

News of the Geneva escapade had already reached Saint Petersburg, where its success won plaudits and an increased budget for the Third Section. At Nicolas's debriefing, Rachkovsky presented him with a rose-gold pocket watch to say thank you.

'The good news is that those two toes entitle you to a significant disability bonus. Good work. And you can get married now,' he says.

'There's something I need to do first. Yulia has something of mine. It's something I need for my wedding. I've been wondering how I can contact her to get it back.'

Fortunately, Rachkovsky's too buoyed up with his latest triumph to notice that Nicolas has inadvertently composed a riddle to which the answer is: *heart.*

'I'll send her a message. It'll take a day or two. We use a

music teacher to communicate in her area. He travels around giving violin lessons. It's rather clever because he can go virtually anywhere without arousing suspicion and he's always carrying a portfolio.'

Wow, thinks Nicolas. Rachkovsky's either accepted him right into the heart of the operation, or he's so pleased with himself that he hasn't noticed that bits of spycraft are practically falling off him.

Nicolas can't wait two days. He's pretty sure that she lives in Ménilmontant or Batignolles, so gets a list of the pharmacies in both from city directories. It takes him half a day to find the right one. She clocks off work at six and he follows her home.

Having made a note of her address, he buys flowers and bribes the doorman to let him in. He pauses on the staircase at the sound of what he thinks is a child crying. A maid answers the door. Nicolas is flummoxed. Who should he ask for? Bessie? Yulia? Ms Gelfman? God forbid, Mrs Verzilova?

A relaxed, unselfconscious version of Bessie arrives distractedly at the maid's shoulder to see who the tongue-tied visitor is, and congeals at the sight of him.

'I need to talk to you,' he says. Bessie nods to let the maid know she should leave them, then joins him on the landing and pulls the door shut behind her. She crosses her arms and waits.

Nicolas experiences the paralysis common to lovers and writers who are daunted by the task of revivifying old words. 'I love you', 'I can't stop thinking about you' and 'We are meant to be together' are phrases that are well past their use-by date, even in 1886.

'I've been thinking,' he says, cleaving to the faint owl-hoot of truth in his heart. 'I've lived in a kind of exile from myself since I was seventeen years old. I've been busy trying to make my fortune and escape from where I grew up. I must have succeeded because the last time I went home I felt like a total stranger. But the thing is, I feel like a stranger here too. The one place I haven't felt like that, the one place I've felt like myself, better than myself in fact, is by your side.' He pauses, not because Bessie isn't listening – she is, and there's a gentle sadness in her eyes – but because a child's voice is audible from just behind the door and it's clearly saying, 'Mama.'

'Come in,' says Bessie. She pushes against the heavy door and leads Nicolas into the apartment. 'I want you to meet my daughter.'

'She had given birth to a crippled child.'

Marianne is three years old, immaculately dressed in a robin's-egg-blue cotton frock and apron; the soles of her satin shoes pristine because she cannot walk. What compels attention is not her pale, sweetly pretty though fretful infant face: it's her huge, distended skull, grotesquely swollen, hairless, frail-looking, and webbed with thin purple veins.

'Leave us, please, Celeste,' Bessie tells the maid, and picks up her daughter, cradling the big head in her arms. Marianne's dark irises have half-slipped beneath her lower lids in a way that evokes a sunset. It makes her look sleepy, and is caused by the pressure in her skull. 'She was born with chronic water in the head,' Bessie explains. She blows a raspberry on the child's neck and elicits a giggle. 'You were saying something on the subject of love, I think.'

Nicolas finds himself struck dumb.

'Let me tell you something that I hope won't sound patronising,' Bessie continues. 'Until I had my daughter, I knew nothing of love.' Using her heel, she slides a basket of toys towards herself and takes out a wooden rattle with which she tries to engage the child's interest, but Marianne seems listless and dull. Bessie puts the rattle in her daughter's hands and closes her fingers around it.

'I'm embarrassed to think of myself as I was before, consumed with the love of revolution, too easily impressed by Pierre's childish dialectics. Of course, the me I was would regard all this as treachery. But the world looks different now. I'm all Marianne has. No god or government will do anything for her.' The child closes one sleepy eye as she gnaws and drools on the rattle. Bessie plants a loving kiss on its big, fragile head. 'People used to say to me, wait till you're older, you'll see that the world is complicated, there's shades of grey in everything. But the opposite has happened. My world couldn't be more simple. There are only two people in it. That's all there ever can be.' The smile she makes is the gentlest she has ever shown him. 'I know you'll understand.'

At the threshold, she embraces him. The cotton of her blouse folds crisply under his awkward hand. 'I'm sorry I was beastly about your Tsar book,' she says. 'You would have made a lovely boyfriend.'

He tries to reply but she stops his lips with her finger. The moment recalls that furious kiss in the doorway, yards from the meeting with the revolutionaries. But this time there are tears and tenderness in her eyes. 'I'm sorry, Nicolas. Now go!'

'Rachkovsky was best man at my wedding.'

Anya's dress, put together in one of her father's ateliers, is the talk of Paris. A pirated pattern is leaked to a dressmaking magazine, much to her mother's delight.

Rachkovsky, pleased as punch to be chosen as best man, organises a surprise stag weekend in Estonia. Ganz, Mulhouse, Nicolas, Rachkovsky and Volchkov hunt ducks and relax in a five-star spa resort in the woods. Nicolas has been feeling strangely unreal ever since he returned to what is, technically, his real life. He'd like to confide in someone, but a weekend away with three of Russia's leading secret policemen doesn't seem like a good moment to open his heart. Perhaps if he had time alone with Volchkov, he could speak to him, but Volchkov is getting on bafflingly well with Rachkovsky. The spymaster and the self-identified bohemian have discovered shared interests in drinking, photography and karaoke. The two of them belt out a surprisingly tuneful version of 'Unchained Melody' together after dinner.

In his king-size bed, under the head of a stuffed elk, Nicolas reads a love letter that Anya has slipped into his suitcase. It's breathless in its anticipation of their coming life together. There's no doubt that she'll be a wonderful wife. Mr Rozenfeld has already dropped hints about bringing Nicolas into the family business. His financial future looks secure. So why does he feel as though he's dying?

In the valise is the pamphlet that Rachkovsky gave him during his panicky midnight visit to 79 Rue de Grenelle. It seems so long ago, but can't be more than six weeks. The title struck him as promising at the time: *A Dialogue in Hell* by Maurice Joly, an author he hadn't heard of.

It's strange, he thinks, how his brain seems to have a special late-night file for things he reads in bed. He'll struggle to remember any detail of them during the day, but open the book again at bedtime, and it all comes back: it's a political satire in the form of a dialogue. The set-up is this: Machiavelli and the liberal philosopher Montesquieu have met in hell and are having an argument about the best form of government. Montesquieu puts the moral case for liberalism; Machiavelli the pragmatic case for tyranny. At first Nicolas was reluctant to read it, because of the title: he thought it might be horror, and he doesn't like reading anything too stimulating at bedtime, but this book presents the opposite problem: two more paragraphs and he's out like a light.

'We spent our honeymoon in Normandy.'

The water of the Atlantic is grey and the beaches are stony. Nicolas knows he's done a bad thing. Out of cupidity, spinelessness and a craving for respectability, he's married a woman he doesn't love. He sits alone after dinner drinking Calvados and then joins Anya in the bedroom, where he perches on the bed in his morning suit, rigid with dread. Anya brushes out her long brown hair in the mirror, a hundred strokes each side, chatting happily about the day.

Nicolas is relieved when there's a knock at the door. A

bellboy brings in champagne and an ice bucket with a note. 'Compliments of the Third Section', it reads in French, and then, in Russian, *'Ne pozor' natsiyu!'*, meaning 'Don't disgrace the nation!' Whether he means the Jewish or Russian one, Rachkovsky hasn't specified.

The alcohol, the long day, the fake telegrams concocted by Rachkovsky conveying the regrets of Nicolas's family from Kiev, the memory of Marianne's swollen, ostrich-egg skull with its downcast eyes like a meditating Buddha: all of it swirls through Nicolas's mind in an unresolvable circuit of images. It's like a problem in algebra he's not clever enough to solve. He steps out onto the balcony to clear his head. The sky is dark and starless, but he can hear the song of the surf on the beach. This water is the last unbroken link with his old life. It flows from here through the Pillars of Hercules, through the Mediterranean, the Dardanelles and into the Black Sea. Somewhere, in the not-so-distant past, a boy stood at a barrel, hearing a version of the same song, but now its tune is irretrievably altered: no Bessie; no redemption; no hope. More salt water spills from his eyes.

As Nicolas closes the door behind him, Anya puts down her brush and looks curiously at his weepy, flushed face. But Special Agent Notovitch is well schooled in the first and fundamental lesson of working with a false identity: you never, under any circumstances, change your story. 'It's just . . . I love you so much!' he lies.

'Mr Rozenfeld offered to make me the manager of a department store.'

Nicolas's in-laws help the newly-weds buy a starter flat around the corner from their apartment. They're used to being very involved in their daughter's life. It dawns on Nicolas only gradually that Anya's desire for marriage was driven by an urge to escape from her parents, as much as by an attraction to her new husband. She talks longingly of travelling far away with Nicolas – to Egypt, or India. But she falls quickly pregnant, and her mother posts an immediate ban on hot baths, soft cheese and heavy lifting. Foreign travel is out of the question.

Mr Rozenfeld takes Nicolas out boating on a lake in the Bois de Vincennes and turns the conversation, not very subtly, onto the subject of his son-in-law's career. In Mr Rozenfeld's view, Nicolas's work in the wine business showed entrepreneurial flair. His literary pursuits, while commendable and a valuable ornament to his other accomplishments, are not a secure way to make a living. Mr Rozenfeld explains that he's selling his shops and he intends to consolidate his business in a single department store. It will be called Étoile du Nord, and he invites Nicolas to manage the haberdashery section.

Sculling through the reedy water, Nicolas thinks smugly of how much he has earned from Rachkovsky in the last year. The work is exciting. There's a trip to London in the offing, to liaise with Scotland Yard. The basement offices have had a long-distance telephone line installed, which can call as far away as Brussels. Rachkovsky's talking about paying for key agents like Nicolas to have their own telephones at home. 'For now,' he says, 'I'd rather keep going as I am.'

'Very well,' Mr Rozenfeld says. 'For now.'

Nicolas, his reputation burnished by the adventure in Switzerland, and having been injured in the line of duty, enjoys increasing status at work. He runs other agents. He gives counterterrorism courses to embassy staff. There are only half a dozen full-time employees in the Third Section, so the work is diverse and interesting. He knows that two people of the six are used to intercept the post. Two run assets and compile intelligence for Saint Petersburg. And Mulhouse is occupied with a hare-brained project that Rachkovsky refers to proudly as 'The Department of Secret Books', which involves meetings with various disreputable-looking right-wing writer types and not much else that Nicolas can make out.

'I was surprised to bump into General Skobelev.'

The hero of the Turkish wars is oddly diminished by the basement offices. Sitting in the reception area, with a laminated badge, a scuffed leather briefcase and badly ironed trousers, he's hardly recognisable as the man who ceremonially accepted the swords of the defeated Ottoman generals.

He's come to meet Rachkovsky. 'It's nice to see your friendly face,' he says, enveloping Nicolas with his ursine upper body. It's 8.15 a.m. Nicolas has just arrived and manoeuvres his arms so as not to spill his paper cup of coffee down the general's back. 'Look at you! How many winters, how many summers?' Skobelev asks, rhetorically. It's a conventional Russian expression for *long time, no see*. 'I'm staying just around the corner. We should have dinner.'

'Absolutely,' Nicolas responds with a similarly hearty warmth.

Time hasn't been especially kind to the general. Trembling hands and a lace pattern of broken capillaries on his face suggest that alcohol's the cause. His thick hair is white, his beard iron-grey. But when he stands up, he's still straight-backed, tall, commanding. And more than that, he represents an important time in Nicolas's life. 'No rush. I'm here for a while. Paris, eh?'

At dinner, the two men call each other *comrade*, polish off half a bottle of brandy and get increasingly sentimental about MacGahan.

'What a woman! She rode better than my officers. You know I offered to put her in charge of a battery at Plevna? She smiled at me and said something about "journalistic objectivity". And the hardships she underwent. For soldiers like you and I, this life is natural. It's quite something for a woman to forgo the pleasures of a home and husband.'

Nicolas is flattered by Skobelev's mistaken assumption that he's a soldier and doesn't bother offering his opinion that a husband was the last thing MacGahan would have wanted.

'How old are you?' the general asks, refilling Nicolas's glass. 'You're young now. You must have been a child then.'

'Looking back, I suppose I was, but I thought at the time that I knew everything.'

'There's no phase of life when that vanity leaves us,' declares the general. 'Right now, I'm sure we can't imagine improving on our understanding of the world. And yet, we must! That is the only meaningful form of progress.'

'I'm not sure about that,' says Nicolas. 'Twenty million former serfs might disagree.'

The general shakes his head. 'Emancipation has been a disaster. Here and in America. Some people are just not ready for the responsibilities of freedom.'

It's a measure of the two men's friendship that they can disagree about practically everything and still get on.

The food is no more than passable, though Skobelev touchingly pronounces it delicious. The room is empty and the smell of stale fat has impregnated the curtains. Nicolas can't help contrasting this place that the general's chosen with the luxurious restaurants Rachkovsky patronises. It turns out Skobelev is having to fund his stay on a measly per diem and is spending his nights in a fleapit hotel. The difference in lifestyle is attributable to one thing: the general is principled and refuses to take bribes.

'What brings you to Paris this time?' Nicolas asks.

'It's hush-hush. I'm supposed to say it's to do with embassy business. The truth is, I'm looking into your boss's financial affairs.'

'Rachkovsky?'

'Yes. It seems he's embezzling. The tricky little Jew.'

For a moment, Nicolas finds himself folded into an origami shape of moral confusion, which he has to unpick: yes, Rachkovsky's an embezzler, but it's not because he's Jewish. Yes, Skobelev is an anti-Semite, but he's also generous-hearted, honest, and a war hero.

'The Jewish thing is neither here nor there,' says Nicolas. 'Someone said that anti-Semitism is the template for all forms of intolerance.'

'Really? Who said that?'

'I think it was Saltykov-Shchedrin.'

'Shchedrin-Schmedrin. The trouble with the Jew,' pronounces Skobelev, 'is that he's only loyal to his own kind. We Slavs are free-hearted people. We're easily taken advantage of.'

Nicolas sees that the conversation is straying once again into difficult territory and suggests dessert.

The sweet-toothed general polishes off a knickerbocker glory and fills Nicolas's glass with the last of the brandy. 'What do you say? Let's order another bottle and get green-snake drunk.'

'I should head home after this,' Nicolas says through a mouthful of cheesecake. 'My wife's pregnant and due in a couple of months.' Nicolas is saddened by the lazy anti-Semitism, by the pitiable state of the general, and doesn't want to witness him coming apart in his cups again. The two men have a good-natured tussle over the bill, and Nicolas promises to pay next time.

Just before they part, Skobelev gruffly mentions that he's brought Nicolas a keepsake. 'A memento,' he says. It's the general's regimental hip flask, battered from service, and engraved with a tribute from the men he once commanded. 'It won't see action again with me, but I thought you might need it one day.' The general's pink eyes glisten in the candlelight as he pats Nicolas's hand. 'Think of me next time you do battle with the Turk.'

Nicolas doesn't know what to say. He looks down at the flask. By some trick of the light, the Skobelev Nicolas sees reflected in the scratched silver is still the White General in his prime. 'Thank you,' says Nicolas. 'I'll treasure this.'

Afterwards, he worries that he was so overwhelmed with gratitude that his thanks came out as gauche and hasty. His sense of confusion is compounded by a feeling that his loyalties are divided between Rachkovsky and the general, between the kind of glamorous Jew he wishes might have been his father and the kind of frail old man who was.

The following morning, Rachkovsky comes in late. 'How was dinner with the general?' he asks Nicolas.

Nicolas looks up from his work – a series of reports on anarchist activities in Manchester, England. 'It was fine, but you know why he's here?'

Rachkovsky cocks his head at an angle that says: *surprise me*.

'He's looking into the way the department's funded. If I had any questionable sources of income, I'd be careful while he's around.'

'And that would be very sensible of you,' Rachkovsky says, and calls Mulhouse into his office.

'Anya gave birth to our first child in March 1887.'

It's a boy: Alexander Notovitch. The first of Nicolas's line for several millennia to keep its foreskin. 'Hello, little man,' Nicolas says, but feels false and fatuous talking to something so inert. Fatherhood is not something he'll ever be especially good at.

The labour was long: fourteen hours, and Anya has lost a good deal of blood. 'He looks like you,' she says, weakly. 'Doesn't he look like Nicolas, maman?'

Mrs Rozenfeld takes Nicolas aside. 'Separate rooms for a while. I know young men have their needs, but give her a chance to recover.'

Nicolas wonders why she's talking to him as though he's some kind of Priapus. Okay, he's managed to give Mrs Rozenfeld a grandson, but the feelings he has for Anya are, mainly, as soporific and comfortable as a night-time cup of cocoa; they don't include the sort of electrical passion that would make such a warning necessary.

Anya stays with her parents for a while. The Rozenfelds can afford lots of servants; their household runs smoothly and luxuriously – much better for a nursing mother. Nicolas lives like a bachelor in his apartment and rather enjoys it. It's big enough for two; for one person, it's enormous. There's more than enough space in the drawing room for the grand piano that Anya has lessons on once a week with Günther, a young music teacher from Vienna.

Middle age is descending on Nicolas quickly. Looking at himself in the full-length mirror, he hardly recognises the fat bourgeois staring back at him. An extra chin has appeared since Anya became pregnant. Office work and all that fine dining with Rachkovsky are the causes. He remembers himself in his glory days in the Balkans; so thin and wiry that he seemed to be able to curl up and nap anywhere. 'You could fall asleep on a clothesline,' MacGahan used to say admiringly. *Must remember to call on Skobelev.* He doesn't want the general's investigation to incriminate Rachkovsky, but on a personal level, he feels sentimental about Skobelev. He loves him, in a way. That anti-Semitism, it's a historical artefact with men of his generation. It's unexamined. Unthinking behaviour, as instinctive as holding a door open for a lady.

The telephone on the stand in the hall emits a steely ring. Only one person ever calls it. Nicolas tugs the rose-gold pocket watch out of his waistcoat. The digital display reads 22.45. Late to be calling. Must be urgent. Rachkovsky's voice: 'How soon can you be ready?'

'I'm ready now.'

'Go downstairs. I'll be there in five minutes. I'll explain on the way.'

He waits under the street light. A rain shower has come and gone. The city gleams as though it's been enamelled. A streetwalker, unusual in this area, sees him in the lamplight, asks him for a cigarette and looks at him brazenly while he strikes a match and cups it from the breeze. He hears the wheels of Rachkovsky's carriage as it turns the corner. Rachkovsky holds the door open. 'Jump aboard. No time to lose.'

From the carriage window, the street lamp seems to trundle backwards, with its attendant prostitute.

'I've had a tip-off from the police. It's Yulia.'

'Yulia who?'

'Yulia. Lizaveta Gelfman. The one you called Bessie. Your contact for the Geneva job.'

'What about her?'

'We're going to her house. There's been some bad news.'

'How bad?'

'As bad as it can be.'

Nicolas unthinkingly exhales, like a man who's taken a punch to the breadbasket.

'Shocking, I know. I need you to go in there. The police haven't cordoned it off yet. I want you to get in and see if there's a note.'

'A note?'

'It was a suicide.'

Nicolas, reduced to a melancholy echo of everything Rach-kovsky says, simply repeats his words.

'Yes. She had an idiot child. It was born with hydroceph-alus.' Rachkovsky holds the carriage curtains apart with his index and middle finger to check their progress. 'Apparently, that's Greek for an absolutely massive head. All her money went on medical treatment. She'd saved a fortune for surgery. Some Kraut doctor called Wernicke, I think, was supposed to put in a shunt to drain off whatever was causing it. Turns out he made a total bish. The poor thing contracted meningitis and died last week. Yulia took it very badly. That's the apart-ment there. Fourth floor. The door should be open. I can't be seen here. You'll have to take a cab back.'

'What's that?'

Rachkovsky has reached into his overcoat and pulled out a sheaf of documents. It's too dark for Nicolas to make out what they are.

'You find the note, if there is one,' Rachkovsky says. 'Then you swap it for this.'

'What is it?'

'Something Mulhouse and I have been putting together. This is our chance to give it a trial run.'

Nicolas's reluctance to take the papers draws a rare flash of anger from Rachkovsky. 'Look, you've got to do it. I don't know if there's a note, but if there is I don't want to be in it. You understand? I haven't got time to redact our business from whatever she's left. This' – Rachkovsky brandishes the papers – 'is simple and will allow us to come out of this mess with something positive. Now take it and go. What's wrong with you, Nicolas? For goodness' sake, *I* can't do it.'

NICOLAS IS OUT OF BREATH by the time he reaches the fourth-floor landing. The door, as promised, is ajar. The apartment feels unlived-in; there's a pair of suitcases un-opened in the living room.

Bessie's lying on the bed in her travelling clothes, still wearing her shoes, her pretty oval face as white and cold as moonlight. The counterpane seems to be made of red velvet. Whatever she was is gone. Nicolas is alone in the room, and that's the thing: this is their final, most intimate adventure, and she's not here for it. The sense of loneliness is mortifying.

He lights the bedside lamp. Her sleeves are pulled up to the elbows and the bedspread is drenched with blood. She opened her veins with a scalpel and bled out where she lay, slipping into unconsciousness as her enfeebled heart fluttered to a stop.

While he's examining the body, he hears a sound at the door. He opens it a crack and sees an anxious face: a woman of about fifty, wearing a dressing gown and slippers. 'Are you the police?' she asks.

'Yes, madame.'

'Thank God. I sent a message an hour ago. There's blood coming through the ceiling.'

'Thank you for your vigilance, madame. The other officers will be here shortly.'

Nicolas closes the door and slides the deadbolt across. Back in the bedroom, another examination of the scene shows what went wrong: Bessie propped an enamel basin underneath her arm to catch the blood, but must have overturned it in her death throes. She was hoping to be found in the morning by the maid. That's to whom the brief note is addressed: *My Dear Celeste.*

The note is brief and businesslike, beginning with an apology, detailing the resolution of her financial affairs, and insisting that she be buried with her daughter. There's no mention of Nicolas, Rachkovsky, or anything do with the Third Section's work.

He pulls out Rachkovsky's papers and reads them in the light of the bedside lamp, at first quickly, then, as his puzzlement deepens, with growing care. They're hectographic copies of a document that's been plagiarised from the book he had on his stag weekend: *A Dialogue in Hell.* That was a kind of broad-brush satire: arch-liberal Montesquieu and arch-cynic Machiavelli meet in hell and discuss politics. This has been altered and reconceived. In the place of Machiavelli there is a sinister figure called the Chief Rabbi. He speaks more or less the same lines as before, but this new draft has turned him into a paradigmatic Jew, boasting of his skill in manipulating Gentiles. It's a crude, anti-Semitic smear, to no end that Nicolas can discern.

He thinks of Mulhouse: like many aspirant writers Nicolas has known, he talked a good game, but this – the padding, the arrhythmic sentences and ill-thought structure – betrays the lazy habits of a hack.

Rachkovsky wants this nonsense planted at the bedside, instead of the dying wishes of the woman Nicolas loves? He stuffs the sheets back in his pocket and blows out the lamp. Already, in his relatively short life, he's faced much thornier dilemmas than this one.

'Rachkovsky demanded total obedience.'

'Come in, sit down. Close the door, would you?' There's no *dear boy*, no tea and chocolates this time. Every now and again, Rachkovsky loses it completely with one of his underlings. The office door closes. There's the muffled sound of Rachkovsky going batshit; a chastened employee emerges twenty minutes later. Sometimes the whole performance is followed by a public reconciliation, an apology and even the gift of flowers.

This time, there's no shouting. Rachkovsky's so angry that the intensity of his focus on Nicolas is almost sexual. 'I've been through all the papers,' he says, in a voice that's singsong with the sound of deflected rage. 'No mention in any of them of the pamphlet I gave you. From this, Nicolas, I conclude that you didn't think it was worth leaving it there.' Rachkovsky closes his eyes and pinches the bridge of his nose between thumb and forefinger. The gesture's a familiar one to Nicolas. The spymaster is fending off a migraine. 'So here's where I am now: you're going to have to help me understand why it is that you would refuse what was clearly a direct order.'

Nicolas, as we know, is quite capable of riffing boldly at short notice. This time he doesn't choose to. 'Look, she left a note. It didn't mention anything about us. It just specified how to wind up her financial affairs and said what kind of funeral she wanted. I thought we should respect the wishes of a dying woman.'

'That's a commendable sentiment in the context of a romance novel. We're not in a romance novel. We're in the middle of a war on terror. The importance of the work we do here seems to have escaped your attention. In the heat of battle, under enemy fire, do you stop to bury your fallen comrades? No, you don't. First you win the war, then you put up the cenotaph. And by the way, since when was it up to you to determine the strategic policy of this department?'

Nicolas starts to answer.

'Don't fucking interrupt me!' Rachkovsky shrieks.

The double bind is, patently, amusing. Nicolas smiles.

'Oh! Oh! This is funny? This is funny! I tell you something, this is not funny!'

'It is funny,' says Nicolas. 'You're funny. Moreover, I quit.'

'If you leave this room, young man, that's it. You will never work for me again.'

It's not just the indignity of being shouted at; it's not just the revulsion he feels for Rachkovsky's obscure plan; it's not just that haberdashery suddenly seems like it will be better for his soul in the long run. It's also that he senses that if he stays in the room, he will be letting down all the people who ever truly cared about him.

Nicolas nods to make it clear that he accepts the verdict, then he opens the door, and walks out of the building without collecting his stuff, leaving Rachkovsky, for once, at a loss for words.

'Rachkovsky would have loved a machine like this one.'

Notovitch is standing to stretch his legs. He caresses the cherry-wood lid of the Imperator.

'My eyesight is not what it was,' he says. 'My hands,

you've seen yourself, are not fit for the task of composition. But I want to leave something other than Rachkovsky's lies behind me.' He gestures at the box of unused cylinders. 'When our work together is complete, I intend to have these transcribed for publication.' His eyes meet Vincenzo's. 'No doubt it seems like an indulgent exercise to you. This is, after all, ancient history, no?' For the first time, Vincenzo sees a twinkle of Nicolas in the old man; he seems suddenly younger, as though refreshed by the memory of his youthful pugnacity.

Vincenzo removes the roll from the dictator and inscribes the date on its sleeve in pencil: 25th March 1933. 'I imagined that was your intention,' he says, diplomatically. 'To make a book.'

This answer seems to please Notovitch. The old man repeats it with satisfaction. 'Yes, to make a book.'

Their work is ended for the day. It is, unusually, a Saturday; one of only two occasions when the men meet on a weekend. Vincenzo asks to use the downstairs lavatory. Its tiny window looks out into the rear garden, a long shady rectangle of damp grass. A lone magpie perches on the bough of a leafless apple tree at the far end. Vincenzo salutes instinctively and then smiles at the absurdity of the figure he cuts: one hand at his temple, the other still directing his aim at the porcelain. It strikes him as a shame that the big garden isn't put to better use. Every available inch of his suburban plot is sown with vegetables each year: trenches of broad beans, potatoes, peas, the tomatoes that his wife loathes. He emerges from the lavatory to find that Notovitch has shed his chapan and put on a grey overcoat and homburg hat: the conjuror transformed into a businessman. 'I have an appointment in the City,' says Notovitch.

Today, the two men leave the house at the same time and end up walking together towards the Underground. Notovitch brandishes his ebony cane like a sceptre.

Two dray horses munch feedbags outside the Royal Oak on Haverstock Hill. A blocky heap of yellow horseshit steams by the kerb. Three men in caps and aprons roll barrels off the cart and down into the beery open mouth of the pub's cellarage. Far to the south, the dome of St Paul's can just be seen rising above the coal smoke of the city. Both men pay the six-penny fare, descend in the lift, and board the southbound train. Their carriage is half-empty. Notovitch sits sideways on a banquette seat, with his feet in the aisle.

'This is not your usual route home,' the old man observes.

'I'm meeting my wife in the city. She wants to buy a new wireless. She likes to keep up with the news.'

'And you?'

'The less I know of what's happening in the world, the better I sleep.'

'I envy the British,' Notovitch says. 'Living under this enchantment – the illusion of eternal peace. Even this underground railway seems of a kind with their thousand years of history, their benign monarch whose power is constrained by an ancient parliament.'

'You told me you hated the British.' Vincenzo has to raise his voice over the rattle of the train.

'As imperialists, they're rascals – all empire-builders are. As a nation, there is a lot to admire them for. No fanaticism. Toleration of eccentrics. A fetish for fair play.'

'I think you are romanticising.'

'That's why I call it an illusion. But would you rather be in Italy or Russia? Or Germany, where they are burying democracy as we speak?'

'I consider myself lucky,' says Vincenzo.

'You can't imagine how lucky. For over a year, I've been corresponding with a German businessman who shares my background.'

Shares my background. Vincenzo thinks: *oh, a Jew.* The electric lights in the carriage dim briefly as the train rounds a subterranean curve.

'He expressed an interest in investing in my business, but with the changes there, he's no longer considering expanding. He wants to sell up and go to America.'

'I heard about the boycott of the Jewish shops,' says Vincenzo.

'That's the least of it. Imagine this: the man I know used to have lunch most days in the same restaurant in Alexanderplatz with friends of his. Some Jews, yes, but not all of them. Now a young Brownshirt begins going there, selling copies of *Der Angriff*. First they think it's funny. It's such a brazen provocation. He comes every single day. My friend tells him to get lost. 'Why would I want to read this insulting propaganda?' Still the young man comes. They ask the proprietor to kick him out. Two days after the election, a whole gang of them turn up, carrying a list of every Jew in the place. They form a guard by the door, read off the list of names, and beat each man unconscious. For the crime of being Jewish. This happened two weeks ago. My advice, Mr Dittami? If you want to sleep soundly, don't buy the wireless. Buy a gramophone instead.'

Vincenzo is out at Warren Street. He turns as the doors close. Notovitch has taken a newspaper from the pocket of his overcoat. Vincenzo sees the homburg silhouetted against the newsprint, gathering pace as the carriage rattles into the darkness.

'I told Skobelev as much as I knew.'

The old general is out of his depth. He's been sent to Paris to satisfy someone's well-grounded concern that Rachkovsky is not to be trusted. But he's too old and drink-sodden, and not clever enough to catch Rachkovsky out. And the sad thing is that somewhere he knows it.

Rachkovsky responds to his requests for information with excessive helpfulness. He sends round so many crateloads of documents that Skobelev is inundated. The general has to stack them in his hotel room, and still they keep coming, piling up into walls, within which Skobelev paces, like a rat in a maze of paperwork.

The general has developed various anxious tics, repeatedly smearing balm on his cracked lips as he sorts and re-sorts documents he hopes will turn out to be incriminating. He adds up the figures over and over again, and each time comes to a different total.

Skobelev senses he's losing his mind. There's mental illness on both sides of his family. Sometimes he hears voices speaking about him through the walls of the hotel bathroom. Sometimes he thinks he's being followed. Sometimes, of course, he is.

Nicolas offers to help. He's got a good sense where the

bodies are buried: start with the mansion in Saint-Cloud – prima facie evidence of embezzlement; request a meeting with the Bourse; get the Russian ambassador onside. It's age-old journalistic best practice: follow the money. But he makes the mistake of telling Skobelev about the document, about Mulhouse's forged paper describing the machinations of global Jewry.

Skobelev is as enamoured as anyone of easy answers. 'The Jews! Rachkovsky's working for the Jews!' He won't let the matter lie.

'The department store never felt like my vocation. Nonetheless . . .'

Mr Rozenfeld's new venture, Étoile du Nord, is a success from the start. It manages to retain the customers loyal to its predecessor boutiques and then add new ones. Cosmetics concessions in the ground-floor pharmacy are staffed by pretty women in lab coats who dole out free samples of anti-ageing serums. Pyramidal displays of macaroons under glass domes stand on the counter of its coffee shop. The whole place smells enticingly of perfume and new fabric.

Nicolas is put in charge of the menswear department. Mr Rozenfeld regards writing as a waste of time, and is watching to see if Nicolas possesses sufficient acumen to succeed him one day at the head of the business. He needn't worry. Nicolas has been working in shops since he was eight years old. He knows how to sell anything, whether it's dried fish, lamp oil, fine wine or shirt collars. Every encounter is a transaction, he remembers his father saying. Everyone who walks through that door wants something. The real skill of business is selling intangible goods: pride, gratitude, health, self-esteem – learn to deal in these and you'll never go hungry. He's a capable accountant, has a good head for figures, can be steely with suppliers, and the soul of charm with customers. He has some good ideas about interior design too, and a spy's eye for window dressing.

One hot day in June – it's Monday the 13th, 1887 – Nicolas takes the afternoon off, telling his secretary to cancel his appointment with a firm of milliners from Nantes. He's been complaining of toothache since he got in. It's a day of pressing heat and intermittent clouds. At a fishmonger's, he pauses to fan the cool atmosphere surrounding the beds of crushed ice onto his face, then hails a cab on the corner, which he directs to Sainte-Geneviève-des-Bois, the Cimetière de Liers: Paris's Russian Orthodox cemetery.

As a favour to Nicolas, Father David has interceded with the bishop to allow the burial of a suicide. The ecclesiastical hierarchy is disposed to look kindly on his wish. Bessie and her daughter will be interred together in the communal plot. But there will be no stone. Celeste the maid and Nicolas are the only mourners. They have to avert their eyes from the child's tiny coffin as Father David sings *Dushe moya*: *Spirit arise*.

It has occurred to Nicolas before, but this time more forcibly, that *he* could be the father of Marianne. The timing of the birth makes her paternity ambiguous. He knows Bessie wouldn't have told him if he was. As the coffins are lowered, he has a sense that an important part of himself is being consigned to oblivion.

A caretaker's lodge guards the entrance to the cemetery. During the service, Nicolas becomes aware of a stranger standing there, keeping a respectful distance. It is Rachkovsky, wearing a pale linen suit and a pair of spectacles with purple lenses. He has a bouquet of gerberas in one hand, which he places beside the grave at the conclusion of the burial, and a walking stick in the other. 'I came to apologise,' he says. 'Shall we walk?' Nicolas falls into step, and the two men tour the avenues of the dead.

Nicolas knows that Rachkovsky has swallowed his pride to be here, and suspects there will be a compensatory attack somewhere down the line. It comes almost immediately.

'I read your book, the India one. I was in bed with Maria – itself a rarity – and I said, that dear boy, something's curiously flat about his style. I thought, what's wrong with him? Where's his panache? Where's his *vim*?' All this without meeting Nicolas's eye. Rachkovsky pauses by a grave and moves some bugloss stems aside with his cane so he can read the inscription. 'When you said you knew her before, I should have guessed then. Since we last spoke, I've made some enquiries and it's come to my attention that you and . . . Bessie . . .' – the slight hesitation signals his solicitude, his desire to accommodate Nicolas's version of the truth – '. . . were closer than I imagined. I'm not a monster, Nicolas. If you'd told me she meant something to you, I would have understood. The document I gave you is a provocation I've been refining with Mulhouse. If I'd known the true situation, I wouldn't have insisted on it.'

Now he looks at Nicolas directly. Rachkovsky knows sincerity is as important to an enchantment as salt to cooking: a judicious pinch of it in everything. But Nicolas can only see his own face in the purple lenses, and what he sees is a sad, middle-aged Jew.

'I appreciate your coming,' Nicolas says.

Rachkovsky reaches out and gives his shoulder a squeeze. He points towards the onion-shaped cupola of the tiny church with his cane. 'You're the wordsmith: would you call that *blue* or *teal*?'

Nicolas squints. The roof has a greenish tinge. 'I might say *aquamarine*.'

'Excellent. *Aquamarine*.' Rachkovsky savours the word like a peppermint comfit. 'Speaking of literary pursuits, I'd love to have your opinion of Mulhouse's creation. It's a work in progress and we're still refining it.'

'I'm not sure I was in a mood to appreciate it.'

'Very true. Context is everything. Let me offer you some.' Rachkovsky leans on a headstone and knocks some dried mud off his shoes with his walking stick. 'Bear this in mind: the ordinary Russian, like the ordinary man anywhere, occasionally feels discontented, occasionally feels disparaged by the way of things. At times like that, he might feel that revolutionary politics says something of interest to him. It would only be natural. What we want to do is to remind him of the profoundly un-Russian character of these people. We want to remind him that the working man has worse enemies than the status quo.'

'But you and I are Jews.'

'What of it? Our ancestors, the Khazars, worshipped the sky god Tengri, and left ribbons on trees to placate elves. We're beyond such fairy tales. You and I are free men. We both realise that God is dead, man is alone, and everything is possible. But that is strong meat which not many people are capable of digesting. Besides, I don't think of our project as anti-Semitism as such; I see it more as a literary device: the Jew as an allegory of modernity.'

'Really? That seems a bit sophisticated for its intended readership.'

Rachkovsky laughs. 'You're being very pi, dear boy. It's unlike you. After all, the thing's a bauble.'

Above their heads, one of the slow-moving clouds drifting to the south takes on the shape of a fish; another thins and momentarily resembles a child with a distended head. 'My future is not in the Third Section,' says Nicolas.

'I'm sorry to hear it,' Rachkovsky says. 'I'd rather hoped you'd reconsider. You're an excellent agent and could look forward to a stellar and lucrative career.'

'My mind's made up.'

'Very well. That's your choice. I don't threaten. It's not my style. But working for the Third Section imposes life-long obligations.'

'I understand,' says Nicolas.

'Of course you do.'

Rachkovsky has a carriage waiting. He doesn't offer Nicolas a lift. As he climbs in, his big, linen-covered backside sticks out awkwardly and Nicolas has an urge to kick it.

'How's your friend Skobelev doing, by the way?' he asks. Before Nicolas can reply, Rachkovsky throws his head back and brays like an ass. The sound is loud, jarring and uncannily accurate. The coachman flicks the reins and the wheels move off, clattering over the cobbles. 'Farewell, Nicolas. And be careful.' Rachkovsky points up in the air with his stick: 'It looks like heavy rain.'

The sky is still blue and the clouds white and innocuous, but twenty minutes later a thunderhead rolls in. Having decided to walk to the railway station, Nicolas is at risk of being drenched. He takes cover under an awning where a newspaper-seller is sheltering too. He hands over a two-sous piece for an evening newspaper, thinking he can improvise a temporary umbrella from its pages while he hails a cab. Then he reads the headline.

'It said, "Murder: Jewish Plot Suspected".'

General Skobelev's body was found laid out on a pile of boxes in his hotel room, killed with a single pistol-shot to the head. The paper decribes him as 'an ardent nationalist and supporter of the Tsar'. The inside pages have a diagram of the crime scene and are full of humiliating details: the hero of the Russo-Turkish War was naked except for his underpants; there was an empty brandy bottle and a book containing 'the most scandalous photographic images'.

The circumstances certainly suggest some kind of honey-trap, but the leader-writers are careful to warn against a rush to judgement. It seems that, departing in haste, the assassin may have accidentally dropped another clue to his identity. The police are reluctant to release too many particulars, but sources say that a document has been recovered suggesting the manoeuvrings of a conspiracy: a cabal of powerful Jews, trying to profit from political unrest.

It is too soon to know, the editorial concludes, whether this will be borne out by the investigation, but the public interest will only be met by a full inquiry. In the meantime, community leaders must make clear where their allegiances lie. France has a proud tradition of offering sanctuary to refugees, and for this to continue, people must be left in no doubt: there is no room in a secular democracy for extremists of any kind. The paper calls upon the nation's Jews to condemn the actions of this fanatical – though entirely putative – minority.

Subsequent newspaper reports suppress the more lurid details of Skobelev's death and the Russian government brings his body back to Saint Petersburg for a state funeral.

Nicolas treasures a single memory of the general in his pomp, ten years earlier, in December 1877, graciously complimenting the defeated Osman Pasha on his defence of Plevna, while the mud around them lay thick with discarded Peabody–Martini rifles.

'I was almost afraid to see him in the flesh,' the general confided to Nicolas and MacGahan afterwards, 'but he had the face of a hero.'

Whatever his failings, with his generosity in victory and personal bravery, Skobelev seemed to Nicolas to epitomise the virtues of manhood. Now the old warrior's body is being carried joltingly by rail back to the country he has defended so long with his life.

'I received a letter from my brother.'

The four foolscap pages of Yiddish contain enquiries for his health, affirmations of brotherly love, and the most harebrained idea Nicolas has ever heard. Avram's planning to leave Kiev for good, with his mother, sisters, wife and children, and emigrate to Palestine.

Some dusty, thistle-strewn patch of desert where camels struggle to find a drink of water? It's called the Dead Sea for a reason. What's wrong with Buenos Aires or New York?

'Israel was promised to us,' Avram writes. 'Here, we'll always be Jews. In a land of Jews, we can be the people. This is our destiny. If you ever feel like joining us, you'll be welcome, brother.'

Nicolas is touched in spite of everything. He misses home, the mess and familiar smells of the family kitchen. Part of him yearns for contact with his former world, with people who really know him. Having gone to such trouble to create a new identity, he finds himself longing for the old one. The people to whom he entrusted important parts of himself – MacGahan, Bessie, even in some way Rachkovsky – have all died or become estranged. All the secrets he's kept have started to feel corrosive. And this shiny-booted shopkeeper is a mask he can't remove.

Today it's Saturday, and he's off to pick out kitchen floor tiles. Standing in the showroom, weighing up the claims of a piece of Spanish slate and some Umbrian terracotta, Anya tearfully reveals she's pregnant again. This is more than a surprise. As far as Nicolas is concerned, it's a biological impossibility. Back at home, he confronts her about it.

She's defensive at first, then guilt-stricken. 'You just never showed any interest in me. You were always at work. You never let me feel like I was part of your life. It was just the once. So soon after the birth that I didn't think I could conceive. I hadn't even started my periods again and I was still breastfeeding.' Nicolas holds out a box of tissues for Anya to dry her tears. He's thinking it was that Viennese piano teacher, Günther, the sneaky little shit.

'I was feeling very vulnerable and lonely. Why couldn't you have just included me a bit more? And anyway, we're Parisians, we're French.' She dissolves into tears as her heart strains to accommodate the rationalisations of free love. She can't bring herself to say it: *what's wrong with a little adultery?*

Cuckold. He never saw that coming. 'That's it,' he says, 'no more piano lessons!'

Puzzlement is etched on her weepy red face. 'Piano lessons? It wasn't Günther, if that's what you're thinking.'

'Who then? I need to know. Surely not Boris *Volchkov?*'

'Oh, gross! No way.'

'Anya, don't make me guess. This is bad enough as it is.'

She's so distressed that he's not able to be angry with her. He knows he's not the husband he ought to have been. He knows that he hasn't loved her in the way she deserves. But he's still a man and his male pride is in tatters.

'It's not even about *him*,' Anya pleads. 'It's about *us*. I just wanted to know what was going on with you. I wanted to know about the man I fell in love with. I wanted to know why he was so distant, so secretive.'

'And you slept with someone else to do it?'

'I wanted a shoulder to cry on. I wanted to know what it was like to be you, to have something separate going on in my head all the time.' She looks at him, pleading with her eyes for him to guess, to spare her from having to say his name.

'Who was it? I'll bloody kill him!' Nicolas says feebly,

feeling he should say it, but knowing he never would.

She replies with a tearful look. And he understands. His anger drains away. A terrible sickliness comes over him, as though he's ingested some fast-acting poison. He stumbles, and steadies himself with a ladder-back chair.

Dear boy, of *course*. The best man. Who else? 'You mustn't worry about him, my child. From time to time, work gets on top of all of us.' The pale hands clasp hers in consolation. That signet ring glints in the candlelight. Is the idea of getting *on top of her* already present in the words' ghostly emphasis? How cunning is he? Can he persuade anyone of *anything*? 'Let me pour you some of this.' A little wine splashes over her fingers as she gestures that it's enough. He dabs the spillage off, and weighs her hand lightly in his palm. 'Motherhood positively suits you, Anyushka. You've blossomed. Let me look at you! My goodness, where has all the weight gone?'

Nicolas sees that big linen-covered rear getting into the carriage at the cemetery, and then getting into his wife. In a hotel room? In the office? In his own bed? He covers his eyes with an involuntary movement of his hand. He thinks he might throw up.

Anya rushes to embrace him. His arms hang loosely down. Her wet face makes a damp patch on his shirt. Her head feels like the hilt of a knife that's stabbed him.

The world is what it is. God is dead, man is alone, everything is possible. I stuffed your wife with my strong meat, Nicolas. And to think that you imagined I was a big neutered tomcat! The sound that his belt buckle makes as he undoes it also says: *Rachkovsky.*

'There are worse things than a new life,' Nicolas says

quietly. 'I forgive you. If it's a boy, we'll give him my name. This will be a secret between us.'

Anya looks at him in astonishment. She was expecting wrath, tears, even blows, not this stoic acceptance. She wonders if he even feels it.

But he does. This is the utmost agony, but he has chosen to accept it. The sense of humiliation encompasses his whole body. It is as though he is being purged by fire, or ice; as though he's fighting for his life in freezing water, trying to keep moving, trying to keep breathing, letting his consciousness contract around the agony, refined by its pain, saying to himself, *There is only this moment, all the rest is a story*, and wishing he could believe it.

3: THE SECRET BOOKS

NOW OPEN YOUR EYES. Take a moment to adjust to your new surroundings. We're standing on a bank of yellow scree that crunches underfoot and slopes downwards from an immense limestone ridge too sharp and steep for snow to adhere to. Miles below us, the stubble of barley fields carpets the valley floor. Prayer flags snap in the breeze, their colours unearthly bright. In every direction, snowy peaks loom above cliffs of striated rock, dwarfing everything we can see. We are never quite reconciled to their presence.

The geography here is mystifying and sudden: alien empires are incongruously collateral. This is the high desert crossroad of Asia: China, Nepal and Tibet beyond those mountains, British India behind us, the expanding territory of the Russian Empire lurking to the north and west.

A train of short-legged, barrel-chested ponies winds its way through the dusty rock, attended by men in umber, ochre, grey. The giddying thin air is hallucinatory. There are visions up here in these mountains. On the farther slopes of the dry valley, something is moving. The men dismount and wait. Nicolas unsheathes a telescope and points it at the distant dots. Traders? Herdsmen? Brigands? 'We'll hold here,' he says. This is a better defensive position. In the folds of his thick overcoat he has a revolver. He breaks the top and counts six bullets in the chambers. This land is claimed by many governments, loyal to none.

'Give the ponies something to eat,' he says, in Pashto, to his guides.

While he waits for the strangers to draw near, he swigs from his canteen of water. The desiccating wind steals moisture from everything without detection. No one sweats in this dry air. Leather cracks and falls apart.

The lead rider in the party of strangers urges his pony up the last fifty yards of scree. He's wearing a Chitrali hat, but distinctive European army boots. He shouts a booming greeting in badly accented Hindi and unwinds the patterned scarf from his head to reveal a wind-burned English face: fox-orange eyebrows, freckles, blue-green eyes. The voice is rough from shouting commands; the diction is a gentleman's. 'Captain Francis Younghusband, King's Dragoon Guards.'

Nicolas saunters towards him to have a better look and to spare himself from shouting. 'Nicolas Notovitch, *Novaya Gazeta* and the *Chicago Herald*.' As he reaches into his breast pocket, he sees Younghusband stiffen in the saddle. What he pulls out is a hip flask. 'Cognac,' Nicolas says, turning the little vessel so its sides catch the sunlight. He offers it to the Englishman.

'After you,' says Younghusband. He's young, perhaps twenty-five, a bluff adventurer type who isn't cunning enough to conceal his unease.

'To Her Majesty's health,' Nicolas proposes, takes a sip, and offers the flask to the Englishman, who accepts it, but doesn't raise it to his lips.

'I had you for a Frenchman,' he says.

'I live in Paris,' says Nicolas, 'but, as must be evident to you, I am a Russian subject.'

'Well,' says Younghusband, 'to the Tsar, then', and turning his head away slightly he touches the flask to his lips and lowers it without swallowing. Nicolas finds himself offended by the half-heartedness of the Englishman's attempt at civility.

Younghusband dismounts. He is wiry, big-boned, a nervous red setter of a man, with a young dog's restlessness and anxious curiosity. He gestures at some bulky objects on one of Notovitch's ponies.

'You map-making? That a theodolite?'

'No, Captain Younghusband. It's photographic equipment. My editors tell me that our readers have a vast appetite for images of exotic locations. We journalists are slaves to the public taste. And as for you, what is the purpose of your expedition?'

'I'm on Her Majesty's business,' says the Englishman. Then, aware how curt he sounds, he elaborates a little. 'I'm adventuring. Bit of a passion of mine. I started in Peking.'

'You've come from China?' The distances involved are so huge that it's impossible not to be impressed. Younghusband concedes he has with a false show of modesty. 'Then the spirit of Drake and Raleigh is not dead,' Nicolas suggests.

'No, and never shall be, I hope,' says the Englishman, with the pomposity that Nicolas has come to recognise as that nation's birthright. He graciously accedes to the wish with a nod.

One of Nicolas's Pashtun guides chooses this pause to break into the conversation. He's wondering how long they expect to stay here.

Nicolas asks him if there's water nearby. The guide indicates a thorn tree half a mile away on the valley floor. Nicolas tells him to head there and make camp.

'You speak the lingo?' says Younghusband in surprise.

'My Pashto is no more than workable,' insists Nicolas, 'my Balti poor, and my Ladakhi practically non-existent. I've told my man to make camp by that spring. I would be honoured if you would be my guest tonight.'

'What spring? The charts don't show a spring,' says Younghusband, unfolding his map.

'The watershed from that range drains into an aquifer which opens there,' says Nicolas. 'You can see by the pattern of vegetation.'

'Well, our casks are bone-dry, so a stop would suit us,' Younghusband admits. 'I'll follow you down.'

The Pashtun servants gather brushwood, and shoot and butcher a wild goat while Nicolas puts up his tiny pup tent.

At nightfall, the air temperature drops to freezing. The sky is vast and moonless: a busy vault of stars streaked with the Milky Way, and Venus stands out as brightly as a pebble.

'I left Peking in March,' says Younghusband, his face yellow from the firelight. Sparks rise from the branches.

Everyone wants to be listened to, Nicolas thinks. He lets Younghusband tell his tale, how he crossed the Gobi by camel, how he travelled by moonlight, how he was bilked by a series of guides. At last, the Englishman is willing to admit to a few shortcomings. Younghusband is rightfully proud of his adventure. He is the first European to cross the Mustagh Pass. The vertiginous ice, which he negotiated in slippery leather footwear, without ice axes, and roped together with his native guides, reduced several of his party to gibbering wrecks. There is no denying the man's hardiness and courage.

Nicolas feels a mixture of emotions: envy, resentment, but also kinship. He senses Younghusband likes it here for the same reasons that he does: this is a simple world. There is no ambivalence about their task; in spite of the secrecy, no murkiness. The interests of the Great Powers are at stake and both men know which side they're on.

And this corner of the world is extraordinary for other reasons. Younghusband understands it too: the Kalmyk and the Tadzhik, the Kirghiz and the Pashtun, the Han Chinese and the Tibetan, the Buddhist and the Muslim. This is the reverse of the neatly embroidered cloth we take for reality; its loose ends and tangled skeins of thread are what we don't see. The swirling mix of colours on its maps are like the marbled endpapers of the secret books. This is a place where stories intersect and grow muddled: stories of Europe and Asia, stories of Cathay and Hindustan; stories of Russia and the British Empire. Borders and endings are fuzzy, indistinct, sometimes incoherent. This would be a good place for a man to make a new start.

'Have you any more of that brandy?' asks Younghusband.

Nicolas offers him the flask. This time the Englishman drinks deeply. 'I say!' It's impeccable stuff. Nicolas chose it in Paris for evenings just like this one: its taste evokes cedar and sandalwood and the consoling feeling of being locked in a cupboard of soft woollen coats. 'The flask's a bit of a relic,' Younghusband continues, trying to read the inscription in the firelight. 'My blasted eyes are going.'

'It's in Russian,' Nicolas says. 'From an old friend, General Skobelev.'

'Skobelev? You know General Skobelev?' The Englishman's surprise is touchingly unfeigned.

'I knew him,' Nicolas says. 'He died this past summer.'

'That's a damn shame,' says Younghusband. 'Every English schoolboy knows his name. The man was a fine soldier.'

'He was many things,' says Nicolas thoughtfully, staring at the tigerish colours of the fire.

'Was he as tall as they say? Blue-eyed?'

Nicolas nods.

'I met some Russian chaps en route. Good fellows. The consul in Abbottabad had me over for dinner. And there was a shopkeeper I drank vodka with who didn't speak a word of English. I toasted every Russian name I could remember, starting with the Tsar. Skobelev's name was the second off my lips. God rest his soul. I'd have been proud to call that man an Englishman. What I mean to say, Mr Notovik . . .'

'Please, Francis, pretend we're in the mess. Call me Nicolas.'

'The point is, as things stand we find ourselves on different sides, but I consider you chaps worthy adversaries.'

Nicolas takes the hip flask and inspects the inscription in the fading firelight: *To our White General. From his grateful men.* An inadvertent sigh escapes his lips and mists the silver. He wipes it with his sleeve. 'I'll drink to that.'

'I say,' declares Younghusband, sprawling happily against some saddlebags. 'There's an Englishman, a Scotsman and an Irishman . . .'

Nicolas watches Younghusband's frosty breath rise into the clear air and listens politely to his dirty jokes. He feels a quiet sort of contentment. Up here, a man can be whoever he chooses.

'. . . my servant Dongmin says it's because I'm a pig.'

Nicolas laughs immoderately at what he takes to be the punchline. Younghusband frowns in puzzlement. 'It's not a joke, old chap. My Chinese horoscope.'

'Of course,' says Nicolas, recovering his composure swiftly. 'A pig.'

Younghusband prods a branch into the fire with the tip of his boot. 'What's yours?'

'Mine? I was born under the sign of the twins, but surely you don't believe such fairy tales?'

'Typical Gemini. But that's not what I mean. In China, the important thing is the year. What year were you born?' Younghusband takes a generous slurp of cognac. 'Come on, play along, old chap. Make it fun.'

Nicolas smiles to himself at the Englishman's lack of guile. It's a transparent stratagem for determining his age. He imagines Younghusband trying the same trick with coy women at the regimental balls. 'I was born in 1858, Francis.'

'1858? Really? I had you younger. That makes you . . . let me see. A horse!' The fact that Nicolas is Younghusband's senior by five years takes the final edge off their rivalry. He offers the Russian some friendly advice. 'I'd think twice about sleeping under canvas up here, old chap. Kanjuti robbers. They could be watching us now. Fiendishly cunning. They'll sneak up at night and cut the guy ropes. Before you know it, you're rolled up in your tent like a length of carpet and being taken off to some slave-bazaar, or worse.'

Nicolas expresses gratitude for Younghusband's concern,

but says he's willing to take his chances. 'Suit yourself,' says Younghusband. Nicolas senses the Englishman's eyes on him as the flames die.

At sunset, Younghusband placed a sheepskin sleeping bag out in the open, ostentatiously; now, he drags it behind a rock to mislead any watching Kanjutis. He gives Nicolas's arm a fond pat as they bid each other goodnight.

Nicolas tends to suffer from insomnia at altitude, but tonight, for some reason, he falls quickly into a deep sleep. When he wakes up, it's still dark and it takes a moment for him to remember where he is. He feels something pressing into his ribs. It's Younghusband, beside him in the tiny tent, and glued closer to the Russian than a beauty spot on a matron's face.

'Mr Younghusband?' Nicolas protests sleepily. 'What in the devil's name—?'

'I thought I heard a noise,' the Englishman says, withdrawing his hand abruptly from Nicolas's sleeping bag, and taking with it the cord from Nicolas's pyjamas.

'The tent is barely big enough for one. If you want it, you're welcome to it.'

'Fine thanks for my concern about your well-being,' says Younghusband, wriggling out of the tent door in his sleeping bag with the motion of a huge and clumsy caterpillar.

The incident is not mentioned at breakfast – rice and mutton stew, cooked by Younghusband's Chinese servant. Like Younghusband's abortive intimacy, the cordial relations of the previous evening are also forgotten. The Englishman is sullen, tetchy, and eager to get going. He also makes a point of being rude about Nicolas's ponies. 'Rather mangy-looking,' he says. 'You'll need to buy new ones, if you can afford to. They'll never make it across the glaciers. Mine are twice as strong, and they kept stumbling.'

'We have special shoes for crossing the ice,' says Nicolas. 'And I assure you these horses have no equal. They are wild Kazakh ponies.' His instincts tell him to leave it there, but his desire to twit Younghusband gets the better of him. He feels compelled to add a provocation. 'An indifferent rider on one of these would challenge an expert like you on a mount such as yours.'

'Really?' says Younghusband, taking the bait, setting down his mess tin of stew and wiping both sides of his hands on his shirt. 'Are you a gambling man, Mr Notovitch? What would you wager for a race against me?'

'I'd do it for the honour of my country,' says Nicolas, 'but I'm not sure what you would have to stake against it.'

'If you're so confident of winning that you feel able to insult my nation, why not wager Skobelev's canteen?' says Younghusband, his voice grown strained and harsh.

'What do you have that could possibly equal its value?'

'I have charts of every valley between here and Peking. Some one-to-fifty-thousand scale. Ordnance-quality. Perfect for someone who was planning military manoeuvres in the area. I expect they'd be appreciated by your paymasters in Moscow.'

'*My* paymasters are in Saint Petersburg. Moscow hasn't been the capital of Russia for a hundred and fifty years, you insular macaroni. Let me see those charts.'

Younghusband throws him a handful of rolled maps from his saddlebags. They are just as he promised: the finest works of British Imperial cartographers. This is intelligence worth having.

'Walid,' says Notovitch, addressing one of his men. 'Saddle Tengri for me.'

The course they choose runs the length of the valley floor, includes a turn at the far end and finishes back at the starting line. There is a delay of twenty minutes while the guides remove hazardous rocks from the course. Younghusband performs callisthenic stretches as they wait.

It is agreed that Walid will signal the start with a pistol-shot.

Tengri has been Nicolas's mount since he bought her in Bishkek. She is grey, with the unflappable temperament of a Buddha, and faster than sunlight. Nicolas is confident of winning this, but, by the look of things, so is Younghusband.

At the pistol-shot, time seems suspended for a second. The sound repeats around the valley. Younghusband is already off, standing up in his shortened stirrups like a jockey.

Tengri hits her gallop and accelerates after the other horse. By the midpoint of the valley, they pass Younghusband easily. Nicolas wants to sing with elation. He delights in Tengri's power. Her urge towards the line is as pure and uncomplicated as the pull of gravity. At the far end, Nicolas is so far ahead that he is able to take a tight course around the rock and speed back, passing Younghusband, who's still twenty yards from the turn. Younghusband's face is tense and grim. He knows he can't win. He knows the maps are rightly Nicolas's, and with them all the precious information they contain. He is a gifted horseman, his mount is decent, but Tengri is a prodigious animal. As Nicolas passes him on the home stretch, Younghusband allows his horse to drift across the line, not enough to collide with Tengri, but enough to test her composure and Nicolas's. It is a desperate gambit. Nicolas, knowing how much is at stake, is the one who panics. He snatches at his reins. Tengri stumbles and rears. Nicolas is afraid he will be crushed. A broken pelvis in this place would amount to a death sentence. He pushes against the mane and jumps clear, lands stiffly on both feet, twists, and feels his right leg give. He falls on his side, expecting to pass out, but doesn't. Younghusband has made the turn, reaches him, and dismounts. 'You all right, old man?'

Nicolas feels the jarring pain as two ends of broken bone clash in his lower leg. The agony displaces his appetite for reproach. He knows Younghusband cheated. So does Younghusband. Part of Nicolas also knows that, were he in Younghusband's position, he would have done the same. But there's also a sense of injustice: Nicolas is suffering because of Younghusband's machismo and hurt feelings; the Russian is paying the price for all the Englishman's bad decisions, beginning with that misguided sortie into his tent.

'Call my men,' says Nicolas, through gritted teeth. The command is superfluous. They're already racing on foot towards him.

Tengri is uninjured, but the fall has pulled her girth to one side and the saddle sits wonkily on her back. She stalks back towards Nicolas and nuzzles his hand apologetically.

'I underestimated his pace.' Younghusband is silhouetted against the sun. 'But he's skittish. Reared up from nowhere. A liability in combat. I'm happy to declare the race a draw.'

217

'She's a mare,' says Nicolas quietly, and finally, gratefully, lapses into unconsciousness.

'We parted there, pioneers of the East.'

When Nicolas comes to, his trouser leg is split open to the thigh. He's broken his tibia. The swelling is enormous, but at least the bone hasn't punctured his skin. He'll need medical help and rest, possibly for weeks. Younghusband waves vaguely towards the south-east and says there's a lamasery where he can be tended to in comfort. 'I need to saddle up,' he says. 'It was a pleasure to meet you.' He doesn't offer his hand in farewell. 'Rotten luck, old man.'

Nicolas has no choice but to ride on. The agony of the jarring, broken leg brings on a kind of temporary synaesthesia: he sees the colours of his pain in the corner of one eye, where it bursts like fireworks: gold, viridian and – for the most breathtakingly awful – purple. At one point, he has to stop to be sick, leaning over the saddlebow to keep the vomit off Tengri's coat.

Walid approaches, looks at Nicolas's bleary eyes and pallid face. 'I have something that will help,' he says. He reaches into a pouch on his belt and pulls out a tiny package wrapped in a piece of canvas. Inside is a pair of clay pipes and a dirty plug of something yellow. It looks like earwax. *'Tryak.' Opium.*

The other men watch curiously as Walid prepares a pipe. It is a novelty to watch Nicolas get high. 'The sahib cheated,' Walid says, as he cuts off a piece of the drug and packs it down in the bowl of the pipe. 'Are all such men dishonest?'

'All men believe in fair play when it suits them,' says Nicolas. 'He'll go home and say he was defending the honour of Her Majesty and that he defeated a Russian spy with cunning.'

Walid dismounts and opens his tinderbox. Shielding it from the wind, he strikes sparks onto its contents: a wad of waxed cotton, which he holds to the opium while Nicolas inhales. He gestures to Nicolas to keep the smoke in his lungs.

Nicolas has the feeling that a tiny dot of sunshine is spreading out through the nerves and ganglia in his stomach and lower back. It is a sensation of warmth and euphoria. 'That must be why it's called the *solar plexus*,' he says. 'Imagine that. Language is clever, isn't it?'

'Yes, master,' Walid replies, and nods to the other men to let them know that the medicine is working. It's time to take advantage of its analgesic properties. The men cluck at the horses and urge them forward with their heels.

Walid is concerned that Nicolas is too relaxed to ride properly. He's sitting slumped in his saddle, with his eyes drooping, a glazed half-smile of drugged contentment on his lips. But Tengri senses his delicate condition and picks her way carefully along the path.

The men ride uphill all morning, through a narrowing defile that rises to the top of a ridge. Nicolas is the last to reach the crest. From here, a vast valley of grey rock is spread before them under the sapphire sky. In the sunlight, the ice on the distant glaciers acquires tints of blue and green. 'It's heaven up here,' says Nicolas. 'Maybe time for another pipe?'

'Not now,' says Walid, laughingly, admonishing Nicolas with his finger. 'Not while you are in heaven. Only when you are suffering in hell!' He kicks the flanks of his horse and heads over to the other guides to repeat his bon mot.

They spend midday in the bottom of the Nubra Valley, out of the sun, grateful for the shade of willows that have been pollarded for firewood. As they rest, a caravan approaches: Bactrian camels, humps waggling under the cargo of pashm they're carrying from Ladakh to Kashmir. The greasy matted goat's wool will undergo an alchemical transformation at the hands of the fabled weavers and become fabric of the utmost softness.

Walid helps his master to his feet to greet the traders. Nicolas is at the limits of his linguistic knowhow, but he is able to convey his predicament in gestures and a few words of Urdu and receive rough directions towards the monastery, which seems to lie somewhere over the next range.

The following morning, just after dawn, they cross into the Indus Valley. Below them, the eponymous river is a ribbon of faded grey silk flowing across the khaki earth, watering barley fields, apricots, willows and skinny poplar trees. All day they descend, with agonising slowness, until they reach the bridge of twisted willow that carries them over the water. They hug the river, following its course downstream, until a narrow entrance opens in the vast wall of the Zanskar Range.

Night is falling when they make the final ascent up the winding path to the monastery.

Walid and the other Muslim guides fall silent. They are strangers here and unsure of the reception they can expect. The lamasery building is huge and squat, like a whitewashed keep or tenement, clinging to the contours of the rocky slope.

Nicolas's last dose of opium was two hours ago and its effects have tailed off. His leg is beginning to throb. He'd like another pipe, but Walid needs him compos mentis. None of the guides speaks the local language. Strange sounds are emanating from the monastery: singing, drumming, cymbals, the demented protestations of brass horns.

Walid and Omar help Nicolas dismount and carry him through the gates and towards the noise. Nicolas senses his men's discomfort – they have fallen among mysterious pagans: the profusion of gods, the sculptures of threatening deities, the colours and strangeness of the temple carvings. The noise grows louder and more disturbing until they emerge into the temple courtyard. Monks in maroon robes, crested red hats and devil masks are dancing in the courtyard before a huge audience of local people who regard the interlopers with intense but unthreatening curiosity.

Nicolas reassures his men: it is the annual festival, an auspicious time to arrive. But he doesn't fully believe it himself.

To his astonishment, a man he takes to be the senior abbot welcomes him in English and indicates to his men that they should bring their master to an upper storey.

Nicolas is carried with great care up two flights of stairs and into a private chamber with a flagstone floor. It is fragrant with the earthy smell of incense. He is placed on a low, soft bed and given a bowl of salty, greasy tea to drink and two pellets of a herbal substance that he can't identify, but which induces almost immediate profound and dreamless sleep.

'I convalesced at the monastery for three weeks.'

Coming to – is it hours or days later? – the first thing Nicolas sees is a smooth young face, as round and congenial as a harvest moon. It belongs to a novice monk in red robes who gives his name as Sonam.

Sonam fusses around Nicolas, propping his leg on pillows, applying a splint, which he fixes expertly in place with tight bandages. The pressure of the dressing immediately relieves the ache in the limb, but Sonam indicates in gestures that Nicolas is not to stand up. He turns his back while Nicolas uses the chamber pot and then carries it smilingly away as though its contents are rare and precious. A few minutes later he returns with a tray of food: barley porridge in a lacquered bowl; a teardrop of barley flatbread; and butter tea, which Nicolas will mentally make palatable by pretending it's his mother's chicken soup.

Nicolas is remarkably hungry, but pauses to bow his head over the tray to say a brief grace. Half a century later, he still can't think about the accident without a shiver of dread. 'Nineteen times out of twenty, such a thing ends in death,' the old man tells his listener.

Vincenzo accepts this estimate is probably accurate, but he also understands that Notovitch is making a grander assertion: his arrival at the monastery was more than lucky; it was providential.

At the end of the meal, Sonam takes the tray and mimes sleep by inclining his cheek onto his folded hands. It will be almost a week before the two men realise that they both speak Hindi.

All day, between snatches of unconsciousness, Nicolas tracks the progress of a square of sunlight from one side of the room to the other. Distant chanting, enforced rest, and the sweet woodsmoke-scented air gradually induce an almost blissful sense of calm. He fondly recollects a languorous childhood convalescence from whooping cough; an oasis of indulgence in the sternness of his early years. When the rectangle of light reaches the far wall, and its shade has deepened to a brassy yellow, the door opens once again.

It is Sonam, this time accompanied by the monk who welcomed Nicolas to the monastery: Nangawan Tanzin, a straight-backed middle-aged man in maroon robes with a shaven head and a face the colour of old canvas. He enquires kindly in English whether Nicolas has been able to rest.

'He had studied in Calcutta and Lahore.'

Tanzin is a man of impressive learning; Nicolas remarks on his fluent English. The monk explains that the chief lama of the monastery took a personal interest in his education. 'The Statsang Raspa Rinpoche sent me to study in Calcutta. Thanks to his patronage, I received a stipend and my fees were paid. In return, he made me promise to come back to the monastery. He died when I was away, so upon the completion of my studies, I returned to teach him in his new incarnation.'

Nicolas is thrown by this revelation, having assumed that he was addressing the chief lama himself. He explains his confusion.

'I am the chief lama's teacher and adviser,' says Tanzin. 'The Rinpoche is of course very keen to greet you himself, but I have pointed out to him that he has homework to finish.

Regrettably, he is not yet a conscientious student. So I am using your presence here to inspire him to greater efforts. I have told him that meeting you is a privilege conditional on his obtaining sufficient marks in his algebra prep.' The monk smiles at his subterfuge. 'In our traditions of meditation, we call this method *using the false to cultivate the real*. I think tomorrow is soon enough for you to make each other's acquaintance.'

Fifty years of constant spiritual practice have given the monk a serenity that can be discomfiting: he is a clear pool, reflecting the character and preoccupations of the people he encounters.

It's a difficult meeting for Nicolas. Twenty-four hours of introspection have been plenty. Already, his mind is troubled with darker reminiscences: Anya, Bessie, Skobelev, Rachkovsky. He doesn't want to lie there another day thinking about them. He feels an instinct to flee which his mind refines into a number of seemingly practical thoughts: he is needed in Calcutta by December; winter will cut off the passes from the monastery; he has half a dozen important interviews to conduct before the New Year.

So, raising himself onto the tasselled bolster, Nicolas thanks the monk for his care in a sincere but formal way that is a prelude to valediction. He explains that he came with a number of men who are probably encamped in the vicinity of the monastery. Would it be possible—? In the first of many eerie anticipations of the invalid's needs, the abbot bows his head before Nicolas has finished his sentence and summons Walid, who is standing just outside the room.

Barefoot, holding his cap in his hand, Walid places his

right palm over his heart to acknowledge the abbot's greeting, and squats down on his haunches by Nicolas's low bed, bringing with him the reassuring but alien smells of turmeric, wool and horses.

Walid tells Nicolas what he already knows to be the case: it would be foolish to continue until the leg has had a chance to heal. The outlook for the weather is favourable. The men are content to wait. He's found a sheltered spot to corral the animals. In the case of early snow, there's a pass to the southwest that has been recommended by a Turkmen merchant.

Nicolas is hardly listening. His face feels hot and there's a buzzing in his ears. He wrestles in vain with this unfamiliar sensation. Opening his mouth, he gives a sob of grief. Once he's started crying, nothing – not shame, not Walid's puzzled face, nor any sense of impropriety – can make him stop.

Tanzin leads the men out of the room. As he leaves, he places a book wrapped in velvet cloth by the bed. When Nicolas inspects it later, it turns out to be a copy of the Bible, a King James on onion skin, printed in Bombay.

'The Rinpoche himself was not yet ten years old.'

Shaven-headed, precociously poised, the boy arrives after supper the following day. He combines the unsettling direct gaze of a self-assured child with the spiritual confidence of his sixteen previous lifetimes. He sits at the end of Nicolas's bed and fires questions at him in Tibetan.

'His Holiness the Rinpoche asks if you have ever travelled on a train,' says Tanzin. 'They are a particular enthusiasm of His Holiness.'

To the Rinpoche's obvious pleasure, the answer is in the affirmative. He turns to Tanzin and says something else. Nicolas thinks he can make out his own name.

'His Holiness asks what it was like,' says Tanzin.

Nicolas takes a sheet of paper out of his writing case and draws the outline of a locomotive. He is a decent draughtsman: his adventures in British India have often occasioned the need for accurate technical drawings. The Rinpoche watches, chattering happily as the train takes shape and Nicolas labels the various parts. In conclusion, Nicolas gives him the drawing.

Delighted, the Rinpoche bows and utters a speech of thanks, which he waits for Tanzin to translate.

'The Rinpoche expresses his gratitude. He also asks if you will be joining your family on their journey.'

'As far as I know, my wife and child are in Paris,' Nicolas replies. 'Ultimately, I will return there, yes.'

The tiny Rinpoche's arms are folded inside the quilted sleeves of his robes. He speaks again, but this time the high, unbroken voice seems to project a strange authority. 'But the Rinpoche says you have a mother living, a brother, sisters?'

Nicolas nods dumbfoundedly. How the devil would he know that? Nicolas has the close-mouthed habits of a well-trained spook. He's a master at not divulging personal details.

'The Rinpoche says they are on a journey.'

Nicolas's face is a picture of astonishment. The Rinpoche laughs, a child again, taking pleasure at the stranger's perplexity.

Tanzin smiles. 'I apologise if we have alarmed you. Certain powers arise naturally as we progress towards enlightenment. In our tradition, we are taught not be distracted by them, but it is a kind of vanity to dismiss them entirely. The Rinpoche has been made aware of the existence of your family and the fact that they are on a journey. He says they are travelling to the land of Issa.'

A gong sounds in a distant part of the monastery. The Rinpoche bows. Before he leaves, he adds another sentence, with the conspiratorial air of someone violating a cosmic vow of secrecy to bring good news. 'He is telling you that they will arrive safely,' says Tanzin.

The abbot follows the Rinpoche out, but pauses at the low doorway to turn again. 'The Rinpoche says there is also Issa in your destiny.'

Tanzin's heavy tread accompanies the rapid steps of the Rinpoche, running down the corridor in his eagerness to fly a new kite.

'I was puzzled by the reference to Issa.'

Walid visits after lunch to give Nicolas a situation report on the men and horses, and also to make sure the master is well. The tears took everyone by surprise. Over the months they've been travelling together, Nicolas has impressed his men with his healthy balance of compassion and toughness. But Walid has seen a few sahibs lose it entirely in the mountains, and it's never the ones you expect. He's gratified to see his boss looking much more like his old self, if a little distracted.

Nicolas gazes out of the window as Walid goes through the likely additional costs of keeping the men on in Hemis.

He nods occasionally, assenting to the disbursement of funds, but appears to be wrapped up in his own thoughts.

At the conclusion of the discussion, Walid picks up his cap and begins to fold his woollen blanket over the shoulders of his kameez. Nicolas turns to him. 'Issa, Walid, *Issa?*'

Walid is momentarily puzzled. There's no one of such a name among the men or the horses. Besides, he's accounted for everyone, from Ali to Zulfugar. Now there's an Issa to worry about? 'Issa, sahib?'

Nicolas nods.

Walid shakes his head. He's never met anyone of that name, man, woman or horse. He reaches for the closest thing he has in the way of a homonym: '*Isa*, sahib?'

'Isa?'

'Isa the prophet. Isa ibn Maryam, peace be upon him.'

'Isa ibn Maryam?'

'Yes, sahib.'

Jesus, son of Mary.

Nicolas turns his head again to contemplate the view from the window. Walid leaves him sunk in thought, feeling less certain now that his master's really on the mend. Is it possible that he bumped his head when he fell?

'The abbot visited me each evening before prayers.'

At night, the monastery is lit with oil lamps. The flames smell faintly sweet and burn yellow – the colour of the butter that fuels them. Studying Nicolas's face in the dim light, the abbot notes a new alertness in the invalid: a blazing in the eyes that could be mistaken for fever.

'Issa – it's your name for Jesus,' Nicolas says. 'Jesus, Yeshua, Issa – the same name in different faiths.'

The abbot lifts a sputtering oil lamp and uses a long metal pin to draw out the wick. 'What you call *faiths*, we call the disguises of the lost reality.' Satisfied with the adjustment, he places the lamp beside its companions on a brass tray. 'Even the greatest sage is uttering truth in whispers. As it passes from mouth to ear to mouth it acquires inevitable distortions. Here, we cultivate stillness in order to regain the clarity of that first breath.' He picks up the Bible from Nicolas's bed. 'More unites us than divides us. In your holy book also, contraries arise from the void – that is the beginning of all. Behind the false oppositions, reality. Behind the ten thousand things, the way.'

The long flames of the butter lamps leave purple afterimages on Nicolas's eyelids when he blinks. The effect recalls the paraffin lantern in his father's shop, by the light of which he memorised human anatomy, learned about the circulation of the blood and lymph, and whose heat awoke the dreams of India that foreshadowed just such a moment as this.

'And what do you know of Issa?' Nicolas asks.

'What you know from your gospel. He was born, he attained enlightenment, he taught, he was put to death.'

'He was born of a virgin,' Nicolas says.

'So it is written in your scripture,' the abbot replies politely. Into the ensuing silence, he projects this unmistakable thought: *whether it is true or not is of no account.*

'He rose again on the third day,' Nicolas asserts, with a touch of defensiveness.

The abbot inclines his head. 'Similarly, it is written.' Light flares from one of the lamps. And then modestly, tentatively, he offers the extraordinary gift: 'And I know also what is written in our secret books.'

'The Bible is famously silent on the subject of Jesus's youth.'

It is the biggest lacuna in all literature: of all the volumes of the secret books, what compares?

From his precocious appearance aged twelve, impressing his elders in the synagogue with his wisdom and maturity, until the beginning of his ministry – at the age, according to Luke 3:23, of about thirty – there is nothing. Almost twenty years of the most significant life in history are missing.

Twenty years: a span that encompassed Uncle Leonard's entire existence – birth, school, nineteen birthdays. How many dawns, how many sunsets, as he hurtled through time towards his premature end? How many hours spent gazing at someone's peachy skin under a Sunday hat in the chapel? How much unconscious delight in being inside his own pale body as he turns in the water of the lido, or rubs his white flesh dry with a rough towel at the poolside? *Shell Wound. Chest and Abdomen. Died 5:30 AM.*

What could possibly have filled those years?

Some, descendants of the haruspex perhaps, have argued that the silence itself is significant: there is nothing to say of that time. Jesus lived a life like all other young men of his class and era. And therefore he was almost certainly married, otherwise the gospel-writers would have bothered to tell us.

Within that gap, drawing from two tiny hints in Mark and Matthew, tradition constructs the fleeting image of a carpenter's apprentice.

The tall young man is muscular and eerily self-possessed amid the knock and song of the woodworker's tools.

But the Greek word translated as carpenter is *tekton*, meaning a craftsman, and that itself is probably a translation of the Aramaic word *naggar*, which can also mean a scholar.

The plane and hammer vanish; and the curls of sweet-smelling cedar disappear. The floor is littered with offcuts of paper and spotted with ink. A less jockish, more bookish Jesus copies an ancient scroll in a clear and distinctive hand.

But why indeed a scholar or a carpenter? Why not something else? The gospels, and the reality that depends on them, alter more or less alarmingly as we reconceive the stories in apocryphal alternatives: the protagonist of the New Testament as a shopkeeper, or a fisherman, a merchant, a glover, a butcher, a former soldier, an ex-pimp, or a repentant criminal. In some volumes of the secret books, He is Himself Judas.

'He ordered the books to be brought to me.'

The abbot lays a bundle in Nicolas's lap and unwraps its layers of coverings. 'These are our only copies,' he says. 'They are slow to make, and . . .' He smiles and shrugs: 'Not all knowledge is for all people.' Within the cloths are two tiny volumes.

Nicolas opens them carefully. They are two codices of brittle paper, made of palm leaves, folded like an accordion, their alien handwritten pages illuminated with images of men and demons.

They are so old as to have shed any sense of human manufacture. They have the same inevitable form as driftwood, and the same auratic power.

'What do they say?'

'Sonam was appointed my translator.'

As Vincenzo sits, watching the needle inscribe Notovitch's words on the wax cylinder, he dimly understands that the two of them are re-enacting an old drama. Notovitch is re-staging what he regards as the formative scene of his entire existence.

There is no doubt about it, this moment represents the summit of Notovitch's life. Everything, from his stowing-away on the *Derby* onwards, has been leading to this point. It is the culmination and vindication of who he is. He has been entrusted with an extraordinary responsibility: a document of incalculable importance. Besides the work of the translation, everything else fades into insignificance. The deaths of Bessie and Skobelev, Anya's adultery, his life back home in Paris – it all seems eerily distant from the place in which he finds himself. Nicolas feels as though he has been raised up physically to a new plane in order to fulfil this task. At this higher altitude, his view of life is Olympian, vast, and no doubt a little chilly.

Nicolas and Sonam work every morning and afternoon in three-hour bursts. According to Buddhist custom, the codices must be unwrapped each time the men begin and wrapped up again when they end their labour.

The volumes are protected by nine different coverings: the outermost is pristine blue velvet, the inner ones increasingly frayed fabric, the innermost mere scraps of ancient canvas that suggest fragments of a sail or shroud. These rags must be painstakingly gathered around the volumes, but Nicolas never begrudges the extra work.

Surveying his whole life, he cannot recall such a feeling of industriousness and well-being. He has perfect mental clarity and a kind of inner calm. Despite the differences between them, he finds in Sonam a congenial collaborator. Since the text is in Pali, a dead language and one completely unfamiliar to Nicolas, he relies on Sonam to make a rough oral translation into Hindi, which he jots down in the shorthand he uses for interviews. The two men then work over sections of five to ten verses at a time, refining the text until it is ready for Nicolas to render into French.

'When I am remembered, it will be for this thing above all others.'

It is a short text – around five thousand words in the original, a little longer in Nicolas's translation, because Pali is a highly condensed language. A few of the pages are illegible. Nicolas feels compelled to take some liberties with the ordering of events to make it more coherent, and reconstructs the Pali verses in a roughly chronological sequence.

From the moment the gospel begins to shed its secrets, Nicolas is in no doubt of the extraordinary nature of the document, but his astonishment finds no reflection in the imperturbable face of Sonam. Yet the revelations the book contains are shattering – for adherents of both the Jewish and Christian faiths.

The Pali gospel opens with a conventional lamentation for Issa's death. News of his crucifixion has reached the author of the work in India (Notovitch presumes the author to be male), who then sets down everything he knows and has learned from Jewish merchants about the life of this remarkable man.

But before dealing with the life of Issa, the chronicler gives his readers a brief history of the Israelites. The people of Israel, he writes, fell into servitude under Pharaoh after losing the favour of their god. Their deliverance, as in the biblical account, was thanks to the guidance of the prophet Moses – in Pali, Mossa. But, in this version, Moses is not a Jew at all: he is a son of Pharaoh. Barely three hundred words into the text, and the foundational myths of monotheism are crumbling.

Lightly skipping over a millennium of history, the gospel-writer describes how, after Mossa's death, the Israelites gradually abandoned their religion; they fought among themselves and were absorbed into the Roman Empire. Humiliated, the Israelites call upon their god for redemption. In verses unmistakably inflected with Buddhist sensibility, the gospel author describes how their prayers are answered.

Forty years on, closing his eyes, Notovitch can still summon up the sonorous French of his translation. His voice sounds rough and oracular in the half-dark of the sitting room. '*Et l'Esprit éternel, qui demeurait dans un état d'inaction complète et de suprême béatitude, se réveilla et se détacha, pour une période indéterminée, de l'Être éternel.*'

And the eternal Spirit, which dwelt in a state of perfect stillness and surpassing joy, arose and unbound itself, for a time, from the eternal Being.

The Pali author writes that Jesus – Issa – is born to a humble family in Galilee. There is no star, no crib, no lowing cattle or visiting magi, but the child's divine mission is evident from the moment he learns to talk.

God himself spoke through the mouth of this child of the woes of the flesh and the glory of the spirit.

While much in the Pali gospel contradicts the Old and New Testaments, there is also much that confirms the biblical accounts. In the childhood of Issa, there is an echo of the moment in Mark and Luke where Jesus confounds his elders in the synagogue. But the author of the new gospel amplifies it into a more vivid and charming scene that evokes Issa's domestic life and his place in Jewish society. The boy holds court in his parents' house, sharing his wisdom with 'rich and well-born people'. Amid the respect and love of his countrymen, the child grows to manhood.

And then, in chapter 4, verse 12 of the Pali gospel, comes the most extraordinary turn. On reaching the age of thirteen, Issa faces the customary pressure to take a wife, but he resists:

And so it came to pass that Issa went forth in secret from the home of his parents, departed from Jerusalem, and in the company of merchants made his way towards India, with the intention of making complete his knowledge of the holy word and of studying the laws of the great Buddhas.

'So we knew: the lost years of Jesus were spent in India.'

'I held the proof in my hand,' says Notovitch. He regards his lumpy fingers with bewilderment. 'I can still see the pages.' He leans forward in his seat and fixes Vincenzo with a stare. 'Everything – everything! – we understood about the origin of Christianity had to be revised in the light of this discovery.'

Vincenzo is moved by the passion in Notovitch's voice. The old man who sits before him blazes with his sense of conviction. Racked with arthritis, he has borne many names and been many things in a single lifetime – a runaway, a husband, a father, a cuckold, a businessman, an author, an adventurer, a spy. But as long as there is breath in his body, he will insist that *this* is who he really is: the discoverer of this lost antiquity.

According to the abbot's secret book, Issa first arrives in India on a merchant ship, laden with glass and gold. He disembarks at a port in the south near present-day Mahabalipuram. Instead of rejoining the ship, he decides to stay on in India, and spends several years travelling among the Hindus, studying their arts of healing. But his monotheism and egalitarianism set him at odds with the ruling priest and warrior castes. 'God the Father made no distinction between his children, who are all equally dear to him,' Issa tells the outraged Brahmins and Kshatriyas.

Their furious response culminates in an attempt on his life and Issa is forced to flee. He travels north, into Nepal, where he shelters in a monastery and applies himself to learning Pali and studying the sacred texts of Buddhism:

Six years having passed, Issa, whom Buddha had chosen to spread his holy word, was perfect in his knowledge of the blessed sutras.

Nicolas can't help remembering what the abbot said: *Behind the false oppositions, reality. Behind the ten thousand things, the way.* The script on the ancient pages of the secret books has given birth to a new history.

There is an olive-complexioned man among the rows of dark-skinned Buddhist monks. He wakes each day at four to bathe and chant the scriptures. He sits long hours in prayer and contemplation. He gives himself to the mundane and often unpleasant tasks of the monastery with mindful humility. The exacting rituals of mealtimes are another form of meditation, compelling attention to the present moment, to the eternal *thou art.* No longer young, and not yet old, he has the eerie composure that comes from having penetrated his vast inner stillness and seen that it is identical with the order of the universe. A decision ripens within him and one day, he awakens to a sense that it is time for him to leave. He visits the chief lama and the two of them sit silently. No words pass between them. Finally, the abbot breaks the silence to grant the adept permission to depart. Jesus the Buddhist passes through the monastery gates for the last time, carrying nothing but his robes, his staff and begging bowl.

Over years of silent meditation, he has lived every one of the iterations of the secret books. Two miles from the monastery, he stops to drink water from a mountain spring that flows out from a cleft in a granite rock. He knows it foreshadows a Roman sword piercing his torso. In its cold pulse he both senses and accepts his inevitable destiny.

His journey west takes him through Persia, where he encounters Zoroastrians – Parsees – whom he cannot shake
from their devotion to a pagan god. Rather than contesting
their errors, he continues on his way, knowing his vocation
lies further on. Finally, aged twenty-nine, he arrives home in
Judea, to be baptised by John into a ministry that is at once
familiar and radically transformed.

'There were losses and gains for everyone.'

'All of us – everyone within the tradition of Abraham – had to
let go of some cherished beliefs,' says Notovitch. 'Father David
had baptised me into the Church of the Risen Christ. From the
Pali gospel, I learned that the resurrection never happened.'

Even for Vincenzo, who takes the claims of religion with
a hefty pinch of salt, this comes as a shock. There are other
big and jarring discrepancies between the Pali gospel and the
authorised texts: no virgin birth, no angels or miracles, and
no Judas.

Upon his return to his birthplace, Issa wanders through
Judea, preaching and attracting disciples. The account the
text gives of his travels and teaching has parallels with the
authorised gospels, but it also echoes other non-canonical
works, particularly the Coptic Greek *Gospel of Thomas*.
Notovitch will never know this extraordinary book, which
is not discovered until 1945 in an earthenware jar in the Nile
Valley by a camel-herder digging for fertiliser.

The authors of the Pali text and the *Gospel of Thomas* were
separated by language, time and vast distances. They can

have known nothing of each other's work. And yet, reading them side by side, one feels as though they are reflections of the same far-off light: an itinerant prophet with rough-spun clothes and dust on his feet, who breaks bread with sinners, and teases his followers towards enlightenment with koan-like riddles.

The Pali Jesus speaks of the kingdom of heaven in the same puzzling terms as the Jesus of the Coptic gospel: it is a mustard seed; it is the union of opposites; it is simultaneously inside and outside you. Both texts make it clear that whatever it is, the kingdom of heaven represents no threat to temporal power. Their Jesus is not the Jewish revolutionary others have imagined, bent on tearing down Roman power and the corrupt religious authority of the Temple.

Nonetheless, the Pali gospel describes how Jesus's ministry begins to arouse the suspicions of the Roman authorities. In the absence of Judas, the intimate betrayer, the villain of the Pali text is the Roman governor, Pilate. Ruthless, capricious, fearing revolt, he grows increasingly anxious that Issa is planning some kind of insurrection. He comes up with spurious reasons to have the preacher arrested, tortures him and then hands him over to the Jewish authorities for trial.

Here is another major departure from the standard biblical narrative. The Jewish elders question Issa and find no grounds on which to punish him. They tell Pilate that none of Issa's teachings contradicts Jewish law. This infuriates Pilate, who orders Issa to be put to death. Powerless to alter the sentence, the Jewish authorities nonetheless register their objection to it symbolically. They adopt the gesture that the gospel-writer Matthew attributes to Pilate:

Having spoken, the priests and the wise elders departed and washed their hands in a holy vessel saying: 'We are innocent of the death of this just man.'

Pilate is unmoved. Christ is taken to Golgotha and crucified between the two thieves. It takes him a day to die. There are no last words, no temple curtain being rent in two, no 'Father, forgive them', no '*Eli, eli, lama sabachthani.*'
The climax is understated and brief:

At sunset, the agonies of Issa came to an end. He lost consciousness and the soul of this righteous man departed his body to become one again with the Holy Spirit.

Upon Jesus's death, Pilate orders the body to be handed over to his family for burial, but then he has a change of heart:

Three days later, the governor sent his soldiers to remove the body of Issa and lay it to rest in some other place, for fear that the people would rise up.

The Pali Jesus dies like any other man, his body subject to the same irreversible biological laws. There is no water-walking, no feeding multitudes with a basket of loaves and fishes, no supernatural powers, no triumph over death to dazzle the wavering unbelievers. Whatever makes his ministry special must be looked for elsewhere.

'What did you expect would happen?'

'Expect?'

'When the document was revealed to the public.'

It is one of Vincenzo's occasional recorded interventions. The exchange is audible at the beginning of the fourteenth roll, the last of four recorded on a single day in March 1933. Hearing Vincenzo's voice, I'm struck by the strength of his Italian accent: *happen* has no *h*; *revealed* is given three distinct syllables.

In the long silence that follows, you sense Notovitch pondering the question's implications: a Buddhist Jesus, a resurrection that never happened, an Egyptian Moses. How had he imagined these revelations would be received? How, indeed?

He closes his eyes, trying to experience the hopes of the man he had been. Half a century later, what he recalls is barely the memory of a memory. *What happened* is a jealous god. It takes possession of the present and puts to death *what might have been.*

Notovitch seems suddenly old. 'I'm tired,' he says, rising and fumbling to turn up the lamp. 'We will continue our work next week.'

The voices cease. The needle begins to drift in the virgin wax.

But Notovitch has not exaggerated the significance of the find. If anything, he's underplayed it. Fate had chosen him to be the emissary of an astonishing truth. Philologists and scholars of comparative theology have long speculated about the origins of Christian thought. What are its debts to other systems of belief? What whispers reached Judea from the East? What echoes of strange thoughts might a bright, curious young Jew have pick up in the bazaars of Galilee? What more insubstantial treasures were brought from India and Han China along with glistening bolts of silk, jade and porcelain?

The pages of the secret gospel finally prove the kinship between the religions of the East and West. Its ecumenical Jesus is a revolutionary figure, steeped in the philosophies of distant lands, capable of speaking to the world in a new language of brotherhood.

And if that were all, it would be plenty. But there is much more. There is the text's extraordinary exoneration of the Jews.

From the authorised accounts of the four evangelists, it's clear who bears the ultimate blame for the crucifixion. There are divergences in the gospel-writers' individual versions, but in each one, Pilate bends to the wishes of the implacable Jewish crowd.

Pilate's reluctance to put Jesus to death varies in intensity from gospel to gospel, achieving its most dramatic form in Matthew. Matthew even informs us that Pilate's wife had a prophetic dream about Christ's innocence and urged her husband to have nothing to do with his killing.

And by the simple maths of storytelling, as Pilate's unwillingness to persecute increases, so does the bloodthirstiness of the mob.

After the handwashing that establishes Pilate's innocence symbolically, the crowd claim responsibility for the execution with a unanimity that, even in the spare writing of Matthew's gospel, seems inflected with a heartless pride. 'And with one voice the people cried, "His blood be on us and on our children."'

His blood be on us and on our children. It's a responsibility that they have recklessly declared to be heritable. This will be a fiction with terrible consequences for their descendants. This will establish the Jews as the people who killed Jesus. This will become the pseudo-theological justification for two millennia of persecution. This will be the glowing centre of a constellation of hatreds that will belatedly acquire a name in 1879: anti-Semitism.

'There can be no expiation,' fulminates the fourth-century saint John Chrysostom, 'no indulgence, no pardon; vengeance is without end, and Jews will live under the yoke of servitude forever.' Generations of Christian tormentors do their best to make his words prophetic.

Growing up Jewish in the Pale of Settlement, all this Nicolas knows, but he now knows too that the charge of deicide was a bum rap; the Jew-haters have got the wrong guys: according to the Pali gospel, the blood guilt rests on Pilate.

*

THE TRANSLATION TAKES the best part of two weeks. Nicolas, usually fluent to the point of prolixity, fusses uncharacteristically over the precise wording of the verses. He struggles to clarify the nuances of the original text with Sonam and to render them accurately in French. After a slight reordering and a final pass for elegance, he pronounces the work complete. Imperceptibly and with eerie speed, his leg has fully healed.

Two days before his departure, Nicolas sets up his photographic equipment in the courtyard of the monastery.

The books are carried outside. In the glare of the midday sun, Nicolas eternises half a dozen of their pages on a series of photographic plates.

Then, having instructed a junior monk on the operation of the camera, Nicolas positions himself, Sonam, the abbot, Walid and the other men around the books. The tiny Rinpoche takes the place of honour at the front, as befits his seniority.

Nicolas returns several times to the camera, burying his head under its cloth and using a loupe to check the borders of the upside-down image for sharpness. Finally satisfied, he tells the monk to shoot a five-second exposure. The men stand, frowning into the lens, with the Himalayan air nipping their nostrils, prayer flags flapping behind them.

This photograph, taken one afternoon in Ladakh, is destined to become an emblem of the new era's zeal for discovery: Howard Carter by Tutankhamun's tomb, Scott's men with vast canvas mittens protecting their frostbitten hands, Mallory and Irvine on the North Face of Everest attaching their rudimentary breathing apparatus, Amelia Earhart, tomboyishly beautiful, perching on the rungs of her red Lockheed.

'My official mission concluded in Bombay.'

Nicolas arrives back in Paris in the middle of January 1888. Heavy snow delays the train from Marseilles and it pulls into the Gare de Lyon just after one o'clock in the morning.

After the long weeks of travel, Hemis, the Himalayan peaks, the glacial light, the smoke and incense of the monastery seem like the recollection of a dream. But in Nicolas's personal valise, alongside the topographic reports that are too precious to consign to even the most secure mail, is his translation of the Pali gospel.

Steam billows around him, rises and dissipates in the cavernous roof as he steps down onto the platform of the eerily cold and empty station. Nicolas has the unmistakable sense that he is walking in the footsteps of the prophets, descending through the clouds of Mount Sinai carrying freshly carved stone tablets.

Eager to be home, he orders his trunks to be sent on after him and takes the only cab in the station forecourt.

For months, Nicolas has been indulging in fantasies about his return and the book's reception. Now he experiences the inevitable bathos of homecoming.

The discoverer of the lost gospel creeps into his house in the sober grey light of a Parisian winter morning, eats some cold tongue from the pantry and goes to sleep on the couch in his clothes.

He is woken by a child poking him in the face with a toy windmill. 'Funny man doing?' says the boy. Instead of being amazed that his son has acquired the power of speech, Nicolas is surprised by how small he is. The boy is still a tiny incontinent child, albeit one with rudimentary powers of communication. Nicolas feels as though he has been away for a decade, while, in reality, he's barely been gone six months. Daylight reveals the filthiness of the cold apartment. Anya has fired the cleaning woman for stealing and been unable to find a replacement. A coffee cup that Nicolas left behind the drapes in the drawing room in July is still there, the desiccated grounds in the bottom resembling a smear of brown varnish.

'Owing to the monsoon rains, my letters home had not been received.'

Or, perhaps, not written? When he picked up his pen in India and wrote the words 'My dear Anya', what went through his head? A spasm of jealousy that he wasn't even entitled to feel, for a wife he had chosen for venal reasons and then neglected? *You're being very dog-in-the-mangerish, dear boy. Uncharacteristically controlling. After all, no one misses a slice off a cut loaf.*

I think he snapped the letter case shut and tried to put the betrayal out of his mind. He'd write to Suvorin instead, or Osip. Sometimes he would get drunk on Madeira and then venture out for a massage in the red-light district. He'd manage to feign surprise each time the Anglo-Indian masseuse put her hand on his penis. At the moment of orgasm, he thought of Bessie, sometimes alive, sometimes bleeding to death on her bed, and then he would leave, feeling as though the transaction had cheapened everyone. Leaving the rights and wrongs of sex tourism aside, it's worth noting how little consolation he derives at this point from the Pali gospel.

With Nicolas back in Paris, the atmosphere in the malodorous flat – steeping nappies, dead mice, decaying food – is unbearably tense.

Almost without realising it, Nicolas is cold and punishing to his depressed, lonely and heavily pregnant wife. It is not his finest hour. He sleeps in a separate room, avoids touching either his wife or son, and is icily polite to both of them. For Anya it is, frankly, a form of torture. One afternoon, while Nicolas is working at his desk, she pours a pot of lukewarm tea on his head. He professes to be mystified by her behaviour, while exulting in the fact that he has reduced her to a parody of unreason and hysteria.

She falls sobbing to the floor, telling him he's a monster.

As Nicolas packs his bag, he feels a kind of relief. And I wonder if the credentials of any aspiring prophet would survive the scrutiny of his domestic life.

Returning to Mère Gigout's, Nicolas finds a stroke has made his old landlady doddery and a surly niece is running things now. The price of the garret flat has doubled and the place is dirtier and damper than he remembers. In the ceiling above the bed is a patch of mould that, in a certain light, resembles Rachkovsky in profile.

This place, when he returned to it in memories, evoked one of the happiest times of his life. Now he asks himself if the past was ever the way we remember it.

'My cousin Osip had come to Paris.'

It's been an age since they last met, but they're immediately so close that there's no question of dissimulation. Nicolas explains that Anya's gone mad. Osip says he's struggling to find work. He's come third-class to Paris in the hope of getting some translations commissioned. His journalism is out of favour and no one will put on his plays. He tells Nicolas that what makes his life tolerable is his wife, Irina. 'Without her, I don't know how I'd manage,' he says. 'Having a helpmeet.

A companion. But if things don't pick up, we'll be forced to do something drastic.'

'Like what?'

'We're thinking.'

Osip's suit is smart enough, but ill-fitting, and his shoes are so worn that they've burst out around his feet.

Nicolas insists he take a pair from his wardrobe and adds a silk tie for good measure. 'See? Who'll be able to refuse you now?'

He feels able to tell Osip about his discovery. His cousin is reassuringly enthusiastic. It's not lost on Nicolas that their positions are reversed. He remembers visiting Osip's cold apartment all those years ago and his blithe confidence then that marriage was a mousetrap he would be clever enough to avoid.

'I had to moderate my impatience to see the book in print.'

There is a long, almost mystifying delay between Nicolas's departure from the monastery and the gospel's first publication in Paris.

He left Hemis at the end of 1887. The quarto volume containing his translation of the Pali manuscript and an account of its discovery will not appear before the public until 1894.

Seven years will have passed since its discovery. Seven years is one of the conventional intervals of myth, connected to some deeper sense of human timekeeping, perhaps even some physiological pace of change. Which of us will be the same after seven years? Who, even now, is Nicolas?

Sometimes I feel I know him well, sometimes I see only a succession of names and masks, sometimes not even that: a cold breeze, a heart that will one day be a heap of ashes, a hand holding a pen. Regretfully, I recognise bad habits that he shares with me, alongside talents that I entirely lack.

Even his surname is a kind of deception. Since his early twenties, he's conspired with the mispronunciation *Know-tah-vitch* in order to move away from the more accurate but more alien *Nah-taw-vitch*.

On his return to Paris, the first person he shows the manuscript to is Father David. No one in Nicolas's circle, perhaps no one anywhere, knows him as well as the Georgian priest who has overseen his conversion, facilitated his marriage and conducted the funeral service of the woman he loved. But despite the closeness between them, Nicolas prefers to let the text speak for itself. He painstakingly copies it by hand – he doesn't want to let the original out of his sight, and he fears the possibility of unauthorised reproductions – and sends it round to the priest with a brief letter asking him to read it as soon as possible. In the exuberance of his dispatching it, he cannot imagine the manuscript eliciting a negative response.

A week passes and still no word from the priest. Nicolas's anxieties have begun to mount. He considers writing, but his impatience won't allow it. Finally, he turns up unannounced after the morning mass and finds Father David in the vestry, putting his surplice on a coat hanger and cinching a thick belt round the waist of his long black robes.

'I read it the day you sent it,' Father David says, raking his grey-streaked beard with massy fingers. A more impartial observer than Nicolas would see steeliness and a certain sorrow in the priest's demeanour. 'Come.' He leads Nicolas into his study and pours each of them a glass of khvanchkara – a sugary red wine from northern Georgia.

Nicolas takes his glass. He is bursting with his desire to know the priest's opinion. From the sacred corner of the room – upper right, opposite the entrance – an icon of the Virgin clutching a prematurely wizened baby Jesus gazes down at him with reproach in her sad face.

'*Gaumarjos.*' Father David raises his glass and looks into Nicolas's eyes over the top of it, as though he's lining him up in a rifle sight.

'*Santé,*' says Nicolas, swallowing half a glass. It's sickly-sweet and tastes like communion wine. 'So what did you think?'

'It is fascinating, certainly fascinating,' murmurs the priest, reflexively touching the heavy chain and crucifix that hang around his neck.

'Oh, it's fascinating, all right,' says Nicolas, proudly. 'It's . . .' He makes the sound of an explosion and with his free hand mimes a bomb going off above his right ear.

'Yes, fascinating . . .' says the priest, already resisting slightly the grand claim implied in Nicolas's gesture. He sits with his legs widely parted, booted feet flat on the floor. Sitting or standing, the soles of his feet always seem braced against the earth's core. It's part of what gives his words such authority. 'Fascinating, but perhaps not so . . . important.'

'Not important? Are you kidding me . . . ?' Nicolas begins to protest, but Father David cuts him off with slow, deliberate words.

The priest wipes his mouth with the back of his hand.

'The world is very simple,' he says. 'Love one another, love God. How many gospels do we need to tell us this?'

'But I'm filling a gap with entirely new knowledge. We have to reconsider the historical Jesus. The roots of Christianity and Judaism will need to be reassessed. There's the possibility of a grander, more inclusive spiritual vision.' Nicolas gropes for phrases that seem to match the importance of his claim. I hear the specious expressions of an advertising copywriter – *brand-new, free gift, improved recipe*. I see worthless money piled up in a Weimar wheelbarrow. He takes another sip of wine. 'I can understand your resistance, but this is huge.'

Father David wrinkles his nose. 'How is the world going to be improved with yet another story? I tell you, as your priest, forget this thing. Go back to your wife. Ask for her forgiveness.'

Nicolas assumes he's misheard. 'I forgave her already.'

The priest sets his wine glass on the table and raises his thick index finger in a gesture which says clearly: *no*. 'You told her you forgave her without meaning it. You treated her coldly and self-righteously. Yours is a soul in peril, Nikolasha.'

Nicolas tries not to smirk at the absurdity of the claim. Souls are betrayed in darkened basements, in front of hooded, sweating prisoners, by spyholes in peeling doors, for gold in moonlit gardens, not in the ordinary contempt of a troubled marriage. Right?

'You need to repent of your pride and cruelty towards her. You need *her* forgiveness,' the priest says, his voice at once urgent and deep.

'Are you serious? Do you have any idea what she did?'

'You took a vow before God. You have duties as a husband.'

'What does my marital status have to do with this book? This is seismic. This is the basis for an ecumenical project that could unite humanity and end suffering.'

'End *suffering*?' queries the priest. He says it without obvious irony, but even to Nicolas the echo of his words sounds like sloganeering, the sort of facile phrase-making the anarchists specialise in and use to justify their violence. 'End suffering,' he murmurs, fondling his beard. 'Well, that would certainly be *nice*.' Father David finishes his wine. 'I'm sorry if my reaction disappoints you.'

In fact, Nicolas isn't aware of any disappointment. His convictions are intact; he's confident of the book's importance. But it's clear that he overestimated the priest's ability to think outside the box. I mean, why *would* he? He's been indoctrinated with two millennia's worth of orthodox thinking. His livelihood depends on sticking to convention. Nicolas needs a broader-minded confidant: a theologian who's prepared to entertain challenges to his own belief system. Sitting opposite the bearded, hidebound old priest, Nicolas wants to facepalm himself for the obviousness of his mistake. He should have gone to someone who's prepared to defy received wisdom. He should have gone to Ernest Renan.

'Renan granted the authenticity of the work.'

Corpulent, white-haired, nearing seventy, Renan is one of the most famous intellectual figures in France. His life, the bare

252

outline of it, reminds me a little of Nicolas's, apart from the Jewishness. There is the same humble background, the gift for languages, the vast curiosity. But while Nicolas has built his career on the sands of hack journalism and espionage, Renan has chosen more solid foundations: the impeccable rock of biblical scholarship. He speaks a dozen languages, including Hebrew and the Greek of the New Testament. His *Life of Jesus*, published in 1863, is – despite the word's over-use – a landmark. In sublime and considered French, Renan painstakingly examines the sources of early Christianity to write the first modern biography of the historical Jesus. It's a grand project that's true to the intellectual foundations of the Enlightenment: sweeping away tradition, superstition and the claims of authority in favour of knowledge and light. To Nicolas's relief, Renan seems inclined to accept the Pali *Life* as genuine.

'I am persuaded by much in your text,' Renan says, with the slow, precise diction of someone whose every utterance is weighed for exactness. The book-lined room where they are meeting is part sanctuary, part monument: evidence of an academic life well lived. Foreign editions of Renan's own books fill the shelves. There are FedExed parcels from up-and-coming writers around the world, all containing galley proofs, all desperate for a career-making endorsement from the master. Every now and then, the computer on Renan's desk emits a glassy ping as an email arrives. He checks them without breaking the flow of his speech. It's nice, Nicolas thinks, to see an old man who's staying current with new technology. A long-haired grey cat curled up on a cushion by the coal fire adds a homely touch to the room.

Seated in an armchair, conscious that he's receiving the great man's benediction, Nicolas savours the pleasurable sensation of a hot cup of tea warming his genitals.

'The gospel-makers were concerned to ingratiate themselves with Rome,' says Renan, pouring himself a cup. 'By the time their accounts were written, the Temple had lain in ruins for decades. The Jewish polity was shattered. There was no future for Christianity as some obscure Jewish heresy. They were aiming for acceptance by the empire. So what do they do? What would *anyone* do in their position?' Renan twinkles his fat hands in the yellow beam of the Anglepoise. 'They begin to make adjustments to their story. Their accounts become friendlier to Rome and less friendly to the Jews.' Renan raises his cup and pauses with the rim at his lips. 'What would you say was the major obstacle to Christianity's becoming the imperial religion?' he asks, his tone suddenly pedagogical as he flings the question to Nicolas, who is momentarily panicked, who is once more a twelve-year-old boy being twitted by a supercilious teacher.

'Monotheism?' Nicolas blurts hopefully. 'The Romans have got loads of gods: Jupiter, Mars. And the other ones.'

'The other ones?' Renan sips his tea and looks vaguely disappointed in his new student. 'I don't think so. It's more simple: a Roman governor put the saviour to death! That, I would say, takes a bit of explaining.'

Nicolas curses inwardly. *Of course! What a dolt!*

'So,' Renan continues, 'the evangelists start to exonerate Pilate and stick the blame on the Jews. By the time you get to Matthew, the account is full of novelistic contrivance: Mrs Pilate with her terrible nightmare; and the tale of the handwashing, which of course is clearly false for many reasons, but not least because it had no symbolic meaning to a Roman.' He lays his hand on Nicolas's manuscript. 'What you have here is much more historically plausible. The account of the arrest, the trial before the Sanhedrin – the gospel versions are nonsensical. The legal procedure they describe contravenes Jewish law. It's just *inconceivable* that things would have happened that way.'

Ping. Renan excuses himself, raises a lorgnette to peer at the screen, and pecks out a response with one hand. The clicking of the keyboard wakes the cat, Porlock, who rises from the cushion and yawns. He is a stiff-legged old brute whose sagging belly sways as he stalks across the rug and stretches, turning his back on Nicolas and flourishing the question mark of his tail and bumhole contemptuously towards the visitor as if to say: ?

'Forgive me,' says Renan, laying down his lorgnette. 'Where were we?'

Nicolas feels emboldened to move on to the major issue. 'I wondered what you made of the earlier chapters, the account of the apprenticeship in India, the implied debt to Buddhism in Christ's teaching.'

'Well, those are very interesting,' Renan says. 'Father David and I are friends, despite our theological differences, and I know he has his doubts about the suitability of publication. As your Buddhist priest puts it: "Not all knowledge is for all people." That's been the official position of most religions for a very long time. As a child of the Enlightenment – if the simile is not absurd for a man of my advanced years – I differ. I have often been struck by the anticipations of Eastern philosophy in the words of the gospel. And what use, after all, is a purely Jewish Jesus? Paul had the good sense to rescue Jesus from his brethren. There is – what is the word? – an *incompleteness* about the Jew. But a truly Aryan Jesus, a Jesus who unites the wisdom of the East with the monotheism of the West. To that I say: *bravo.*'

'I'm delighted you see things that way.'

Renan scratches his blotter to draw the cat's attention. Porlock's ears turn towards the sound and then the rest of the cat follows, padding across the rug and hauling himself into his master's lap.

'You are a very lucky fellow,' Renan says, rubbing his finger against the bar of Porlock's cheekbone to incite a purr. For a moment, Nicolas thinks he's addressing the cat. 'Not many people have an opportunity like yours. It's quite an honour to bring a text like this into the world.'

Nicolas mutters something insincerely modest.

'Having said all this, you'd do well to bear the laws of physics in mind. It won't pass without resistance. The text you have is too . . . naked. It requires appropriate clothing in order to be welcomed into polite company: a foreword, footnotes, and a substantial afterword by an eminent scholar.'

'I was intending to add all that. I just haven't had time since I got back. Things have been a bit hectic at home.' Nicolas feels a pang of guilt as he recalls the smell of nappies, his wife's misery, and his son wearing a moustache of congealed snot.

'By an *eminent* scholar.' Renan is uninterested in Nicolas's domestic arrangements and repeats the words more coldly, as though they're a lesson his student has failed to heed. 'The introduction you have written here is very pretty, very *journalistic*, but, to risk mixing metaphors, you are venturing into choppy waters. Something more seaworthy is needed. Your little craft needs to be better caulked, otherwise it will be overwhelmed before it gets out of port.' His fat fingers drum the manuscript. 'A book like this should have a champion. I'm offering to put my lance at its service. Better that, I think, than to face me in the lists.' Renan raises his sly face and looks Nicolas in the eye as he delivers the *coup de grâce*: 'I'm afraid all the gods of Rome couldn't help you then.'

The smile on Nicolas's face glazes into a rictus of anxiety as it dawns on him what the old man's about. It's a threat. Renan's ambition is undimmed. He wants his own name to be on the book. Either he'll take credit for the discovery, append one glorious finale to his list of other achievements, or he'll turn his intellectual gifts against the project and destroy it. As if aware of his master's intentions, Porlock has curled up on the manuscript and gone to sleep.

'That's a very generous offer,' says Nicolas. 'I really wasn't expecting that. If it's all right with you, I'll take some time to think it over.'

When Nicolas tries to remove the manuscript, the cat opens one sleepily malevolent eye and refuses to budge. Renan rubs Porlock's ears and once more ignites the throaty rumble of a purr.

'It appears that Porlock cherishes his own hopes of being a biblical scholar one day,' says Renan in a mild tone that conceals its pointedness. 'It is a surprisingly common dream among both cats and humans.'

'My daughter, Hélène, was born in February of that year.'

The child is premature. Nicolas doesn't receive the telegram until two days after she's born. It's been directed to various addresses across Paris before ending up with Boris Volchkov, who brings it round in person.

Thinning hair shorn, thicker in the waist, soberly dressed, Volchkov looks exactly like the respectable, middle-aged art teacher he's become. He waits while Nicolas opens the telegram and reads the news of the birth.

'Shouldn't you be over there?' Volchkov nags. 'Moral support? Being absent for the birth is one thing; if you miss the christening, tongues will wag. It's going to be tougher on Anya than it is on you.'

'Rachkovsky's the father, you know,' Nicolas says with an indifference that conceals how heavily the words weigh on his heart.

Volchkov shrugs. 'It's the eighties, things are different now. No one's going to think any the less of you. I expect you left a couple of fair-skinned bastards behind in India on your visits.'

'I don't think so, Boris.'

'You don't *think* so. But you don't *know* for sure.'

Nicolas is one hundred per cent sure, but he doesn't see the point in continuing the discussion. He needs to conserve his energy for more significant fights.

'I've got a cab outside,' Volchkov continues. 'Let's go.'

Nicolas allows himself to be persuaded. Anya is in a private room at La Maternité, the lying-in hospital that used to be the convent of Port-Royal. The baby lies in a wooden box, a *couveuse*, lined with sawdust and heated from below by a pan of hot water. The hospital's head of obstetrics is a pioneer in this treatment for premature babies. The infant is visible through the glass lid of the incubator, bearing no obvious sign of her paternity and wearing a tag on her ankle that says 'Baby Notovitch'.

At the sight of Nicolas, Anya's eyes fill with tears. 'You came to see us.'

By the chilly standards of nineteenth-century fatherhood, there's nothing noticeably frosty about Nicolas's deportment. Our great-great-grandfathers didn't make playlists for the birth, insist on snipping the umbilicus, or pull off their shirts in the delivery suite for some vital skin-to-skin with the neonate. The duties of a Victorian dad are not onerous: distant benignity; a whiskery kiss at bedtime; an embarrassed and probably inaccurate account of human sexual relations when a boy reaches puberty; safeguarding a daughter's virtue until marriage and then handing her over to the custody of a son-in-law: surely Nicolas can manage *that*?

But Nicolas is not sure. The sense of mortification is so mystifyingly primal.

Anya's mother, fussing over a selection of presents that she has brought to the hospital on behalf of friends and relatives, gives her son-in-law a perfunctory kiss on each cheek and leaves the room, indicating to Volchkov that he should follow.

'My waters broke three weeks early,' says Anya. 'In any other city, she would have died.' Her voice contains an unsayable regret, Nicolas understands: some part of her wishes the baby were gone so that he would be able to forgive her.

'Modern medicine is a wonder,' says Nicolas, coldly.

A nurse bustles in to give the baby her feed: warm donkey's milk, the nearest approximation to a human mother's, delivered expertly with a spoon. The swaddled child with its round pink face resembles a clothes peg or a skittle. The nurse offers the bowl and spoon to Anya. 'Would madame care to . . . ?'

Anya turns her face to the wall.

'Come, come,' says Nicolas, woodenly patting her hand.

One thing is becoming clear: Anya really loves him. So why cheat on him with that poisonous cretin he can't bring himself to name? He wishes he could talk to MacGahan. What would she say? 'Love, however it comes, is too rare to be tossed in the trash', perhaps. He knows she'd side with Father David.

But Nicolas's jealousy, reactivated by the sight of Rachkovsky's child, shuts him off from any insight into Anya's predicament. Viewed with more compassion, her infidelity makes perfect sense. For her it was a way of taking charge, of becoming the protagonist in a version of her life where she was the betrayer, rather than the betrayed.

The heart has its own way of knowing. She must have seen and been wounded by Nicolas's more profound betrayal. She knew that he had never been straight with her: there was neither desire nor love from his side, just weakness, a liking for convenience, and a certain social ambition.

Perhaps she even instigated it, surprising Rachkovsky with a forward gesture, placing her hand on his knee, emboldened by the wine she's grown unused to. She enjoys the power of conjuring desire in a formidable man.

*

AFTERWARDS, DRINKING COFFEE at a Formica table in the foyer with Volchkov and Mrs Rozenfeld, Nicolas keeps glumly silent. Volchkov tries to fill the pauses with chat but Mrs Rozenfeld keeps turning the conversation back to her son-in-law. She knows something's up. 'Anya says your work has taken you outside Paris again. Is it very hush-hush? When will you be back? She's missing you terribly.'

Nicolas mumbles something non-committal. He is too full of self-righteous anger to notice how touching it is that Anya's lied to protect him from the charge of neglect.

'The hard thing is usually the right thing,' says Volchkov, as they leave the hospital.

'Thanks. As it happens, I'm collecting mottos for fortune cookies,' Nicolas says sourly.

'I'm just saying. People don't cheat to be *with* someone else, they cheat to *be* someone else.'

'You're on fire, Boris. What is this, the Platitude Olympics?'

'Clearly, you'd prefer to be alone,' says Volchkov, touching the brim of his hat and bowing with a certain dignity before setting off at a run to catch a tram.

Nicolas walks aimlessly across the city to try to calm his mind. He has the feeling that he is a riot of selves, between whom he must somehow adjudicate. Even in this version of the secret books he can't live all his possible lives. Who shall he be? What is his duty to Anya? What is to be done?

He knows that by pursuing the gospel's publication, he's cut himself off from the possibility of orthodox salvation, of dropping to his knees in an exhausted heap in front of Father David and handing things over to God. It's dawning on him that his discovery will turn out to be a terrible burden.

Nicolas is weary of the mess of living, of not knowing what to do, which choice is right. For the first time in his life, he feels a pang of envy for his brother, Avram, clearing thistles from fields outside his moshava in Palestine. The members of his organisation, Hovevei Zion, have been sponsored to make a new start, surrounded by their families and like-minded Russian Jews. Nicolas envies the fullness and certainty of their existence, if not the hardship and manual labour. How wonderful to be at the centre of a complete story, instead of having to make your own identity every day, of having to wake up and figure out who to be.

Nicolas's feet have led him towards the Jardin des Tuileries. What has summoned him? Chance? Fate? The instinctive lure of the green space? The crocuses are in bloom, poking through the earth like the beaks of tropical birds. Glancing away from the flowers, Nicolas sees a familiar rotund shape in a silk hat, promenading through the formal gardens.

It is the first time since Bessie's funeral that their paths have crossed.

Nicolas bows his head with an inclination so slight that he hopes it can be interpreted as contempt. Rachkovsky goes one better, sweeping along with no acknowledgment of Nicolas at all. As they pass, Nicolas can clearly hear Irina Rachkovskaia say, 'Didn't you know him?' and her husband reply, 'He's a shopkeeper now.'

After a few more steps, Rachkovsky turns his head in the direction of the box hedges and says, loudly enough for

Nicolas to hear: 'There, my love, the first one of the spring: cuckoo!'

No, Rachkovsky hasn't taken up ornithology. He intends a play on words which works better in French than English: *coucou* is the bird, *cocu* a deceived husband. Rachkovsky means clearly to insult Nicolas, knowing that gossip about the child's paternity is current in the intersecting social circles they inhabit.

A dozen swift heartbeats later, Nicolas has caught up with them.

'Were you addressing me, sir?'

'Monsieur?' Rachkovsky turns and smirks at him. His moustache quivers as though he's barely able to suppress laughter.

The look is intended to be provocative, but perhaps Rachkovsky has underestimated Nicolas's hot-headedness. Nicolas slaps his face so hard that the sound rings across the gardens. A woman gives an audible gasp. Two bystanders intervene to separate the men with their walking sticks. Rachkovsky's cheek is tomato-red and a thin thread of blood is visible in one of his nostrils. His eyes glitter with a strange anger.

Irina Rachkovskaia yells a foul Russian expletive and tries to assault Nicolas with her furled umbrella.

'How very impetuous of you,' says Rachkovsky, dabbing at his nose with a gloved finger. 'I'll give you until tomorrow afternoon to apologise.'

'Don't hold your breath, wankstain,' Nicolas hisses shakily, in a regrettable departure from the chivalric code.

That evening, Nicolas compounds the insult with a libellous letter in which he vents all his anger toward Rachkovsky.

He's so enraged that the nib of his pen tears right through the paper and his handwriting, usually impeccable, is full of jagged peaks and savage hyphens, like the cardiogram of a heart attack.

He has umpteen reasons to hate the man, but it is clearly unwise to twit him so openly with accusations of bribery, forgery and murder. Then as now, the Russian secret services have a habit of dealing ruthlessly with disgruntled former employees.

'A duel was inevitable.'

Volchkov, the natural choice for Nicolas's second, tries to persuade him to back down.

'You don't want to do this. It took Pushkin three days to die. If it's not the bullet, it's the bits of clothing that get caught in the wound. You'll suppurate to death.'

'I've weighed it all up,' says Nicolas calmly. 'If things go wrong, I'll need you to settle my affairs.'

He places an envelope in front of Volchkov. In a steady hand that has fully recovered its poise, it reads 'To be opened in the event of my death'.

Volchkov has never seen this side of his friend and is a little in awe. Although he knows rationally that duels are a stupid display of machismo, Volchkov's inner romantic stirs at the prospect of a fight. Some small corner of the art teacher is still the self-mythologising bohemian of ten years earlier, and the idea of participating in a duel recalls the works of Lermontov: gun smoke rising from a Dagestani valley, young men ready to lay down their lives to avenge a trivial insult.

Plus, laughing in the face of death is all the more attractive when you're in a final-salary pension scheme and someone else is doing it.

'It's my duty to warn you of the consequences,' Volchkov says resignedly, pocketing the letter.

In the days leading up to the duel, Nicolas feels unexpectedly content. His story has become gratifyingly simple. This is the part in the drama that has been written for him. He is a dishonoured husband. He is striking a blow for a dead friend.

Volchkov and Mulhouse, Rachkovsky's second, meet to finalise the details. The duel will take place at dawn in the Bois de Boulogne. A surgeon has agreed to make himself available. According to protocol, Nicolas has the choice of weapons. It's an easy decision. The arthritis that will plague him in later life is already beginning to take hold. Swords are out of the question. Lots will be cast to determine who has the privilege of shooting first.

Discussing the arrangements for the duel in whispers at the back table of a cafe, Volchkov begins to contemplate what it might mean if Nicolas dies, or is horribly injured. It is widely known that Rachkovsky is an expert shot.

Over the years, Volchkov has found Nicolas arrogant, inscrutable and patronising about his photographic projects, but he considers him a friend nonetheless. And as a reformed libertine, as a painter and photographer of the naked human form, he has an intuitive sense of the vulnerability of flesh.

Seated in the cafe, Volchkov is troubled by a sudden vision: he sees a man's naked body lying in a brimming bathtub, the sea cucumber of his penis lolling in the pondweed of his pubic hair. He sees the pale belly jarred by the impact of a bullet, a calamitous wound opens, bloody shadows obscure the water, eyes grow glassy with death. Suppressing a shudder, Volchkov fondles his paunch through his waistcoat and feels its reassuring warmth. No, it is his duty to be Nicolas's better angel. 'So, Mulhouse,' he says. 'You know how these things work. I mean, *really* work.'

Mulhouse sips his canarino – a joyless beverage comprising hot water and a screw of lemon peel – and shoots Volchkov a puzzled glance.

'We're not really going to let these guys fight,' Volchkov continues. 'Right? I see this going one of two ways. Way number one: my guy gets the first shot and discharges his pistol in the air. Way number two: your guy gets the first shot and . . .' Volchkov pauses and prompts Mulhouse with his raised eyebrows.

Somewhat belatedly, Mulhouse understands what's required of him. 'Right. I'm with you. My guy discharges his pistol in the air,' he says.

'*Exactly*. After that, another shot in the air and honour is satisfied. There's just no point anyone getting hurt. You cool with that?'

'Naturally,' murmurs Mulhouse. His unblinking composure suggests straight-arrow honesty. 'I was going to suggest something similar myself.'

The two men shake on it. Later, Volchkov will recall that Mulhouse's hand seemed to shrink a little from his touch.

'On the morning of the duel there were nine degrees of frost.'

The unusual weather reminds Nicolas of February in Saint Petersburg. The low mist can barely creep above the tree roots. Sharp yellow sunlight pierces the branches. Trundling in a carriage towards the appointed place, Nicolas thinks of his cousin Osip, of his brother in Palestine, of Suvorin and all the others he has neglected. Perhaps this is how it ends, he thinks. He has slept poorly, naturally, contemplating the imminent possibility of his death. The idea of pain bothers him. How could it not?

Beside him, Volchkov is praying that Rachkovsky draws the lot to fire first so he doesn't have to explain his subterfuge to Nicolas.

Neither man has considered a more troubling possibility: that Nicolas has fallen hook, line and sinker for one of Rachkovsky's stratagems. Nicolas thinks he is fighting for his wife's honour, but Rachkovsky has other business to resolve. He has been gifted an opportunity to tidy up some loose ends around the Third Section's affairs: specifically, the problem of an unreliable ex-employee with questionable allegiances who knows where too many of the bodies are buried.

The guns are swimming in grease, necessary because of the extreme cold. Mulhouse offers the choice of them to Nicolas, as the duelling code demands. Nicolas weighs them both in his hands and favours one, more or less arbitrarily. Mulhouse walks back to Rachkovsky and Nicolas passes the gun to Volchkov to wipe clean. As Volchkov towels off the grease, he broaches the possibility of resolving this whole thing with a handshake. 'I'd rather have you alive, Nicolas,' he says, touchingly.

Nicolas snaps the gun open and looks along the chamber. After a day at the practice range, he has greatly improved his accuracy: he can hit a large melon at twenty paces with better-than-even odds.

'What if *I* kill *him*? That's a possibility – and a good one. He's doing appalling things. He's got a plan to frame the Jews. He's a hatemonger.'

'Let's be clear,' Volchkov says. 'You're doing this because he impregnated your wife.' The look he gets from Nicolas suggests that perhaps this is more honesty than the occasion demands.

Mulhouse calls the principals together to draw lots for the first shot. Nicolas avoids meeting Rachkovsky's eye. When he picks the longer straw, he's surprised to see Volchkov wince.

As Volchkov helps Nicolas off with his overcoat, he whispers into his ear, 'I have a confession to make. Mulhouse and I made a gentleman's agreement. That *finita la commedia* shit sounds very romantic, but it was devastating for Russian literature. Nowadays, it's more like wrestling matches – the whole thing's arranged in advance. It makes a better spectacle. And there's less chance of being hurt.'

'What are you saying, Boris?'

'I'm saying it's all been agreed. You fire in the air, he fires in the air. We all go home.'

'You are kidding, right?'

'Why would I kid? Nicolas, this was my decision as your friend,' says Volchkov.

Nicolas's face freezes in a jack-o'-lantern of incredulity.

Volchkov falteringly continues. 'I gave Mulhouse my word of honour.'

Nicolas's indignation is too enormous to articulate in the time available. Mulhouse calls the principals to their marks.

Rachkovsky has kept on his overcoat. If Volchkov were thinking straight, he'd object to this: Nicolas has stripped to his shirt and waistcoat. His hands are blotchy with the cold. He raises his gun and aims it slightly down and left of Rachkovsky's chest, knowing that the trigger pull will cause the muzzle to drift the other way. All things being equal, he has a better than fifty per cent chance of causing death or serious injury. Knowing what we know, we would be inclined to take those odds.

Steam rises from Rachkovsky's bare head. He is chillingly unafraid. Say what you like about him, he knows how to carry himself like a man.

One bullet through Rachkovsky's centre mass will pierce the leather padding he's packed cheatingly around his midriff. At a minimum, it'll incapacitate him. There'll be no hope of a shot in response. Even with the surgeon standing by, the chances are good he'll bleed out in ten or fifteen minutes.

So what's holding Nicolas back? It's Volchkov. If the gentleman's agreement is violated, and if he misses, then Volchkov is answerable for the breach. Mulhouse will be entitled to his own satisfaction. There will be another duel between Mulhouse and Volchkov. Rightly or wrongly, Nicolas feels able to gamble with his own life, but not with Volchkov's.

Giving an exasperated sigh, Nicolas raises the barrel of his gun and discharges it into the air. Birds start from the trees at the sound. Nicolas is enveloped in a savoury cloud of cordite.

'That was a very sporting gesture,' Rachkovsky shouts hoarsely through the smoke, taking the loaded gun from Mulhouse and aiming it. Nicolas has turned slightly to his

right to pass his empty weapon to Volchkov. Despite Volchkov's best efforts, the butt is still slippery with grease and
the gun falls from Nicolas's grasp. Instinctively he stoops to
gather it from the frosty grass. The accident probably saves
his life. Rachkovsky's bullet tears through his shoulder instead of his ribcage and misses his heart by six inches. It is a
miraculous escape.

The surgeon rushes to attend to the fallen duellist while
Volchkov loyally squares up to Mulhouse. The men have to
be separated from one another by Rachkovsky, who claims
the gun went off by accident. There is no evidence that will
prove things either way.

'Anya came to my bedside.'

Pale from her own convalescence, post-partum figure
strapped tightly into a corset, Anya brings flowers and copious tears to the hospital ward.

Nicolas is propped up on starched pillows, doing a cross-
word puzzle. He looks surprisingly well, considering how
much blood he's lost. The fragments of bullet that have been
removed from the wound make a grisly still life in the ashtray beside his bed. Anya takes his hand. He can't doubt the
sincerity of her remorse.

'He told me you were in love with a revolutionary. He said
there was no place in your heart for me, but that I shouldn't
be sad about it, that the best marriages worked like that.
That you'd given me the gift of freedom.'

What can Nicolas say? It's largely true. 'I've been weak,'
he says. 'I've been—'

Anya presses a finger on his lips. Even at this tender moment of reconciliation, he seems fated to recall Bessie.

But the bloodshed gives them a fresh start. Nicolas's gesture, which actually comprised both homicidal and suicidal instincts, is recast as a profoundly romantic deed.

'We date our true marriage from the day of the duel.'

Date. It's definitely the present tense. And yet the inscrutable old man wrapped in the worn blue folds of his chapan doesn't project a woman's care. There seems a notable absence of flowers or perfume in his life. The chilly hallways of the house smell of gravy and coal-tar soap. One day, when the downstairs loo is blocked, Vincenzo takes a peek at Notovitch's bedroom on his way to the upstairs one: the lonely single bed, the teetering stack of books on the side table, watery London light trickling through the net curtains. The bathroom cabinet contains pills and unguents for arthritis, half a bottle of aftershave from a Jermyn Street chemist, and a device that turns out to be a nostril-hair trimmer, but nothing that hints at a female presence. Where is Anya now? Perhaps not dead, as Vincenzo has presumed. What kind of marriage did they have, he wonders? How close could they possibly become? How close could anyone get to Notovitch, with all his secrets?

'Out of the inauspicious rubble of our marriage, we made a fresh start,' says Notovitch. 'Neither of us expected much from the relationship, but we were not poor. Anya was unlucky with her health, but things could have been worse.'

Does that mean good or bad? Or was it just an ordinary

marriage, composed of all the compromise and ambivalence that one supposes to be normal?

I think it was better than that. On the first anniversary of the duel, Anya invites Volchkov and his wife, Babette, to dinner. She gives the maid the evening off and cooks a leg of lamb that she leaves to rest on the hostess trolley she received as one of her wedding presents.

She is a little flushed and proposes a toast before they take their seats at the table. Even in this company, it is a surprisingly unconventional suggestion. The chatter stops. 'It's not every woman who can say her husband fought a duel for her honour,' she says. 'So I'd like us to drink to Nicolas, my husband, the bravest man I know.'

'Hear, hear.' Volchkov slaps his thigh approvingly. Babette touches his shoulder. She's shy, knows the stories of her husband's misspent years, senses he's drunk, and doesn't want him to make a scene.

Nicolas, as custom dictates, raises his glass but doesn't drink.

'And one further toast,' says Anya. 'To Boris, his brave second.' She turns to Volchkov and gives him a sweet smile. 'Boris, if you ever let him fight another duel, I'll shoot you myself.'

Over dinner, Volchkov retells the story of the duel with a degree of licence that will increase annually at subsequent anniversaries of the event. By 1900, Rachkovsky shakes with fear as he awaits Nicolas's shot. In 1903, Volchkov will claim that the spymaster actually soiled himself.

Anya and Nicolas share a tender glance across the table. Nicolas has an announcement of his own. He gets up to fetch a bottle of red wine that is standing on the sideboard.

Volchkov wipes his mouth with his napkin and winks at Babette, as if to say: *get ready for this*. He has already told her that his friend keeps a fabulous cellar.

'I never thought I'd be serving this,' says Nicolas. The bottle was uncorked two hours ago to breathe. Nicolas pours the wine into fresh glasses. Volchkov holds out for a large measure. It is cherry-coloured, young. 'It was made by my brother, Avram.' The liquid glugs enticingly in its passage to the crystal. 'So: to first fruits and new beginnings.' Nicolas looks at his wife as he drinks it.

Even when Volchkov swirls the wine in his glass, the bouquet is surprisingly reticent. He strains his nostrils to detect a whiff of fruit, but there's nothing, Now he takes a sip and feels his mouth pucker. Thin, sharp, tannic: it's loathsome. But apparently not to Nicolas, whose usually reliable palate seems to have become clouded with a layer of sentiment. Nicolas savours it dreamily, approving not the wine, but some more abstract quality: its unlikeliness, perhaps. 'It was made by Jews in Palestine,' he murmurs, incredulous.

'Honour was satisfied.'

During the years following his return from India, Nicolas prospers in retail. Étoile du Nord flourishes under his increasingly direct guidance. Grey gives his temples a distinguished air. He learns to tolerate his children. Another one, a boy named David, arrives roughly nine months after the first anniversary of the duel.

These uneventful years – the best for humans, but worst for novels – drift into the 1890s. The big gap bothers me a lot.

Notovitch insists to Vincenzo that his anxiety about Renan explained the delay. But it doesn't quite work. Why not let the old man take credit for it anyway? What's the big deal? The important thing is to publish, right?

If it were entirely up to me, I'd do things differently: compress the interval between the return and publication, maybe cut straight from the hospital bed to the title page of the book, or find Nicolas, still injured from the duel, looking with obvious pride at a display of *The Unknown Life* in a bookshop window.

But after all that hope for the book, all that excitement, Nicolas continues to prevaricate. It's not until 1892 that Renan dies, freeing Nicolas from the obstacle he claims he feared. At the end of 1893, the book goes to press. It is published the following spring.

'The auguries were good.'

The launch is scheduled to be held in the bookshop of a friend, but buzz around the publication is so huge that a larger venue is required.

Suvorin comes. Osip sends his congratulations from Saint Petersburg, but his finances are too squeezed for him to make the journey in person. Five hundred people pack into a hired ballroom and Nicolas is introduced by his publisher to a smattering of applause.

Standing in front of a big map of India, Nicolas shows the audience the route of his journey and identifies the location of the monastery with the red dot of a laser pointer. Its slight wobble betrays his nerves.

'Thank you for coming,' he says. Looking out into the crowd, he sees friendly, curious expressions. In the face of a man handing round canapés, he suddenly recognises his own father. The vision flusters him momentarily. He glances down at his index cards and shuffles them to buy time to compose himself.

'I have written many books,' he says, 'as some of you know. They cost me much toil and in the course of working on them I have lost good friends: Margaret MacGahan and General Skobelev are two people who I would give almost anything to have with me now.' He raises a glass of water with a shaky hand and takes a sip. The sound of his swallow is as loud in his ears as thunder. 'It is strange, I think, that after a career of writing books, I should be proudest of all of one I *didn't* write. Perhaps, before I read from this book, it would be useful for me to say something about the manner of its discovery.'

Rapt, the crowd thrills to the story he tells. His confidence grows and his modest manner enhances the power of his narrative. He describes the pain of his injury, his first impressions of Hemis, his encounter with the abbot and the Rinpoche, the extraordinary moment when he held the secret books for the first time and intuited their significance.

Finally, after reading a section of the gospel, he closes the book. 'I think of this book as an invitation,' he concludes. 'An invitation to consider what we believe and why we believe it, and whether or not there are other beliefs that might be richer, truer, fairer and kinder.'

Familiar with events of this sort, and the low wattage of their usual audiences, Nicolas waits in the ensuing silence for a few hands to rise timidly. If he's lucky, there might be one loudmouth who'll kick things off, who'll channel the curiosity of the others and encourage them by example to overcome their inhibitions. But there's nothing. The silence drags on. Wearily, he realises that this is going to be like all his previous experiences of publication: the book on which he slaved for years will vanish like a coin dropping into a bottomless well with not so much as an answering plink.

Nicolas is just beginning to consider reading another extract when a man at the back of the hall gets to his feet and begins applauding with deep, slow claps. Around him, the entire audience gradually rises. The ovation lasts for what seems like eight or nine minutes, during which Nicolas feels disembodied, as though he and everyone in the room is weightless, floating. Over the course of twenty-four hours, the entire print run sells out.

Ten further impressions are required before the end of the year. For the first time in his life, Nicolas has written a bona fide bestseller.

'Renan had been prescient about its reception.'

The story of the newly discovered gospel spreads quickly beyond France. Word of Nicolas's book is picked up in March, a week after publication, in MacGahan's old paper the *London Daily News* and then reported in the *New York Times* in April. A month after that, the *New York Times* publishes an ill-tempered review of the book, suggesting that Nicolas has been hoaxed.

The lamas were not as clever as they pretend, or as is pretended for them, if they were not able to compile from their 84,000 rolls of lives of Buddhas which are not accessible to the people a relation as flattering to themselves as is this relation of the life of Issa.

But controversy about the book does nothing to endanger its fortunes. An English-language edition is in preparation by the middle of the summer. It is published to excellent sales. German, Italian, Spanish, Russian, Yiddish and Hebrew editions are soon underway. Everywhere the book appears, much discussion centres on whether the gospel is authentic, the nature of its message, and the reliability of the messenger. It is to be expected. These are the birth pains that accompany any new truth. This is what Renan warned of. Nicolas welcomes the debate as evidence that he's being taken seriously. The book is launched. He has every confidence that its success is in the hands of some higher power.

The Unknown Life of Jesus Christ meets its first serious obstacle at the end of 1894 in the pages of *The Nineteenth Century*, a literary periodical, which publishes a long, discursive essay about the book.

Nicolas's publisher, a constitutionally nervous man called Alexandre Soubsol who has edited the book with the lightest of touches, is panicked by the article. He calls on Nicolas one morning and, finding him out, leaves a copy of the magazine with his housekeeper. Nicolas reads it later that afternoon.

The piece is by a man called Max Müller, a professor at Oxford University. German-born, Müller is a linguist and a scholar of comparative religions. His review strikes a weary, supercilious tone: the contemptuous manner of a highbrow academic stooping to dismiss a foolish popular enthusiasm. Nicolas's hackles rise. He has to take a break from reading to calm himself. But when he picks up the article again, with a cooler head, he sees that, behind the snarky rhetoric, the classical allusions, and Müller's complacent references to his own expertise, the attack only has two prongs. Nicolas opens his writing case and prepares to counter his opponent robustly.

Müller's first charge is that the account contained in the text rests on an unlikely coincidence. According to the opening verses of the Pali gospel, the Jewish merchants who bring news of Issa's death to India almost immediately meet people who knew him during his sojourn there. This, Müller insists, is so improbable as to engender disbelief.

Nicolas matches Müller's disdainful tone as he makes short work of this objection. Yes, there's a coincidence in the Pali gospel, he admits. But you don't need a professorship from Oxford to know that none of the gospel-writers was reporting for a wire service. The so-called coincidence is very likely to be a form of elision or foreshortening. The gospel-writer is trying to get across a complicated story with some economy and grace. 'The gospel is not operating according to Professor Müller's notions of non-fiction or historical accuracy. We cannot know what kind of conflation, compression and licence the Pali author considered appropriate,' Nicolas writes.

I'm struck by his restraint in choosing this line of response. He could equally well have said, yes, there's a coincidence. But so what? Coincidences stretch credulity. That's exactly what they do. But in a vast, complicated world, they're arithmetically inevitable. What would be statistically odd would be a world with none. The things that actually happen are very often the product of the unlikely, but they are not fictional.

Müller's second objection is another paper tiger. It's meant to cast doubt on Nicolas's credentials as a scholar but really it's the lamest of rhetorical tricks, an appeal to authority – in this case, Müller's own. The professor describes the extensive catalogues kept by Buddhist libraries, which he has studied himself in detail. According to Müller, these are exhaustive lists of all their holdings of both sacred and secular texts. In none of these, Müller says airily, is there any mention of the manuscript that Nicolas claims to have found: how could something as important as the Pali gospel be absent from their catalogues?

It's a spectacularly open goal, Nicolas realises. Müller's reasoning is circular. His fallacious argument boils down to this: there can't be any significant texts the professor doesn't know about, because otherwise the professor would already know about them.

Of course, the professor's not a fool. Behind the smoke and bangs of his assault is an intelligence that has considered the attractiveness of Nicolas's claims. Müller clearly senses that a credulous public is inclined to be seduced by the tale of the lost gospel. And he understands that part of the story's appeal is the exoticism of its setting: an unknown corner of India, a snowbound monastery, a mysterious manuscript. A large part of his article is devoted to correcting this impression. But in his eagerness to demystify Nicolas's story, to drain it of its exotic character, Müller goes much too far the other way. He makes it sound as though Hemis Monastery is just like a public lending library in Manchester, with all its treasures itemised in a card catalogue.

In his counterblast, Nicolas has great fun with what he calls Müller's 'Teutonic literalism'. One section of his reply is especially interesting to people like us who have come to know something of Nicolas's other lives. 'It seems Professor Müller has no notion of the obligations of the occult,' he writes. 'Just as there are hidden parts of government, and, if Monsieur Charcot is correct, hidden parts of our own natures, there is also hidden knowledge which by definition appears in no index or catalogue. There are, like it or no, secret books whose presence exerts an unacknowledged power on the visible books in which the accounts of human endeavours take their authorised forms.'

It is the first time that Nicolas makes explicit the understanding he will carry with him to his grave. Confronted by a man who insists that the world behaves in ways that are comprehensible and inevitable, Nicolas has begun to formulate his alternative notion: the world is a flux of events out of which we contrive the stories we call *reality*.

There is one additional sidelong attack. In his introduction to *La Vie Inconnue*, explaining his delay in publishing the book, Nicolas had mentioned his encounter with Renan and hinted, perhaps too broadly, at his sense of the old man's covetousness. 'Whatever else Renan was, he was certainly far from jealous,' Müller says, snottily. Nicolas lets it pass, but he wonders if this, perhaps, is the source of the professor's animosity. There are few men in the field who do not owe some debt of loyalty to Renan.

Nicolas saves his most defiant gesture for the close of his rebuttal: 'I will shortly be making another trip to Tibet to find the originals of those documents. I propose to start at the end of the present year.'

'But you had the photographs?'

It is Vincenzo again. Notovitch makes a fleeting grimace. His lips part with a regretful smack. 'It was a very curious thing,' he says.

Those photographs, faded to sepia with age, should by rights be hanging in Notovitch's living room. He should pass one to Vincenzo now to pore over: the guileless face of Sonam, the abbot, the tiny Rinpoche with his eyes crinkling against the sun, Nicolas himself, heartbreakingly youthful – all of them arrayed around the priceless gospel.

Most precious of all would be the images of the text itself, sharp enough to be legible when enlarged, to be shared around the world not just for authentication, but for fuller understanding of its subtle shades of meaning, for comparison with related documents, to enrich the intellectual life of the planet.

Before he left Paris for India, Nicolas had undertaken a crash course in photography with Volchkov. He'd chosen the robustest technology: plates that could, according to the testimonials, survive immersion in water, extremes of temperature and scrutiny by an airport's X-ray machine.

Volchkov sternly warned him off letting anyone handle them in India. So, soon after his return, Nicolas took his plates to be processed by a chemist whom Volchkov had recommended, an Italian called Giuseppe Balducci.

Balducci made detailed notes about the temperature, altitude and atmospheric conditions in Hemis and promised to have the plates printed within forty-eight hours. But when Nicolas returned two days later, Balducci told him the plates were blank.

Nicolas was so irate that he summoned Volchkov to the shop. A triangular argument ensued between the men. Nicolas was further incensed that Volchkov's allegiances seemed to be wavering. He kept implying that Nicolas was somehow at fault.

'You're sure you loaded them correctly?' Volchkov asked. 'Like I showed you?'

Finally, in a show of conciliation, Balducci agreed to try the process again, this time with Volchkov working alongside him. Together they were able to conjure a single image from one of the plates: a view of Simla, showing bungalows ranged across the terraced hills and an Anglican church rising incongruously in the distance; a suburb of London in the foothills of the Himalayas. But of the gospels, of Hemis, of the abbot, Sonam, Nicolas himself: nothing.

'It was bad luck,' Notovitch sighs, with alarming understatement.

'Then the real attacks began.'

Nicolas feels quietly confident about the way he has dispatched Müller. Other opponents will surely be more wary now. His complacence is soon shown to be baseless. As 1894 draws to a close, the tone of the opposition to *The Unknown Life* grows fiercer and more personal.

Correspondents – some named, some anonymous – begin to pop up in the letter columns of the British press, writing from India, claiming to have been to the monastery and to have found evidence that contradicts Nicolas's account.

Fortified with these additional testimonies, Müller publishes a revised version of his piece. This time, he includes fresh material in an appendix that purports to debunk Nicolas's claims completely. There is a report from an anonymous woman traveller to Hemis who says she could find no record of a Russian ever visiting the monastery. More damaging still is a long account written by an Englishman named J. Archibald Douglas, who says he has interviewed the abbot. According to Douglas, the abbot disowned any knowledge of Nicolas, the gospel and Issa with a vehemence that seems deeply out of character for such a contemplative man.

Similar attacks proliferate in the French and English press.

'When I was a professional liar,' says Notovitch, 'I was rewarded financially, I was acclaimed as a hero and a patriot. Now that I was telling the truth, I was denounced everywhere for my falsehoods. It was very curious.'

Getting to his feet, he pulls from the bookshelf a bound copy of another periodical, *The Journal of Contemporary Philosophy*, and shows Vincenzo the text of an article repeating Douglas's claims and calling Notovitch's integrity into question. He draws Vincenzo's attention to the name of the author. 'Karl Marks! Imagine! Even then, he could not resist his silly games with me. Probably he had Mulhouse write it for him.'

'Rachkovsky?' asks Vincenzo.

'Who else?' Notovitch puts the magazine back on the shelf, clearly disdainful of Vincenzo's naivety. 'Remember, they had agents throughout the region. These letters that Müller quotes from so approvingly. Who are they? Who was this redoubtable Victorian woman? Who was Douglas? Who was this absurd character Karl Marks? They were creations of the Third Section, they were glove puppets of Rachkovsky himself.'

'You think so?'

'Of course. He was determined to destroy me. I accept that was his role. He used my enthusiasm for this discovery to disparage me in the eyes of the world. It was a classic Third Section manoeuvre – you find what is most pure, most characteristic of a person and with that you annihilate them. What is unforgivable is the complicity of a man like Müller, who should have known better, who should have been more open-minded. Why was he so willing to believe these spurious accounts? Because their testimony comports with what he is inclined to believe? Because their evidence was better? Or is it more basic? Is it because he was unwilling to trust the word of some shady ex-Jew from Crimea?'

The question lingers. It feels like the first time Notovitch has acknowledged his past so directly.

At the beginning of 1896, Colonel Younghusband publishes his account of his travels across Central Asia, *The Heart of a Continent*. Seeing the book in the publisher's catalogue, Nicolas requests a galley proof – a journalist's prerogative. He gets no reply and has to order it through a specialist topographic bookseller. He tears the parcel open as soon as it arrives and finds his name in the index. Reading the scant and tendentious section dealing with the encounter at the Skardu Pass, he is inflamed with rage. Younghusband has dismissed Nicolas in two brief paragraphs, portraying him as a devious, self-important fraud. Unsurprisingly, he does not mention the horse race.

I walked up to him with all the eagerness a traveller has to meet a countryman of his own after not seeing one for nearly seven months. But this time it turned out the stranger was a Russian! He announced himself as M. Nicolas Notovitch, an adventurer who had, I subsequently found, made a not very favourable reputation in India. I asked M. Notovitch where he had come from, and he replied that he had come from Kashmir. He then asked me where I had come from. I said from Peking. It much amused me, therefore, when on leaving he said, in a theatrical way, 'We part here, the pioneers of the East!'

This same M. Notovitch has recently published what he calls a new 'Life of Christ', which he professes to have found in a monastery in Ladakh, after he had parted with me. No one, however, who knows M. Notovitch's reputation, or who has the slightest knowledge of the subject, will give any reliance whatever to this pretentious volume.

Nicolas considers the possibility of a libel action. He even travels to London to meet a firm of solicitors. The imperial capital is a disorientating place of Dickensian fogs and extra-ordinary ethnic diversity. The winter temperatures, while never below freezing, have the peculiar rawness that is London's contribution to the lexicon of cold. Nicolas enjoys the trip, visits the British Museum, is entertained by a musical version of *Les Misérables* and tours the city on an open-top double-decker bus, but gets little encouragement from the solicitor who advises him, a cadaverous man named Nigel Corduroy.

'Perhaps you are familiar with him?'

Vincenzo shakes his head. 'Is he famous?'

'I do not believe so, but he lives, as you do, in the south of the city.'

Vincenzo has to suppress a smile. It's hard to shake the small-town conceit of believing that two people you know in a foreign city must be familiar with one another.

Corduroy advises that the chances of success in a lawsuit are small. Younghusband's assertions may not be factually accurate but are protected by the legal defence of fair comment. 'Your problem, Mr Notovitch, is that others are saying what he's saying.' On his desk is a copy of Müller's article. For this depressing and unhelpful advice, Nicolas is invoiced twenty guineas.

Nicolas writes a furious letter to Younghusband, care of his publisher, dismissing his account as the predictably one-eyed opinion of an embittered jingo. He encloses a return address but receives no reply. His anger is heightened by a growing sense of desperation: he is beginning to fear that, barring some unforeseeable reversal, the opinion of Younghusband and Müller will become his epitaph.

Calling on his publisher, Monsieur Soubsol, to find out about foreign sales and plans for a paperback edition, Nicolas finds him increasingly unable to meet his eye. Sales of the book are still healthy, but nothing like those heady weeks of publication. Some miasma surrounds the book, some stain of dishonour. The conventional way to dispel this would be a duel, but he can't duel everybody. The unspoken word he hears on everybody's lips is *Jonah*. He is the unlucky passenger, the object of whispers and pity. Everybody wants to— He can no longer think of the word in Russian. The sense of his memory failing is another blow to his self-image. He knows it in French: *s'éloigner*. They're distancing themselves.

Two years after the book's publication, the *New York Times* rounds up the evidence against Nicolas and administers the *coup de grâce* to his reputation:

> Professor Müller has suggested that M. Notovitch may
> have been hoaxed by the monks. Professor Douglas
> denies him even this loophole for escape and declares that
> he is simply a notoriety-hunter and reckless forger who
> trusted for safety to the remoteness of the scene in which
> he laid his fable.

'*Not one person came to my aid.*'

Interest in Nicolas and his discovery peaks and dwindles abruptly. The appetite for new stories is ceaseless and the public that has been enjoying the kerfuffle around Nicolas's gospel now grows restless, moves on, and turns its collective gaze to different dramas. In fact, the publication of Nicolas's book coincided with the beginning of another scandal and it is with this that much of the Parisian intelligentsia now becomes preoccupied. In 1894, a young French officer was charged with treason for handing military secrets to the Germans. The whole thing has the feeling of something dreamed up by the Third Section: a cleaner in the pay of the French intelligence service claimed to have found top-secret information in a wastepaper basket in the German Ministry. The French officer alleged to be the spy has been cashiered and sent to Devil's Island.

The issue of his guilt or innocence will divide the country for years. He is innocent, in fact. It will subsequently become impossible to escape the conclusion that the officer, Alfred Dreyfus, was framed because he is a Jew.

'Scapegoat.'

'You remember the etymology? Few people do. It's in Leviticus. One of the stranger passages of the Old Testament. You recall the conflations of sin and disease; holiness and purity; the obsessive washings and anointings? They are pathological, no? You know about Charcot? Krafft-Ebing? Freud? Anyway, they made Dreyfus one of those.'

Talk of French values being under threat is a coded signal that Nicolas is particularly alert to. And what are French values historically anyway? Liberty, equality and fraternity? Or monarchy and a hereditary elite? Science and reason, or faith and the authority of the Church?

It seems to Nicolas that what is now known as the Dreyfus Affair has become a proxy war between the peddlers of competing fictions, between humans finding more and more orotund ways to justify their versions of 'bad' and 'good'.

To a less jaundiced Jewish writer-journalist, it's the impetus to start dreaming afresh. Writing in his private diary, Theodor Herzl begins sketching the outlines of a new state, a homeland for the Jewish people. At this stage, he's not sure whether it's a political programme that will lead to the founding of a new nation or the plot of a speculative novel. In fact it ends up being both.

'My cousin Osip became a Zionist.'

On what's to be his final trip to Paris, Osip makes the pitch. 'This Herzl, the Jew from Budapest. He's a visionary. Why shouldn't the Jews have their own land? It's the natural ambition of a nation. Your brother had the right idea. I wish I'd done it twenty years ago. We're going out to look.'

Nicolas snorts in contempt: 'Keeping the sabbath? Dietary laws? Purifying your wife after menstruation? We were about to enter the twentieth century last time I checked.'

Osip has the tenacity of someone who's used to struggle. 'It'll be a secular state. All welcome. It'll be for Jews like us. We'll be what Jews were meant to be: the conscience of the world, sticking up for the weak and the dispossessed.'

Nicolas sees the zeal in his eyes. He looks incredulously at his pigeon-chested cousin and thinks: *you've never used a tool in your life. It's too late to become a pioneer.* But he doesn't want to trample on Osip's hopes, so he curbs his dismissiveness. He feels there must be another way. 'Anya was born in Paris – she's determined to live here forever. Besides, she loathes travel. She doesn't even have a passport. A dusty city in the Middle East? I can barely get her to the seaside.'

'I gave up writing for a time.'

The failure of the book kills Nicolas's appetite for letters. He doesn't really enjoy reading any more. Instead, he surrenders to the routine of work and family. He feels happiest nowadays overseeing the business of the department store, choosing between fabric samples, deciding that season's hem length, commissioning buttons. He is a good employer, capable of discerning and rewarding talent. He has an eye for the people who can give themselves over to a task, who are at home in the physical world, who have an intuitive grasp for the laws and aesthetics of cutting fabric or wrapping a purchase.

Eventually, he finds his way back to writing. First he tries a historical novel, which he embarks on enthusiastically. But when he comes back to it, the antiqueness of the style strikes him as ersatz – competent fakery, like some falsely aged furniture. He decides to turn his hand to theatre and composes a farce involving a marriageable heiress, twin suitors and lots of wordplay, which he takes to a hot young director called Hippolyte who's respectful but non-committal about staging it.

'What sort of plays do you enjoy?' the director asks.

'Shakespeare, Molière, Gogol's *Revizor*,' Nicolas replies.

'Ah, the classics!'

The director gives Nicolas house seats to his newest production, a play with the unlikely-sounding title *King Bubba*. Anya finds a babysitter and puts on one of her most astonishing silk dresses. Nicolas wears black tie. They find themselves wedged in between hirsute young people with denim clothes and facial piercings. At curtain-up, a man in a fat suit wearing a crown and carrying a lavatory brush makes his way to the middle of the stage and hurls incomprehensible abuse at the audience: 'Cornswoggle! Pisspots! Vomit!'

Anya digs Nicolas in the ribs with her fan. 'Very modern,' she whispers, approvingly.

'The twentieth century arrived on a Monday morning.'

The effort to keep faith with his discovery has exhausted Nicolas. He never realised how much of his life he had spent avoiding the pain of humiliation until he was forced to confront it repeatedly. At big gatherings, it's hard for him to endure the whisperings, the pointed fingers, the eyes that linger on him but withdraw swiftly to avoid meeting his.

He'd like to celebrate the new century at home with a handful of friends and some excellent burgundy. But his father-in-law, now sixty-five, is hosting a huge event in the department store. The mannequins in the window displays have given way to dioramas of French history: Charlemagne on the battlefield; Joan of Arc putting the English to flight; the Declaration of the Rights of Man; Napoleon emancipating the Jews; Louis Pasteur in his laboratory. Inside, a sabreur dispatches a balthazar of champagne with a gleaming blade and its sparkling contents pour into a fountain of goblets piled in the shape of the Eiffel Tower.

Volchkov turns up with his wife, Babette, and wearing a tartan waistcoat that he says is intended to honour his Scottish antecedents – like the poet Lermontov, he claims to have roots in the Highlands. Nicolas's remark that they seem very high-spirited provokes a gale of laughter.

'That's because we're off our faces,' says Volchkov.

'You don't seem drunk.'

'We're not. We're high as kites!' says Babette.

Volchkov flourishes a snuffbox. 'Want some?'

'What is it?'

'Cocaine.'

'Cocaine?'

'Keep your hair on. It's harmless fun – and perfectly legal.'

That evening is one they'll all have cause to look back on. Despite anxieties about the health of the economy, despite the perennial rumbling of personal discontent, the coming century is something that inspires general optimism. Of course, the ostentatious and rather brash event won't impress the topmost layer of Paris's upper crust. These people with their hire-purchase ballgowns and brand-new jewellery are arrivistes with foreign names and recent fortunes. The recollected whiff of the shtetl and slum may put off the beau monde, but it's also what gives these people such hope for the future. How much better can things get?

The plan is to gather on the roof at midnight to watch the firework display. Nicolas goes up early to smoke alone and avoid another long business-related conversation with his father-in-law. Mr Rozenfeld is considering gambling the fortunes of Étoile du Nord on a rage for fur: fur-trimmed dresses, muffs, fur hats. His thinking is that economic crisis in Russia plus Nicolas's language skills should get them the pelts at the best possible price.

At five to midnight, the press on the roof is close to hazardous. From his vantage point, Nicolas can see the crowd on the fire escape locked in virtual immobility. One figure is determinedly pressing her way through them, wriggling through impossibly tight gaps, ignoring the admonitions from the stewards in their high-visibility jackets. It's Anya. 'I wanted to be with you for this,' she says. She's out of breath from the climb, her ballgown crushed and disarranged from her struggle through the throng. He's moved at her sentiment and the effort she's gone to and squeezes her hand as the first volley of fireworks lights up the night sky. 'I love you,' he says, just at the moment when a huge explosion tears a gash of purple into the velvet night.

'Oh, look at that one!' she says, as a waterfall of stars pours out over the city. 'What did you say, sweetheart?'

Nicolas chooses a pause in the barrage to speak again, but this time he's interrupted by a cry of alarm. He recognises Mrs Rozenfeld's voice. She shrieks in panic: 'My husband! Someone, help!' Bending awkwardly in her ballgown, Mrs Rozenfeld tugs the arm of her recumbent husband, who has fallen and is clutching his chest.

'I succeeded him as head of the company.'

Upon Mr Rozenfeld's death, Nicolas is introduced to a second set of account books, whose liberal red ink reveals that Étoile du Nord is heavily in debt. Cavalier borrowing and a pressure to keep up the appearance of solvency are behind the subterfuge. The problem is compounded by a global financial panic, which drives up interest rates. The tills ring healthily, footfall is excellent, but everything the business earns is still not enough to pay off creditors. Nicolas is compelled to lay off staff and close two loss-making departments: sanitaryware and the pharmacy. He tells the board that he wants to focus on the core business and honour his late father-in-law's plans to develop opportunities in Russia.

He finds he relishes the challenge. He reconfigures the shop, resists the temptation to take it too downmarket, and from his homeland he sources various products that give Étoile du Nord a sense of luxurious eccentricity that chimes perfectly with the public mood: not just fur, but embroidery, lacquered brooches, amber – even Russian yoghurt, which is blended into smoothies in the juice bar. On frequent trips to Russia, he develops relationships with textile factories in Ivanovo, the mill town that's gaining a reputation as the 'Russian Manchester'.

'Looking back, I chide myself,' the old man sighs. 'I was intoxicated by the business. I lost sight of my true purpose. Now and again in dreams I saw the face of the young Rinpoche wearing a look of childish disappointment. I knew I had failed to fulfil the task I had been given: I had betrayed the secret gospel.'

'It was to be another book that captured the popular imagination.'

There is no formal launch for this one, no prosecco and canapés, no speeches, no hopes of making the shortlists of prestigious literary awards. It seeps out, bubbles up like a belch of swamp gas, and then, very slowly, almost imperceptibly, acquires an eminence and a solidity that its creators could never in their wildest imaginings have predicted for it. Nicolas comes across it for the first time in Russia.

It's September 1905. He's making a business trip to Ivanovo. Strikes have been holding back textile production, but Nicolas's supplier is at pains to reassure him that it's all resolved and talk of revolution is overblown. On his way home, Nicolas rewards himself with a stopover in Saint Petersburg, where he enjoys the crisp hints of autumn in the air and the middle-aged pleasure of wandering around the city with his cousin Osip, arguing about books and politics. Nicolas listens politely while Osip gives him his take on *Crime and Punishment*: 'You can't understand the book if you haven't lived through a Saint Petersburg summer. Raskolnikov goes mad from a surfeit of light. His compassion is displaced by too much thinking. You see, there's such a thing as an excess of reason.'

They bribe a guard to let them into the unfinished memorial church on the Catherine Canal that will come to be known as the Saviour on Blood, and survey the progress of the mosaics that show scenes from the gospels picked out in bright polychrome tiles.

'Imagine how these will look when your Pali gospel is accepted!' says Osip.

Nicolas glances over to see if he's being teased. Anything to do with the gospel pains him. But Osip is entirely sincere.

They've got the place to themselves. In a preacher's dramatic voice, Osip sketches out the alternate images as he gestures towards the walls: 'Christ in saffron robes, the lamasery. Issa chiding the Brahmins! Himalayan peaks. The

Sanhedrin washing their hands!'

'That *will* look pretty good,' Nicolas concedes. He's touched by his cousin's enthusiasm. The church is going to be lit with electric light. The colours of the mosaics have a vividness he's never seen before. The whole thing is like a happy fusion of French art nouveau and Slavic soul. 'When do you think that will be?'

'It's religion,' says Osip. 'It moves at biblical speed. Three hundred years? Two, if you're lucky.'

At the front of the church, the gold iconostasis is yet to be fitted with its precious pictures. 'I prefer it like this,' says Nicolas. 'Without the icons. I just don't get them. What's the point? There's no perspective, no historical accuracy, the colours are weird. Everything's too bright and the baby Jesus always has the eyes of an old man.'

'But that's just it,' says Osip. 'They're not supposed to show things as they are. They're windows into other worlds, into God's world, where other rules apply. If your gaze rests on that world long enough, what truly seems unreal is this one.'

By the western wall of the church, they contemplate the spot where the Tsar fell. Both men are silent. 'The Raskolnikovs who killed him have a lot to answer for,' says Osip.

'Anarchists,' says Nicolas.

'It's because of them that Jew-hate has become the fashion,' says Osip.

Nicolas smiles. 'Jew-hate has been the fashion since we built the pyramids.'

'Not like this. If he hadn't died, things would have gone so much better for us. Since then, only bad things. This year has been the worst. I tell you we're not staying around to see how bad it gets. The change that's promised now won't be enough for those that want it, and it will be too much for those that don't. I'm hearing it already: *Blame the Jews.*'

As he looks at his passionate, thoughtful cousin, it dawns on Nicolas that this is the friend he should have had. For twenty years, theirs has been a persistent missed connection. Perhaps it's not too late? He takes his cousin's arm. 'Forget this silly dream of Palestine, Osip. Why don't you move to Paris?'

Osip shakes his head. 'Too many reasons.'

'Seriously. We could help you get started. I could find you work at the shop – interesting work. Irina would love it. I think she and Anya would really get on. Anya's always saying she wishes she had more Russian friends. In fact, the more I think about it, the more it makes sense.'

'Irina doesn't speak French and I don't have your gift for business,' says Osip.

Nicolas, ever the negotiator, is not deterred by the flatness of his cousin's refusal. He asks Osip to hear him out and begins a long homage to his adoptive city that starts with bistros and ends with sunsets over the Seine.

It's too much for his cousin. 'You don't get it, Nicolas. Paris is marvellous, I'm sure, but Paris is no better than here. You saw what they did to Dreyfus. At least the Russian anti-Semites have their unique ecology to excuse them: tyranny, the knout, serfdom, an ignorant clergy, long winters, vodka. But if this crazy religious hatred can flourish in the land of Voltaire, if an assimilated Jew can be persecuted in the way that poor man was, then truly nowhere is safe. You heard

about the pogrom in Kishinev? This Nilus's book is seriously bad news. There is something new in the world, a terrible
and mendacious form of an old evil, and I tell you I fear it
deeply.'

'Steady on. I don't even know what book you're talking
about.'

'You haven't heard of these *Protocols*, as they call them?'

'Nope.'

Osip sighs. 'You will.'

*

NICOLAS ARRIVES at the station at ten the following day
for his journey back to Paris. A train just in is disgorging
passengers from the Asiatic depths of Russia. Half a dozen
men with sunburned, high-cheekboned faces squat on their
haunches outside the station and split sunflower seeds with
their teeth.

Inside the station bookshop, Nicolas's gloved hands turn
the creaking carousel of paperback bestsellers: guides to doing business, award-winning fiction embossed with foil med-
als, political memoirs. The plenitude of books once excited
him, now he finds it oppressive. He searches half-heartedly in
the current affairs section for something with 'Protocols' in
the title, but can't see it. He chooses a biography of Chekhov
instead and a book of word searches and takes them to the
cashier with some breath mints, bottled water and an inflat-
able neck pillow.

The train eases out of the station at eleven on the dot with
a hiss like a fresh-forged horseshoe going into a blacksmith's

bucket. Nicolas has a first-class compartment to himself. He perches on its oversprung red velvet seat, his books neglected, watching the city recede. Haymaking is underway. The cut grass has been bound in sheaves and set in stooks. A hawk circles the stubble on the rising currents of warm air, searching for mice. A middle-aged peasant in soft boots, scythe slung across his shoulders, lollops home for lunch down a track of dried ruts, and turns his head to stare indifferently at Nicolas's passing carriage. The train enters a tunnel of green trees. There's a flash of white skin, shouts and splashes as the tracks cross a river where youngsters are bathing.

Nicolas's eyes close. The sunshine is orange through his eyelids. Suddenly, he's in India: tracking that square of sunlight from his sickbed in the monastery, the air perfumed with the smell of goat's wool and incense. When he opens his eyes again, a voice is shouting: 'All off, all off.' It's still light outside. His nap has made him docile. He dismounts from the iron steps before he's even registered what's happening. The train is making an unscheduled stop in a forest. He wonders where they are. They must be beyond Pskov? The trees give little clue: beech, elm, birches, pine. He peers down the curved length of the train: his carriage and its neighbour are in a glade. Beyond them, he sees the passengers' descent is complicated by the trees that almost abut the track. Hats and dresses are being snagged in branches. In the other direction, the locomotive is out of view around a bend. Shafts of dusty apricot sunlight pierce the foliage. At the other end of Nicolas's carriage, a family gets out: spherical bewhiskered father first, then his son, a skinny youth of fifteen or so. The two men help out the boy's sister, a sulky, hunch-shouldered beauty about two years older, and finally, the mother, who lets out a whoop of surprise as she's hoisted to the ground.

The father offers Nicolas a cigarette. 'Saboteurs, the guard said.'

'Saboteurs?' says Nicolas, declining the smoke.

'Or terrorists. Comes to the same thing,' says the man, lighting his cigarette. It's a Turkish one, very fine indeed, and the man's suit, though crumpled, is silk.

The boy wanders to the edge of the glade and crouches down beside a fir tree. 'Not too far, Lyova,' says his father, 'in case it goes suddenly.'

His father introduces himself as Vassily Kuryagin. He owns a textile mill in Ivanovo. Nicolas explains he's just been there himself and asks about the strikes.

Kuryagin shakes his head and picks some loose tobacco off his tongue. 'They need their heads examined. Stepping on the throat of their own prosperity. You'd better believe someone's pulling their strings.'

Nicolas nods. It's the kind of talk he's heard before. Professional agitators are rumoured to be busy in the Russian Empire's industrial centres. Security has been tightened on the railways – especially ones like this that cross parts of Poland now under Russian rule.

Kuryagin goes on. 'Our country finally starts resembling other countries and this is the thanks we get – chaos.' Nicolas nods. He still feels light-headed from his unexpected nap, and there's something bizarre about all the passengers trying to make their way off the train in the middle of the woods, but he doesn't disagree with Kuryagin. The new factories of Ivanovo turn out an excellent product at a good price, but the political upheaval is making it impossible to do business with them. 'Lyova! Come meet the gentleman!' Kuryagin whistles over at his son.

'One sec, dad.'

'Now!'

The boy jogs over from the edge of the clearing, dragging his toes as he runs. 'Look.' He holds out his handkerchief in front of him. He's got six big yellow mushrooms. Nicolas remembers the name for them when Kuryagin says it: 'Milk caps! Clever boy.' Kuryagin looks at Nicolas. 'You can take the boy out of Russia, but you can't take Russia out of the boy. Say *how do you do* to the gentleman, Mr . . .'

'Notovitch.'

'How do you do?'

'Very pleased to meet you,' says Nicolas.

'The thing about these mushrooms,' says Lyova, with the finality of a judge handing down a sentence, 'is that you must never fry them in butter. Oil yes, but never butter.' The boy's rawly broken voice and enormous Adam's apple are joined to an inexplicable self-assurance.

'That's good to know,' says Nicolas.

'Lyova speaks Latin and Greek,' says his father. 'Tell him, son.'

'*Amo, amas, amat,*' the boy says, wiping his nose on his sleeve.

'See?'

Passengers from either end of the train are showing up in the glade. The mood is light; a woman laughingly swats her husband with a teasel. It adheres to his velvet jacket, long stalk dangling.

A pale-faced young guard jogs along the track behind them, holding his signal flags.

'Hey, what's going on?' shouts Kuryagin.

'The police are searching the train,' the guard says. 'We're waiting to be informed. There was a rumour about a bomb . . .'

At the word *bomb* a gasp goes up from the assembled passengers. The woman with the teasel starts to cry.

The poor guard raises his voice desperately. '. . . a bomb on the Baku train, not this one. It's purely a precaution.'

Now no one believes him. While one group of passengers buttonhole the guard and quiz him, the unflappable Mrs Kuryagina spreads a rug on the grass and invites Nicolas to an impromptu picnic: a flask of cranberry squash, cheese, sausage, black-bread sandwiches. Nicolas is happy to accept and he tells her he admires her sang-froid. 'What can we do?' she says with a philosophical shrug. 'What will be will be.'

'Fifty grams would be good,' says Mr Kuryagin, flashing a bottle of spirits and two glasses. 'Will you join me?'

Nicolas thinks: *why not?*

Neither mother nor daughter drinks, but their questions grow bolder as the single shot of vodka inevitably becomes two, then three. 'You're not married, Mr Notovitch?'

'My wife and children are in Paris. I say *children*, but they are grown up now.' Alexander is eighteen, Hélène seventeen, David, his youngest, is sixteen. Their childhoods have flashed by. Nicolas feels momentarily baffled: where has it all gone? At this instant, as he sits on a soft rug in a beech forest, mildly drunk, time seems to have stopped altogether. The smell of wood mould, warm grass and coal smoke is eternal. Nothing has ever changed. And yet back home in Paris the three squalling infants have all become adults, who dote on their mother and keep the same guarded but respectful distance from their dad.

'Your wife,' says Mrs Kuryagina with the merest hint of disappointment. 'That's good. I took you for a widower.'

'A widower?'

'Your band.'

Nicolas glances down at the wedding ring on his left hand.

'We do it the other way.' Mrs Kuryagina holds up her ringed right hand.

'I see. I wear it in the French style. Fortunately my wife is very much alive.'

'I'm glad to hear it.'

'We *thought* you were French,' says the pretty daughter, shyly, not meeting his eye.

'I am Russian, but I reside in Paris,' says Nicolas with a courteous mock bow.

'Paris! Goodness!' says the daughter with a blush.

'The thing about the French,' says Lyova sagely, 'is that the women are beautiful, but the men are cowards.'

'Knock it off, Lyova,' says his father.

'But it's true, Dad, you said so yourself.'

'What *I* said,' says Kuryagin, by way of clarification, 'is that when it came to it, our Russian muzhiks sent the Frenchmen packing. But they'd conquered half of Europe before they made the mistake of coming to Moscow.'

'But you said . . .'

'That's enough, Lyova,' he says fiercely. Lyova takes the telling-off in good part, without any visible petulance. 'Headstrong,' says Kuryagin, his mouth full of black bread. 'Like his grandfather. My father was a serf, you know. Bought his freedom. He squeezed every drop of serf out of his own veins. That's what a Russian does. We're taking the boy back to his school in Germany. "Backwards. Russia's so backwards," the other boys tell him. Bring them home to Ivanovo and I'll show them how backwards!'

'The thing about the German boys is that they love discipline,' says Lyova.

'What the blazes is going on with this train?' his father asks, to no one in particular.

Just then, a group of policemen make their way through the glade: a short one who's clearly their leader, and four stockier ones with swagger sticks and sly, bribe-taking faces. 'All clear, back on,' says the short one.

'What was it, my friend?' Kuryagin tugs the man's sleeve. 'Your men thirsty?'

The junior policemen look hopefully at their boss.

'We'd better not drink in uniform, citizen. But you're very kind.'

'Take the bottle.' He slips it into the officer's pocket. 'What happened?'

'We had a tip-off. Better safe than sorry.'

'Reds? Or terrorists?'

The officer touches his cap. 'I can't say, sir. We'll make a full report.' He leads his men away.

'It seems you can cause almost as much trouble with a pretend bomb as a real one,' says Nicolas.

'Yid terrorists,' says Kuryagin. 'Trying to bring this nation to its knees.'

'Vanya, really,' his wife admonishes him. 'Spare the gentleman.'

'What makes you think they're Jewish?' Nicolas asks. He wonders if Kuryagin meant to be rude, or is simply the kind of bigot who is not good at identifying the presumed enemy. 'As it happens, my parents were Jewish. And I don't think any ethnic group has a monopoly on making trouble.'

'You're a gentleman, sir, and I don't mean you any offence. But the chaos they're causing is no joke.' He pulls something from his pocket. 'I used to think like you, but this book shows me I was naive.'

'The thing about the Jews,' says Lyova, 'is that they don't respect our Russian culture.'

'You're mistaken,' says Nicolas, hotly. 'You're mistaken, young man.'

'With the greatest respect, individual Jews may be all right. I have nothing against them personally,' says his father, leaping to the boy's defence. 'If I met a Jew now, I'd shake his hand and say "How do you do?" I admire the Jews, the way they look out for each other, their business sense. Tough negotiators. But some of them – not all of them, but some of them – once they sense weakness, it's over. Our government hasn't been strong enough. Now look at us: it's like woodworm. Look how we collapsed against the Japs. How can the Russian army that defeated Napoleon have been turned to cream puffs overnight? Look what's happened to the nation: the drunkenness, the liquor shops run by the Jews, the collapse of decent values. The rot goes deep, my friend . . .'

Nicolas wants to argue, feels obliged to argue, but the vodka has slowed his brain down and while he watches the man's mouth move, the voice he hears is Rachkovsky's: *Russia's destiny is special. Liberalism is a Western fad. Submission to authority is the message of Eternal Rome. We reject the decadence of Eternal Carthage.*

'. . . whores and ladyboys. Inverts marrying one another and adopting children. Everyone thinks it, but people are afraid to say anything because what good will it do? After all, it's the Jews who run the media.' He claps Nicolas on the back by way of friendly conclusion.

The guard waves his flag and calls the passengers back on the train. Kuryagin dusts the crumbs off his knees. Nicolas helps the women up the steps.

'You keep the book,' says Kuryagin. 'I've ordered plenty. We're changing for Baden-Baden in the morning. My doctor has told me to slow down. I'm taking a rest cure but my wife will be giving my credit card a good workout. If you have no plans tonight, why don't you join us in the dining car?'

'I have to go through some paperwork,' says Nicolas.

'That's the spirit. We'll look you up in Paris one day. The next time you need textiles, write to Kuryagin and Son.'

'It was Rachkovsky's book.'

Sitting in the darkening carriage, Nicolas reads it with a creeping sense of recognition that begins in his neck hairs. He can't account for it at first. And then he knows: he's read this book before, albeit in another language and another century. A work that was once fiction is being served up as historical truth. What was once political satire is now being passed off as the secret minutes of a conclave of Jewish elders.

Capitalised slogans scattered through the text form a hysterical poem in free verse that gives as good a précis of the book as any:

WE SHALL DESTROY GOD

MASSES LED BY LIES

MONOPOLY CAPITAL

WE SHALL ENSLAVE GENTILES

JEWISH SUPERSTATE

CHRISTIAN YOUTH DESTROYED

OUR GOAL – WORLD POWER

POISON OF LIBERALISM

WE NAME PRESIDENTS

WE SHALL DESTROY

WE CONTROL THE PRESS

ONLY LIES PRINTED

GENTILES ARE STUPID

WE FORBID CHRIST

WE SHALL BE CRUEL

WE SHALL CHANGE HISTORY

WE CAUSE DEPRESSIONS

GENTILE STATES BANKRUPT

WE ARE WOLVES

It should be laughable. The plagiarism from Maurice Joly is still as plain as daylight: whole chunks are verbatim quotes from the original. But somewhere in Nicolas's being a tocsin bell is tolling. The wheels of the train beat out a single verse from Job: *For the thing which I greatly feared is come upon me, and that which I was afraid of is come unto me.*

*

THERE IS AN INEVITABLE FORCE behind the clamour for more rights. In a world of telegraphs and flying machines, the claims of divinely sanctioned rule and the status-sustaining myth of a hereditary elite look crumblier than an old brocade. Rachkovsky knows this. He knows too that People's Will are fanatical and violent (brave and unsentimental, they'd say, of course), but small in number. A bigger worry is what's happening now: mass-based movements, moderates on the march, calling for a shake-up of the status quo. How might one counter that? What would blacken their reputation at a stroke? How might you seed doubt about progress in people's minds?

Huge inequalities of wealth, unanswerable elites, hunger, plague, violence, the care of the sick and elderly, economic change scouring away old ways of life, unhappy would-be migrants desperate for a new homeland: these raise big and complex questions. To answer them, people would need to think deeply, talk to one another, ask which stories they'd prefer to live by.

The questions that need to be answered are the ones that have exercised the great minds of political philosophy for millennia: What is fair? What is the right way to be in this world, and what are its uses? How ought we to be governed? How do we reconcile the claims of faith and state, of law and conscience? How do we balance our freedom with our security? What is our obligation to the weakest in our society? How much responsibility do we bear for suffering beyond our borders?

Not one of them is easy. And there is a more troubling possibility hovering behind them: people are pursuing these questions as if they have answers, but what if they *don't*?

Rachkovsky intends to make things simpler, to save people the effort of thinking too hard. Instead of politics and mess and many dispiriting questions, just the one: *what do you think of the Jews?*

Behind it is a sound too shrill for human ears to acknowledge, a minatory whistle of alarm, an atavistic shriek, which goes in deeply and activates an ancient portion of the mind. 'Strangers in camp!' it says, summoning up the fear of the not-us, the brown or white, or mysteriously bearded, or clean-shaven, the men who smell of foods we do not recognise as wholesome: it plays on all the fictions of difference; and there are infinitely many.

Rachkovsky, I'm afraid, is an enchanter and artist too. There is no necessary moral value in telling stories. And like all artists, he doesn't just create things from thin air. He works within a tradition he's inherited, guided by his predecessors, but choosing when to follow them and when to make his own way. He sees what's already there, and what has the potential to exist.

Here are the ingredients – they're very promising: two millennia of distrust, fictions of race, a stateless people; the accusation that the Jews killed Christ, poison wells, kill Christian youths to drink their blood, or to bake it into unleavened bread. And Rachkovsky can draw on the strange and undeniable fact that many of Russia's would-be revolutionaries are Jewish.

Rachkovsky himself has barely picked up a pen. He's worked like the master of a Renaissance studio, supervising a team of junior craftsmen, or a surgeon who makes a few key incisions and steps back to let his underlings suture up the patient. But there is no doubt that this dark masterpiece is his. He has created a literary golem, a book that will be known as *The Protocols of the Elders of Zion,* that will become notorious as a warrant for genocide.

'The Tsar himself was one of its first dupes.'

Nicholas II is taken in completely by its tale of a power-hungry Jewish elite manipulating popular discontent. He makes notes in the margins: 'What depth of thought!' 'Everywhere one sees the directing and destroying hand of Judaism.' The Metropolitan of Moscow orders extracts to be read in all of the city's Orthodox churches.

The Tsar's most fanatical supporters, the Union of the Russian People, an organisation of violent anti-Semites more commonly remembered as the Black Hundreds, ask the Russian government to fund the printing of the *Protocols* for use as propaganda.

Shortly after Nicolas arrives back in Paris, the worst pogroms in Russian history erupt across the country, inaugurating decades of bloodshed.

'I felt obliged to do something.'

'This is a surprise,' says Rachkovsky, leading Nicolas into his private office. The spymaster has aged well, as plump people often do. His face is unlined and his curly hair still thick and black, though the somewhat lifeless matt texture suggests the assistance of dye.

The outer offices gleam with brass, ivory and polished rosewood. Twisted electrical wires hang in swags along the walls. Technology has moved on so quickly in the almost twenty years since Nicolas was last at Rue de Grenelle that he scarcely knows what he's looking at. In humming cabinets, reams of data are being transferred to punchcards to have their secrets extracted by patented algorithms. Brass encryption machines ensure that no one can read the department's correspondence. A bank of Belinograph transmitters spit out whole documents and even images that have been communicated across vast distances by electrical pulses.

'I read your charming novel about the lost gospel,' Rach-kovsky says, faintly accompanied by the tic-tac sound of a young telegraph-operator entering text on a Baudot keyboard that resembles a piano.

'It's not a novel,' Nicolas replies sharply.

'Come, come. Remember: I dabble a little in fiction myself.'

Nicolas arrived here determined not to be sidetracked, not be distracted by old conflicts, but now he feels compelled to defend his discovery. 'If you took the trouble to examine the evidence I presented in the text, you'd find—'

Rachkovsky's delighted to have provoked a reaction so easily. 'It isn't the *evidence* that I took issue with, in fact. The story might or might not be true, but what it lacked, novelistically, is a certain *enchantment*. It was too tentative, got moving far too slowly, was far too preoccupied with the fauna and flora of the Himalayas.' He reaches for a box of Turkish cigarettes and lights one up, blowing curls of perfumed smoke across the desk. He leans back in his chair, cigarette held aloft, left hand cupping his right elbow across his paunch. 'The thing I've realised about you, Nicolas, is that you lack the imaginative gifts to be an artist of the first water. A real writer would have said, "Stuff all that scene-setting." A real writer would just say, "*Fiat lux!*" and win us over with the power of his vision. The sad truth is that you lost your real vocation when you turned your back on the Third Section. Though by the look of that lovely suit, business at the department store is good?'

Shaken by the attacks, Nicolas feels his face flush and the

adrenaline rise in his body. He has to compel himself to stick to his task.

'I've been in Russia for business. I came across this.' He shakes it out of his valise onto the desktop, not trusting himself to hold it in his hand without shaking.

Rachkovsky regards it with a shrug of boredom and barely asks: 'What is it?'

'*The Great in the Small*, by Sergei Nilus. But the last section, the *Protocols*, is the provocation you created with Mulhouse.'

'And? So what?'

'This book is being used to stoke anti-Jewish hatred. It's a death sentence for people like our families, people we grew up with.'

'How disappointing if you've come here to be tedious, Nicolas. The one thing you never were was boring. But now *you*, with everything you have, somehow feel the need to stick up for a few Hymies in Odessa?'

'I'm going to expose it as a lie.'

'You needn't bother. The Tsar already knows it's a forgery. He's had the whole affair looked into. They all know it's made up. Anyone who cares to examine it can find out the truth. But the thing about a work like this one is that those who believe don't care about the *facts*. It doesn't have to be true, because it *feels* true. That's the lesson you've never learned as an author. How hard you are on people, expecting them to grasp little nuances and details, boring them with your history lessons, fussing over your overworked sentences.' Rachkovsky lets his features drop into the slack face of a dullard, tongue protruding from his lips as he inscribes a word in the air with the glowing tip of his cigarette. 'Just one idea is all you need. Mine's unstoppable: a black-hat baddie with a yarmulke and side curls rubbing his hands as civilisation burns.'

'Yours is a calumny against the Jews which is causing bloodshed.'

Rachkovsky smiles. 'Mine is a calumny against the Jews which is *preventing* bloodshed. We are witnessing the death struggle between order and anarchy. You don't have the wit to grasp this, but if killing my own mother would secure stability in Russia for another ten years, I'd be morally obliged to do it. You should be thanking me for this book. In fact, you should be doing all you can to shore up the Tsar because if history shows anything, it's that the Jews will suffer the most if he goes. Right now, His Imperial Majesty is the only force capable of holding back the Black Hundreds—'

'Murderers who've been inspired to kill by your book!'

'You and I both know that collateral damage is as inevitable as it is regrettable.'

Nicolas replies with a curse too filthy to print.

Rachkovsky's unperturbed. 'What are you going to do? Attack me with your book? Bore me to death with talk of "interfaith dialogue"? Make us all join hands and sing "Hare Krishna"?'

'You're a liar, an embezzler and a murderer!' shouts Nicolas, with commendable, but slightly hysterical, vehemence.

Rachkovsky lifts a brass mouthpiece from the cradle on his desk. 'Show my guest out, please.' With an expression of bored distaste he grinds his cigarette out in the crematorium of his ashtray. 'Just think of this: if I believed you posed any real threat to me or my work here, I would destroy you and your family without a second thought, starting with your feckless firstborn, Alexander, who's racked up such terrible gambling debts. Wouldn't your moneylender father be horrified about *that*? Dear me, from the look on your face, this *is* unexpected news.'

'*Tokonoma.*'

It's the corner alcove in a Japanese teahouse: a recessed space that faces the entrance. It is sacred and easily defiled. Only a single object is displayed there: a calligraphic scroll, a painting, a vase, a spare arrangement of flowers.

'There is a place of honour in every mind and every system of thought that pretends to be a culture and in it is placed its defining good: god, family, the race, wealth, personal liberty,' says Notovitch. 'What's in yours, Mr Dittami?'

Vincenzo answers without hesitation: 'My children.'

The old man nods. 'Then you understand my predicament.'

'*There was nothing to be done.*'

It's not entirely true. Nicolas still *chooses* to be silent. Like everyone who's ever made an ignoble compromise with his conscience, he finds plenty of good excuses not to kick up a fuss about the *Protocols*. What would it achieve? The die is cast. Rachkovsky's right – their truth or falsehood is beside the point.

The real reason is preverbal – the heart's unease when his children leave the house, when he thinks of them being stalked by Rachkovsky's spies. Every now and then, one reports an encounter unusual enough to be a sly message: 'A very friendly Russian man, Papa. He said he knew your family from Kiev and to say hello.'

'I confronted my son about his debts.'

Nicolas finds him in his bedroom: at the top of the house, tennis clothes on the floor, posters of cavalry regiments and adverts for patent medicines decorating the walls. Exasperated by the boy's failure to be tidy, Nicolas and Anya have declared the room off limits to the maid. The result is deepening chaos and a precocious, bachelor funk. Nicolas averts his eyes from a calendar of nude images poking out from beneath the unmade bed. 'I've become aware of the fact that you're in financial trouble,' he says.

Alexander's first response is lies and stonewalling. The boy is eighteen and has his paternal grandfather's black hair and skinny build. 'It's not true, Papa. I swear on my mother's life!' Enraged by the boy's brazenness, terrified by his knowledge of Rachkovsky's reach and cruelty, Nicolas slaps his face. It is the first time he's ever raised a hand against one of his children. It's hard to say which of them is more surprised.

'At your age, I was writing dispatches on the Turkish wars!'

'We can't all be heroes, Dad!' wails his son, with snotty and plaintive irony.

The truth comes out in a hiccoughing, tear-stained confession while Anya pounds on the locked door and demands to know what's going on.

'I'm handling this,' Nicolas insists.

Alexander has fallen in with a fast set of boys. It's clear they tolerate his presence because he is from a wealthy family and easily milked of money. Nicolas listens with a toxic sense of guilt. He knows it's his fault. The boy is insecure and craves acceptance. He's failed to instil either self-belief or self-reliance in his son. It feels like a shameful echo of his own flight from his identity, the struggle into manhood that began aboard the *Derby*.

'These boys are not your friends,' says Nicolas. 'I'm going downstairs right now to ring their parents.'

'No, Papa, no!' The boy howls inconsolably. 'I'll pay the money back!'

Another bitter recognition: like Nicolas, what Alexander fears most is losing face.

The aftermath is a series of pained phone calls and sulky personal apologies from the other boys. Nicolas pays back the money to their parents, but keeps a tally of what Alexander owes. He uses the debt as leverage to make his son drop talk of an army commission and accept a junior role in the family business. The boy is inevitably cold-shouldered by his so-called friends, but embraces his new reality with a kind of relief. Nicolas wonders whether things might have turned out for the best.

On his eighteenth birthday, Nicolas's youngest son, David, announces that he's going to Argentina to seek his fortune. His mother pleads with him not to go, but Nicolas recognises his own stubbornness in the boy and has a sneaking admiration for the plan: it's clear that Argentina is poised to be the next economic superpower. 'If I were eighteen again,' he murmurs to his wife, 'I'd do the same.'

As a concession to his mother, David remains in Paris long enough to attend his sister Hélène's wedding to a widower called Xavier de Fronton, who has two infant children from his first marriage. From Nicolas's point of view, Xavier's previous offspring, rustic accent and plain face are demerits all offset by his *particule*, good nature, and profitable canning business in Marseilles.

A few days before the wedding, Nicolas receives a letter from Rachkovsky. It feels fat and the handwritten return address has an unguarded looseness. Nicolas rings the office and is put on hold. Rachkovsky comes on the line.

'Nicolas.'

'I received your letter.'

'And?'

'I haven't opened it.'

'Oh.'

This is the reason Nicolas called: if Rachkovsky needs a favour, he wants to hear him beg for it.

Rachkovsky clears his throat. 'I was merely writing to ask if you would pass on a wedding gift to your daughter.'

Nicolas makes no reply. Is that the sound of Rachkovsky sighing, or the static electricity on the line?

'I would like to help secure her financial future,' Rachkovsky continues. It's impossible to know his motives, but a streak of sentimental concern for his natural child is not beyond all probability; after all, Hélène's a piece of him.

'That's neither necessary nor possible,' says Nicolas. After years of being bested by Rachkovsky, this feels like a minor victory.

'I didn't think so. But I needed to ask. Goodbye, Nicolas.'

Nicolas hangs up the phone.

The wedding goes off well. They erect a marquee at Anya's mother's country place, hire a band, and send the newly-weds to Rome for their honeymoon. Dancing with his daughter, slightly tipsy after a successful speech and relishing the sense of a meaningful occasion, he looks at his surroundings in wonderment. *This is plenty*, he thinks, as the band play a selection of 1880s cover versions: 'Love's Old Sweet Song', 'Sweet Violets' and 'Is She Not Passing Fair?' Nicolas is so thoroughly immersed in this role – proud father, successful businessman – he almost forgets that he once aspired to change the world.

'Then war.'

Time passes too quickly. Nicolas and Anya age. Their faces lose the high contrast of youth, their colours fade. Year succeeds year. When war breaks out in 1914, Nicolas loses his best tailors, seamstresses and milliners to the national drive to make military and naval uniforms. Worse is to come: his son Alexander announces he's signed up to fight. At twenty-seven and unmarried, he still yearns to make his own mark in the world. In spring 1915, he is one of more than 100,000 French soldiers killed in the Second Battle of Artois.

Nicolas receives the telegram at work. Before returning home to tell Anya, he goes to speak with Father David for guidance. Neither man brings up their differences over the Pali gospel.

Father David has lost a great deal of weight over the past ten years. He looks wraithlike and close to death himself. His deep voice sounds like it's coming out of a vault. 'It is the primal bereavement,' says the priest. 'Numberless parents have suffered it. It was the test of Abraham. It was Our Lady's loss. It was the sacrifice God undertook Himself.'

'What use is theology to me?' says Nicolas, reproaching the priest with his red-rimmed eyes. 'I want my boy back.'

Father David knows that sometimes the wisest speech is silence.

'It's my fault,' says Nicolas. 'He was looking for a short-cut to become a man.'

'Not at all. He made a choice. It's sad for us, but now your son is free.'

'No, no.' Nicolas weeps openly. It's the thought of the boy in pain. He has seen enough of war to understand the hideous butchery, the things shells do to human bodies. 'There were so many things ahead of him.'

Nicolas leaves the church contemplating something drastic: he has an urge to harm himself – not just to commemorate the loss, but to give it physical expression, to put it in something less cheap than words.

Outside, a man is sticking propaganda on a Morris column; a roll of posters under one arm, glue pot and brush in the other. The posters call on loyal citizens to support the war effort by buying government bonds.

At a zinc table in front of a cafe across the street, a British soldier, a private, in a peaked khaki cap and hobnailed ammunition boots, tastes a café au lait with obvious distaste and adds sugar.

Nicolas, though now fifty-six and almost half a lifetime away from his years in journalism, still hasn't lost the professional knack of striking up casual acquaintances. He does it now as a form of displacement, to avoid thinking of his loss and the terrible task awaiting him at home: breaking the news to Anya. He thanks the soldier warmly for his sacrifice and insists on buying him a brandy.

The soldier, eighteen years old, five feet five and a half inches tall, sallow complexion, grey eyes, reminds Nicolas of someone he once knew, but whose name he cannot now recall. Grateful to meet an English-speaker, the soldier talks excitedly about his upcoming leave. He's headed back to London to see his sweetheart and has come via Paris to buy her a present. He wanted to get her a miniature Eiffel Tower, but the war effort has pushed up the price of metal and all but the tiniest are unaffordable.

Nicolas orders more brandy and becomes unusually unguarded. 'I've seen war myself,' he says.

'You were a soldier?'

'A journalist. The Russo-Turkish War.'

The British corporal nods, purely out of politeness. The old fellow's a decent sort but like all old men inclined to reminisce about an irrelevant past.

'I expect the name Skobelev means something to you?'

'Oh, yes,' agrees the nice young man. 'Oh, yes.' He follows nothing of the long anecdote that follows: troop formations, unpronounceable foreign names, a man or woman named after a day of the week.

Nicolas sees the grey eyes disengage. 'Another drink? I insist.' He orders Marc de Bourgogne this time, the closest he can find to the vintage he drank with Younghusband. It is different from what he remembers: the flavour carries notes of leather boots warming at firesides, roasted chestnuts, old book bindings.

'I never drank before I came to France,' says the boy. 'My parents would be horrified. We get rum in the trenches twice a day.'

'What is their objection?' Nicolas asks.

'They're Baptists. They don't believe in it.'

'You can remind them Christ's first miracle was turning water into wine.'

The boy's curiosity is piqued. The alcohol encourages him to overcome his ingrained habits of discretion, his instinct to avoid controversy. 'May I ask what religion you belong to, sir?'

'I'm a sort of Christian myself.' The subtle qualification is a storyteller's gambit. A slight misalignment, a raising of tension that demands resolution, a seventh chord yearning for a tonic. 'Years ago, when I was travelling in India . . .'

The young man listens to Nicolas's story as the afternoon unravels and pronounces it most interesting. His drinking slows, Nicolas's continues at a steady pace. Before he knows it, Nicolas is drunk and venturing to give the young man advice. 'What are you fighting for?'

'For king and country. The Kaiser's a tyrant.'

'Go home,' Nicolas announces. 'There's nothing here worth dying for. Find someone you love, be good to them. Lead a simple life. That's all there is. Listen – your sweetheart, what's her name?'

The boy blushes as he says it. He hasn't told his parents and it feels like violation to be uttering her name to a stranger.

'What's she like? I mean, short, tall, dark, fair, slim, full-figured?'

322

'It's hard to say.' The boy looks in consternation at the clock. The old coot has crossed a boundary.

'The reason I say, monsieur, is that women's clothing is a speciality of mine. If you can give me some idea of size . . . I'm the general manager of the Étoile du Nord. I would be honoured—'

'Really, it's not necessary. I'd better go. I have to catch a train.'

Nicolas makes another sally, but the boy is unbudgeable.

'Before you go – your name?'

'Leonard.'

Out of unsteady eyes, Nicolas watches him leave and orders one more for the road. Walking home he is assailed by a frantic grief. He thinks: *my son's dead.* The earth seems to open beneath his feet. Later, trembling and hung over, looking at his bloodshot eyes in the mirror, he will remember Leonard's affronted expression and wonder where he has seen it before: Volchkov, Alexander, Skobelev, someone, but when?

'1917 brought further calamity.'

Seduced by the high rates of economic growth in Russia, but fearing the sporadic turmoil of its urban centres, Nicolas has invested in a huge farm outside the northern city of Vologda and spends more money acquiring the land that adjoins it. He intends to build an industrial dairy plant with refrigerators and automated milking machines. Whatever happens, he thinks, people will still need to eat.

He greets the March revolution with restrained optimism: perhaps this is the change the country needs. But after the

Bolshevik coup in October, his land is expropriated. He makes a frantic and ultimately fruitless trip to Moscow at the end of 1918, where he embarks on a weary circuit of temporary offices, beseeching the new regime's zealous young bureaucrats to return his property. Their reactions vary between open contempt and mere annoyance.

It is the last time he will visit his homeland. Osip has already left with his family for Palestine. The new Soviet Union is fighting for its life in a bloody civil war. At Kazan station, Nicolas observes Red Army recruits being mustered before setting off for battle against their White opponents.

In his rough, parade-ground shout, their brigadier tells them to stand easy. A special visitor has come. The whisper among the troops grows louder as a black Daimler pulls up on the station forecourt. Bodyguards in fur-lined leather jackets flank the figure who emerges. A cry of joy goes up from the assembled soldiers. 'Lenin!' The new country's revolutionary leader is coming in person to address them! Hang on – he's wearing spectacles. 'Trotsky!' Recruits nudge each other – in a way, this is better: Trotsky's known for his brilliant oration. But wait – Trotsky's skinny as a greyhound. He can't have changed so quickly. Even the Politburo aren't eating *that* well.

Clad in a hat of black astrakhan, wearing a red armband on his grey coat, the plump dignitary raises a brass megaphone to his mouth. 'Representatives of the working class, vanguard of the proletariat, I'm afraid Comrade Lenin is unable to be here. He has sent me in his place. My name is Ilya Nevin, Commissar of Information.'

Nicolas's jaw grows slack with disbelief. His suitcase slips

324

from his grasp and lands upon the pavement with a thud. He leaves it where it is as he skirts the gathering to get a better look at the face of the speaker.

'Let us be in no doubt about the immensity of the struggle that faces us,' Nevin continues, his frosty breath swirling around the megaphone. 'We are assailed on all sides by the forces of bourgeois reaction.'

His face has been shaved clean, but there's no mistaking those green eyes, that catlike look of self-content. It is Rachkovsky, sleekly triumphant in a seal-fur coat. Nicolas watches, not hearing the words, as his old nemesis whips the troops into a froth of revolutionary enthusiasm and then tops it with three lung-bursting cheers.

The brigadier marches his men double-quick to the troop train as Rachkovsky waves them on from the running board.

Nicolas walks towards the Daimler at a speed that arouses the concern of Rachkovsky's bodyguards. One grabs his lapels while the other puts him in a headlock. 'Where are you going, citizen?'

'I'm a friend of the commissar.'

'Sure you are. You look like a reactionary parasite to me.'

'Peter! Rachkovsky, it's me.'

Rachkovsky steps off the running board. 'Do I know you?'

He approaches Nicolas, who's been hauled off balance by the bodyguards, who's using all his strength to stand upright and not to tumble to the ground at Rachkovsky's feet.

Rachkovsky looks at him for a long time. 'Do you presume to know me, citizen?'

Nicolas is seized by a frantic hatred, by a desire to immolate them both. Like Samson, he will pull down the world on both their heads. 'I know you from Paris,' he shouts, with a demented yell, 'where you were the head of the Tsar's secret police, where you murdered revolutionaries, fornicated, and undermined the working people.' The last words are interrupted by a flash of light. The front of his face goes numb. One of the bodyguards has broken Nicolas's nose with the palm of his gloved hand. Blood spatters the pavement. He's lying on the ground. He sees the bodyguard's felt boot an inch from his eyes. He hears the sound of a revolver being unholstered.

'Shall I finish him, chief?'

'No need. I'd know him anywhere. It's the well-known Menshevik sympathiser Max Schneiderman. Stay here and see he gets on the train to Paris.'

'I have to salute his resourcefulness.'

After decades ruthlessly defending the Tsar's interests, Rachkovsky ought to have been undone by the revolution. The Tsar's abdication left him with neither a protector nor a *raison d'être*. If there were any justice in this world, he'd be skulking around a labour camp with a spoon in his boot, running demeaning errands for the terrifying Thieves Guild who control everything inside the prison walls.

But a man who knows everybody's secrets is never as weak as he appears.

The Chinese scholar-poet Chuang Tzu famously claimed to be uncertain if he was a butterfly who dreamed he was a man, or a man who dreamed he was a butterfly. Rachkovsky has exploited a similar but less charming ambiguity.

He claims that during all those years spent as a government agent, his real sympathies lay with the revolutionary terrorists.

Returning to Moscow in 1917 with a big fat file listing anyone who's ever informed on anyone, he finds himself in a surprisingly powerful position. There's barely a person in the new government who wasn't compelled, at some time, to sell a piece of their integrity to Rachkovsky, either for money or to settle scores with colleagues.

Reflagged with a hammer and sickle, Rachkovsky seeks out the opponents of the new regime, enforces ideological purity, and puts his storytelling talents at the service of his new masters.

Meanwhile, his old masters are being executed in a basement in Ekaterinburg. The Tsar and Tsarina, their son, their five daughters, and the courtiers who accompanied them into exile are shot and bayoneted to death. Three books are discovered among the Tsarina's possessions: a Russian Bible, a copy of *War and Peace* and *The Protocols of the Elders of Zion*.

'I returned with a black eye and wounded pride.'

When Nicolas gets home to Paris, he finds a letter waiting from his brother in Palestine. He has guessed its contents before he opens it, but is still shaken to see the facts in black and white: his mother's dead.

He wonders why they didn't telegraph. With a war on, it would have been hard to make the trip, but he would have tried. He's overwhelmed – not so much with grief, but a sense of guilt. What a bad, neglectful son he's been. What a lot of pointless resentment he's carried towards his parents.

Loss piles on loss. Nicolas's wife and daughter contract the terrible strain of influenza that tears through the world, spread by demobilising armies, killing almost a twentieth of the global population.

Disregarding the risk to himself, he nurses Anya through what he fears will be her final hours. Sometime around three o'clock in the morning on 15th December 1918 she wakes up. The fever's passed. But his daughter, Hélène, dies on Christmas Eve.

Nicolas grows close to insanity with grief. He thinks of Hélène's last visit in the summer with his grandchildren. It made him sad then to see that she too, at thirty, was visibly ageing. In a certain light, he glimpsed incipient crow's feet and an image of the old woman she would now never be.

*

IT IS APRIL. Outside, the city is wearing its new green.

Notovitch suggests moving the Imperator to the conservatory where the light is better, but is not strong enough to offer more than token assistance. The old man seems vulnerable. His arthritis is worse. Once or twice he loses the thread of his recollection and admits he's been sleeping badly.

The knowledge that the dictation machine is much too heavy for him to move safely on his own awakens an obstinacy in Vincenzo which topples over into a kind of rage. 'Stand back,' he shouts, as he propels the Imperator across the parquet on its squeaking legs. By the time Vincenzo's negotiated the door to the hallway, the old man has changed his mind. The sun, shining through the fanlight above the front door, makes Notovitch look weak and spindly. His slippered feet make a pathetic sound on the hall tiles. One panel of the machine has been scratched against the doorjamb. Notovitch looks at the mark with wary eyes, but says nothing. Vincenzo drags it back into position.

'Emerson says the English have no faith in God. Do you find that to be the case?'

Where Vincenzo lives, the nonconformist churches are full on weekends, Salvation Army bands play hymns at the Tube station, and he tells Notovitch so.

'That's a pity,' the old man says. 'I was rather hoping to find a nation of agnostics. An absence of dogma would make them more receptive to the Pali gospel. It's easier to fill an empty cup. The Great War, of course, turned many back to religion.'

Seated in a wingback chair, Notovitch shuffles the papers in his lap. 'I will be going back to Paris, the week after next,' he announces. 'I am sorry to be leaving, but the venture that brought me to London has not met with success. I was hoping to find a buyer for my business. However, this – our more important work – is close to its conclusion. I will need to ask your help in arranging for a transcription of the cylinders. It will be much easier to find an English stenographer here than in Paris.'

Vincenzo nods, wipes his forehead with a handkerchief, and starts the Imperator.

'Did I mention to you that I saw Kuryagin again?'

The Bolshevik coup in 1917 brings a flood of Russian refugees to Paris. Nicolas is bewildered to hear the unfamiliar sound of his native language being spoken in the streets of his adopted city. One day, in Montmartre, he sees Kuryagin, the mill-owner from Ivanovo, walking uncertainly in a fine but threadbare suit, arm in arm with his daughter.

Without a second's hesitation, Nicolas approaches them and greets them in Russian. His salutation dies in his throat when he sees how much they've altered. The daughter's fresh beauty has burned up in the fire of revolution. Her face is haggard. Kuryagin stares sightlessly though glaucomatous pupils the colour of cooked egg white. His hand tightens on his daughter's arm. 'Is it a friend, sweetheart?' Even his voice has altered: more weak, more tremulous.

Moved by their obvious destitution, Nicolas opens his wallet and pleads with the young woman to take fifty francs. She accepts the money tearfully.

'The French are so kind,' her father murmurs. 'We are obliged to your goodness, sir.'

Kuryagin's daughter thanks Nicolas repeatedly in broken French. He senses that she knows exactly who he is, but is too humiliated by the change in circumstances to admit it. To bring the uncomfortable reunion to a close, Nicolas touches his hat and bids them farewell.

Even after decades of literary silence, Nicolas still thinks of himself as a writer. It's a fantasy that he'll never abandon. It's one of the stories he's staked his life upon. But in reality, he's settled for a comfortable life and recognises, when he's honest, that his later work is facile dabbling. The value of anything equals what you will give up to possess it.

What you write sincerely must cost you pints of your own blood.

As his body exhibits the irreversible symptoms of senescence, he allows himself a smile at his youthful hysteria about ageing. At the same time, he understands his precocious panic was justified. It seems like five minutes ago that he was carousing with Volchkov, scribbling hopefully in his garret, awaiting the footsteps of a messenger who might dispatch him across continents in pursuit of a story. But the triumphs of his youth are mere puffs of dust on an aged uniform that now seems quaint and small and strikingly handmade. The city that he knew before the construction of the Eiffel Tower looks at him with an imperial indifference. He says the things that old people say: remarking on the sudden changes in children, the folly of politicians, the high prices of everything, the cacophony of modern music. He bemoans the state of the world in predictable jeremiads, confusing – as old men tend to do – the end of his life with the end of civilisation. And yet, death seems as distant as it ever was.

Looking back on his life, he consoles himself with two things. One is *The Unknown Life*. He still feels singled out by his luck in making that discovery. Few are chosen for a task as important as that. The other, and more surprising, consolation is his love for Anya. The two of them share the unspoken sympathy of people who have suffered and rejoiced at the same things. He finds solace in her mere presence. A secret book; his wife's love: he wonders if he was worthy of either.

'I expect you are wondering, "Why now?"'

Notovitch tosses his papers onto the floor, then rises from his seat to request a pot of tea from the housekeeper.

Vincenzo stops the dictation machine and waits. The door furniture clicks heavily to announce Notovitch's return.

'For everyone else, the interest and controversy of my discovery is barely a memory,' says Notovitch. 'The general excitement, the incredulity, the vituperation and mockery that followed it – all faded into silence now. I was surprised to come upon a mention of it a few days before our first meeting while leafing through the pages of *National Geographic* magazine at the dentist's. It was an aside in an article about a recent find of Scythian treasure. The allusion was in the context of great archaeological hopes that prove finally false. I was particularly amused to read its description of me as a "mysterious Russian nobleman". How pleasing to be thought mysterious! And how much that ennoblement would have tickled my father!' The curtain rail utters a sharp rattle as Notovitch pulls the drapes shut. 'In that very same issue, I read an advertisement for your company, Dictascribe.'

'Scriptovox.'

'As you say. I'm a great admirer of Anglo-Saxon ingenuity. Verne and Robida may have dreamed the future, but Manchester and Birmingham have built it.'

As an Italian, Vincenzo doesn't feel like the intended object of this flattery.

'The coincidence crystallised an intention I have been carrying with me for some time. I feel an obligation to leave my own testimony. Events in Germany have given my task fresh urgency. Its new chancellor is a great champion of the *Protocols*. Despite the cowlick and improbable moustache, he's

332

the manifestation of something that we ought to be taking very seriously.'

The brass lever of the door dips and the housekeeper enters with the tea things. Vincenzo takes the tray from her and places it on a footstool by the fire to steep.

A silence falls which neither man is keen to break. The ghosts slip from the room: Bessie, Skobelev, Volchkov, Alexander, Leonard. The last to leave are Notovitch's other selves: Naum, Kolya, Nicolas; the named and the unnamed, the ones that have clamoured to be heard, the ones that have chosen not to speak at all.

Finally: 'It's to be expected that a man my age should look back at his life and ask what question it has posed, and whether he has answered it.' The old man sighs. 'I have to own up to a dereliction of duty. I was entrusted with a task by the lama. Instead of disseminating that gospel, I was distracted, I was too easily disheartened. I shirked my destiny. In the time that remains to me, I intend to correct that error. I will share the hope promised in the Pali gospel – the hope of a spiritual life beyond the dogmatic assumptions of any single creed.'

Vincenzo rotates the teapot in the way his wife has shown him and pours. There is the near music of two ascending notes as the cups fill and the clouds of fragrant steam rise.

'Transcription of these cylinders is the first step. I have been corresponding with the keepers of the antiquities at the British Museum. I have suggested another expedition to search for the original text as a matter of urgency. I'm hoping for a reply shortly.'

'But you never went back to India yourself?' Vincenzo asks, handing a cup of tea to Notovitch.

The old man shakes his head. 'After Anya's father's death I was compelled to take over the running of the firm. My responsibilities to the company, my duties to my wife, fatherhood, all made it impossible. There were practical obstacles. And, besides, what would it have achieved?'

'You could have brought back the original gospel. You could have proved your critics wrong.'

'Perhaps. Perhaps not,' says Notovitch mildly. 'To begin with, I'm not certain the abbot or the Rinpoche would have consented to let the text leave the monastery. But ask yourself this: was there *any* evidence that would have satisfied my critics?'

The younger man begins to list things that might have been adequate – copies of the text in Pali, testimony from Buddhist priests, photographs – but Notovitch dismisses them instantly.

'Mr Dittami, the world is stories in arms. In my own lifetime, I have seen history altered by the power of stories. But it was never their likelihood or any positive proof that gave them victory. Rachkovsky knew this. Herzl knew this. They understood the power of a simple story – the simpler the better. And more than this, they understood in an uncanny way which existing stories had the power to be shaped, to be rewritten in ways that would alter how we live.'

'You didn't go back,' says Vincenzo again, now almost wonderingly; it's no longer a question.

'No,' agrees Notovitch. 'What would have been the point?'

'None,' Vincenzo says. 'There was no evidence you could have brought back—'

'Precisely.'

'—because there was no evidence.'

Notovitch's eyes narrow. He sets the cup in the saucer with a click and glances over at the Imperator. It's not recording. 'Our work is concluded, Mr Dittami. I don't wish to keep you from your family.'

Vincenzo is not so easily put off. The questions in his mind are not the ones that Notovitch has posed. He's not wondering why the old man chose this moment to dust off his old, derided story. Since Hemis, since the Rinpoche, or thereabouts, he's started to have misgivings about Notovitch's basic truthfulness. It arose as a suspicion so slight that at first he didn't have a word for it, only a visual image: a fox, sniffing cold air for an unfamiliar scent, nostrils subtly dilating, catching – what was it? – a faint whiff of falsehood?

'There was no evidence,' Vincenzo persists. 'There never was a gospel. I doubt you even broke your leg. I expect there was no duel. Perhaps no Bessie either.'

'Yes, and no Paris, no Third Section. You also are a figment of my imagination,' says Notovitch, calmly. 'This whole room is the creation of some gnostic demiurge and visible reality is a cruel joke.'

Vincenzo ploughs on, disregarding the icy look that has lowered the temperature in the room, formulating the thoughts that are finally taking shape. 'Perhaps the Third Section is real. Perhaps you really did some work for them. But you didn't care about Renan's objections. I think something else happened to you. Who knows what? At some point in your life, you realised that what Rachkovsky said and what you believed was wrong. You realised that none of us is free to choose exactly who we are.'

'You seem very sure of this, Mr Dittami.'

'I know this, sir, if I may. Perhaps I may tell you something of myself. Some things I have understood from my own life. I was raised in an orphanage. It's merely a fact. I don't want your sympathy for it. I'm free to marry a duchess. If I have money, I can send my children to the finest school. Who knows? But I am not free to tell my story in any way I like. Whatever I do, Vincenzo Dittami will always be the priest's bastard from Genoa.'

Notovitch nods, like a fencer acknowledging the unexpected speed of a circling parry that instantly turns defence into attack. He is even more surprised by the directness of the thrust that follows.

'You will always be a Jew from Crimea. Nothing can change that. You wanted to be a writer, you chose to convert to Christianity, but some part of you, maybe the best part of you, kept faith with the child you were. You couldn't stop being a Jew, but you could try to change what being a Jew meant.'

'Laughable. Almost, may I say, Rachkovskyan in its contempt for the truth.'

'I think you wrote a version of the gospel that you thought should be true.'

'That's your story.'

'And what is yours?'

There is a pause. In the silence, the sound of a woman's laughter is audible from the pavement beyond the window. Notovitch looks down at his hands. In this moment, he is suspended between two distinct versions of himself. He sees the outlines of his other lives, ghostly possibilities that will

336

never be fulfilled in this world. His resistance has been briefly weakened. Something about Vincenzo's honesty has moved him, his willingness to embrace the humiliation of his own identity. *The priest's bastard from Genoa.* Notovitch glimpses the relief of confessing everything. It would be so easy. But that isn't what his life is about. It's partly the acquired habits of spycraft, the unwillingness to let go of an assumed identity because only bad will come of it. But it's also an act of faith, the belief that by willpower our stories can overcome the laws of nature. The world is sustained by myths. One replaces another. There are only better and worse. The stone rolls back, the body's there. The stone rolls back, the body's gone. One small adjustment and the contingent reality is completely altered. You can't give up now, he thinks. The future depends on it. This has cost him too much. *There must be a best story.*

'You've heard my story, Mr Dittami. I translated the Pali text as accurately as I could,' Notovitch says. And then, with some of the pedagogical huffiness of Renan: 'Reality doesn't care whether you choose to believe in it, Mr Dittami.'

'But there is no evidence!'

'Evidence! What evidence would satisfy you?'

That's when Notovitch took off his slipper to show Vincenzo his ancient wound – the livid skin, the missing toes – beneath the strange frugality of his darned sock.

There is a whole genus of tokens that are offered in stories to redeem the inflated currency of words: handkerchiefs dipped in blood, wounds, strawberry marks, the livers of slaughtered animals, heads on silver plates. Sincerity is generally made visible through someone or something's suffering. 'I cannot believe in Western sincerity because it is invisible,'

337

said the writer Yukio Mishima, 'but in feudal times we believed that sincerity "resided" in our entrails and if we needed
to show our sincerity, we had to cut our bellies and take out
our *visible* sincerity.'

Examining the old man's mutilated foot, Vincenzo allows
himself to be persuaded. But doubts remain. And possibilities almost too dark to contemplate.

*

I'VE LIVED WITH NOTOVITCH for a very long time, I've
wondered about his motives, his aims, and how best to tell
his story. There's no question that his gospel has become an
idée fixe – for both of us.

His complete works are memorialised in the frontispiece
of the volume on my desk. It's the one he inscribed to the
Duchess of Kent one January night in 1939, in which the list
of previous publications has been slyly and almost imperceptibly defaced with the word *jésus*.

'Why, Notovitch!' the duchess said afterwards, as his
identity dawned on her. 'The scoundrel who claimed Jesus
was a Hindu!' Her inaccurate judgement is not the unkindest
verdict we need to consider.

In some volumes of the secret books, He is Himself Judas.
Nicolas Notovitch and the tale of his lost gospel are real.
It's my fascination with him that has drawn me into this
enchantment. The events he's described to Vincenzo – fore-
shortened, condensed, assuming the liberties of fiction – im-
pinged on the history we know roughly in the way he said
they did.

The figure who bothers me is Mulhouse. Who is this thrusting young writer, so Gentile in origin and yet, in other ways, so close on the palette to Nicolas? As Notovitch has told the story, he's pinned the blame on Mulhouse. But when you see them side by side, are they two different men, or one, gazing at his reflection in a pool of mercury?

No one knows who composed the *Protocols*. The strong evidence is that it was written on Rachkovsky's orders, with aims much like Notovitch has described. Various candidates for authorship have been proposed. Mulhouse's name conceals an author whose identity is, in fact, unknown and probably irrecoverable. If we could pull off that mask, who would we find behind it? A converted Russian Jew named Élie de Cyon, perhaps. Rachkovsky himself. Perhaps. But at the time the *Protocols* were composed, there was another bright young writer of Jewish ancestry in Paris, consumed with a frivolous attitude to words and stories, who believed that a writer could alter reality with his pen. I often wonder if Nicolas himself was the sorcerer's apprentice who unwittingly unleashed poison and spent the rest of his life remorsefully searching for its antidote.

᛭

THE HOMELY FUG of a 1930s kitchen. Blacked stove. The crimson arms of Vincenzo's wife, Peggy, in the washing copper. Everything covered with a layer of damp. The new Pye wireless, paid for with Notovitch's guineas, warbles a dance tune. Shirt collar off, suspenders dangling, Vincenzo drinks sweet milky tea from a saucer. The little girl beside him with chapped red cheeks and hand-me-down woollen clothes is Francesca herself, future custodian of Notovitch's memories.

'You told him he was fibbing? What did you do that for, love? That's looking a gift horse in the mouth,' says Peggy.

Having confessed his outburst, Vincenzo has no sensible reply and takes refuge in his native tongue. '*Vieni qua, tesoro*,' he says to his daughter. '*Prendi il cestino.*' He closes her hand round the wicker handle of the basket.

Outside in the garden, he picks the fat pods of the broad beans and passes them to Francesca.

He knows he needs to make amends.

Hatchards on Piccadilly is a ten-minute walk from the Scriptovox showroom. Vincenzo goes there one weekday in his lunch hour. A book is a good present for a writer. He looks at the table of staff picks by the entrance and reads: 'I heart this eye-opening account of life at the bottom by one of our brightest young progressive writers!! Must read!', written in passionate scrawl beside a new book called *Down and Out in Paris and London*. The title makes him smile. That might work. As long as Notovitch gets the joke. He picks up a copy. It's a good-looking volume, but priced rather steeply at eight shillings and sixpence.

'Can I help you?'

A man in brilliantined hair and shiny spectacles. As a fellow salesman, Vincenzo has reservations about the assistant's method: he's moved too early and too forcefully.

'I'm looking for a gift.'

Vincenzo's accent suddenly sounds as strong as Gorgonzola. The man hovers in an unfriendly way. Now and again this happens to Vincenzo, despite his smart clothes and affable manner – his foreignness inspires instinctive distrust in someone. He dips into the book and reads: *Have I ever told you, mon ami, that in the old Russian army it was considered bad form to spit on a Jew? Yes, we thought a Russian officer's spittle was too precious to be wasted on Jews* . . . Another dip: *in a corner by himself a Jew, muzzle down in the plate, was guiltily wolfing bacon.* He puts the book back on the table and addresses the suspicious salesman. 'Perhaps something less . . . political?'

*

THE TWO MEN MEET for the final time on a warm morning in May 1933.

Notovitch waits in the sunshine outside the house. Vincenzo and Pierre Thibaut, still alive, still more than a decade away from his death in France, arrive in the Scriptovox truck to take the Imperator and the cylinders to their temporary home in the warehouse. Notovitch will be in touch about having them sent on to Paris after the transcription.

'What word from the British Museum, Mr Notovitch, about the expedition?' Vincenzo asks, when the machine is wrapped in old blankets and roped tightly to the bed of the truck.

'Nothing yet,' the old man says. 'But I live in hope.'

Pierre cranks the engine. The truck judders into life. He drives away alone. Vincenzo is seeing the old man off at the station. They travel together in a cab south through the city, past Lord's cricket ground, where the first test match of the summer is being held, and through the leafiness of Regent's Park.

'Thank you for your scepticism and honesty, Mr Dittami. They have been very instructive to me.'

'I was perhaps too sceptic, sir. If so, I meant no offence.'

'Not at all. It's important that I don't underestimate the obstacles that still confront the gospel. I intend to acknowledge my great debt to you in the book.'

'That is very kind but not necessary.'

'Of course, if you prefer to be anonymous, for any reason, I will respect that.' Notovitch's look is weighted with a wounded heaviness. He's authorising any future denial. At that instant, Vincenzo feels a terrible pity for the old man and his vast loneliness. He remembers the hostile salesman in Hatchards. The distrust based on nothing. He recognises a commonality with Notovitch. A line from Deuteronomy: *Love ye, therefore, the stranger, for ye were strangers in the land of Egypt.* 'It would be an honour to have my name in your book.'

'Very well. As soon as I reach home, I will wire you the money for the transcripts. In the meantime, keep the cylinders safe.'

At Victoria station, a porter checks the luggage tag on Notovitch's steamer trunk and hoists it onto a trolley. The concourse is spotted with pats of dried chewing gum.

After agonising over the parting gift, Vincenzo settled on a book from a dealer on Charing Cross Road: a copy of *The Divine Comedy* in Italian. Notovitch seems genuinely surprised and moved. He whistles at the porter and gestures for him to return. He unclasps the trunk and opens the lid. From inside, he removes an object which he presses into Vincenzo's hands. Skobelev's flask.

342

Too much? I think so. It feels a little Hollywood. Perhaps it's MacGahan's chapan instead, tied into a bundle with knotted string and naphthalene-impregnated paper.

That doesn't seem right either.

How about this: perhaps he takes out a billfold, removes two five-pound notes and hands them to Vincenzo?

No, that's completely wrong – that last gesture only demeans both men.

Perhaps the precise detail is unimportant.

Do they embrace? Definitely not. They shake hands with a certain guarded respect, knowing there is no basis for friendship and little chance of meeting again.

The guard blows his whistle. Notovitch gets aboard. The train departs.

4: CONVOY SIXTY-EIGHT

LOOK: A COLOURED MARBLE TURNING IN A SEA OF INK.
As it rotates, slowly, anticlockwise, the dark line of approaching sunset gobbles a continent puckered with mountains and vast belts of olive forest. Distant wind shirrs the blue enamel of its oceans. It is an earth. Not exactly *the* earth, but a planet very much like ours.

You recognise this church. In our world, it's called the Saviour on Blood. Here it has other names: *khram Khristusa neschetnykh del*, the Church of Christ of Myriad Things, or, more formally, the Church of the Pleroma.

Inside, the walls are covered with mosaics that tell a story you're familiar with: a shaven-headed man drinks water from a cleft rock; here, he sits in contemplation among orange-robed adepts.

Here's one of Notovitch himself. It shows our hero in the library at Hemis, examining the volumes of the secret books. Its intent is narrative rather than devotional – in other words, you're not supposed to pray to it. And yet the depiction of the lama pushes the orange of his robes as close to radiance as Church doctrine will permit. The artist seems to have been influenced by images of Joseph Smith encountering the Angel of Moroni: there's the same surprise on the young man's face, the same transfiguring light surrounding both figures. It's probably just a coincidence. I expect all annunciations are vaguely alike.

347

This is one world where the fates of Rachkovsky's and Nicolas's books have been reversed: where the *Protocols* sank like a stone and *The Unknown Life* swept across the world and acquired believers. It is a world where a set of poisonous certainties has been exchanged for the inclusive story that Nicolas found. This dream seems close to what Notovitch hoped for. But the fantasy is so remote that the dream threatens to grow thin and colourless before our eyes. The world where this happened is quite another story.

Quick: pick your goods. No war? No poverty? A spirit of tolerance, community, better stewardship of the planet? Since human nature hasn't altered in any fundamental way, any change is bound to be accompanied by new opportunities for suffering. Only a fool would be certain that this will be better than our world. But, knowing the twentieth century, it seems unlikely to be worse

In this other world, there are many changes from our own. To take one of the most minor: here, my great-uncle Leonard died at the much riper age of eighty-two.

I only met him once: at my grandparents' ruby wedding anniversary in 1977 – the year of the Queen's silver jubilee.

What I remember is this: his liver-spotted hands, the somewhat reddish colour of his remaining hair, his nut-brown skin and distinctive accent. When he said my grandfather's name, Ray, it sounded like *Rye*: the strange – to me – vowels a product of long decades working at a steel mill in Wollongong, Australia.

The official history of Leonard was one of pioneering spirit, risk-taking, trials undergone, and a fortune made. He'd defied a long-running family tendency to insularity, uprooting himself and moving to Australia after the war. With the money from the steelworks that he earned and saved, he bought a general store: at one exhausting stage, he'd worked at both, subsidising his foray into retail with night shifts smelting ore. He'd had five children with a local woman. They and their offspring were too numerous to join him for the reunion. His brief visit left a little residual envy. It was felt he'd been too showy with his money and too openly critical of the British weather. He'd also spoken sharply to one of the catering staff at the pub where the anniversary was held for bringing him the wrong main course. This was a significant demerit in the eyes of my grandparents, who abhorred, above all, a fuss.

The largely wholesome version of his life was punctured when we received the order of service sent by his daughter after his death. It detailed the obsequies for one Leonard *Price*.

Our informal inquest was held at the dinner table that Christmas lunch. My father, who always took unseemly pleasure in provoking his in-laws' discomfort, led the prosecution.

'Why would he do a thing like that?' my father asked. 'Was he ashamed of his *name*?'

'I think he did it for our sake,' my grandfather said. 'We don't blame him.'

'No, we don't blame him,' said my grandmother, siding with her husband instinctively. She doodled on the tablecloth with her fork and let out the noisy sigh that, even at the age of ten, I identified as the sound of her anxiety.

My father's notable glee, my grandmother's cornered expression, my grandfather's efforts to dispense judgement with thoughtfulness and sobriety: all of it was at odds with the paper hats that they were wearing from the Christmas crackers.

'He had shell shock,' my grandmother said.

'He had shell shock?' queried my father, with mocking incredulity. 'Did it make him forget his *name*?'

'Whether he had shell shock or not, he'd been through hell,' said my grandfather. 'It's not up to us to judge.'

'*You're* in no position to judge,' my mother said to my dad, trying to defuse the tension with mockery. 'America wasn't even in the war until 1917.'

In this world, that one chance meeting, a stranger's kindness, altered the points on Leonard's destiny. He never spoke of it, but I know what happened: the old man (always old to Leonard) who poured him drinks at a zinc table in Paris, whose words and obviously broken heart persuaded a wavering young soldier to desert.

The choice Leonard made, the shame, the cost to his family's respect, the necessary change of identity – this is the stuff that novels are made of; novels, whose purpose is to reconstitute our lost potential, to restore the worlds that might have been.

Do you like this Leonard less? Inevitably. But you only have to think of yourself answering the door in your pyjamas or nightdress, opening it to see the pale, panicked face of your young son wearing a stolen greatcoat over his torn uniform, desperate for money and forgiveness, glancing both ways down a wet provincial street, and you know you would have hidden him as long as necessary in an upper bedroom, and emptied every last coin from the cashbox, to see to it that he was able to start a new life somewhere, under a new name.

*

EVEN IN A MUCH LESS radical departure from the facts, there's still bathos and awkwardness about Leonard's resurrection. What if he'd merely survived, simply been more circumspect about the dangers – not volunteered for the sortie into No Man's Land that, by family tradition, is how he met his end? If he had not died then, some other version of the secret books would have been fulfilled. Would it be better or worse? Our lives, separated in reality by half a century, might well have overlapped.

I imagine the ring of the brass bell above the door on Moyser Road, the shelves of paint and sandpaper. A familiar, unfamiliar face above a cash register. With a feeling of disappointment, I realise the narrow congruence of our interests. We've got virtually nothing in common. Perhaps we would talk about football or swimming. I understand that I don't know him at all. I can see that other lives have depended on his, that his survival has been a boon to many people; but unless the whole tragedy of the war has been averted, the saving of Leonard seems unsatisfyingly arbitrary, more meaningless, in fact, than his death.

The fact is that Notovitch's intervention came too late. It's signing up in 1914 that does for him; no, it's further back yet: it's the accident of being born in 1897, in that unlucky cohort for whom the shot at Sarajevo waits like a terrible summons.

351

THE WORLD WE INHERIT is composed of the dreams of
the dead. We can never wake from them entirely. I have inhabited the dreams of an Irish-language teacher in Trieste,
an impotent librarian in Buenos Aires, a consumptive doctor
in a room that overlooked the lilac sunsets of the Black Sea.
From them, and writers like them, I have learned to ask certain questions: whose stories are we in, to what end are they
told, why are they believed?

It's not my fate, I realise, to write a restrained, considered
book in the third person with immaculate sentences. What
a pity. I love lean, tight prose, neat periods that glisten and
overlap like the scales on a snake. I love writing that is aus-
tere and poised, inflected with the seriousness of past-tense
narration, but I understand too that it is a kind of rhetorical
trick. A feeling of timeless profundity is created by leaving
out what is most messy and most characteristic of ordinary
human lives. Gravitas is achieved by exclusion, by not acknowledging the monarch's farts, the lover's bad breath, the
piles of Lego in the living room. It's the trick of those photographs of the pyramids that detach them from the sprawl
of the Cairo slum. I reread my own pages with a kind of dismay, but it is at least the same kind of dismay I feel when
I see my ageing face in the mirror. This is me. And I know
enough about myself to know that I can't do ten pages on a
dying preacher sanding the door of his chapel. So I cling to
the self-serving belief that you will be more authentically you
if I'm more authentically me.

Habitually, I do my work in daylight. These are my steady

hours, the time to undertake the slow, patient business of accumulating words. But as the end draws near, evenings are better. Darkness is suited to endings.

We know what the ending needs to do: it should achieve some resolution or insight; answer some question implied in the journey of the central character; return us to the opening chord, but with it or us changed. But what actually *is* an ending? Which thresholds are truly final? Which are even real?

As we put the cylinders away, as we look forward to ascending from the basement, it feels as though we should consider the possibility, at least for a moment, that Notovitch was telling the truth; that on a certain day in 1887, he discovered a lost gospel in an Indian monastery.

We could go right now, if we wished, to Ladakh to check. Packing a bag with warm clothes and setting off immediately, we might reach Delhi tomorrow. We could be on the runway at Leh the day after, having overflown the astonishing Zanskar peaks and descended over Spituk Monastery on our approach to the city. Peering down from the aircraft window, we're low enough to see monks in yellow robes and masks performing sacred dances in its central courtyard.

Such a sudden arrival at high altitude is, of course, foolhardy. The Bakula Rinpoche airport is two miles above sea level. Your head spins as you take your luggage off the carousel.

We hire a car and driver at the airport, follow the course of the Indus through the mud-brick villages that line the valley: Choglamsar, whose inhabitants are refugees displaced by the invasion of Tibet; Shey; Thiksey; Ranbirpura.

Hemis Monastery stands in a dark adjunct running south of the main valley. Winter is stubbornly entrenched.

Despite the bright sun, snow and ice cling to the road that winds up to it. You may need to shovel sand from the verge and spread it to help your tyres grip, while your ears sing at the altitude. Without the chance to acclimatise, your lungs and body will protest at the thinness of the air. The feeling of weakness in your oxygen-starved body is like a bitter foretaste of old age.

The low lintels of the monastery doorways will threaten to brain you. Sitting by a wood-burning stove in an upper room much like the one that Notovitch described, the present abbot will acknowledge that he has encountered the rumours before. You're not the first to put the question: a Russian visitor, yes, a manuscript, yes, Jesus.

The story has altered over the years. In some you'll hear Issa himself studied at Hemis. That's not, as you know, the tale that Notovitch told.

Cross-legged on a soft mat, you take a dried apricot from the bowl in front of you, eat a cashew, thank him for the tea, ask to see the library.

The books, you're pleased to see, are treated with veneration: their loose-leafed pages folded in cloths, pressed between boards and each one stored in a separate glassed-in niche. These are the Buddha's teachings; these the commentaries. That's what you're told, anyway. Unless you read Tibetan, you'll have to take their word for it.

'Among all your books, could there be such a manuscript as Notovitch described, in Pali?' How *badly* you want to believe!

The monk shakes his head. A secret book? 'I don't know,' he says. It seems like the most unlikely answer of all. But you feel he is too honest to claim the book exists; too attuned to the motives of tourists to scotch the story once and for all.

There is one person he says you could ask for a definitive answer. The current Statsang Rinpoche. You jot down the address: Lhasa, People's Republic of China. In an act whose cosmic wisdom is impenetrable to you, the present Rinpoche chose to be incarnated in Tibet, an occupied country, and is stuck there for the foreseeable future.

*

AT THE HOTEL IN LEH, an American contractor from Boston who's working at the air force base receives the information that your father is from Medford with surprising indifference. He's not keen to talk about his work. It dawns on you later that he thinks you're a spy. Your English accent, bonhomie and unlikely claim to US citizenship are something he seems to have been briefed about. Habits of distrust, it appears, have persisted at this altitude.

Chagrin gives way to darker contemplation.

So much of Notovitch's story isn't quite right. The monastery's books you've seen are all in Tibetan. There aren't any at all in Pali. Why were his men speaking Pashto? Turn the map of Ladakh which way you will, you can't fit his route plausibly on the landscape, or see where he might have raced Younghusband for the charts.

Are you content with a mystery? Do you want to press on? How much does final knowledge mean to you? If there is no book, it implies scenes different from the ones he revealed; the gaps in his story obscure another Nicolas: one who never shed a final allegiance to his father's faith, who, as Vincenzo guessed, envisaged and created a text that might undo the bloody fictions that had pursued his people for centuries: a man who never gave up searching for the better story.

And for this man's end, how much further will you look? Cast handfuls of powder in the flame? Heat volatile metals in the alembic? Apply to the mayoral rolls in Paris? Search in back issues of old newspapers to find an article about his son, a wine merchant, inaugurating a Franco-American trade association in New York? Examine the livers of animals without a mark on them?

Here, on the rocks beside the road south to Manali, is a tent, the abode of an oracle, the shaman of a group of Ladakhi nomads; it smells of goats. Put silver in the thin brown hand. Cast the bones. Her eyes roll back in her head. The temperature drops below freezing with the sunset. In your deranged state, it appears that smoke is issuing from her mouth. She's speaking in the language of the secret books. What is it *exactly* that you need to know?

*

IT IS 1939. All that's left of Étoile du Nord is the shuttered premises. Inside, there's damp, loose carpet and horizontal mannequins where wealthy Parisians once tussled over the spring collections. A decade of economic blight has eaten away at the business. Nicolas's trip to London failed to turn up a buyer for the store and depleted precious savings, making any hope of transcribing the rolls impossible. Nicolas and Anya are compelled to economise. Old age, shame and

356

increasing poverty combine to bring about a contraction of their circle. On a rare social excursion, Nicolas has his troubling encounter with the duchess. Father David died years ago. His replacement is a young émigré called Father Gerasim, who has left Russia to get away from the communists. The experience of religious persecution has, paradoxically perhaps, made him more narrow-minded and intolerant. He's a stickler for convention. Father Gerasim has a thick sable beard that he likes to gather in his fist like a pigtail when he's listening. In his eyes, there often seems to be a secret joke, but it's never clear at whose expense.

There's none of the wisdom and chatty intimacy that Nicolas enjoyed with his predecessor. In any case, Nicolas rarely goes to church these days – now and again at Orthodox Christmas, and mainly because he likes the music.

Volchkov has moved to Lyon. Rachkovsky's gone entirely. He vanishes from this story, leaving a mask to be worn by other antagonists.

Paris falls in June 1940. Anya is too frail to leave. Since her terrible decade of loss, she's found it increasingly hard to leave the house. Unfamiliar places seem full of unspeakable menace. It is a form of mental illness. Nicolas has long since given up attempting to reason with her delusions. He cares for her in their apartment: a much smaller one, in which piles of his books form teetering internal walls.

In the aftermath of military defeat, an old theme emerges. There has already been some grumbling that the Notovitches' remaining son is abroad and not doing his bit for France. Now the recrimination is more overt: '*On nous a vendu,*' goes the muttering. '*Sales youpins.*' *They sold us out. The dirty Jews.*

By October, Jewish businesses are forced to display bilingual signs in the windows. *Entreprise juive. Jüdisches Geschäft.* Under the *Statut des Juifs*, foreign Jews must register their names and places of birth at the police headquarters.

Nicolas wisely chooses to ignore the order. He tries once more to sell the department store with the hope of raising money to emigrate. Someone offers him a ten per cent down payment, changes the locks, and then reports him as a foreign Jew to avoid paying the rest.

He reassures Anya. Father Gerasim will have proof of their baptisms and marriage. They will straighten this thing out: perhaps join Volchkov in Lyon while the unpleasantness subsides. He finds Gerasim in the vestry. The priest listens without expression and replies unhurriedly.

'You've not been to church for a while,' he says. 'I have a proposal: I'll find the paperwork that shows your parents are Orthodox believers from beyond the Urals, born east of the Pale, in the land where no Jew ever set foot. In return, you repudiate the lies in your book.'

How long has Gerasim been cooking up this plan? He's an opponent of heresy, innovation and woolly thinking. The position of the Church is very clear: submit to tradition or take your chances on Judgement day. Religion is not a menu à la carte.

The old man blazes, suddenly young. 'You whippersnapper! How dare you!' Gerasim turns his back until he hears the door shut.

Upon reflection, Nicolas realises he must do as the priest asks. If he's drawn a conclusion from his life, it's that a human being is worth more than any mere idea. But now it's too late.

On 7th June 1942, Parisian Jews are legally obliged to buy and wear the yellow six-pointed Star of David. They pay for it with clothing coupons. Jews are banned from public places and subject to curfew between 8 p.m. and 6 a.m.

On 16th July 1942, Anya and Nicolas are rounded up with 13,000 other Jews and confined to a velodrome on the outskirts of Paris. A single jury-rigged standpipe supplies dirty river water for washing and drinking. Anya contracts dysentery and is taken with Nicolas to the Rothschild Hospital on Rue Santerre.

He holds her hand at the end. She is gaunt, unrecognisable. There is no trace of the shiny, squirrel-bright girl he courted with all that torment and ambivalence five decades earlier, in another life, another century. He strokes her face.

'Remember our wedding?' she says.

He says he does.

'Remember I called to you on the balcony? I thought you'd never come in. You were crying. It was our wedding night. *Remember?*' She squeezes his hand. Her flesh is yellow, her fingers cold and dry.

'Because I loved you so much,' he says.

'Really?'

'Yes.' There is a catch in his voice. She closes her eyes.

Thousands of the interned Jews are transported out of France, but Nicolas is briefly reprieved. He is transferred to Drancy, and carries his tiny cardboard suitcase into one of the modernist five-storey blocks that remind him a little of the blocky lines of Hemis. From the rooftop, beyond the barbed wire, he can see the dome of Sacré-Coeur in Montmartre.

One by one, convoys depart. There are seventy-eight in all. Number sixty-eight leaves from Drancy on 20th December 1943. The passenger list gives family names, first names, dates and places of birth.

He is the oldest in his convoy, but not the oldest of all. The names, hailing from Algiers, Budapest, Salonika, Karlsruhe, Lyon, Kishinev and Kiev include children and octogenarians. One, Betty Ruben, from Altmark, dies at the camp in Récébédou in her ninetieth year. Another was born in 1849. The birthplaces of the Mittelsteins, scattered across Europe, track the spread of the family like tree rings: Novo Radomsk, Paris, London, Paris, Nantes.

They are recorded among the 76,000 names listed in Serge Klarsfeld's *Mémorial de la déportation des Juifs de France*, a kind of compendium of secret books, of lives that might have turned out otherwise.

NOTOWICZ, NIKOLAI   13.06.58   KERCH.

The mind recoils from the name in print. The record is terse. *Upon arrival at Auschwitz on 23 December, 210 men were selected to receive the identification numbers 173708 to 173917 as well as 61 women (75340 to 75400). 1229 people were gassed immediately.*

A tale so familiar and so strange. Sidings at dawn. Sealed stock cars opening with a rush of warmth and human smells. Guards in grey overcoats. Leafless trees. Laughter and lamplight from the windows of its headquarters. A gramophone playing 'Stille Nacht', the simplest and sweetest of carols, over a landscape that beggars imagination. An SS officer assigning life and death with the most casual gestures. There's no way a man in his eighties would survive the sorting. Notovitch is getting ground up in the implacable machinery that he tried to sabotage. But the enormity of what's happening is a terrible vindication of his gospel: if this is possible, surely all things are possible?

In those last minutes, he distracts himself from the misery around him with images of calm and transcendence: a cube of lapis lazuli from a certain mine in Badakshan, a lake in Ladakh reputed to bestow immortality, rain falling; for a tiny moment he senses the miraculous possibility of eternal life, swimmers and sinners alike, tumble-turning forever in the azure mercy of divine love.

He gazes down at his naked carcass and waits for the icy waters of history to close over his head.

Briefly these are his memories: the cubbyhole on the *Derby* where he slept; a crisp morning in Saint Petersburg; the sand dunes at Otrar and the sun in his eyes; dancing with his daughter at her wedding while the band played 'Is She Not Passing Fair?'; the grey glass roof of the Vélodrome d'Hiver; holding his dying wife's hand in the ward of the Rothschild Hospital. It is almost finished. He remembers that he too was loved. Now he goes, with all the dignity he can muster, towards the place where all stories end.

There is no body. But someone has to read the eulogy.

History – one of the powerful fictions he had little use for – in so far as it recalls him at all, considers Nicolas Notovitch a buffoon who did a grubby thing; I have come to regard him as a kind of hero.

We can think of him in the aftermath of the war. At Nuremberg, we will have cause to remember what he said: 'Mr Dittami, the world is stories in arms.'

He foresaw as well as anyone the violence that happens when we follow the instinct to inflict our stories on other people. He was ahead of his time in wondering how we can begin to live in a world where we truly understand nothing. He doubted humanity would be able to let go of its stories: the new tales of progress and nationhood; the old ones of history and religion, of God and the devil. So in their place, he tried to offer a better one.

He was not, as he is sometimes portrayed, a self-interested liar possessed with a contempt for the truth. He was motivated by despair. He knew that no weapon had yet been devised that was as deadly as a typewriter. Men follow orders. But the authority of a command dwells in a story. He understood that few people were capable of living in his thoroughly disillusioned reality. He wanted to improve the fictions people live by, because he knew it was the most human thing in the world to make up stories and start fighting over them.

There are many particulars of his life that remain unclear; generally not through vagueness, but because he offered so many competing versions of it. His paradoxes are legion. An unbeliever, he consoled himself in those final seconds with the words of Isaiah: 'For a small moment have I forsaken you; but with great mercies will I gather you.' And in the shape of his disillusioned life, we catch the echo of another: a Jewish boy growing up by an inland sea, infatuated with dreams of the East, who saw that the world was made up of stories in arms and wanted only to invent better ones – stories of love and compassion and forgiveness.

AFTERWORD

THE NOVEL IS A LUNAR ART, borrowing its light from drama. Along with epigraphs and dedications, I'm sceptical of the need for afterwords and acknowledgements. I'm not persuaded of the value of seeing the sweaty actor-manager of a novel's tiny theatre returning to the stage to give special thanks to their confidants and supporters. It always feels vaguely like boasting and, as a reader, I'm usually affronted that anyone could be more important to the author than me, the paying customer.

But if it *were* me reading this for the first time, I'd wonder how much of what I'd just been told was true.

The *Protocols*, of course, are all too true. Only circumstantial evidence connects the book to Rachkovsky – though it is very strong. Its baleful influence lingers. Norman Cohn's *Warrant for Genocide* was my chief source and I winked at its title in the text. I also drew inspiration from Stephen Eric Bronner's *A Rumor About the Jews*.

Rachkovsky was real, as was the Third Section, and the basement offices at Rue de Grenelle. I owe a big debt to Alex Butterworth's excellent *The World That Never Was*. The CIA have made available online a declassified history of the Russian secret service in nineteenth-century Paris. I have taken huge liberties with the facts, but the essential truth of an arch-schemer working on the Tsar's behalf profiting from a war on terror is, I believe, accurate.

Skobelev and MacGahan are loosely based on real characters. Januarius MacGahan (a man) was a correspondent for the *London Daily News*. Two volumes of the paper's anthologised war correspondence were my chief sources for the Russo-Turkish War. The account of the massacre at Batak I drew from its pages. Skobelev was a Russian war hero but his later life took him to Central Asia, where he died. I have merged him with a character called Seliverstov who was murdered, probably on Rachkovsky's orders, in Paris in 1887.

Bessie is a fiction, but the woman I've described as her sister, Gesya, was a conspirator in the assassination of Nicholas II and her death and that of her baby happened much as I recounted it.

Nicolas Notovitch and the tale of his lost gospel are real. It was my fascination with him and his motives that resulted in this book. Its method – slapdash, wilful, knowingly anachronistic – will not conceal my vast ignorance of many of the subjects I've touched upon. I've been guided by the precepts of Novalis and Tolstoy, who said, respectively: 'Novels arise out of the shortcomings of history,' and 'History would be an excellent thing if only it were true.' I blame Flaubert among others for propagating the misconception that stories exist and writers find the best way to tell them. I believe that writers – and in this sense, we are all writers – construct everything, including their own identities as writers.

It wasn't until 1965 that the Second Vatican Council issued the document *Nostra Aetate*, which included these words: 'What happened in His passion cannot be charged against all the Jews, without distinction, then alive, nor against the Jews of today. Although the Church is the new people of God, the Jews should not be presented as rejected or accursed by God, as if this followed from the Holy Scriptures.'

In case any ambiguity remains: my great-uncle Leonard Castle was killed in action in 1916.

If you close this book moderately entertained, more suspicious of assertions of expertise and alerted to the seepage of the modes of fiction into areas of life that conventionally claim to be concerned only with the facts, then I've exceeded every hope I had for the book. The method I commend to you, though perhaps the outcome of such an exercise is already obvious at the outset: pursue someone, anyone, into the worlds that might have been, and the soul you glimpse can only be your own.